That
Spring in
Paris

CIJI WARE

Cover design 2017 by The Killion Group, Inc.
Cover and colophon design by Kim Killion.
Paris photo credit: Carol Gillott;
Artist photo credit: Michael Svoboto.
Formatting A Thirsty Mind Book Design

ISBN: 978–0–9889408–6–4 ebook editions;
ISBN: 978–0–9889408–7–1 print edition

Additional Library of Congress Cataloging-in-Publication Data available upon request.
1. Women's fiction   2. Paris 3. San Francisco 4. Landscape painting 5. Post-Traumatic Stress Disorder 6. Military and commercial drones 7. US Air Force pilots 8. Graphic Art 9. 21st century Contemporary Fiction. 10. Romantic Fiction 11. Terrorist attacks

e-Book Edition © May, 2017; Print Edition © May, 2017

Published by Lion's Paw Publishing, a division of Life Events Media LLC, 1001 Bridgeway, Ste. J-224, Sausalito, CA 94965.

Life Events Library and the Lion's Paw Publishing colophon are registered trademarks of Life Events Media LLC. All rights reserved.

For information contact: www.cijiware.com

PRAISE for Ciji Ware's Historical and
Contemporary Fiction

"Ware once again proves she can weave fact and fiction to create an entertaining and harmonious whole." *Publishers Weekly*

"Vibrant and exiting…" *Literary Times*

"A story so fascinating, it should come with a warning—do not start unless you want to be up all night." *Romantic Times*

"A mesmerizing blend of sizzling romance, love, and honor…Ciji Ware has written an unforgettable tale." *The Burton Report*

"A romantic tale of intrigue…a compelling story line and fascinating characters." *The Natchez Democrat*

"Ingenious, entertaining and utterly romantic…A terrific read." JANE HELLER, *New York Times & USA Today* bestselling author

"I read straight through…" MARY JO PUTNEY, *New York Times* bestselling author

"Oozes magic and romance…I loved it!" BARBARA FREETHY, #1 *New York Times* bestselling author

"Fiction at its finest…beautifully written." *Libby's Library News*

"Thoroughly engaging…*Booklist*

Also by CIJI WARE

Historical Novels
Island of the Swans
Wicked Company
A Race to Splendor

"Time-Slip" Historical Novels
A Cottage by the Sea
Midnight on Julia Street
A Light on the Veranda

Contemporary Novels
That Summer in Cornwall
That Autumn in Edinburg
That Winter in Venice
That Spring in Paris

Contemporary Novellas
Ring of Truth: "The Ring of Kerry Hannigan"

Nonfiction
Rightsizing Your Life
Joint Custody After Divorce

DEDICATED TO

My husband, **Lt. Anthony P. Cook**, U.S. Navy
My brother, **Chief Petty Officer Richard Harlan Ware**, U.S. Navy
My uncle, **Seaman Leon Ware,** U.S. Navy
My father-in-law, **Major Howard Bell Cook,** U.S. Army

Men who served their country honorably on land and sea.

Chance meetings are almost always soon forgotten,
like shoppers riding upwards on an escalator
passing other strangers traveling in the opposite direction.
And then there are those split-second encounters
when paths cross—and lives are changed forever.

CHAPTER 1

November 13, 2015

Engrossed in a book since dinner, Patrick Finley Deschanel was oblivious to the late hour as well as the gentle slap of water against the steel hull of *L'Étoile de Paris*. That is, until he heard the loud, staccato sound of rushing footsteps arriving on the barge's deck. In an instant, the American expat's head snapped up and a rush of adrenaline coursed throughout his body. Jumping to his feet, he immediately went into a combat crouch. Head lowered, he peered out the window of the pilothouse that formed one half of his living quarters on the 110–foot stationary vessel that once had hauled oil products along the canals of France.

A few seconds later when he had absorbed the scene outside his cabin, Finn inhaled a couple of deep breaths as he'd been taught in his 'special' yoga class prescribed by his shrink.

A harsh voice in his head commanded, "Stand down, you idiot!"

By that time, he'd recognized the familiar figure of his elderly landlady's grown son, Pierre Grenelle, accompanied by his wife. Both were hurrying in the direction of Madame Grenelle's more commodious compartments, forward on the barge.

The former U.S. Air Force Major let out a low curse. Once again, Finn Deschanel had instinctively gone on Red Alert in Paris—not Afghanistan. And once again, he had to remember where he was. *Who* he was. A civilian, now…taking cover from the world outside his windows that faced the Seine and the Eiffel Tower, whose twinkling lights mocked him from across the river.

At least he had finally become accustomed to the barge's gentle rocking as, daily, the world's sightseers in their open-air long boats glided past and under the bridges. These vessels, along with commercial craft sailing up and down the Seine, constantly sent waves toward the embankment where the barge was permanently moored. Most days, now, Finn was even able to ignore the pedestrians on the quay that were forever peering toward the portholes on the land side of this barge that had been his Paris address for the last seven months.

A condo on the water.

Then the rueful thought occurred to him that a "hideout" was probably a more accurate term for his current accommodations, located not far from the Trocadero Gardens, a lush green expanse of park on the Right Bank. He cast another glance out a plate glass window in the main cabin—formerly the pilothouse—that faced a full-on view of the glowing tower not two hundred yards across the water. The mighty filigree of iron girders, bathed at the four corners by the beams of huge spotlights, pointed skyward into inky darkness.

The moment he'd seen the iconic beacon across *L'Étoile's* bow that shined every evening until 1 a.m., he knew his search for the perfect place of refuge was over. Within minutes of his arrival, he'd handed Madame Grenelle a small bundle of euros to secure the lease. Since then, his nightly routine had been to head for his bunk in a stateroom in the stern when the tower's lights went out. Once in bed, he'd pray to God the next eight hours would be uninterrupted by night sweats or the recurring dreams of horror etched in his brain.

He glanced down at the second-hand copy he'd been reading of *Hemingway: The Paris Years* that he'd purchased at one of the bookstalls along the river. He'd been engrossed in its pages since consuming a supper of steaming *coq au vin*. He'd taken pride in the chicken dish doused in red wine that he'd managed to produce from a single pot on one of two burners positioned next to a minuscule stainless steel sink that had been built into a table doubling as a desk. In fact, in recent months he'd discovered that taking cooking classes *à la Française* and reading good books were better than prescription drugs or booze for avoiding re-runs of certain, highly disturbing scenes often playing in his mind's eye.

His glance took in the barge's beautiful teak floors that were partially carpeted with a well-worn Persian rug. A large, wooden wheel, motionless and locked into place, had once steered the barge, but now served as a hat-and-coat rack.

Trust Claudine to find me a unique and *reasonably priced haven in which to lick my wounds...*

His elderly unmarried aunt, Claudine Deschanel, was well aware that her nephew had broken a tradition by resigning his commission at the ripe old age of thirty-seven. No matter that there had been a male Deschanel serving in the United States military from the time their celebrated ancestor, Emile Deschanel, had arrived in America as a member of the Marquis de Lafayette's entourage in the American War of Independence. Aunt Claudine had accepted without rancor that two centuries of Deschanel career servicemen had come to an abrupt end.

However, on the day Finn had landed in the City of Light in such terrible shape, the seventy-seven-year-old retired editor of *Paris Vogue* declared matter-of-factly, "You've quit the military? So be it. You've done your duty to History, to God, to Country, and to my almighty baby brother. If Andrew doesn't like your decision, too bad! Be as fearless with that tyrant father of yours as you were in all those deployments in the Middle East, Finn, to say nothing of that damned airbase outside Las Vegas. I say it's time for a new chapter, *mon cher. Vive La France!*'

Promising not to reveal his whereabouts to anyone, she'd rung her longtime friend, Eloise Grenelle, and secured him a place to live in the stern of the old lady's black-hulled barge. Then Claudine made an appointment for him with a shrink she knew.

I'll get through this...I just need more time. I'll deal with Dad...eventually.

And as for certain other members of his family circle...maybe in a few months he'd bite the bullet and get back in touch, but for now, he needed to be just where he was.

If only I could get one decent night's sleep!

Through the bulkhead wall of bookcases at the far end of the wood-paneled pilothouse he was suddenly aware of an exchange of agitated female voices alternating with an equally excited masculine speaker. Despite the rising volume in the compartments next door, Finn couldn't quite make out what was being said—either due to his fledgling grasp of French or the rapidity with which everyone was speaking. However, he clearly heard the loud sounds of a woman weeping, and then a low male voice crooning in a tone that Finn assumed was meant to be soothing.

The sorrowful wails instantly flung him back to the sight of smoking rubble in a well-remembered village compound. He could still see—

Stop! You are on the barge. This is Paris. This is today. Like they told you...think of something else!

But it was hard to do that. From Eloise Grenelle's section of the boat, the echoes of distress being suffered by the kindly woman raised the hairs on his arm. Soon, he could hear that her cries had turned to moaning, but that, too, reminded him of the women and men who had haunted his dreams these last years.

A few moments later, Finn heard the sudden sound of footsteps on his deck outside his end of the barge that swiftly switched to a fierce pounding on his front door. His well-tuned senses brought an absolute awareness of the here-and-now.

"*Monsieur, monsieur!*" a voice shouted in anxious waves. "*Ouvrez la porte, s'il vous plaît! Ouvrez! Ouvrez!*"

Finn knew enough bare-bones French by now to cross the pilothouse in three strides and fling open the wooden door. At the sight of the stricken expression of Madame Grenelle's son, every word of the language that Finn had struggled to acquire since coming to Paris suddenly evaporated.

"What's the matter, Pierre? What's happened? Is Madame ill?"

Pierre stood, frozen in place.

"*Mon fils…*my, my son…" he struggled in English.

Tears had begun to cascade down his cheeks, and in a torrent of French he wailed, "*Jean-Pierre! Il a été abattu…les terrorists…les—*"

"Madame Grenelle's grandson has been shot?" Finn translated, wanting to be sure that the word '*abattu*' meant 'shot' and not 'killed.'

Pierre spoke about as much English as Finn spoke and understood French. Madame Grenelle's son shook his head, his eyes assuming a haunted look.

"*Oui! Une attaque terroriste! Comme Charlie Hebdo, comprenez vous? Beaucoup d'attaques!*"

Finn struggled to understand. "You're saying it was a terrorist attack…like in January at the cartoon magazine in Paris, yes? Many attacks on civilians tonight?"

"*Oui!*"

Finn could feel the blood begin to pound in his head.

He comprehended most of Pierre's further explanations: that someone from a hospital had called with news that Pierre's twenty-nine-year-old son, Jean-Pierre, had been dining with a friend in the 10th *Arrondissement*. Pierre named half a dozen other locations around Paris, including a concert hall, where coordinated bands of black-suited Muslim extremists had reportedly killed with abandon.

"I must go to find my son!" Pierre finished, tears still streaming.

Finn felt his heart begin to thrum in his chest as he sensed his entire body going into well-schooled commando mode from his days when he jumped into real aircraft at a moment's notice.

First thing: get the facts. Second—

The Frenchman, framed by the entrance to the pilothouse, raised his hands to cover his face, his shoulders heaving.

Finn pushed all other thoughts aside and asked in the best French he could muster, "Pierre, how can I help? What do you need me to do? Stay with your mother?"

"No, no, my wife will stay here with her while I go to find Jean-Pierre. I don't want them to see Jean-Pierre, until I know…"

"I understand," Finn said with a brusque nod.

Then in half-French, half-English, Pierre told Finn that Saint Louis hospital was directly across from the café *Le Petit Cambodge* where his son had apparently been shot, but for some unknown reason, Jean-Pierre had been taken, instead, to the American Hospital on the outskirts of Paris proper.

Pierre looked pleadingly at Finn. "Since you are *Américain*, I thought…if you—"

"*Oui!* Of course," Finn replied. "The American Hospital on Boulevard Victor Hugo. I'll go with you. I know exactly where it is."

"Oh, merci, monsieur. You are most kind to come with me," Pierre murmured, his relief evident.

Finn dismissed the man's thanks, grabbing his Air Force flight jacket off a spoke of the ship's wooden wheel. Through the barge window, the Eiffel Tower suddenly plunged into darkness. He glanced again at the ship's clock. It was just 1 a.m. He wondered when the lights of Paris would come back on after this night of terror, along with what variety of horror would confront them at the American Hospital?

The biggest question of all for Finn was...would he embarrass himself if he witnessed a bloodbath again?

"Let's roll," he barked in English, as if commanding a member of his former aircrew, adding, "my car—*ma voiture*—is parked quite close by."

Finn waited until 3 a.m. Saturday morning outside the Intensive Care Unit until twenty-nine-year-old Jean-Pierre was wheeled back to the ICU after surgery for wounds to his back and head. Finn then went home to shower and called his Aunt Claudine at her apartment at dawn to give her the terrible news about her friend's grandson. All day Saturday, the two Deschanels sat vigil with Jean-Pierre's family in the waiting room.

Finn would never divulge to the Grenelles, however, that he was quite familiar with the hospital at #63 Boulevard Victor Hugo. It was an institution established in a chic Paris suburb, Neuilly-sur-Seine, in 1906 by a group of philanthropic Americans to serve the burgeoning expatriate community. Its visitors and patients had included literary luminaries like Hemingway, Fitzgerald, and Gertrude Stein. Thank God Claudine knew a nice lady shrink there, skilled in treating returning vets with "curious forms" of Post-Traumatic Stress Syndrome.

Early Saturday evening, Finn looked up as the trauma doctor who had operated on Jean-Pierre approached, beckoning him to step to one side for a private conference in English. With an eye to the flight jacket of the former serviceman, the surgeon whispered to Finn that he had never seen injuries like those suffered by the patient except on a battlefield of war. Fortunately, Claudine and Eloise Grenelle didn't hear the doctor's remarks as the two old friends sat conversing in French.

"Why was Jean-Pierre taken to this hospital, so far away the restaurant where the attacks occurred?" Finn asked, trying to keep the criticism from his voice. He knew better than most that immediate treatment could make an enormous difference with wounds as acute as Jean-Pierre's and he sought an answer to the question that had been plaguing the young man's family since Friday night.

"Saint Louis Hospital—near *Le Petit Cambodge* and the concert hall—was overwhelmed with casualties," the doctor explained with a shrug. "The other person in the ambulance was an American and conscious, as Jean-Pierre was not. She apparently demanded to be brought here when the line of emergency vehicles ferrying victims to the nearest medical treatment backed up more than a block. We have an ER here, too, so the emergency responders agreed to her wishes, given the jam-up near the scene of the attacks. It was anybody's guess how long they would have waited to get help at St. Louis versus the twenty or thirty minutes it took to drive at top speed here to Neuilly."

Finn nodded, and resumed his seat next to his aunt, repeating to the assembled group what he'd learned.

Nearing midnight that endless Saturday, the Deschanels were urged to go home to get some rest. Then again on Sunday mid-morning and into the afternoon, Finn and his aunt stayed with the family when Jean-Pierre was taken for a second time into the operating room for an emergency procedure to relieve the building pressure of blood leaking into his brain cavity.

Their huddled little group had watched in silence as orderlies wheeled the patient, his head and upper body swathed in bandages, out of the trauma ward and down the corridor toward an unknown fate. For Finn, a bizarre wave of relief came over him that the scene greeting them now and when they had initially arrived at the hospital was so antiseptic that it had spared him the sight of the bloody slaughter he'd seen so often in the Middle East. Reflecting how thankful he'd been to stay at a distance from the carnage the last two days, he was overcome with shame.

As Sunday evening approached, the lights came on in the hospital's waiting area, rousing Finn from his viciously circular thoughts and sending Madame Grenelle and his aunt once again into a rapid-fire exchange of French. Listening intently, Finn gathered that the Grenelle matriarch urged him and his aunt to return home for a second time and await a phone call when there was word as to the outcome of this latest medical procedure. Claudine, her weariness reflected in her lined face, nodded in agreement and beckoned to Finn to obey Eloise's bidding. The pair walked out the hospital's impressive glass and brushed-steel revolving door and into the cold, dark, November night. Claudine paused, allowing her nephew to keep a grip on her arm.

"Why don't we both go to my place for something to eat?" she suggested. "I'll make us some scrambled eggs and then you can go back to the barge, feed Eloise's cat, and get some sleep. Monday may be a very long day."

"Sounds good."

"As for tomorrow, shall we plan to meet here at the hospital, say around quarter to twelve?"

"Don't you want me to pick you up?" he asked,

predicting the answer of his feisty, septuagenarian aunt.

"No, not at that hour. It's faster for both of us Monday if I take the metro or the bus." She regarded her nephew for a long moment then said, "You heard the American doctor describe Jean-Pierre's injuries earlier today. Given what you know about these things, Finn, what chance of survival does poor Jean-Pierre have, do you think?"

Finn hesitated. He debated whether to hold off giving his dire prediction. His opinion was based on the ravages of similar heavy-arms fire he'd witnessed in his time in the military. He could only assume that the bi-lingual surgeon treating Jean-Pierre had described in more detail to the Grenelle family the seriousness of the victim's wounds— and their likely outcome. Why should he voice the grim probability that the young man had only a slim chance of pulling through—and in heaven knows what shape?

"Well," he replied carefully, "let's hope a second surgery will do some good."

"But you don't think there's much, at this point, that can help, do you? Even if he lives, he'll be little more than a vegetable, given his head wounds?"

Finn held her gaze. "We're in a Catholic country, so I suppose we shouldn't rule out miracles."

"And I suppose we should pray for one," Claudine noted acerbically, "but alas, we've missed Sunday Mass— yet again."

Finn could think of several miracles they should probably be praying for.

CHAPTER 2

November 16, 2015

Juliet Morgan Thayer had no notion of what lay ahead as she stepped off an all-night flight to Paris from San Francisco a few minutes before ten a.m. on that Monday morning in mid-November. Hers had been one of the first planes to land after De Gaulle Airport had reopened following the terrorist attacks. An eerie stillness permeated the nearly deserted terminal and she was struck by the pinched, pained expressions on the faces of her fellow passengers, still reeling, as she was, from what had happened in France less than three days before their arrival.

Turning left with the crowd, her knee-high winter boots treaded soundlessly along the close-cropped red carpeting that led from the jet way into the central section of the airport. Military police in full battle gear lined the corridors in all directions, stone-faced beneath the tilt of their berets. Everywhere she looked, a forest of menacing black assault rifles were pointed at the floor, trigger fingers extended along the gun barrels. She could feel the eyes of the security forces giving her the once-over as they warily scanned arriving and departing travelers passing by their assigned positions.

Her senses on high alert for anything out of the ordinary, Juliet pulled her 21-inch wheeled carry-on behind her, more convinced than ever that if a terrorist suddenly appeared, there was nothing she could do to protect herself.

Just like poor Avery…

The minute Juliet had heard her longtime friend's thin, reedy voice message from Friday on her cell phone, she'd gone online to purchase a one-way ticket to Paris. Avery's call for help had been amongst seventeen messages that Juliet had been too swamped with work to answer until the weekend. When she finally heard it, the sound of screaming sirens had been in the background nearly obliterating the first words of Avery's rasped plea to come to the American Hospital in Paris—and then her phone had abruptly cut off.

It all seemed so surreal. Avery Evans in the wrong place at the wrong time, shot by a bunch of terrorists who didn't even know her name, let alone that she was American.

Juliet hadn't slept a moment as she hurtled six thousand miles through the air at 33,000 feet. Whenever she closed her eyes, horrifying images she'd seen on CNN danced on her lids: sirens wailing…police massing outside a concert hall, their bodies encased in bullet-proof uniforms and helmets with opaque shields…first responders in Day-Glo vests carrying blood-drenched victims on stretchers on that most unlucky of Fridays, November 13th. Just before Juliet had boarded the plane, the latest estimates were that 350 had been injured and some 130 souls had lost their lives suddenly, randomly, and with absolutely no warning to family or friends.

Oh, God, is Avery alive…or is she *one of the fatalities?*

Juliet scanned the overhead signs for directions to Passport Control and then simply surrendered to the line of travelers funneling down a long corridor as her thoughts rehashed the unhappier aspects of her departure from San Francisco the previous evening. Everyone at home had denounced this trip and thrown roadblocks in her way. Juliet's father feared for her safety, given she spoke such poor French. Her mother—as usual in solidarity with Juliet's eldest brother—was of the opinion that her only daughter was being rash and overly dramatic. "For pity's sake, Juliet! You're crazy to launch into such a wild goose chase for a wanna-be portrait artist with little talent who left a real job here to dabble in Paris."

"She has *lots* of talent," Juliet had hotly defended her friend. "You're just parroting what your sainted eldest son said when Avery quit working for him."

Another major detractor regarding Juliet's dash to San Francisco International Airport had been her on-again-off-again boyfriend, Jed Jarvis. At the ridiculous age of 36, they were still tap-dancing around whether or not they were even an actual couple.

"Don't be stupid," Jed had declared when she told him of her plans to depart immediately. "You don't even know for sure where Avery is. Let her family play rescue ranger. Brad said her dad's rich enough to medevac her outta there if she needs it."

But the reaction from Bradshaw Thayer, IV, her eldest brother, was the worst, hands down. A former Stanford track star, the Thayer family Golden Boy and current CEO of a successful family start-up had stormed into the art department after her staff had departed for the day. She'd been toiling over a sketch of a roadside bomb blowing up a hum-vee before creating it electronically in her computer-assisted design program. She liked to work out her ideas on paper, first, but for this assignment, she'd felt nothing but a sense of loathing both for the project—and her participation in it.

"Shit, Jules!" Brad had yelled, stomping across the room to stand next to her slanted drawing board. "I just got your email. I don't care what's happened in France! No way can you take time off right now. You're on deadline, remember?"

"But I can't get Avery to answer her phone!"

Brad had shot her a look of outrage mixed with disdain when Juliet announced she'd already booked the first available flight to Paris. He'd slammed the side of his fist on the top edge of her big computer screen, nearly tipping it over.

"I said *no*, God dammit! We've got two new video games in production and I need you to get on the stick and work out the final packaging. I just got another big reorder from the Air Force wanting to use the next *Sky Slaughter* release in their latest flight-training program. It's been the number one video on Amazon for six months now. Every kid in America wants the next version for Christmas. You can't leave now, even for a *day*!"

Juliet's temples began to pound as they did so often in confrontations with her eldest sibling.

"The woman ran our computer graphics department for four years," she'd protested. "She's a large part of why you *got* that reorder!"

"So?"

An insolent 'so' had always been Brad's go-to non-answer, but by then, his eyes were slits of blue ice and his lips had all but disappeared as he scowled at his sister.

"When she called me, she was in an ambulance!" Juliet protested. "She begged me to come."

"*So?*" he repeated. "Your supposed best pal left the company at the exact moment our video sales went viral and we were about to take GatherGames public! She was a key employee. She could have jeopardized *everything*."

Juliet threw the pencil she'd been sketching with onto the table. "And you're comparing the run-up to GG's public offering on the hallowed New York Stock Exchange with someone who's been shot in a café by *terrorists*?"

"Whatever…" he said, with a wave of his hand.

"Well, I'm going to Paris to see if my best friend is still

alive, so just deal with it!"

She'd grabbed her tote bag and exited her office before he could answer or threaten to fire her, which he did, anyway, in a subsequent text message.

Just thinking about that conversation with her brother provoked a bolt of anger in Juliet's solar plexus so potent, it nearly knocked her flat. And now, here she was, in the supposed City of Light that had entered one of the darkest periods in its history. In near-panic mode, she wondered how she would navigate the next few days with her lousy command of French, a factor that her other brother Jamie had also pointed out—although more gently than her father—when he drove her to the airport.

James Diaz Thayer…the one person always in my corner— and Avery's, too. If only Jamie had come with her.

Just then, Juliet caught sight of the sign guiding travelers to the airport's immigration checkpoint. By this time, her rolling suitcase felt as if it were full of rocks. She was dizzy from both jet lag and lack of sleep. The wave of anxiety gnawing in the pit of her stomach made her fear she might be sick right in front of all those French police clad in riot gear. Additional men in army uniforms were posted in front of airport shops and cafés that were abandoned and shuttered tight. The passenger next to her on the flight had said that several routes of the underground metro had been closed until further notice. Fortunately, a helpful flight attendant had told her where she could most likely find a taxi—if there were any to be had.

The small crowd already gathered at immigration stood silently waiting their turns. She wondered how many people in line had rushed to Paris like she had in search of loved ones whose fate it had been to end up in a Paris hospital—or worse—after Friday's attacks? Glancing at her watch, Juliet felt another wave of anxiety assault her.

How long would it take her to get to the American Hospital? And where the heck was it, anyway?

"*En avant!*"

Juliet hadn't noticed who had barked the order, but she was being waved forward to one of several glass windows. The blue-coated officer stamping passports scrutinized her face and auburn, shoulder-length hair, comparing them with her picture ID. He asked in clipped tones in English why she was entering France at such a perilous time.

Juliet responded in her halting French, hoping to convince the officer of the importance of her mission. "M-my friend...she's like a sister to me. She was shot on Friday and I've come to try to—"

"*Est-elle morte?*" he replied, switching to his native language.

Did the officer actually ask, "Is she dead?"

Juliet sucked in her breath. Her father was right. Every word of French she'd learned in one of the few academic courses she'd taken in art school flew out of her head.

"I don't know," she answered, remembering suddenly, "*Je ne sais pas.*"

The immigration officer's expression softened, his pen poised over Juliet's documents. Despite the man's civil inquiries, however, she felt as if she were treading through a movie that was set in Nazi-occupied France during World War II.

"You haven't noted how long you'll be staying in this country." He pointed to the form she'd filled out on board the plane.

"I don't know...it depends on—"

"Just an estimate will do. Shall we say a month?"

"Maybe less...but yes...a month is probably best to put down."

Brad's most recent text said he would "fire her ass" if

she stayed in Paris more than a week.

If Avery has died, though, it'll take time to have her body shipped and—

Stop! she ordered herself. The only way to get through this was to keep calm, put one foot in front of the other, and see where things led.

The officer glanced at the line of travelers standing behind her as he stamped her passport and handed it to her through the window.

"I will pray that your friend is all right," he said, surprising her with his kindly tone. "So many are not."

"I know," she murmured. "Thank you."

Juliet knew at that moment she was not in a movie. This was real. Perhaps the immigration officer also knew someone who had been injured or killed? Six degrees of separation. Maybe less.

With her passport restored to her, Juliet blurted, "I am so sorry for what has happened in France, *monsieur.*"

The man behind the plate glass nodded and their eyes met.

"It will likely be called our Nine-Eleven, don't you suppose?"

Juliet nodded without reply, thinking to herself that the brutal attacks at the French cartoon magazine, *Charlie Hebdo,* the previous January had come close to qualifying as a French 9/11. Poor France, she thought, pushing through the turnstile to her right and sprinting through the Arrivals door, her suitcase in tow.

Once outside the airport in the cold November morning air, she was assaulted by the disconcerting sounds of whirling helicopters hovering overhead. Fortunately, there were a number of taxis waiting for passengers and Juliet raced to join the short line. Everywhere she gazed, scores more military and local police looking like Star Wars warriors patrolled the entrance and the airport's perimeters.

The driver of the car she was assigned gave a perfunctory nod and loaded her suitcase into the trunk. She showed him the address she'd pulled up on her mobile phone and attempted to ask in French how long it would take to get to the American Hospital. Within the torrent of his reply, she gathered he'd said that it was located on the outskirts of the city and was about a half-hour drive, given the light traffic.

Juliet sank into the back seat and closed her eyes. Half an hour. In half an hour, she would find out if Avery had survived.

The car left the airport complex and entered the nearly empty streets. Rousing herself from her stupor, Juliet noted that flags everywhere were flying at half-staff. More helicopters were buzzing overhead. She tried to ignore them, along with her copy of the *International New York Times* that she'd tossed on the seat beside her. The blaring headline declared that the remaining terrorists who hadn't blown themselves up had not yet been apprehended.

Don't think about that now…just think about getting to Avery…

Juliet drew a shaky breath when the taxi turned off a quiet, tree-lined residential road and sped up a cement ramp, halting in front of a stone and red brick-fronted building that turned out to be the entrance to the American Hospital. The driver, having gathered from their halting exchanges en route that his passenger knew someone wounded in the recent attacks, bounded from the car and lifted her small suitcase from the trunk.

"*Bonne chance, mademoiselle,*" he said with a melancholy smile, refusing to accept payment for the trip.

Moisture welled in Juliet's eyes at his gesture of kindness and she attempted to smile her thanks in return. She had never felt so exhausted in her life and thought she might keel over right there on the sidewalk and have to be carried into the *L'Hôpital Américain de Paris* on her own stretcher. Inhaling deeply again to steady her nerves, she made a headlong dash toward the chrome and glass revolving door, her wheeled suitcase bumping along behind her.

She never even noticed that a tall figure clad in a worn leather flight jacket was heading in precisely the same direction at the same moment she was—equally in a hurry.

"Oompf! *Oww!*" Juliet cried, her elbow plowing into a man's mid-section.

A split second following this collision, a large, strong hand grabbed her upper arm, only just preventing her from collapsing across her suitcase and perhaps even landing on the cement in front of the revolving door.

"I am *so* sorry!" apologized the man who had been both her victim and, now, her rescuer.

By this time, he'd grabbed her other arm and righted the two of them. The stranger appeared close to her in age. His slightly Gallic profile made her assume he was French. Embroidered on the chest of his leather jacket on the left side was the name "Deschanel." However, the words he'd said in English were spoken in a perfectly normal American accent, which startled her.

"Are you okay?" he asked with a worried frown.

"*Yesss,*" she hissed between clenched teeth. "Barely."

She rubbed her elbow that still smarted from the impact. He removed his hands from her shoulders and studied her briefly. Towering above her by at least a foot, and broad-shouldered, the man had closed-cropped, jet black hair. The angled planes of his face were smooth-shaven and his starched, blue cotton collared shirt beneath his jacket gave him a squeaky clean appearance.

He said, "I didn't see you until the last second when you just suddenly appeared, barreling toward the door." He paused, adding, "Like I was." Then he asked for a second time, "Are you sure you're all right?"

The near pile up was her fault, she knew, but she didn't have time to apologize.

"I'm okay!" she insisted, and made a grab for the handle of her suitcase, propelling herself and it through the door of the hospital without a backward glance.

Would Avery be a patient here, she wondered as she sped through the lobby at a dead run—or would her best friend be lying in the morgue?

CHAPTER 3

Avery was alive!

Juliet kept her eyes glued on the hospital's receptionist at the Information kiosk as she waited impatiently for directions to her friend's room. She sensed the tall individual she'd literally run into outside the hospital a few minutes ago had just come through the revolving door and was now crossing the lobby behind her. He strode with some urgency down a corridor to her left, past the sign "Intensive Care Unit" that featured an arrow pointing in the same direction he was headed.

He sure looks like he's late, she thought. If he was a doctor, she hoped for his patients' sakes he was not scheduled to perform any tricky procedures today.

The other best news of the day, as far as Juliet was concerned, was that the entire staff at the American Hospital was apparently required to speak a passable amount of English that certainly bested her own abilities in French. After a brief exchange, she was astonished to learn that hers was the solitary name on the approved-visitors roster for Ms. Avery Evans, noting "Juliet Thayer" as "next of kin." More good news: Avery had been assigned a private room on the post-surgery ward and her condition had just been upgraded from "critical" to "serious."

At least she's not in the ICU, Juliet considered, feeling relieved that she wasn't being told to go down the same corridor as the man in the leather jacket. She should have offered an apology for rolling over his foot with her suitcase, but then surely, current circumstances excused her?

The receptionist gave a nod in the direction of Juliet's luggage.

"You've only just arrived in Paris, *oui?*"

"Yes. I flew from the States as soon as I received word that Ms. Evans had been shot in the attacks."

"You must be exhausted," the young woman offered sympathetically, "but your cousin will be overjoyed to have you here, I expect."

Cousin? Juliet almost smiled. Trust Avery, after only six months of living in Paris, to be schooled in the ways of French bureaucracy and to list her friend as a close family member in hopes it would gain Juliet easy entry upstairs if she'd raced to France as Avery had so poignantly summoned her.

A few minutes later, Juliet hesitated at the door to Avery's darkened room, not wishing to wake her. The still figure cloaked up to her neck in crisp, white sheets, was either asleep or sedated following the three-hour surgery that, according to the nurse at the desk, Avery had endured in the early hours of Saturday morning. Juliet tiptoed across the room and took a seat on a metal chair beside the bed. Within seconds, Avery's eyes flew open.

"Jules! Oh my God…you came!" she murmured, her voice hoarse.

"Well, don't you think you took some awfully extreme measures to get me here?" Juliet replied in the usual teasing way they had with each other.

"You wouldn't come with me the first time I asked," she said, the faintest of smiles tracing her lips, "so…a pal's gotta do what a pal's gotta do."

Avery's eyes fluttered shut and she appeared to drift back to sleep. Juliet settled into the chair next to the bed, her mind shifting to the day when her best friend left San Francisco for Paris. Juliet had driven her to the airport. All the way there, Avery had pleaded they should exchange the profession of commercial art for a further and more serious study of landscape and portrait painting, respectively. "Video war games are your brother's obsession, not yours," she had implored. "Designing illustrations on boxes of this crap wasn't the reason we went to art school."

"I know, I know!" Juliet had retorted. "Don't rub it in."

In the beginning, their graphic design work had been an easy way to pay off their student loans while making good money creating the illustrations used on the packaging for innocent little games like electronic tic-tac-toe. Then, all of a sudden, Brad decided to launch his own version of a digital World War III and life at work became crazy. The first in the series of violent games where players gained points by electronically blowing up "high value targets" that were clad in the distinctive clothing of citizens of the Middle East was an immediate hit and received millions of dollars worth of free advertising on Facebook and Twitter from its enthusiastic fans—mostly male. GatherGames' meteoric success, in turn, prompted the move to take the company public with the stock debuting high above predictions. Immediately the pressure was on to come up with more games to keep fans, Wall Street, and the investors happy.

"Not even Jamie can stand to watch the footage anymore, the poor guy!" Avery had said that last day before she'd boarded her flight. "Do you actually think your younger brother likes editing animated blood and guts all day long? '*Sky Slaughter...Death by Drones*'," she mimicked in sepulchral tones. "Gimme a break!"

"Jamie claims he's getting Post-Traumatic Stress Disorder just from staring at all those mythical kill sequences for hours on end," Juliet had agreed with a mirthless laugh.

"He probably *is* getting PTSD! Just because he's mastered the technology side of the video game business doesn't mean he meant this to be his life's work, does it?"

"God, no!" It seriously jerked Juliet's chain that Brad had pressured Jamie away from his editing job at Pixar studios in the East Bay by both demanding family solidarity and making him Chief Technology Officer when the Thayer family business was first being bootstrapped. "Without even asking, Brad slotted my poor baby bro into editing these horror shows to save money, I guess. By that time, Pixar had hired his replacement and he was stuck."

Avery's parting comment before she boarded her plane for Paris that day had returned to haunt Juliet this past weekend.

"Has anyone at GatherGames ever thought about the implications of what they're slinging out there into the Universe?" she'd groused. "'G.I.s pitted against the Muslim world!' Jeez...I couldn't believe it when Brad ordered us to print that phrase on the outside of the box."

"Oh, you mean how *Sky Slaughter* desensitizes pimply teenagers into thinking that killing other human beings is a w-a-a-y cool, patriotic sport?"

"That," Avery said, "and the fact that anyone can use the encrypted messaging between players to communicate anywhere in the world—and not even the F.B.I or the C.I.A. can crack the codes."

"Or so we think," Juliet had quipped. "Brad says the government's National Security Agency *has* been trying to crack private codes from telephone calls and bank records and Google searches, sucking up all our data to turn us into a police state."

"Brad thinks NSA is cracking *hundreds* of individually-invented encryption codes?" Avery had scoffed. "That older brother of yours is paranoid."

Since Friday's attacks, the newspapers and TV reports

were full of speculation that the Paris terrorists had used encryption technology embedded in video games and cell-phone messaging applications to exchange communications during the run-up to their devastating assaults on French civilians. Bolstering Avery's contention that encryption was hard to crack, even by the NSA, authorities were bemoaning via the media that they couldn't decipher pre-instructions that had been transmitted, terrorist-to-terrorist.

And given her acrimonious parting from her employer six months ago, Avery had made no effort to conceal her disdain for the way in which hotshot Stanford Business School graduate-cum-CEO Bradshaw Thayer IV had morphed into an "arrogant, insufferable, dot-com asshole."

"Look, I'm sorry," Avery had apologized one time. "I know he's your flesh-and-blood—if it's possible you were born from the same loins—but really, he's a total jerk."

And now, gazing at Avery in her hospital bed—eyes closed, face pale as the pillow behind it—Juliet was forced to admit that she completely agreed with Avery's assessment of Brad's behavior since the company had gained success producing video war games particularly noted for their realistic violence. Juliet recalled how tempted she'd been half a year ago to hop on the plane alongside her former "cubicle captive"—as Avery had described their working environment. But, of course, Juliet hadn't gone to Paris, citing the irrefutable fact the Thayer clan was dangerously up to its eyebrows in debt helping her older brother launch his electronic empire.

But why, Juliet wondered, had she allowed Brad's arguments to convince her to take over Avery's former position as design director? Why hadn't she made the break at that moment and pursued her true love, landscape painting? She had allowed herself be convinced that, as a member of the hallowed, fifth-generation Thayers of San Francisco, family loyalty came first. After Friday's attacks, she wasn't so sure she still bought into Brad's line that encryption was the bulwark of free speech—and freedom, period—and that there was more at stake than just a job she'd grown to despise in a company whose recent products she now hated.

Why did life have to be so complicated?

Juliet heaved a sigh and glanced around at the sterile surroundings. To the right of the hospital bed, a machine hummed rhythmically as it dispensed the proper amounts of intravenous painkiller for a patient who had had several bullets removed from her right shoulder and upper arm, both of which were swathed in multiple layers of bandages.

Juliet shifted her weight on the metal chair beside Avery's bed and felt her own lids grow heavy. She closed her eyes as the accumulation of stress and travel fatigue pulled her under, and soon she fell fast asleep, sitting bolt upright.

Avery stirred restlessly in her bed and looked over at her sleeping friend.

"Jules?"

In an instant, Juliet awoke and sat up straight, but her eyes remained at half-mast for a few seconds longer. "Hey there," she murmured. "How are you feeling? Can I get you something?"

Avery lifted her head off the pillow and winced. "They had to set my arm in a couple of places in order to get the bones back in line. I have no idea what they did to my shoulder, but it hurts like holy hell."

In a show of sympathy, Juliet leaned forward and lightly patted her friend's good hand lying on top of the bedcovers. "I learned from the receptionist that you told them I was your next of kin, and a first cousin, no less," she teased.

"Well, that's practically true," whispered Avery. Her eyes fluttered shut once more as she added, "I would have said 'sister'—but we look so different."

It was laughably true. Avery was short and a little stocky, with a truly arresting set of breasts and a mop of wildly curly dark hair, while Juliet's slender height and shoulder-length auburn mane were a complete give-away as to her predominately Irish-English ancestry.

"Well, I'm honored to be named as your cousin," Juliet said, giving Avery's uninjured hand another small squeeze.

"I figured that you'd be the only one to show up," Avery muttered, barely awake.

Juliet knew that Avery had very little hope that her mother, an aging hippie growing medical marijuana somewhere in the wilds of northern California, would come riding to the rescue. And, sadly, the same was probably true for her father, Stephen Evans, a Wall Street investment banker whom Avery hadn't seen much of since her parents split up when she was six. Avery had once disclosed that at least her father had granted her a modest trust fund at age thirty-five, which she'd apparently used to "jump ship," as Brad had termed it. Given the crazy pressure they'd both endured at GatherGames, Juliet hadn't blamed her friend one bit for leaving and, in fact, had nothing but admiration—and a good dose of envy— that she'd had the means to do so.

Juliet would never dispute the truth that Avery had been the leader in their relationship from the first day they'd met as undergraduates at the Art Center in Pasadena, a decade and a half ago. Gazing at her friend, now, immobilized in a hospital bed in a foreign country,

Juliet could hardly believe the chain of events that had reunited them.

Avery moved her head from side to side, uttering apologetically. "Sorry. I keep dozing off. It's the meds. Did I mention yet how glad I am to see you?"

Juliet felt her lips curl in a smile. "Yes, you did. And by the way, the nurse told me how lucky you are regarding your shoulder, as opposed to your right arm. They extracted two bullets lodged in tissue, only. No bones there were affected at all."

"Even so, that's the kind of luck I could certainly do without."

"Thank heavens you're left-handed and you'll be able to paint your portraits as well as you always did," Juliet said, trying to find something cheerful to offer.

As Avery closed her eyes once more, a tear from each corner slid down her cheeks.

"The meds aren't helping?" Juliet worried that the pain had increased.

Avery's voice caught. "How will my friend ever paint again?" she cried. "He was shot in the back when he threw himself on top of me right after the guns started spraying bullets everywhere!"

Avery, whom Juliet had never once seen cry in the years they'd known each other, began to weep quietly.

"I can't imagine what that was like..." murmured Juliet. "Who were you with?"

"Someone from painting class. We were sitting side-by-side on the left side of the restaurant, our backs to the door. We both heard a commotion and some shouts and saw this guy come in with this huge, long gun, and then everything exploded. The next thing I knew, I was on the floor with a bunch of bodies heaped on top of me, including my friend, closest to me, and also the waitress who'd been serving us...and I don't even know who else."

She continued in a strangled whisper, "I was having Asian noodle soup...and the noodles were everywhere... dripping with blood."

"Oh, Avery...I am so sorry this happened to you. I-I—"

Juliet was at a loss for a way to comfort her friend. Meanwhile, Avery began to toss her head back and forth against her pillow, tears now streaming down her face.

"A hospital was across the street, but the line of ambulances stretched a block..."

"Thank God you got yours to take you to this one."

"I must have passed out after I yelled at them that I was an American and wanted to come here. I don't even remember the trip," she said, choking on a sob.

All Juliet could think to do was hold her friend's good hand more firmly. She rang for the nurse, who immediately administered an additional sedative. The thickset, no-nonsense woman motioned for Juliet to follow her out of the room.

"Your cousin is not only suffering physical pain from her wounds and surgery," she explained, "but she's still in shock and can't stop reliving the moments she was shot. Before you arrived, she demanded to know what happened to the young man that was brought in with her."

"She just told me he threw his body over her to protect her."

The nurse heaved a heavy sigh. "I had to tell her that the poor boy remains in acute, critical condition in Intensive Care."

"Is he going to make it?"

The nurse gave a shrug, raised an eyebrow, but didn't hazard an opinion.

Juliet thanked her and returned to Avery's bedside. Several hours later, the wounded young woman awoke suddenly and immediately rang for a nurse. Once again, she demanded to know from the staff member who'd just come on duty the current medical status of the young man brought in the ambulance with her on Friday.

"Unless you are a family member, I am not at liberty to tell you, *mademoiselle*," the new nurse declared in heavily accented English.

"But we were together having dinner when the men started shooting!" protested Avery. "We're good friends, damn it! You've got to find out what's happened!"

Tight-lipped, the nurse merely shook her head disapprovingly and left the room.

"*Merde!*" swore Avery, reaching for the covers with her good left hand and throwing them aside. "I'm going down there!" she announced, and then cried out in pain as she struggled to sit upright.

Juliet bolted from her chair and put a restraining hand on Avery's good shoulder.

"Look, sweetie, I completely understand why you're anxious to know about your friend, but if you get out of bed, you'll hurt yourself and that won't help anything, least of all, you. I'll go and try to find out how he's doing and come right back, I promise."

Avery collapsed onto her pillow while Juliet fretted that any bad news could be even more upsetting than not knowing how the young man was faring. Clearly, though, either Juliet went on an intelligence-gathering mission, or Avery would injure herself trying to find a way to sneak down the hall.

"Tell me his name and I'll see what I can sleuth out," Juliet offered, adding with a wink, "and shall I say you're his fiancée or something?"

Avery snorted and then winced from the pain it caused her arm and shoulder. "He's eight years younger than me," she answered, "and there was no romance between us at all, but he's a hell of a good portrait painter and has been a wonderful friend to me from the day I walked into *L'École des Beaux Arts.*"

Avery's eyes again filled with tears.

"So what's his name?" Juliet asked, preparing to depart.

"Get a piece of paper," Avery directed, her voice choked. "You can write it down and show it to the charge nurse to find him when you get down to the ICU."

Juliet slipped unnoticed past the nurses' station on Avery's floor and sped downstairs. She was grateful to have previously spotted the sign indicating the location of the Intensive Care Unit at the far end of the corridor. Clustered outside that area were knots of people with anxious expressions, all speaking various languages in hushed tones. Juliet supposed each group was holding vigil until they had news of loved ones fighting for their lives inside the ICU.

Were they all victims of the shootings on Friday, she wondered, or was it the usual collection of tragic circumstances that could snuff out life from accident, sudden heart attack, or a deadly disease?

As she approached, a familiar figure came into focus—the person she'd practically run over with her suitcase when she'd made a dash for the hospital's entrance. He had his arm beneath the elbow of a stylishly attired older woman with blondish-grey hair wrapped in a chic chignon anchored at the nape of her neck. Juliet couldn't help but admire the woman's trim figure clad in a classic, black pants suit, her neck artfully swathed by an orange, black, and gold Hermes scarf. Her eyes were luminous behind large, black-rimmed spectacles in the style of Jackie O's sunglasses that had been fashionable a good fifty years earlier.

Both the elderly woman and her escort were listening intently to the words of a white-coated doctor whose attention was directed at another man and woman of middle years. Standing next to the quartet was a second elderly person with wispy, steel gray hair who leaned on a cane.

Juliet halted a few feet away, chagrined to deduce that the man she'd collided with was no arrogant doctor, but was someone who'd rushed to the hospital, just as she had, because of a sick or injured friend or family member.

The physician was speaking French and Juliet could see that Flight Jacket Man, as she decided to call him, was concentrating, laser-like, on the conversation, as if struggling to understand what was being said. The doctor then turned toward him and the woman in the elegant black pants suit. "I was just saying to the family," he volunteered in English within earshot of Juliet, "that the young man is not doing at all well, post-surgery, and we've had to initiate a life support system." He paused, and then added, "I must warn you that the outlook is bleak. We know, now, that he was shot fourteen times."

"Oh, God, no!" murmured the woman whose elbow was still held firmly in her younger escort's hand. She turned swiftly toward the woman with gray hair and spoke in rapid French. "*Eloise, ma chèr amie, je suis terriblement désolé...*"

Juliet recognized the empathy and sorrow laced in the woman's words addressed to her "dearest friend, Eloise"—the part of the exchange Juliet comprehended.

The doctor then continued describing to the English speakers what he had just told the patient's parents and grandmother: that despite a second surgery to remove more shrapnel and ease the swelling in the cranium, the shooting victim remained in very critical condition, having suffered devastating wounds to his upper torso and skull.

"I'm afraid your friends, the Grenelles, are faced with a very difficult decision."

"About whether to keep Jean-Pierre on life support?" interrupted the tall figure in his American accent.

Juliet emitted an audible gasp that drew his attention. In the next second, the two exchanged glances—his of recognition, hers of dismay that the name she'd just heard matched the one she'd jotted down at Avery's behest. "Jean-Pierre Grenelle."

They're speaking about the same young man Avery was with on Friday!

Meanwhile, the doctor nodded to the Americans, adding "We will continue to monitor him closely, of course, but…"

His voice trailed off. Juliet studied the look of sorrow infusing the faces of the Grenelles' two family friends. The slight curve of the nose belonging to Flight Jacket Man reminded her of a young Yves Montand, the late, handsome star of classic French films.

He turned to the elegantly dressed older woman standing beside him. "I've seen these cases countless times, Claudine. It would be merciful to just pull—"

His companion cut in.

"I agree with you, of course," she said, speaking in low tones with a warning glance in the Grenelles' direction, "but this is a decision that only Eloise and her son and his wife can make. Perhaps they will ask us our opinion…perhaps not. Jean-Pierre is their precious boy and a superbly talented artist. Can you imagine what it's like to be the ones to simply switch off a life with such promise?"

Meanwhile, the physician volunteered that he would keep everyone informed as to any change. Addressing the Americans, he added, "You have been good to stand by them all these long hours. Please forgive my brevity, but I must return to the ICU." He inclined his head to include the assembled group and retreated through a pair of double doors.

Juliet stood frozen to the spot. Flight Jacket Man pivoted toward her and extended his hand. "I didn't introduce myself before. I'm Patrick Deschanel," he announced. "'Finn,' to my friends." His direct gaze told her he'd instantly recognized her, just as she had him. She seized his hand as he gestured with his other toward his companion and Jean-Pierre's family members. "This is my aunt, Claudine Deschanel, and our friends, the Grenelles."

"I'm Juliet Thayer. I just got here this morning from San Francisco to be with my friend...who was also wounded in the attacks."

"I *do* remember your arrival," Finn said with the ghost of a smile.

For some reason Juliet continued to clasp his hand. It felt warm and comforting to hold on to something, even if he were a stranger.

"I owe you an apology," she said, staring into electric blue eyes that seemed a startling contrast to Finn Deschanel's tanned face and dark hair. Black Irish, she'd guess, mixed with French, obviously, with a name like Deschanel. "When I jumped from the taxi, I was in a tearing hurry to find out if my friend was alive or—" She halted mid-sentence, not wanting to distress the Grenelles any more than they were already "I-I wasn't looking where I was going. I'm really sorry. And I'm sorry that my suitcase ran over your foot."

"It was my good one, so no harm done."

"Oh, gosh! I'm *so* sorry. I was just horribly worried and jet-lagged and—"

"I'm joking," he reassured her. "I'm perfectly fine."

Juliet didn't know whether to be relieved or annoyed by Finn Deschanel's teasing, so she let go of his hand. The others in his group were closing in on the two of them as if she were now a member of their circle. Finn's slight smile faded as he made introductions to the Grenelles, who stood slightly apart from the Deschanels and Juliet.

"I saw your strong reaction when you overheard the doctor describe the seriousness of Jean-Pierre's wounds," Finn said. "Do you know him?"

"No. As I said, I-I've just flown from California to be with my best friend, who's recovering from gun-shot wounds in the surgery ward." She pointed in the opposite direction down the long corridor that stretched behind them. "Her name is Avery Evans. She...well, actually, she sent me down here to...to try to find out about the man in the ambulance with her. From what I just overheard, it sounds as if he's the same person."

Finn turned his back slightly, placing himself between Juliet and the others and spoke in an even lower voice. "Were they together Friday night?"

"Avery just told me that Jean-Pierre Grenelle was her dinner companion at some Asian restaurant that night. She said that he threw himself on top of her to try to shield her when the shooting began..."

"At *Le Petit Cambodge*?"

"Avery only said it was a restaurant near a hospital—but the ambulance brought them to this place, instead."

Finn's aunt had stepped forward to hear their conversation and was staring at her with a look of astonishment.

"Your friend and Jean-Pierre were *both* at *Le Petit Cambodge* Friday night?" Claudine repeated.

Juliet nodded. "Yes, I think that's right. Avery and Jean-Pierre Grenelle are apparently friends from art school, *L'École des*—"

Juliet stopped speaking and fought back a wave of emotion that had begun to choke her. Avery would be devastated to learn that her poor friend was on life support and it sounded dire. She swallowed hard, waiting until she thought she could continue in a normal tone of voice. Claudine laid a comforting hand on her arm.

Finally, Juliet managed to speak once more. "Avery's French isn't great and I imagine she thought the American Hospital would be…well…better—that is, if she didn't die first."

Finn disclosed quietly, "Apparently, the hospital close to the restaurant was clogged with ambulances. The reason that Jean-Pierre's injuries are so severe is that he was shot many times in his back and head. His chances of survival were probably never good, but we'll just have to wait and see."

"Oh, no!" Juliet said barely above a whisper. "Avery said he smothered her with his body to protect her."

"What is your friend's condition, now?" Finn asked somberly.

"Avery's been badly wounded in one arm and her shoulder. They've upgraded her from 'critical' to 'serious,' though, and the nurse told me that she'll recover."

"Well, that's a blessing…" murmured the elder Deschanel.

Juliet turned to Finn and said in a rush, "My French is horrible. Could you please tell Jean-Pierre's family that Avery considered him a wonderful friend at *L'École*. She's been studying portrait painting in the same class there. He saved her life by knocking them both to the ground when the guns went off."

"*Mon Dieu!*" murmured Finn's aunt. Speaking French, she quickly translated the news of Jean-Pierre's heroism to his three family members who were looking confused by the rapid exchanges that had just taken place in English.

Juliet's gaze traveled from Claudine Deschanel to the stricken expressions of the Grenelles, and finally settled on

Finn. His look of deep compassion enveloped and supported her like the steadying hand she'd seen him place earlier beneath his aunt's arm. She pulled him to one side and spoke quietly. "How can I ever tell Avery that Jean-Pierre is on life support?" she agonized. "She's been through such hell herself, and spoke of nothing else but how wonderful Jean-Pierre has been to her since she came to Paris. She's still not out of the woods with her own injuries. As soon as I walk back in that room, she'll demand to know what I found out." Juliet looked beseechingly at Finn and spoke in a whisper to avoid upsetting the Grenelles even more. "What in the world can I say when I have to tell her that...t-that...his prognosis is so bad? It will be the worst, possible—"

"Shall I go with you?" Finn intervened.

For a long moment, Juliet simply stared at him. A virtual stranger was willing to help Avery when, by-and-large, Juliet's own family had abandoned a former friend and colleague to her fate.

"Would you?" She felt another knot of emotion welling into her throat. "I'd be hugely grateful."

Within seconds, the choking sensation had traveled to her chest, and she could feel moisture brimming her eyes. She raised her hands to her face as the first sob ripped from her throat. She felt a strong arm encircle her. Then Juliet began to weep, whether from jet lag, lack of sleep, or the tragedy of a brave, young French portrait painter clinging to life a short distance from where they stood outside the ICU. She leaned into the expanse of Finn's leather jacket and dissolved into tears that she simply could not keep inside any longer.

CHAPTER 4

Juliet's acute embarrassment over her public meltdown outside the ICU lasted the entire length of the hallway that led back to Avery's hospital room.

"I don't know what came over me," she apologized.

"You're exhausted and most likely in shock yourself," Finn replied. "Don't beat yourself up about it."

"But I still don't know what to tell Avery about Jean-Pierre's condition. *How* should I tell her?"

"Tell her as much of the truth as you think she can handle right now."

"Given how fragile she is, I don't think she can handle any of it."

By this time they had reached Room 203. Avery's hospital bed had been positioned so she could sit up at an angle. She was holding a small paper cup filled with ice chips. Her eyes widened when she noticed a complete stranger had entered her hospital room beside Juliet.

"Who's that?" she demanded weakly.

"Avery, this is an American friend of the Grenelle family... Finn Deschanel. Finn, this is Jean-Pierre's friend from art school, Avery Evans."

Avery fastened her eyes on the newcomer and pleaded, "Have you seen him?"

"Yes," Finn said with a slight nod. "He's had two surgeries and he's still under the anesthetic."

Avery glanced over at Juliet and murmured, "Two? Oh, Jeez...that sounds bad."

Finn added, "Like yours, his wounds from that kind of ammunition can do a lot of damage. The doctors are still assessing everything."

"But will he be okay?" pressed Avery. "Eventually, I mean?" She jutted her chin in the direction of her own arm in its protective sling.

"We won't know the outcome for a while, but Juliet told his family what a good friend he's been to you, and sent your best wishes, which they deeply appreciated."

Avery demanded, "Juliet, did you tell them he *saved* my life?"

"I told Finn and his aunt, who is a good friend of Jean-Pierre's grandmother, and she told them in much better French than I could have." She forced a smile she didn't feel.

"I think it really helped the Grenelles a lot to hear how bravely he'd behaved under fire like that," Finn volunteered.

Juliet was struck by Finn's gentle approach to softening the blow that would eventually come down when Avery was stronger and could better bear the truth about Jean-Pierre's life-threatening injuries. As he stood beside her bed, he had exhibited a kindness and empathy that Juliet hadn't experienced since she couldn't remember when. Here he was, wearing a military flight jacket, and yet he seemed so different from the hard-ass, cynical, game-playing macho men who'd been part of her life in the last decade. What was this man doing in Paris, she wondered? And why was his aunt also here and so amazingly fluent in French?

Before she could speculate further, Avery closed her eyes and Juliet hastened to rescue the tilted paper cup in her friend's hand.

"Sleepy?" she asked.

Avery nodded. "At least J-P's still alive. I was so worried..." she murmured, and then she began to breathe the even breath of a drug-induced sleep.

Finn motioned for Juliet to step out of the room and

into the hallway. Just then, Claudine appeared at the other end of the corridor, heading in their direction. The closer she drew, the more troubled they could see her expression had become.

Finn almost appeared to stand at attention as if he would salute someone. "What's the matter?" he demanded of his aunt. "Has something happened?"

Claudine halted beside them with a glance at the room number over their heads.

"The Grenelles cannot bring themselves to detach Jean-Pierre's life support. So they're just sitting vigil outside the ICU. They told us to go home and await word."

"Has the doctor said how long this could go on?" Finn asked in a low voice.

Claudine shook her head. "The doctor's in surgery with another patient. The machine is breathing for Jean-Pierre and beyond that, it's just a big question mark what happens next. Eloise won't budge, and neither will Pierre and his wife, so I think we should do as they say and go home."

"Really? Leave them here?" he asked, concern etching his features.

"Yes, I think we should," Claudine replied with a weary sigh.

Juliet imagined that the older woman was feeling the long hours she'd been awake keeping her friends company, to say nothing of the horrific strain on everyone living in Paris that began the previous Friday and hadn't let up.

Meanwhile, Finn had turned his back, his arms folded tightly across his chest. Juliet was startled to see the scowl that now clouded his face.

"The doctor described wounds as severe as any I saw in Kandahar," he said, his voice sounding raw and ragged to Juliet's ears, "and likely as fatal. The guy's entire upper body and head have been ripped apart by heavy-arms fire.

Why don't they put the poor bastard out of his agony!" he declared, slamming one fist into his other hand.

Claudine's look of alarm shifted instantly to Juliet, who gazed back at her with a feeling of both shock and compassion. Finn had just acknowledged he'd served in the U.S. military in the Middle East and undoubtedly had seen horrific acts of war—in stark contrast to the simulated carnage she'd witnessed in her brother's video war games. The flight jacket he wore made sense, now.

She put a tentative hand on Finn's forearm. "You both must be absolutely exhausted...and I'm about to drop myself from either hunger or jet-lag. I agree. I think all three of us need a break. Let's leave."

Finn nodded, a kind of detached coolness masking his features.

Claudine glanced worriedly at her nephew and then said to Juliet, "Finn has his car here and can drop us both off. Where are you staying?"

"Avery doesn't know it yet," Juliet replied, "but I'm going to borrow her apartment on the *Rue de Lille*." She turned to address Finn. "I hope that won't take you too far out of your way? I could easily just get a taxi."

As if shaking himself out of a trance, he replied, "No, no...not out of our way at all. *Rue de Lille* is not that far from Claudine's place on *Rue Jacob*. They're both on the Left Bank."

"Great. Give me a sec to find Avery's house key. I saw her purse on the bed stand. The emergency responders must have gathered it up when they put her in the ambulance."

Fortunately, Avery's keys were easily located at the bottom of her handbag next to her cell phone. Juliet scribbled a note and tucked it under the paper cup half full of melted ice chips. It was early evening by now and it had grown dark outside the hospital windows. Juliet imagined that the nurses would soon be coming in with Avery's evening cocktail of sedatives and pain pills. She wrote:

> *I'm at your flat, a cell phone call away*
> *and not too far by metro, I'm told.*
> *Otherwise, I'll see you in the a.m.*
> *Love, your Cuz...*

She dangled the keys in one hand and pulled her suitcase by her other as she emerged from Avery's room. "For once, something was easy around here," she announced, and then halted in her tracks. "Where's your aunt?"

"Claudine decided the quickest way to get home was by metro, since her line is back up and running again. I expect by now, the stations are swarming with cops."

"Oh, gosh! I hope your driving me to Avery's didn't—"

Finn laughed. "God, no! My aunt at seventy-seven prides herself on her independence, and it really *is* faster for her to take the metro." He grabbed the handle on Juliet's suitcase. "For some reason," he said, a sly grin spreading across his face, "she found it significant that you and I literally crashed into each other outside the hospital."

"You told her about that? Did you mention how rude I was not to apologize on the spot the way you did?"

"No," he replied, deadpan. "I told her it was all my fault."

Juliet pointed a finger at the worn patch on the sleeve of his jacket.

"Oh, I get it," she teased him. "An officer and a gentleman?"

"By Act of Congress, no less," he replied.

"Huh? How's that?"

"I'll explain later. Let's get out of here."

Finn gestured to a minuscule car parked in the hospital visitors' area. Juliet absorbed the sight of a vintage, low-slung MG's forest-green body and black canvas top and began to laugh.

"No wonder your aunt wanted to take the metro!" Finn swung open the passenger door and she pointed to the camel-colored leather interior. "A two-seater with a tiny bench for a back seat? Does this vehicle actually drive? It must be fifty-years-old!"

"Sixty-four years," Finn replied with obvious pride. "It's a 1951 model."

Juliet bent at her waist to have a better look inside.

"And just how were all three of us, plus my suitcase, going to fit in this chariot?"

"I could have strapped your bag to the back," he insisted. "You're slender enough to have squeezed onto the bench behind Claudine riding in the passenger seat."

Juliet looked at him with undisguised skepticism.

"I bet your aunt just chose the subway to avoid feeling like a clown at the circus."

Finn held up his hand like a Boy Scout. "I swear…on my honor…my aunt volunteered that she admired your loyalty to your friend Avery, flying here all the way from California. Her exact words were, 'With the time change and all this stress, the poor girl must be about to drop. I'll take the metro and give her my seat.'"

"Hmmm…." Juliet murmured, unconvinced. She tapped the MG's soft canvas top. "But…don't get me wrong," she hastened to add, "I'm very grateful for the ride."

"When I bought the car seven months ago on a sunny spring day with the wisteria and cherry blossoms in bloom, it seemed like a swell idea," he noted, stashing her suitcase on its side behind their bucket seats. "I should have been a little suspicious, though, that it came with a bearskin rug. Hop in and you'll see. It can be quite cozy."

As soon as she was settled, he tucked a very brown, very heavy, very furry blanket around her feet, legs and shoulders.

"No heater, right?" she asked when he'd folded

himself into the other seat. "Where did you get this antique? And a right-hand drive, no less."

"Someone from England sold it to a friend in Paris who sold it to another guy, who—after about twenty-five or thirty years—sold it to me."

"But at least the French are sensible like us. They drive on the right side of the road while the British drive on the left. Isn't it kind of terrifying to maneuver a tiny, English sport car like this in Paris traffic?"

"Oh…like most inconveniences, you get used to it." He turned the key in the ignition and Juliet was alarmed by the odd sounds that burbled forth. She observed Finn in profile as he wiggled the key, his brow furrowed in concentration. "Come on, baby…come *on*!"

A second later, the MG seemed to respond to his commanding tone and the engine turned over. Juliet covered her eyes as they pulled into traffic.

"Whew," she breathed when the car appeared unscathed in the flow of vehicles advancing down the road. Despite the heavy bear rug, she could see her breath within the close confines of the passenger seat. She wondered if tonight it would start to snow and the security helicopters would be grounded?

Finn handed her his cell phone. "Can you pull up Avery's street address on my GPS? I vaguely know where *Rue de Lille* is, but I don't know where the apartment number shows up."

Juliet took his phone in hand and murmured, "Let's see…number seven."

"How did your friend happen to land a place to live there? It's a great neighborhood, but pretty fancy."

Tapping the address into his phone she replied, "Actually, I was the one who told her to see if there was an apartment on *Rue de Lille*, or nearby."

"You've lived in Paris before?"

"No, but my great-great grandmother did." Unable to keep the pride out of her tone, she added, "She was one of the first women to gain a certificate of architecture at *L'École des Beaux Arts* at the end of the nineteenth century. After the big San Francisco earthquake in 1906, she designed and built the small hotel my family owns and still lives in."

Finn glanced briefly at the Google map on the phone that Juliet held in her hand.

"That's impressive," he said with an admiring nod. "Is Juliet a family name?"

"Julia…Juliet…both are. We alternate generations to keep everyone straight at family get-togethers. Great, great granny's mentor was another pioneering California woman architect named Julia Morgan who built a slew of buildings out West."

"Well, Juliet is a beautiful name," Finn replied as he made a right turn across a bridge and drove along the Left Bank of the Seine. "Very romantic." The outlines of the Eiffel Tower rose in the night sky, its silhouette beautiful and ominous in the darkness.

She pursed her lips, wondering if Finn were teasing her, as had so many others all her life, about the connection to Shakespeare's *Romeo and Juliet*. Meanwhile, he returned his gaze to the street ahead.

"It's so strange not to see the tower lighted after dusk," he murmured. "But you were saying that you recommended Avery find a place on *Rue de Lille*?"

"Yes. When Avery decided to quit her job where I worked too and come to Paris to study portrait painting, I told her about the student quarter near *L'École*. Amazingly enough, there was an apartment at the top of number seven, and Avery took it."

"Well, the neighborhood is pretty posh now. French gentrification, et cetera."

"It is?" Juliet asked, somewhat deflated.

"The lower apartments, especially, but I imagine there are still some *bonne chambres* on the top floors."

"What are *bonne chambres?*"

"Maids rooms," he translated.

Juliet took in the sight of the massive former train station they were passing that Finn identified as the *Musée d'Orsay*. She remembered from her art history studies that it housed one of the world's greatest collections of Impressionist paintings.

"So," Finn said, turning onto the *Rue de Lille* behind the museum, "for the first time today you'll be seeing where your great-great grandmother lived—what, a hundred-plus years ago? That *is* pretty great."

"It is." She smiled at his joke, stirred by the thought she'd be staying at Avery's flat in the very building where her talented forbear had lived. She glanced across the space separating them, her spirits lifting a notch. "I want you to know, Finn, that I really appreciate you're doing this...driving me to Avery's."

"Happy to oblige," he replied, scanning the street numbers passing by.

"No, truly," she insisted, "and also, you were great the way you handled telling Avery the absolute minimum about Jean-Pierre's condition. You saw for yourself how fragile she is right now. I can only imagine how terrible it is for you and your aunt to know that...well...that the Grenelles' boy probably isn't going to make it."

She noticed Finn taking a firmer hold of the leather-covered steering wheel, but all he said was, "Glad to be of help."

"Are we very near *L'École des Beaux Arts?*" she asked.

"It should be at the far end of *Rue de Lille*. Ah...and there's number seven."

Miraculously, there was a parking place within a block

of Avery's apartment that was just large enough for the diminutive car to slip into next to the curb.

"No wonder you like driving *cette petite voiture* in Paris," Juliet said admiringly.

"Ha-ha! You *do* speak French. I understood: 'this little car,' right?"

"Yes, but as I said before: my French is horrible-to-non-existent. Only what I was forced to learn while in art school. That's where Avery and I first became friends, and then we both got jobs at a San Francisco start-up—which actually belongs to my family, too."

Finn reached for the door handle, and then hesitated.

"Ah…interesting. A hotel *and* a family business. What did you two do there?"

"Commercial graphic art. Not a first choice for either of us, but we both needed to start paying off our student debt. My dad always says that five generations of Thayers have lived from hand-to-mouth in a *big* way and we're 'land poor.' Educating three kids, each two years apart, at private colleges cost plenty."

"What was your first choice with art?" he asked, leaning back in his bucket seat.

"My goal has always been *plein air* landscape painting, and Avery, obviously, is passionate about portrait painting. They teach both at *L'École*."

"*Plein air* means…painting from real life, right? Outdoors…in the plain air?"

"Yes, basically landscape painting." Then she teased, "Hey, you speak French about as well as I do!"

Finn again reached for his car door handle. "Well, I'm betting that despite what you say, you're probably way ahead of me in that department. I studied Arabic at the Academy."

"Army or—?"

"Air Force. My appointment to the Academy in

Colorado Springs was the 'Act of Congress' thing I kidded about earlier. A senator from your state has to recommend you as a candidate and it gets voted on."

"You're an actual pilot?" She glanced at his flight jacket.

"Not anymore." He paused. "I got shot down a couple of years ago on my second tour in Afghanistan," he added with no further details. He swiftly opened his door and went around to help Juliet out of the car, seizing a corner of the heavy bearskin blanket and folding it into a thick square. Pulled to her full height, she shook a finger at him in the chilly evening air.

"You can't just drop something like that on me! Shot *down*? Thank God you're okay! What happened?"

Finn took his time placing the blanket on her empty seat and then offered matter-of-factly, "A mission to evacuate soldiers hurt in Kandahar. I only ended up with a broken leg and a thigh full of shrapnel. Four of the guys didn't do so well when we crashed."

"Meaning?"

"They died."

"Oh God, I'm so sorry."

Finn ducked his head and reached into the back seat of his car to liberate her suitcase from the bench seat where he'd secured it.

"After I got hurt, I couldn't pass the flight physical. When I recovered well enough to walk without a limp, I was transferred to a States-side division for three years. Last year, I resigned from active duty—period." He set her suitcase on the ground and pulled up its telescoping handle. "And that's the story, morning glory."

Juliet guessed Finn had probably told that version of his departure from the service many times and wanted to get it over with as quickly as possible. Maybe he was working for NATO or something, she speculated, which accounted for why he was in France. What would he say if he knew that she had designed the packaging for the top-selling video war game that offered "pretend" aerial combat of the most violent kind to kids as well as to amateur joy-stick jockeys like her brother Brad and his Stanford buddies—men approaching their middle years who had never served a day in uniform?

"So, no more Air Force?" she commented, falling in step beside him as he led the way down the street.

"Nope." He took her arm as they approached number seven and she was startled by how comforting it felt to have this stranger by her side. "Let's get you upstairs and turn on the heat in Avery's flat," he said. "In November in some of these old buildings, it can actually be cold enough to freeze fish."

CHAPTER 5

Avery's apartment building was in a fortress-like structure with ten-foot-tall wooden double doors on the street level that were flanked by panels of glass protected by wrought iron scrollwork. An outsized brass slot for mail punctuated the right door's central panel—and there was no keyhole to be seen under the knob on the left door.

"So *now* what do we do?" she asked in some dismay, holding up Avery's set of keys. Just then, another helicopter could be heard patrolling a few streets away.

Finn swiveled his head, eyes darting to the sky. Juliet observed him inhale a deep breath, let it out slowly, and inhale a second one. He pointed to a panel of buttons affixed to the right-hand stone doorframe. "Do you know the code?" His voice was tense and he shot a glance to the right and left of the two of them, as if something sinister was very nearby.

Unnerved by everything happening around her, Juliet shook her head. "I-I never thought to ask."

"Okay," he said in a clipped tone. "Let's ring for the concierge."

By this time, Juliet's hands were both shaking and numb with the cold. She pushed the lowest button on the panel, waited, and got no response.

"Here, let me try," Finn offered.

Methodically, he pushed the top button for an unknown apartment, waited, and when no one said, "'Allo?" he proceeded to push the next five until there was a loud buzzing sound and he swiftly pressed his leather-clad shoulder against the heavy door.

"So much for security," he commented. "Quick, get

inside." He held the door for her to enter a narrow, stone-paved foyer that muted the sounds of the helicopter overhead.

Juliet turned around slowly, grateful to be inside where it felt safer.

"Just think…" she murmured, pointing to a set of stairs. Her voice echoed in the passageway. "My great-great granny, Amelia Hunter Bradshaw Thayer, strode up and down those stairs every day she went back and forth to architecture class at *L'École*…" She shivered in the cold. "I hope she owned a fur coat! This place is the North Pole!"

"Avery lives on the fifth floor, right?" Finn asked, taking a tighter grip on her suitcase. "That means it's six flights up. The French count the bottom floor as the 'ground floor,' and one flight up is the *first* floor."

"Really?" groaned Juliet. "We have six floors to climb? That cancels the goodness of the French driving on the same side of the road as we do in America."

Finn gave a snort of laughter and reached for the banister. The pair trudged up the circular stairway in silence, passing door after oak door, until both of them were out of breath, puffs of steam spewing from their nose and mouth in the frigid air by the time that they reached the top level.

"Let me try opening her door," Juliet said between gasps. "I have to master all this sometime."

Fortunately, the modern key fit smoothly in the lock, easily admitting them into Avery's apartment. Once inside, however, they exchanged startled glances, neither speaking at first as they both gazed at the walls surrounding them. Finally, Juliet declared, "This is not even a maid's room. It's an attic. Watch out, Finn! If you move from the door, you'll bump your head."

The interior of Avery's flat could not have been more than three hundred square feet, with much of it useless space for anyone but a midget, due to the sloping angle of the roof and deep-set gables cut into two walls.

During the next twenty minutes the pair tried everything possible to get the heater to work. Leaving Finn to continue fiddling with the dials on the radiator under the window, Juliet crossed the one-room space to inspect the half-fridge that was narrower than an ice cooler—and probably less efficient, from the look of its rusty interior.

"There's not a thing that's edible in here," she complained. "Not even any take-out Chinese!"

"Well, remember…Avery and Jean-Pierre were having dinner at *Le Petit Cambodge* together last Friday," Finn noted over his shoulder as he squatted next to the heater. "Maybe she mostly ate out, although I thought art students lived in a garret because they were penniless and cooked *la soupe* on one tiny burner."

Juliet pointed to a half-empty bottle of red wine on the windowsill next to the heating unit. Finn picked it up and gave it a shake.

"Mostly frozen," he announced.

Juliet was puzzled. "As of a year ago, Avery has a private income. It's not huge, but she didn't have to live like *this*."

"Decent apartments are hard to come by in Paris," Finn explained. "This is in a great neighborhood, close to *L'École*, and there's a great restaurant, *La Calèche*, just opposite. Down the block is *Le Bistro de Paris*, which is very *belle epoch* and looks as if it might have been around when your great-great grandmother lived here." He gazed at Juliet with a thoughtful expression. "Maybe Avery doesn't stock any provisions because she has a boyfriend she stays with…but it's probably not Jean-Pierre. He's gay and lives with his parents."

"She told me today that he was just a pal she'd gotten to know in portrait class."

Finn rose to his feet and inadvertently grazed his head on the ceiling. "Oww!" Rubbing his forehead, he moved to the center of the vaulted chamber where his six-foot frame had some breathing room. "I can tinker with my MG's engine, but I'll be damned if I can figure out how this French heating system works."

"See, I *knew* landing in Paris wouldn't be so easy," Juliet grumbled.

"Do you know any hotels or B and Bs near the hospital?' he asked.

Tired and discouraged, Juliet retorted more sharply than she intended. "No, do *you?*"

Finn settled his hands on his hips and appeared to be turning something over in his mind.

"I noted one or two hotels on *Rue de Lille*...but I expect they cost a bomb. I-I guess you could always sleep on my couch for a couple of days. At least until we can figure out this heating system."

Juliet's gaze narrowed. From his stance and the tentative tone of his invitation, he didn't seem at all convinced it would be a good idea to make such an offer.

"Thank you," she said, tight-lipped, "but I don't think so."

She could sense that her jetlag had risen to a serious level and she was unreasonably put out with Avery for living in such a disgusting hovel.

The wine is frozen? Give me a break, Avery!

Then she was overcome with guilt. The woman had been recovering from gunshot wounds in the hospital for four days! So what if her apartment was a mess?

Finn titled his head.

"So what do you want to do?"

His abrupt question and Avery's unfit living conditions made Juliet ready to hit someone on the head with the wine bottle.

"I'll just sleep in my clothes and coat tonight and find someplace else to stay in the morning," she replied more crossly than she intended.

"That's ridiculous!" Finn exclaimed, not bothering to hide his own exasperation. He was exhausted too, she guessed, from being up all night with the Grenelles and from all the stress of the previous few days.

"I'll be fine," she insisted.

"You won't be fine," he countered. "You'll end up with pneumonia in a hospital bed next to Avery's."

"I'll be *fine*!" she repeated. "You're perfectly free to go."

"That's not the point," he shot back. "Why won't you be sensible and sleep on my couch?"

"Because I can tell you really don't *want* someone to sleep on your couch! Or you don't want *me* to."

A long silenced stretched between them. They hardly knew one another, and here they were, having their first fight.

Finn appeared taken aback by her direct answer, which they both knew rang true. He inhaled deeply once again, turned to one side and stared up at the low-slung ceiling.

"It's nothing to do with you at all, but you're right," he admitted to the sloping roof. "I didn't. Think it was such a good idea for you to stay at my place, I mean." He shifted his gaze, addressing her. "But I do, now." He took a step forward. "Truly. I'm sorry for extending such a half-ass invitation. You must be beat. It's just that no one has ever stayed at my place since…since I've been in Paris."

"Well, far be it for me to ruin your record."

A good-looking guy like him has been celibate as a monk? What gives with this ex-airman? she fumed silently.

"You obviously can't stay here," he insisted, "and honestly, I'd enjoy your company."

"Why the sudden change of heart?" she challenged him.

The sound of an approaching helicopter rent the air once more and flashing lights from its fuselage winked as it passed above the gable. Finn's eyes darted toward the window in the roof where the drone of the helicopter grew louder, his expression grim.

"Why the change?" he repeated. "Because I agree with my aunt. You shouldn't stay here alone at a time like this."

She glanced at Avery's iron bedstead. Its thin, rumpled quilt looked as if it wouldn't even keep a polar bear warm. Then she pointed to the helicopter making another pass by the window before it disappeared from their view. "You're taking pity on me in an emergency, are you?"

Finn cocked his head and stood rigidly at attention, as if poised to duck and cover. "Yes," he said between clenched teeth. "It's not very safe until the cops find the other terrorists, and who knows when that will be?" Juliet gave a nod, her own, intense fight-or-flight response now matching his. "And, besides," he added, appearing to relax slightly as the loud sounds of the rotors began to fade, "I'm also taking pity on myself. My French is so bad, I could never hash out the heating issue with Avery's landlord or the building's concierge. I'll ask Aunt Claudine to help us tomorrow."

"Who said you were expected to sort out Avery's heating?"

"Nobody. But I feel I ought to. Helping out a fellow American in a time of war, and all that."

She could tell he was trying to make light of their former, mutual testiness toward each other.

"And also," he added, a faint smile tracing his lips, "I live right across the Seine from the Eiffel Tower. It would be nice to have someone to wait with until the lights on it come back on—as long as you won't post anything on

Facebook while you're here," he finished, his tone now dead serious.

"Nothing on Facebook? How weird is that? But I hate it!"

"Not posting stuff on Facebook?"

"No, I *hate* Facebook. But, tell me...are you in hiding or something?"

Finn ignored her comment. "The lights across the water have been off since Friday. *That's* what's so weird."

She nodded at him soberly. "San Francisco City Hall's been lit up in blue, white and red in sympathy with France since last Friday."

"Really? That's nice. I haven't seen the news at all."

"Don't watch it. It's horrible."

"Why don't you stay at my place at least as long as Avery is in the hospital?" he proposed, and Juliet felt that this time, his offer was genuine. "And another thing," he continued. "As it happens, I know the Grenelles well, because I live next door to Madam Grenelle, J-P's grandmother, on a barge moored on the Right Bank of the Seine."

"You're kidding! You live on the same boat as Madame Grenelle?"'

"I'm not kidding, and you'll be pleased to note it's moored permanently to the dock, has heat, and hasn't gone anywhere in twenty years. Besides, it will take a village to comfort that family, along with your friend Avery, if Jean-Pierre..." He allowed his sentence to dangle in the frosty air.

After a long moment Juliet murmured, "Okay." And immediately she was filled with sheer relief that she didn't have to stay alone atop a frozen attic in a city where security helicopters were on constant patrol. She realized how scared she was in a place with aircraft buzzing the roof every five minutes. It was terrifying to be where she knew no one other than the man standing two feet from her, along with a friend who'd been shot by terrorists—some who had yet to be hunted down.

"'Okay' means you'll stay on the barge?" he confirmed.

"Yes. And thank you. As you say, I should be sensible."

"I'm glad."

"Really?" she asked, arching a skeptical eyebrow.

"Really."

"So…?" she said on a long breath that spun mist in Finn's direction.

"So," he echoed with a brusqueness Juliet imagined he'd employed as an officer in the U.S. Air Force, "let's roll. And just pray that I can get the MG to start again in this disgusting weather."

Mercifully, the little sports car started up with reasonable ease. Finn soon crossed the river once more and parked the vehicle half on the sidewalk near the quay that paralleled the Seine's Right Bank where several canal boats were moored end-to-end.

"You live tied up to a dock next to 'New York Avenue?'" Juliet exclaimed when she caught sight of a nearby blue and white enameled street sign.

"Technically, where I've just parked is a spur road, *Georges Pompidou.* To be exact, I live in the Sixteenth Arrondissement on the River Seine adjacent to Avenue New York and across from the Eiffel Tower. Conveniently hard-to-find, yet in plain sight." He glanced over his shoulder. "Still no lights on the tower tonight."

Juliet could only nod as once again, Finn took charge of her suitcase, commanding her, "C'mon. Let's get you on the boat and warmed up, and then I'll make us something to eat."

Finn led the way down a cobbled ramp toward a black-hulled barge whose square upper section, the pilothouse, he explained, consisted of a series of large, plate glass windows framed in amber-colored wood and topped with a roof painted white. A large black cat sat on deck, meowing loudly as they approached the gangway in the shadows of early evening.

"Meet Mademoiselle Truffles," Finn declared.

Once they'd mounted the metal ramp and stepped on deck, he stopped to give the feline a scratch behind her ear. The cat immediately rubbed against Finn's pants leg, begging for another caress.

"You named her after the chocolates—or the smelly mushrooms that fancy chefs grate on scrambled eggs?"

"The smelly stuff. She's a barge cat and supposedly belongs to Madame, but she hangs out wherever the spirit moves her along this stretch of the Seine. Don't be startled when she pops into the pilothouse from time to time through a window cracked for air."

Walking along the narrow deck, Juliet noted the boat had been christened *L'Étoile de Paris* in gold leaf letters.

"Star of Paris," she noted aloud. "Is she? A star, I mean—as in comfortable?"

Finn feigned insult. "If you're inquiring whether she has the necessary amenities like a kitchen and a toilet, you'll be happy to hear the answer is a resounding 'yes.'"

Juliet halted her progress toward the pilothouse and stared in awe at the murky outlines of the Eiffel Tower jutting above them across the water, not two hundred yards away.

"So close," she breathed, her eyes scanning its height. "It's amazing, even without lights."

She turned and allowed her gaze to follow the Seine

along another line of barges stretching in the distance toward a bridge on her left. Looking to her right, the water flowed to another bridge that she'd noted on Google maps had the odd name of *Bir Hakeim*. She turned toward Finn in an effort to reassure him that the beauty of the scene didn't mean she assumed she could become a permanent guest.

"You'll probably be happy to learn that my imposing on your hospitality shouldn't be for too long. Even if Avery isn't released from the hospital very soon, I'll have to get back to San Francisco in a week."

Finn turned around with a look of surprise.

"I thought you said you worked in your family's company. Why the pressure on you to get back right away? Isn't this what most people would call an *emergency?*"

"Did I not mention that I work directly for my big brother?" she replied with a short laugh. "He said if I don't get back on the double, I'll lose my job."

"Even given what's going on with your friend Avery? Why would he do that?"

Juliet hesitated, and then gave an answer in as neutral a tone as she could muster. "It's a public company, now. He's a hard-ass and worried about meeting Wall Street's expectations for this quarter—and the expectations are unreasonably high."

Finn pulled out a key from his jacket pocket. He slid it into the lock of a door that was richly paneled wood on the bottom and, on its top section, boasted a square glass window protected by a rattan shade on the inside. Over his shoulder he said, "Sounds like a guy with all heart."

"Bradshaw Thayer the Fourth's heart?" Juliet said, trying to sound nonchalant. "It's not been confirmed he actually possesses that organ, but I'm hoping he does have one, somewhere."

Finn merely raised an eyebrow as he pushed open the

door. Over his shoulder, Juliet caught a glimpse of a large room, flanked by big windows on the waterside as well as the side that faced the street. In the center, open space was a large wooden wheel that obviously once must have steered the barge. In a corner stood a small, iron fireplace with a stovepipe punched through the roof.

"And, what is it you do for your brother's company that requires your presence so keenly," Finn asked, "despite Europe having just experienced something approaching America's 9/11?"

He deposited Juliet's suitcase beside the arm of a three-cushioned couch covered in white sailcloth and littered with a few, comfortable-looking back pillows.

"Brad's the CEO of this family enterprise of ours. And what do I do, exactly?" she repeated, wondering how best to answer a former Air Force pilot who'd been shot down in combat. "Well, I...uh...I'm the graphics design director. I create packaging and branding for the games the company produces. We have a new one about to launch, which is the reason my big brother wants me home as soon as possible."

"What kind of games," he asked. "Board games? For kids?"

"Uh...no. Electronic."

"You mean like electronic solitaire or...like video games?"

"Video," she said shortly, glancing out the window at the shadowy Eiffel Tower.

She shifted her focus to what she assumed was called the main cabin and made a show of admiring the sapphire blue and garnet Persian carpet that covered two-thirds of the teak flooring beneath their feet. "Very nice digs, by the way," she said, giving the room the once-over.

Opposite the sofa were two Marie Antoinette-looking armchairs covered in deep red velvet. A brass-studded wooden chest served as a coffee table and, to the right of this grouping, a comfortable leather chair the color of cognac took up the rest of the corner on the side of the barge that faced the land. At the far end of the room was a built-in desk incorporating two burners and a sink—an area that Juliet concluded doubled as a kitchen.

"I have Aunt Claudine to thank for this place," Finn acknowledged, with a sweep of his hand. "She persuaded Madame Grenelle, who lives on the other end of this bucket, to allow a burnt-out drone pilot to crash here until he figures out the rest of his life."

Juliet stared at her host, stunned by this announcement offered so casually.

"After you stopped flying real aircraft, you operated unmanned *drones*?"

"Yep…although what we were doing was 'real' enough, in that we shot Hellfire missiles from those fixed-wing planes at live, human targets in Iraq and Afghanistan—all from the comfort of our leather-lined cockpits in a trailer on Creech Air Force Base outside Las Vegas."

His tone had dropped several notches and was filled with self-loathing.

"You flew drones…remotely…from Nevada… that were based in the Middle East," she said, unable to keep the shock out of her voice, "…aimed at targets over there?"

Finn's mouth had assumed a straight line and his eyes were shuttered, though he met her glance. "That information is no longer classified. Just look on the Internet."

"Goodness," was all she could manage to reply.

"So, since you seem to be familiar with drone warfare, I'm curious," he said with a steady glance. "What *kind* of video games do you design packaging for?"

Juliet crossed to the sofa and sank down on its sturdy cushions. She wondered where she'd ultimately lay her head this night after she answered his question.

"How's this for irony?" she said, staring up at her host. "The company my family owns is called GatherGames. These days, we produce war games. Our latest little offering is *Sky Slaughter...Death by Drones.*"

Not surprisingly, she figured, a long silence blossomed between them.

Finally, Finn said softly, "Holy hell. You and your friend Avery were in the video *war* games business and worked for the company that produced *Sky Slaughter?* Really? The new guys in our unit were training on that when I left, for God's sake!"

Naturally Finn might be familiar with the games, she thought, as a feeling she identified as shame filled her chest. Flying real drones had been his business until very recently. However, his response seemed to reveal his astonishment that she'd been involved in such an enterprise—or was it disgust, she wondered? She wouldn't blame him. Finn spun around and walked to the far end of the main cabin. He announced without preamble, "I'll scramble us some eggs. I don't know about you, but I'm bushed."

"Yes," she agreed, recognizing Finn's deliberate and abrupt change of topic. Meanwhile, she began to wonder how either of them was still standing upright after the last few days of high stress. "Let's eat and go to sleep."

Finn shot her an odd look but merely nodded. Within minutes he handed her a plate with buttered toast and surprisingly tasty eggs sprinkled with fresh thyme. He pointed to a small table for two under the pilothouse window and they sat down. Juliet sensed they both were basically giving out a dial tone. She made no attempts at chitchat, and neither did Finn. When they had finished, he gathered both plates in his hands.

"Let me help," she offered.

He handed her the plates and nodded in the direction of the ship's tiny galley.

"Just put them in the sink. I'll go get the bedding for the couch."

Finn disappeared to his stateroom a few steps below the main section of the pilothouse and in the stern. After rinsing the plates, Juliet stood waiting patiently beside the sofa and considered the irony of their two lives intersecting in front of the American Hospital in Paris—an event that seemed utterly preposterous, given the oddly similar, yet dissimilar worlds each had been living in prior to their collision.

Finn mounted the short ship's ladder with his arms laden with sheets, a towel, and a blanket. "I'm going to give you the bed, below, and I'll sleep on the couch."

"Absolutely not!" she protested. "Having me here is not exactly what you signed up for, and besides, I'm at least a foot shorter than you." She glanced at the three-cushion sofa. "I'll fit quite nicely on this thing." She extended her arms. "Here, give me the bed linen." She grabbed a top sheet that she swiftly folded over like an open-ended hot dog bun, and within minutes, she'd arranged the blanket and pillow. "There. See? That's perfect," she declared. "Okay if I use the facilities and then dive in here?"

Juliet didn't wait for Finn's answer but grabbed a pair of black tights and a T-shirt out of her suitcase, along with her cosmetic case, and retraced his steps below to the cabin at the rear end of the boat.

"The head—I mean, the toilet—is on the right, behind that narrow door," he called. "The sink and shower are in the corner, behind the canvas curtain."

"The head...the galley. Boat Speak. Got it. Thanks."

When Juliet returned less than five minutes later, Finn hadn't moved from where she'd left him standing beside the sofa in the main cabin. She wondered if he even was aware she'd come back because his eyes gazing out the pilothouse windows at the shadowy hulk of the Eiffel Tower across the water were fixed in a thousand-yard stare.

"Well…I guess we should—" she began.

Finn swung around sharply as if she'd startled him. After a long pause he said, "The lights never came on tonight on the tower."

"They usually stay on this late?" she asked, noting the ship's clock on the shelf said it was nearly ten p.m.

"Yes. Till one o'clock in the morning. It's probably considered a target now."

Juliet sucked in her breath.

"So no lights is a precaution?" she ventured, feeling her heart speed up.

"Maybe," he answered, his gaze focused again out the window. "At least until they catch the terrorists that got away." He turned to meet her glance. "You going to be okay up here? I'm fine if you've changed your mind and—"

"No! The least I can do is let you sleep in your own bed. I'll just say goodnight." She lifted the edge of the sheet and pulled it back. Then she met his gaze once more. "And thanks, Airman Deschanel. I really appreciate this."

"Major Deschanel to you, *mademoiselle*," he corrected with a faintly sardonic smile, adding, "for what that's worth. Let's just hope we can both get some sleep."

Juliet silently wondered if she would be able to block out the sounds of the air patrols sweeping up and down the Seine outside the windows every so often, or shut off the images of the last few days that were swirling around in her mind.

The next morning she would recall, to her later amazement, that she didn't even remember her head hitting the pillow.

CHAPTER 6

As was so often the case, Finn figured he hadn't slept at all. The helicopters overhead certainly hadn't helped. He'd almost dropped off when the sounds of approaching aircraft rotors roused him to full alert, his heart pounding. Before he realized it, he'd leapt out of bed, blindly rummaging in the closet next to the toilet for his assault rifle—a weapon he didn't possess any longer. It had taken him at least thirty seconds of deep breathing to talk himself out of the belief that he was still in Kandahar. He couldn't even shower off his sweat-soaked body for fear of waking his guest upstairs.

Finally, at six o'clock the next morning, despite the darkness outside the porthole above his bed, he slipped into his jeans, T-shirt, and leather jacket, and tiptoed up the ladder from his stateroom. Silently, he padded in stocking feet to the pilothouse without waking his visitor and put on his shoes and jacket outside the door.

The morning air was as glacial as it had been the night before and he could see his breath as he trotted up the incline from the quay to the street level and continued up the hill to his local *boulangerie*. Finn had mastered enough French in the previous six months to order a couple of croissants and select his daily baguette, along with drinking his first cup of coffee of the day. He sipped it slowly, standing in a corner and watching the stream of Trocadero residents file into the shop to make their own morning purchases. His thoughts drifted to the sight of the woman curled up on his couch and wondered if he'd get any sleep at all while she was staying onboard? It wouldn't be great if he awoke in the middle of the night with one of his full-blown—

Don't go there!

He forced himself to shift his thoughts and concentrate on the babble of customers while consciously inhaling the rich scent of baking bread. He'd been advised to latch onto anything in his immediate surroundings that would keep his thoughts from spiraling into worry or flashing back to scenes he was being schooled to put out of his mind. He took another gulp of his coffee, swallowed, and breathed deeply again. Glancing at his watch, he decided that he should purchase some extra croissants to deliver to Madame Grenelle, next door, and got back into the line. By that time he returned to the barge, perhaps Ms. Juliet Thayer would have awakened and another bizarre day would begin.

Juliet awoke to the sound of river traffic sending waves slapping into the hull on the other side of the couch where she'd been out like a light. In the distance, another helicopter churned through leaden skies. She stayed very still, trying to get her bearings and pull together her scattered thoughts of the previous twenty-four hours. She was on a barge. Her host was a former drone pilot. Her friend was in terrible shape in a Paris hospital. Jean-Pierre was at death's door. Terrorists were still at large. Wonderful.

Her breath caught at the thought that nothing felt safe, except perhaps in the company of the Major, and actually, not even then.

She heard the ping of her cell phone from the depths of her tote bag. *Is that what woke me up?* She reached in and read the latest text message.

> **Jules…are you really here,**
> **or did I dream you came to Paris?**
> **AE**

She quickly texted Avery that she'd be at the hospital in half an hour, then sprang off the sofa, folded the sheets and blanket and put them with the pillow into a neat pile. She could see by the open door leading to Finn's stateroom that his bed was empty, so she raced downstairs, accomplishing her ablutions in record time. Quickly scribbling a note of thanks to her host, along with her cell phone number so they could coordinate their comings and goings by text, she sprinted down the gangway and headed for the street above the river. She had no doubt she'd see him later in the day with his landlady outside the ICU where poor Jean-Pierre was fighting for his life.

Amazingly enough, a taxi was the first car to drive past on the street flanking the river. She hailed it, directing it to take her to the American Hospital in Neuilly-sur-Seine. The streets were filling up with more cars than she'd seen the day before, yet she felt as if her entire body was still on high alert.

At the hospital, Avery's day was filled with tests, medications, naps, and a ten-minute period of sitting upright in a nearby chair. Juliet did her best to boost her friend's morale, but felt at a loss for how to comfort Avery as she constantly asked for information about Jean-Pierre. Juliet pretended she'd inquired at the nurses' station—she actually was afraid to ask, just telling her friend, "No further news, I guess."

Finn and his Aunt Claudine looked in on Room 203 in the late afternoon when Avery had fallen asleep again, exhausted from her recent exertions sitting up. When Juliet noticed the visitors standing in the doorway, she tiptoed across the room and motioned for them to follow her a few steps down the hallway.

"How's Jean-Pierre doing today?" she asked.

Claudine merely shook her head as Finn said, "The same, which is bad."

Juliet glanced back over her shoulder and was relieved to see that Avery remained sound asleep. Maybe she could avoid answering her questions for one more day.

Just then, one of the nurses came by and announced visiting hours were over and that the evening meals were due to arrive at any moment, an obvious hint the visitors should be on their way.

Claudine looked as weary as Juliet felt, announcing that she was going to take the metro home, heat some soup, and fall into bed.

"Is it really safe to do that?" Juliet asked. "Take the metro, I mean?"

"When one is seventy-seven, it's safe enough," Claudine responded with a shrug.

Juliet agreed with a heavy sigh. "After Avery has her supper, that's what I'd like to do, too. Just have soup and crash."

The nurse spoke up. "Ms. Evans probably won't wake up for an hour or more, as we've given her additional sedation after sitting up in the chair for the first time."

"Why not leave Avery a note like you did yesterday?" Finn suggested. "You can come with me now, which will be easier all around."

Juliet was relieved to hear this plan as—unlike Claudine—she didn't feel up to negotiating a strange subway system guarded everywhere by men in full battle gear.

"Just give me a sec," she answered, fatigue starting to invade every pore.

To everyone's relief, the number 82 bus was idling, curbside, just outside the hospital and Claudine gingerly hopped aboard. All three of them were glad she had the choice of riding it home to her apartment, rather than braving the metro. Finn stopped briefly at a shop he knew near the barge and emerged with a carton of *Soupe au*

Pistou—a concoction made of carrots, zucchini, green beans, and button mushrooms in a rich chicken broth topped with a green sauce resembling Italian pesto.

"It's the French version," Finn explained, "made—as is pesto—from finely chopped fresh basil, garlic, and olive oil." The two were soon seated at the small table in the barge's "salon," as Finn called the main section of the pilothouse. Besides the soup, he provided a basket with heated slices of bread, along with butter in a small crock.

"You seem pretty up on French food," she commented, taking another spoonful of the rich, steaming liquid. The helicopter patrol along the Seine had lessened somewhat and conversation was easier, now.

"Cooking is my newest hobby, although I'm too beat to make anything tonight," he allowed. "On a normal day, I find it very relaxing."

"Even on two burners?" She nodded in the direction of the tiny stovetop.

"It ups the challenge," he replied with a faint grin. Finn appeared to study her across the table for a long moment. "I've been meaning to ask you… You alluded yesterday that the family company your brother runs didn't always produce video war games when you first started in the art department. What *did* it produce?"

Juliet wasn't surprised that a former rescue helicopter and drone pilot might be curious about the evolution of her brother's firm.

"In the beginning, which was five years ago, we were doing our version of Angry Birds and electronic tic-tac-toe types of products. As I mentioned before, Avery and I both had student debt to pay off. We figured when my eldest brother, Brad, offered us jobs, it was the quickest way to get on with the type of art we really wanted to pursue."

"Well, if you don't mind my asking, has your brother-the-boss ever flown a drone, or any aircraft?"

"Just simulators."

"Was he ever in the military?"

"No. Make that *God*, no." Juliet suddenly felt that a deep freeze colder than Avery's frigid flat had descended on the barge. "And if you can at least view my friend Avery in a decent light, she quit in protest last spring as head of our graphic arts department when the videos became increasingly violent."

"But *you* didn't quit?" After a moment's silence he added in a tone that softened his words, "You just don't seem very war-like."

"You're right, I'm not." She met his glance. "Maybe in your world you'll think it's a lame excuse, but my parents' entire future is at risk right now. Just as I was managing to pay off my college debt, my father took out a huge equity loan against our family's hotel. He did it to help our resident Golden Boy launch this new video war games phase of the business. My parents also run a small architectural firm in addition to overseeing the hotel, and they're nearing retirement age. I haven't left GatherGames because I want to make sure Brad pays Dad back, now that the drone series is doing phenomenally well and the stock is sold on the open market."

"So you took over Avery's job when she quit?"

Juliet nodded. "I need the leverage of being design director to make sure Brad makes good on that loan. His excuse for not paying back the money is that he needs Dad's funds to keep reinvesting in the company to 'scale it,' as he insists we should."

The truth was, Juliet had been stunned when she'd found out that her father had wagered the family's celebrated boutique establishment atop Nob Hill on such a risky venture spawned by his first born. However, such was the strange power that brother Brad seemed to wield over everyone, especially Juliet's parents.

"So you're genuinely worried that your brother won't reimburse your father?"

Finn's doubtful expression prompted Juliet to offer a fuller explanation. "Oh, eventually he will, I'm hoping—if he can—but he burns through cash like a hot knife through butter and he's always chasing the new-new thing. Paying back our father is not high on his personal priority list, I guess. I'm just afraid we'll have another dot-com bubble burst before he gets around to it...which would be disastrous for the rest of us, including my other brother, as well as my folks."

"Is this other brother also involved in the family firm?"

"Yes, my younger brother Jamie, who's a total sweetheart. He edits the videos."

"That does sound complicated," Finn noted diplomatically.

To Juliet's relief, her host's tempered expression seemed to indicate he apparently understood a bit better the quandary in which she found herself.

Finn rose from the table and gathered their soup bowls, heading the few steps toward the small sink embedded in the desk where his laptop stood open.

"How about I make a fire tonight?" he suggested. He glanced out the window where evening had closed in around the dim outline of the Eiffel Tower on the opposite shore. Then he stooped down and reached for some kindling and a few small logs from a brass bucket to throw into the iron fireplace that dominated one corner in the main stateroom. "And do Brad's simulated war games involve encrypted messages between the players?" he asked, his back to her.

Oh, boy, here it comes...Finn probably knows way more than Brad about the implications of private encryption...

"Yes," she admitted, watching Finn's broad back as he crumpled up newspaper.

Finn glanced over his shoulder. "You know, don't you, that French authorities are pretty sure the terrorists, here, employed encryption used in video game technology and phone apps? The theory is they disguised their messages sent back and forth between their members as they planned and executed what happened here last Friday."

"Yes, I know that. I read the same article in *The New York Times* this weekend that you probably did." Brad's counter-arguments surged into her mind. "Our world is now *based* on encryption—and certainly the military is."

"That's true," Finn agreed.

Juliet said, "Look, we all know that banks use encrypted software to keep people's accounts secure. The airlines use it, companies use it, and every government agency in the universe needs encryption to keep information protected."

"That's also true." Finn poked at the fire to encourage the flames. "And it's getting damn scary to think it can be turned against us by some bad actors."

"Yeah, but how would Americans feel if some foreign power used unmanned drones to drop a bomb on a bad guy next door to them...and it just happened to kill a couple of innocent neighbors in the process?"

Finn fell silent. His face, in profile as he tended the fire, had become an expressionless mask. Finally he said, "This latest terrorist attack is going to bring about a big public reaction because evil people can use drones and encryption for evil purposes. But in a strange sense, encryption may be the one thing that's defending our freedoms from governments that use it to invade our privacy and control people."

"But look what damage the really bad guys can do," Juliet said glumly.

"A tiny minority use knives to kill people," Finn

noted, "but that doesn't mean ordinary citizens should be forced to turn over all the knives in their kitchens to higher authority."

Juliet looked at her host with amazement. "So, I take it, you are not in favor of law enforcement demanding ways to decode the encryption used by terrorists, despite what's just happened in France? Despite what's just happened to our *friends?*"

"No, I'm not in favor. Once powerful authorities have that ability, what's to stop them from sucking up our private data without warrants in the name of national security—which they do already—and then having the means to crack the codes and know every single thing about each citizen? At the end of the day, I've come to think that secure, private communication is a good thing. It's the only thing that stands between citizens and an authoritarian, militarized regime, whichever country they're in."

"Wow," murmured Juliet, "You sound like Brad— only nicer. I can't believe you were career military."

"I'm not anymore. And besides, encryption is only one piece of this mess."

"No kidding," Juliet said with some heat. "For sure I respect your service, Finn, but I happen to think the U.S. attacks in the Middle East that killed so many civilians are the very events that created this international hornet's nest in the first place. You're right. You can't blame it all on encryption."

Finn threw another log on the fire with a thud.

"Nope. And what about the lies we were fed that Saddam had yellow-cake uranium and that he was ready to use nuclear weapons? If you can't trust top officials in your country to tell the truth, we're in a pretty sorry state."

Juliet was shocked to hear a former military man agree with her own opinion on the U.S. government's faulty reasons for the build up to the war in Iraq. She said, "*I* was certainly persuaded by those fake arguments back then to support the Iraq invasion, more's the pity."

Finn threw another log on the pile with another show of force. "Weren't we all? I went into the military thinking I was one of the good guys."

"And now?"

Finn rose to his full height and turned around. "As you've just pointed out, civilian and military uses of encryption have created issues that aren't easy to sort out, and anyone who sees the disaster that defines the Middle East simply in black-and-white is a fool. Why, exactly, have we been fighting wars for a decade and a half—and still counting? *Was* it just about the oil? Was it multi-national corporations only caring about their profits? Was it radical Islam wanting to wipe out all other religions? Was it the revolving door between our military and U.S. weapons makers that kept the merry-go-round spinning? No one has the corner on truth anymore." He wiped the dust off his hands onto his jeans. "You know how your family tends to produce architects and artists? Scores of men in *my* family were in the military, back to the dawn of the country. It's what we Deschanels *did* for God and country. My dad wrangled me an appointment to the Air Force Academy, and off I went, like the Eagle Scout I'd been in high school. Back then, who knew about drones and targeted killings?"

Finn sounded self-mocking and bitter.

"How long did it take for you to become…aware, I guess you'd call it?" she asked.

"It's taken me a *long* time—too long, in fact—to see behind the curtain about a lot of issues and think things through for myself, based on some very first-hand reality checks." He pulled a box of matches off a nearby table and stepped back to the fireplace. "After I finished flight training, I flew those combat rescue missions, and it was all about the guys in my unit and trying to save lives. I didn't have time to consider misinformation about Saddam Hussein having yellow cake to build a nuclear bomb. It was all about avenging 9/11 and protecting the homeland."

He lit a match and leaned down. The flames were soon licking the crumpled paper he'd stuffed under the kindling. He prodded the logs with an iron poker. "When I spent eight months in a VA hospital recuperating after my helicopter was shot out from under me, I had plenty of time to think about how America got into these wars."

"That was when the four other soldiers died?"

Finn nodded. "When I failed the regular flight physical, but I was fit enough to pilot drones, I figured I owed those guys…something. I accepted the assignment at Creech in Nevada, which I did for three years. So you see, I responded to peer and family pressures just like you. I drank the Kool-Aid. I followed orders. I did as I was told—and as my father and my entire family back to the founding of this country would have expected of me."

As Finn rose and stood in front of the fire, Juliet slowly shook her head. "So, while my brother was teaching horny teenagers to shoot pretend enemies, you were actually killing *real* enemies."

By this time, the fire in the iron stove was burning brightly and throwing off heat. Finn closed the glass doors and sat down on the leather armchair.

"By the time I got to Nevada, our forces had already made many tribal factions in the Middle East into our enemies, so yes…they were my targets."

"Do you miss it?" Juliet asked, holding his gaze.

"Killing people?"

"No!" Juliet recoiled, absorbing his admission that he'd killed other human beings. "Flying *real* aircraft. Being an Academy grad and all that goes with that? All the macho, military stuff," she pressed. "Because that's what I think has hooked my brother as if he was main-lining heroin. He and his friends are pretend big shot warriors who get a huge rush from all this high-flying hardware."

"Heroin?" Finn repeated. "Well, I can tell you that what I did sitting in those unmarked trailers in the desert, killing by remote control, never delivered a 'high' as far I was concerned. It was soul-destroying, and I couldn't wait to get away."

Finn was staring at his hands in his lap, his face now a mask.

"But at least you were getting rid of some very bad guys," she ventured.

He looked up. "Yeah, that, but we were not just shooting down psychopathic killers. My job included pointing our high-powered eyes in the sky at the aftermath of those Hellfire missiles, right down to the scenes of innocent sheep farmers whose legs we'd blown off."

Juliet saw the haunted look that invaded his eyes.

"God, Finn," she murmured, "what an awful thing to have seen."

"It was worse to be the cause of it. Regular pilots just drop their bombs and fly on. There are always women and children who inadvertently get caught in those explosions. *You* try ending your duty shift writing up the gory details in the daily reports about the dead six-year-olds whose deaths you witnessed and know you caused."

He compressed his lips as if willing himself to end this confession.

"God, Almighty," Juliet said, barely above a whisper.

Finn stared out the large, darkened window on his right that faced the river. "I have no idea why, but you are the only person I've ever given *that* particular detail to."

"Accounting for the children?"

"Yes."

Finn had the same look she'd seen earlier, an unseeing, thousand-yard stare.

Juliet murmured almost to herself, "It would be hard to ever erase those kinds of images from my mind. I have trouble trying to forget the grisly, make-believe scenes in the junk *we* make."

Finn abruptly rose from his chair and reached toward a standing lamp, flipping the switch. He began prowling the room like a panther, turning on a few other lights with military precision.

"I got to a point where I wanted to put a bullet through my head if I had to drop any more hell on people seven thousand miles away from the God-damned Las Vegas Strip." He clicked on a wall switch with a vengeance. "When I'd finally fulfilled my obligation, I walked out of those trailers and resigned my commission without a word about it to anyone. When the paperwork was finally processed, I caught the first plane from Vegas to New York, and flew straight on to Paris where I collapsed on my aunt's couch and didn't even speak to *her* for a month."

"That must have been a terrible time," Juliet commented quietly.

"Drone pilots are quitting by the scores," he announced in a flat voice. "Any self-respecting pilot hates these jobs that 'keep us out of harm's way,' as the Pentagon folks are fond of putting it. It got so I could barely drag myself to the antiseptic, air-conditioned control room where we steered our Hellfires toward 'high value targets' seven thousand miles away and watched 'em die."

"It sounds as if your Aunt Claudine understood what you were going through," Juliet suggested cautiously. "She's obviously helped you get back on track."

Finn halted in the middle of the stateroom. "It'll be quite a while before that happens," he replied with a warning look, and for a moment, Juliet felt a chill run down her spine.

"Are you getting…help for…?"

She wondered how to politely ask if a person was a human time bomb?

As if he read her mind, Finn said, "Claudine got me to admit I probably had a full-blown case of PTSD, whether anyone else believed it of drone pilots or not. If you don't have blood spurting out of your ears, the military thinks you're fine."

"What about your father?" Juliet challenged. "Wouldn't he—"

"No, he wouldn't," Finn interrupted her roughly. "He'd never believe a drone pilot who quit wasn't anything but a weakling, but I've seen guys who *really* flipped out and—" He shook his head. "Never *mind* what I've seen." Hands defiantly on his hips, he continued to gaze across the stateroom as if he expected her to rise from the sofa and walk off the boat. "So, Ms. California," he asked with one eyebrow cocked, "are you sure you're still okay about sleeping on my couch another night?"

CHAPTER 7

Finn's fists were clenched against his thighs. The length of his entire frame was as stiff as the poker he'd been using to stir the embers into flames in the iron fireplace. Despite his defensive stance, Juliet's mind flashed on the many kindnesses he'd extended to her, her friend Avery, his aunt, and the Grenelles during these first tumultuous days of their acquaintance.

No, she considered, she had no fear of being an onboard guest of Major Patrick Finley "Finn" Deschanel. It was plain to see that the man was grappling with some very tough issues in his life, but he was clearly a stand-up guy—and when had she last experienced *that?*

"I'm fine with sleeping on your couch," she declared, "that is, if you can give me a glass of wine tonight to settle my nerves. Do you happen to have any?"

Finn's shoulders relaxed. He cocked his head, as if correctly interpreting the message she'd sent him that she didn't consider him a particularly dangerous character. He shrugged and said, "I know I've got some Scotch and...let me see what else." He crossed to the bookcase to survey the collection of liquor he had on the bottom shelf. "Yes! An unopened bottle of *Arbouse*, a nice French Rhone."

"A red. Perfect!" She slipped off her boots and tucked her feet under her legs on the couch. "I need a little self-medication after the last couple days. Join me, will you?"

"Not for me, but how about a slice of brie and some grapes?" he suggested, and their world had returned to spinning in a normal orbit.

"You know," she said, hoping her words sounded as if she were just making polite conversation, "I actually read a bit about drone operators and PTSD when we were preparing to release our first video war game."

Finn looked up from the bottle he was in the process of opening. "You mean the interview with that pilot who wrote the piece in *GQ* magazine a while back? He was the first one publicly to break silence about what it's like to pilot unmanned missions remotely."

"That's the one," she nodded, "and wasn't there also a government report that drone pilots had higher rates of PTSD than regular pilots because they were exposed to seeing and assessing in detail the carnage their explosives created, like you just told me?"

"That, and working twelve hours at a clip in front of those glowing screens under high stress at a base in the middle of nowhere—followed by going home every night, forbidden to talk about anything that happened while we were on duty."

"God, it sounds absolutely awful," Juliet sympathized, accepting a stemmed glass of wine the color of garnets.

"Cheese, et cetera coming right up." Finn strode to a cupboard and rummaged within its shelves. With his back to her, he said, "I was lucky that Claudine marched me over to the American Hospital soon after I got here and threatened to kick me out of her apartment if I didn't sign up for help...which I did."

"Has it made a difference?"

Finn set a plate with offerings on his coffee table.

"Some. I got diagnosed 'PTSD,' all right. I'm totally off the meds and the booze, as you can see." He waved a glass filled with carbonated water. "I see a shrink two times a week who's trying to retrain my brain not to 'go there' when there are trigger events that throw me back to that trailer or...some of the things I experienced in the Middle East. Believe it or not, I even do a special kind of yoga designed for PTSD folks. I still have nightmares, which I hope I won't subject you to while you're here, but after seven months hiding out, as you called it…yes, I think I *am* better. Not cured. Better."

Juliet could sense that Finn was waiting for her reaction to his candid disclosures. *He wonders if I now think he's a crazy person…or a wuss…or a coward.* She sank back on the couch while Finn remained standing, looking down at her. She met his gaze, murmuring, "How can life get so friggin' complicated, Major Deschanel?"

"It sure is a bitch, at times, ain't it, Ms. Thayer?"

Juliet closed her eyes, her head cushioned by the back of Finn's couch. No one at GatherGames would believe that she was sharing a barge on the River Seine, however temporarily, with a Major in the Air Force who'd flown drones—real ones—and admitted to having actually killed people and suffered anguish in the aftermath of his military service. Did Finn now hate the video war games industry as much as she did? The handsome man standing two feet away from her with a look, at times, of such desolation in his eyes had been an integral player in a *real* war with its *real* devastation. He also just confessed that being party to it had nearly destroyed him.

"Juliet? Have I scared you?"

At the sound of his voice, low and vibrating with intensity, she opened her eyes. "Absolutely not." She sat up straight and took a sip of her wine in order to think through a more complete answer. "It's just that I'm trying to take it all in, you know? How I got here. How you did. What happened in Paris last Friday. How scared I feel whenever I hear the helicopters overhead or I'm on the street by myself. What the last years have brought about for everyone. The fact you flew drones. Killed some people. The fact that, even though I hated what I've been part of, and knew it couldn't be good for kids, I kept doing it—not *just* because I was I worried about my parents' getting their investment back—but because I also earned a very good salary, plus stock options, using my artistic skills to make drone kills look real...'cool'—"

"Hey! Whoa, there!" Finn interrupted. "Before you feel too guilt-ridden that the junk your company produced is polluting the youth of America—"

"It is!" Juliet interrupted, slapping the palm of one hand against the sofa cushion.

"Maybe so," he said, taking a seat on top of her closed suitcase standing next to the couch, "but you should probably know that I spent most of my teenage boyhood playing video war games and stuff like *Grand Theft Auto* given to me at Christmas by my father."

He pointed to a picture on a nearby shelf showing a group surrounding a young man in uniform with the Colorado Rocky Mountains serving as a backdrop.

"That's you and your family, right?" she asked.

"Yep, at graduation." He pointed to an officer in a uniform with a chest covered with five square inches of colorful service ribbons. "Your dad owns a hotel?" he commented with a grim smile. "My dad, Andrew Deschanel, is a three-star general."

Juliet stared at the framed picture of the Deschanel family gathered in Finn's honor at the Air Force Academy. "Your dad has three stars? Wow. In the Air Force?"

"Army. And, incidentally, I was really good at video war games. I loved them because I beat my father all the time."

"So were you two addicted to them, the way my brother and his buddies are?"

Finn paused, giving her question some thought. "Yeah. Probably. I played nonstop all through high school. But let me hasten to add, I soon discovered that the real deal is no game. Too bad your brother hasn't experienced sitting in one of those innocuous-looking trailers parked in the middle of nowhere. Maybe he wouldn't want to spend his life making money off bending the minds of oversexed boys like I was, training us to think killing other humans, long-distance, is a kick-ass occupation—and a substitute for getting laid when you're fourteen."

Finn remained perched on her upended suitcase. Maybe he thought she didn't want him to sit that close to her on the couch? He returned his gaze to the plate glass window just as the Eiffel Tower was suddenly illuminated with blinding brightness in shades of blue, white, and red.

"Oh, look!" Juliet exclaimed, swiveling in her seat on the sofa. "How beautiful! They've turned the lights back on in the colors of the French flag! Isn't that a good sign?"

The enormous structure's colorful outline was reflected in the water below it.

"It'll never look the same to me."

"No...not to you, it probably won't," she agreed. "Just like the space where the Twin Towers once stood in Manhattan has never looked the same to New Yorkers." She reached out and placed a hand lightly on his sleeve. "Finn, I've been living in a glass house atop Nob Hill, so...just so you know... please don't think I'd ever throw stones at you because you fought in the Middle East or flew drones."

Finn pulled his gaze from the shining beacon across the water to observe her sitting on his couch. His blue eyes crinkled faintly at the corners. He gently chucked her chin with the fingers of one hand. "And I'd never throw them at you, either, Ms. Design Director. Maybe at your brother, but not at you."

Juliet grew very still. The sensation of this brief encounter between his flesh and her face sent an electric current buzzing in her jaw. She almost leaned against him like the barge cat, Truffles, wanting to be petted again. An unexpected wave of relief washed through her that he didn't judge her as she didn't judge him. It felt like the same reprieve Finn had granted her when he insisted she not spend a night shivering in a frigid flat in a strange city where terrorists were still on the loose.

He gave her nose a brotherly tap with his index finger as if to retract any feeling of intimacy that might have briefly been flowing between them. Rising from his seat on her suitcase, he crossed to the leather easy chair where a copy of *Hemingway: The Paris Years* lay open, upside-down, on its arm. He closed the book, set it to one side and turned to face her. "It's lights out time for this guy. What about you?"

Juliet nodded, wondering at the lingering memory of his touch against her face. "Okay if I brush my teeth and use the head?"

If Finn Deschanel and Juliet Thayer had known each other better, both would have confided the next morning that their second night on the barge together in their separate sleeping quarters had resulted in the most peaceful eight hours' slumber that either of them had enjoyed in a very long time.

For Finn's part, he opened one eye in his stateroom and stretched his body in the double bed that was built into the bulkhead. Amazed that the clock on the table at his elbow registered six a.m., he hadn't woken up once in the night, which was a first in more than three years.

He donned his jeans, a T-shirt, and his jacket, and tiptoed out the door, shoes in hand. His mission, per usual, was to secure fresh croissants and his daily loaf of bread to offer the sleeping beauty on his couch, along with a second cup of coffee he'd concoct in his French *presse* glass pot when he returned.

Walking swiftly along the cobbled quay in the chilly

morning air, Finn judged his mood was actually bordering on cheerful as he recalled the sight of the lovely young woman with reddish-brown, shoulder-length hair that was one shade shy of the color of the Rhone wine he'd served her the previous evening. He'd been surprised and even gratified by the jolt of sensation he'd experienced gazing down at her, sleeping so peacefully. She was curled on her side beneath the covers on his sofa in a posture he could easily imagine a man mirroring, a protective arm cast around her shoulder.

In fact, he'd almost chuckled aloud to see Juliet's hand tucked under her chin like a feminine version of The Thinker, the colossal statue dominating the gardens of the Rodin Museum on the *Rue de Varenne* where he'd often walked since arriving in Paris. Given the horror of the last few days, it felt strange and not a little curious to Finn to be enveloped by the comforting thought that a very attractive artist from San Francisco who had loyally raced to the rescue of a close friend was asleep in his home—and would be there waiting for him when he returned.

The first thing Juliet heard when she swam to consciousness her second morning on Finn's barge was the rattle of a key in the door across from the sofa where she'd conked out the minute her head had touched the pillow the night before. Sunlight, bright and cool, poured through the large picture window above her head, and when she rose up on one elbow, her breath caught once more at the sight of the Eiffel Tower soaring into an azure sky across the water dotted with river traffic moving in both directions.

And then she remembered why she was here, but before a cascade of worry could plunge her thoughts into all the troubling aspects of Avery's injuries, a broad-shouldered figure loomed in the doorway. Finn held a waxy paper sack in one hand, as well as a *baguette* that was nearly two feet long in a paper sleeve stashed in the crook of his arm. In the hand clutching a dangling key, he also gripped a newspaper.

"Good morning, Sleeping Beauty," her host greeted her.

"Here! Let me help you," Juliet exclaimed, jumping out of bed, only to realize she was skimpily clad in her black tights and matching T-shirt with no bra underneath.

"No worries, I got this." Finn headed for the other end of the main salon. He deposited his packages on the desk with its two electric burners and small, stainless steel sink and faucet. Nearby rested a toaster oven, a small tin cupboard, and Finn's open laptop. "Sleep okay?" he asked with his back toward his guest.

"I don't remember even closing my eyes."

"And how do you feel this morning?"

Juliet watched him store his purchases in the limited space and answered, "I feel okay, I guess. Better than yesterday. I didn't even dream, which is unusual for me."

Finn's head rose abruptly and he said over his shoulder with a short laugh, "Me, too. Didn't dream. Very unusual for me as well. I guess we both had hit the wall, given everything that's been going on since last Friday."

"I *do* feel better," she reflected slowly, "but I still feel a bit jumpy. Do you?"

He turned, arched an eyebrow without answering her directly, and crossed the room, handing her the newspaper. "Here's a copy of the *International New York Times*. The cops raided an apartment in the suburbs early this morning and killed two of the remaining terrorists. They're still looking for the guy who threw away his vest with the explosives in it, undetonated. He may have escaped to Syria. I'd say it's normal to feel jumpy, but the situation's definitely improved. Want some coffee with your croissants?"

"*Oui, oui, oui!* You are a total hero," she murmured with a grateful sigh. "Gotta have my caffeine." She grabbed a pair of jeans that she'd pulled out of her suitcase the previous night. "Okay if I use the head down below?"

"And here I thought I'd have to drill you on nautical terms while you're aboard."

"I live on San Francisco Bay, remember?" she teased as she descended the few steps to the stern compartment. "I'm a sailor and know my share of nautical terms. But can you teach them to me in *French?*"

"*Mais non,*" he called to her, "but that's a good suggestion for my next lesson with my language tutor. Coffee will be waiting."

For the next half hour with Juliet tucked into one end of the couch and Finn sitting on the other, the pair settled in, sharing flaky crescent pastries and strong, dark coffee. It was too early to head for the hospital, so Juliet gave herself permission to relax for an hour and enjoy the company.

"Want more hot milk to top off your coffee?" Finn asked, and Juliet obediently held out her mug, watching him pour the frothy mixture he'd heated on his burner into her cup.

She took a sip and leaned her head against the back of the couch. "Hmmm...I think I feel myself relaxing for the first time in a week," she declared. "The croissants are fabulous and this is about the best coffee I've ever tasted—and in my hometown, we're coffee fanatics."

"Studying French has led to my haunting the open-air food markets which, in turn has led to taking some cooking classes for novices at the *Cordon Bleu,*" Finn disclosed. "Making a decent cup of coffee was one of the first things they taught."

"And you cook on those two little burners," she marveled once again.

"The challenge keeps me on my toes."

"I'd love to study French cuisine," she ventured, aware, suddenly, of how wistful she sounded. "I grew up with room service at our family's hotel, but I adore good food and learning to cook it is on my Bucket List, believe it or not."

Her thoughts were suddenly filled with imagining what it would be like to be living and painting in Paris and taking trips to all the wonderful open-air markets, to say nothing of seeking out some of the stunning landscapes France had to offer. She could practically see herself shopping with one of those string bags to put her purchases in and eating her way across the city, sampling the fare produced by hundreds of charming bistros and cafés. She stole a glance in Finn's direction. He was so easy to be with, she mused, and so considerate, even to getting up early to provide breakfast and securing a copy of an English-language newspaper on a day when every tourist in France was probably looking for one. If Jed Jarvis were here, he'd probably say, "Babe, how 'bout going out and finding us a box of Cheerios, okay? I hate all this French stuff."

She realized with a start that this was the first time she'd given Jed a single thought since she'd arrived in France and gotten her passport stamped.

As she munched slowly on a bite of her croissant, its buttery goodness virtually melting in her mouth, she glanced out the window at the soaring magnificence of the Eiffel Tower. What a change from her normal life, having a leisurely breakfast with a man who, even when they weren't exchanging a word, felt so...*compatible*. Then, her eyes were drawn to the newspaper filled with stories of tragedy and terror and she felt guilty for enjoying anything during this terrible time.

Finn, who'd returned to reading his section of the

newspaper, sensed her looking at him and glanced across the space on the sofa that separated them. Embarrassed to be caught staring, Juliet said the first thing that came into her head. "God, I was so tired again last night, weren't you?"

"Totally bushed," he agreed. "And before you rush anywhere, we can check with the nurses' station to see how Avery is doing this morning. No point going over there if she's still sleeping or they're sending her for tests, or something."

"Sounds like you know hospital routines pretty well."

"My leg took its own sweet time to heal," he said with a shrug, pointing to his left thigh. "I learned that I might as well do it 'their' way and not get all agitated by the medical staff's sticking to their routines."

"Was it a bad break?"

"Breaks. Three of them. Plus the shrapnel."

"Ouch! No wonder you seem like such a patient man," Juliet responded, and took a deep sip of her delicious brew. "I suppose not getting a call in the middle of the night about Jean-Pierre from Madame Grenelle is a good sign, don't you think?"

Finn's cheerful demeanor altered somewhat. "I expect it only means J-P is still on life support," he said, his eyes drifting back to the newspaper page he'd been reading, although Juliet could tell he wasn't really paying attention.

When they'd both finished their breakfasts, Finn rose from the couch, gathered their plates and cups and took them to the sink. Juliet glanced down at the page of the newspaper he'd abandoned with its headline:

MORE EVIDENCE THAT TERRORISTS LIKELY USED
ENCRYPTION TO PLAN PARIS ATTACKS

A shiver slid down her spine and she was unable to take her eyes off the bold letters. She wondered if Brad was reading the same reports. Did he have one iota of remorse about the sort of violent video games he'd developed in the last two years and from which he planned to make his millions? Her unhappy reverie was abruptly interrupted by the sound of a cell phone ringing in Finn's bedroom. He bolted down below to retrieve it, and as soon as he answered, his voice lowered. Juliet reached for the newspaper article, but she couldn't concentrate due to the indistinct but heated exchange between Finn and his caller. A few minutes later, he emerged and immediately returned to rinsing the plates in his tiny sink without looking in her direction.

"Can I help?" Juliet called. "I can dry—"

"Thanks," he cut her short. "I got this."

When he again settled on the sofa a few feet from where she sat, she hastily handed him back the section of the newspaper she'd appropriated. He merely folded and wedged it between his thigh and the arm of the couch. A long silence ensued. Juliet felt the earlier pleasant mood had completely altered. She pointed to the picture of his family on the bookshelf that Finn had shown her the previous evening. "I probably shouldn't ask, but how did such a veteran soldier react to your decision to resign from the military?"

"Not well." Finn's voice had an angry edge and his gaze was aimed over her head in the direction of the Eiffel Tower across the water.

"Ah…right," Juliet murmured, adding in what she hoped was a casual, conversational tone, "I suppose that's not very surprising for a general. And is that your mom?" she asked, pointing. "She's so pretty."

"Yes. This was taken two years before she got cancer. She passed away when I was on my second tour in Iraq, before I was redeployed to Afghanistan."

"Oh, Finn. I-I'm so sorry…about your mom, I mean."

"Thank you. It was rough. And that's my sister, Maureen." He pointed to a young woman in a pale blue pants suit. Juliet could tell he was trying to sound more cheerful. "She married an Army guy…a colonel, now."

"And that?" she said, pointing to a very attractive blonde with a drop-dead figure clad in a crisp cotton lavender-and-white print dress and a wide-brimmed straw hat.

"That's Kim. She was my girlfriend at the time."

"Well, she's a stunner."

"She still is."

At his clipped words, Juliet felt her heart lurch for some reason. She laughed nervously and attempted to joke, "She's still pretty…or she's still your girlfriend?"

Finn continued to look at her with a steady gaze. "In the spirit of full disclosure, you know that phone call I just took?"

"Yes." Juliet was astonished to realize she was holding her breath.

"That was my lawyer in Nevada."

"Do you have some legal issues left over from leaving the military?" Could he be in some sort of trouble? Might that be the reason he'd moved to France?

"No, not that," he replied. "It's a different kind of legal issue—having to do with ending my marriage. My lawyer is in the process of negotiating my divorce."

You're *married?*' Juliet blurted, her eyes drawn to his left hand, devoid of a ring. "To Kim?" she confirmed, pointing once more at the picture he'd returned to the shelf.

"Technically…yes."

"Technically, married is married," she repeated firmly, doing her best to hide a wholly embarrassing rush of disappointment that made her cheeks grow warm.

Jeez, Juliet! You only met this guy exactly forty-eight hours ago! Cool it!

Meanwhile, Finn was explaining, "We've been separated for quite a while. I'm just trying to finalize everything."

"Why? I mean, why are you separated?" Juliet was even more embarrassed by this inane outburst. "Man, am I nosey! You don't have to answer," she added, feeling ridiculous, a sensation that was soon replaced by irritation. *Why hadn't he mentioned he was married the first night I stayed on the barge? Perhaps that was the true reason that he was so reluctant, at first, to have me stay when Avery's apartment turned out to be uninhabitable? Divorcing couples are usually still very much emotionally involved.*

An avalanche of questions began to bubble up. As far she could observe, Finn was one dishy guy. Why would his wife split with her husband after all he'd been through? And why would he leave her—unless something really bad had happened between them. *And who was greatest at fault? Why did every single thing in life have to turn out to be so f-ing complicated?*

Finn cocked an eyebrow from across the couch. "As they say, an officer and a gentleman never speaks of the misdeeds of a lady."

Juliet felt herself bristle. "Oh, so they were all *her* misdeeds, were they?"

"If you knew the whole story, you'd probably agree that most of them actually were."

Before she could respond, they were startled by a sharp series of knocks at the door. Outside stood a teenage girl with purple streaks in her black hair and bangs.

"I am so sorry to disturb you," she apologized, her English excellent. She glanced over Finn's shoulder at Juliet on the far side of the cabin. Flushing slightly to see that he obviously was entertaining company at breakfast time, she explained for Juliet's benefit that she was Colette, Eloise Grenelle's granddaughter, and thus Jean-Pierre's sister. "Can I trouble you to come speak to us at *Grandmère's?*" she asked Finn, adding that the entire family was gathered next door. "It's quite urgent, I'm afraid."

With a look of apology to his guest, Finn excused himself to follow Madame Grenelle's messenger to the opposite end of the barge. Juliet listened to the sound of their retreating steps. Then she jumped to her feet, as if shot out of a canon, and began to pack.

CHAPTER 8

Juliet couldn't even explain to herself why she felt she had to leave the barge in such a hurry. She simply switched into automatic pilot and next thing she knew, she was snapping shut her small suitcase.

Yes, after staying on his barge for two days, she was frankly shocked to learn that Finn was a married man—however technical or un-technical he might consider his status to be. As far as she was concerned—and despite the fact that she supposedly had a guy of her own that she saw exclusively at home—she could not deny the quiver of excitement she'd experienced in the former pilot's company, or the hope that she might, at the very least, have met a kindred spirit.

Yet, something else was in play that instantly had convinced Juliet she could no longer remain a visitor aboard Finn's boat. She swiftly folded the sheets and blankets and placed them neatly on the couch. As a postscript to her very proper thank you note, she offered a little fib to make her departure seem less abrupt.

> *Avery just called. I can stay at a small hotel near the hospital until they release her, which sounds sensible for all concerned.*
>
> *We'll keep tabs on J-P and pray for the best. Again, thanks for everything,*
>
> *Juliet*

Carrying her suitcase by its handle instead of rolling it noisily along the deck, Juliet bolted down the gangway and sprinted along the quay toward the city street that ran above the stonewall overlooking the Seine. Miraculously, a cab came into view just then and she jumped into it. By the time it deposited her in front of the American Hospital, the reasons propelling her hasty exit from Finn's abode finally had begun to form sentences in her mind.

Finn Deschanel's life is just as complicated and out of control as mine!

Like her, he was still involved in an intimate relationship. He had a friend who'd gone through a horrible trauma and would need his help—if the poor guy lived. Even more amazingly coincidental, Finn had been part of a hated profession. If she were brutally honest with herself, the last thing she needed was getting entangled emotionally with a married man suffering from PTSD who lived in a foreign country!

Even a man who said he was in the process of getting *un*-entangled…

By this time, Juliet had arrived in the hospital lobby and paused to sign in. Despite her good intentions, however, as the elevator rose to the second floor, her mind kept reviewing every enjoyable instant that she'd spent on *L'Étoile de Paris*. When she reached the door to Avery's room, a nurse in the hallway explained the patient had been taken downstairs for another X-ray.

"Could you please tell Ms. Evans that I'm grabbing a coffee in the cafeteria and I'll be back in twenty minutes?"

"*D'accord*," nodded the nurse.

Juliet left her suitcase in Avery's room and soon settled in a plastic chair clutching a paper cup containing a surprisingly decent brew. The cafeteria was filled with doctors and nurses coming off the night shift, along with the usual cluster of friends and relatives of patients waiting to gain entry to the hospital rooms when official visiting hours began. As she slowly sipped her third cup of caffeine that morning, she found her mind circling back to everything she had observed about the airman she'd met two days ago. She was positive that Finn had felt the same spark she had when they'd been talking late into the night and so compatibly for an hour more this morning—that was, until the phone call from his lawyer had so clearly upset him. Timing was everything, and her timing with Major Deschanel was lousy. Tempted though she might be, she knew for sure that if she took a single step in Finn's direction, things would just get messier than they already were.

She rose from her chair, tossed her cup into a trash bin, and made her way back toward Avery's floor. As she approached Room 203, a stab of deep sadness and regret took hold, convincing her—though she knew without a doubt, anyway—that she was missing out on something that might have been quite wonderful.

But facts are facts, kiddo.

Juliet was scheduled to leave Paris in a few days' time. Sadly, she'd never have a chance to find out where the path down the embankment to Finn's barge might ultimately have led. And then there was Jed Jarvis, the supposed man in her life. *One good thing to come out of all this,* she thought, heading toward Avery's hospital room: *I knew, for sure, now, what I intend to do about him.*

Juliet stood in the doorway to Avery's hospital room. "Hi, brittle bones, how're you feeling?"

"Like I got shot and then was run over by a truck," Avery answered with a weak grin and her own stab at gallows humor. "Who knew having an X-ray could knock the stuffing out of a person?"

Juliet advanced to her bedside and gently placed a waxy paper bag with two croissants fresh from the hospital cafeteria on top of the bedcovers.

"Well, you're still among the living, which means you're healthy enough to eat a little contraband," she announced. "I snuck it past the authorities at the nurses' station."

"You are a total champ. *Café crème*, too?"

"Of course," Juliet said with a sly smile. "Next time, I'll stop at a real *boulangerie*." She grinned at her friend. "Takes me back to the days when you used to demand your daily *latte* from the GatherGames commissary, remember?"

"*Café crème…latte…*it's all the same. I need my caffeine fix to feel human, and this might start me on the road to that. You are truly my rescuing angel."

Juliet crept back to the door to Avery's room and closed it quietly, praying a nurse wouldn't walk in and eject her for not following the rules. She removed the puffed pastry from the bag, tore Avery's into bite-sized pieces, and uncapped her "take-away" paper cup of coffee laced with hot milk.

"Just put it there," Avery indicated, pointing to the rolling tray that fit over her bedcovers. "I can manage with my good arm."

Juliet had also brought a cup of orange juice with her, so the two friends nibbled their pastry and sipped in companionable silence as they had so many times when they'd sat at their computers at work.

"How was the apartment?" Avery asked after several minutes.

"Honestly? A frigid cell in a prison tower! The heater wouldn't work, so I spent the last two nights on a barge moored on the Seine near the Eiffel Tower, thanks to a very nice friend of the Grenelles." Juliet proceeded to tell the story of Finn's escorting her to Avery's apartment, only to insist she come back to his place to avoid freezing to death.

Avery, with a mouthful of pastry, acknowledged, "It took me a week to learn to master the heat at my place."

"Well, before I came here today, I booked myself a room at a small hotel nearby until they let you out of the hospital and we get someone to fix your heat." Juliet smiled with false cheer and added, "I can get into my room around noon."

Avery's eyes were suddenly rife with anxiety.

"Did you hear anything more this morning about Jean-Pierre?"

"Not anything beyond what we were told before."

Juliet swiftly shifted away from the dangerous direction the conversation was taking by volunteering to contact Avery's parents, "To let them know you're okay."

Avery abruptly set down her paper coffee cup. "Now why would I want to do that?" she said with a scowl on her face.

"Because they'll be worried with all the news, knowing you're in Paris and they haven't heard from you since Friday."

"They don't know I'm here and haven't heard from me in the six months I've been living here, nor me from them." She stared at the last morsels of her croissant. "Trust me, I could be on death's door and my mom would make what's happened to me be all about *her.*" Avery's voice took on a mimicking tone. "'Flying to Paris is such a strain on the immune system, to say nothing what a complete bummer it is to be missing the marijuana harvest.'"

"C'mon, Avery," protested Juliet.

Avery's face became redder as she enumerated the predicted reactions of her parents if they were informed of what had happened to their daughter.

"Oh, and of course, my mom would bemoan the food and water upsetting her delicate digestive system, and, besides, 'the French are so rude!' And, for sure, she'd insist that her expenses coming to look after me should be reimbursed by my father's zillions, and that would cause its usual uproar and—"

"Avery, no…really, it can't be *that* bad."

Pain shot through her friend's eyes. "Honestly? It is," she stated flatly. "And when it comes to my father, I don't imagine that he would think what's happened to me was such a big deal, given that I didn't actually *die* Friday night."

In the silence that followed, Juliet felt an enormous rush of sympathy. She knew absolutely that her brother Jamie and her father—and even her mother—would immediately fly to her side if it had been her who'd been gunned down. She pulled a tissue from the box on Avery's side table and handed it to her, alarmed to see her friend's eyes had filled with tears. Then she dug into Avery's handbag, resting on the bedside table, and pulled out her cell phone.

"C'mon, Av, can't *I* call or write them a short note about what's happened? Do you have their email addresses in this?" She waved the phone. "All I'll do is tell them you were wounded in the attacks but are expected to make a full recovery. At least they should know what's happened to you!"

"No! Please don't."

Juliet heaved a defeated shrug. Avery's estrangement from her parents was not news to her, but the depth of their family dysfunction was alarming. "Okay, then." She reluctantly replaced her friend's phone inside the purse where she'd found it. "The 'non-event' view of last Friday's events also sounds like someone else we both know."

Avery shot her a knowing look. "Your brother Brad was pissed that you came to Paris, am I right?"

Juliet wished, then, she hadn't brought up the subject of her elder brother or had to acknowledge that he'd ordered his sister not to come to France, but Avery and she had built their relationship on total honesty.

"GatherGames' newest piece of dreck is to be released

soon and he needs me to—"

"No need to go into details," Avery snapped. "I know: 'Work comes before life.' What comes after *Sky Slaughter – Death by Drones? Revenge of the Space Terrorists?*"

"Not quite...but you're close."

"No holding back, Juliet. What's the title of Brad Thayer's latest masterpiece?" Her mouth was set in a straight line.

"*Sky Slaughter Two–Drones in the Desert.* A real shoot-'em-up. Brad says every male under thirty-five in the world has asked for it for Christmas, but it won't be released until after the first of the year. Too many back orders for *Sky Slaughter One.*"

Avery shook her head in disgust. "I ask again, Jules, how could you and Brad be from the same family?" She pursed her lips. "And how are all our other dear colleagues enjoying life at our South of Market headquarters?" she asked, referring to Northern California's second Silicon Valley.

The simple truth was that no one from the company Brad ran dared voice their sympathy for Avery Evans or even about the terrorist attacks in Paris within their boss's earshot, nor had anyone even asked to convey best wishes for their former co-worker's recovery when they'd heard Juliet was dashing out the door to the airport. Their CEO was obviously displeased by his sister's actions, and his many minions were not about to appear to disagree with him. Wishing to change the subject, Juliet pointed to a vase of beautiful cut roses that must have come from a Parisian friend's garden.

"Who are those from? They're gorgeous!"

Avery reared back on her pillow in surprise. "I have no idea. They must have arrived when I was down getting X-rayed. Can you look at the card for me?"

Juliet crossed to the small bureau and peered at a note

penned in French that was nestled in the stems.

"*Let me know when I can come see you. Alain Devereux,*'"
Juliet read. She looked up. "At least I think that translation
is right. Who's he?"

"My professor at *L'École* who teaches the portrait
master class." Avery's voice suddenly wavered. "That's
how I became friends with Jean-Pierre. J-P speaks excellent
English, and Alain asked him to help me get adjusted at the
school the first week I enrolled."

Avery pushed away the tray with her coffee and the
crumbs of the croissant she'd consumed. She lay back with
her head on the pillow, and closed her eyes.

"Tired?" Juliet said with a rush of sympathy. "Why
don't you take a little nap and I'll go get settled into my
new digs."

Avery barely nodded as Juliet tiptoed out the room.

Juliet returned to Avery's beside after her first night in
a nondescript hotel near the hospital that could just as
easily been a Holiday Inn—bland, efficient, and without
much charm, but the price was affordable by Parisian
standards. She was startled and pleased to see that another,
rather impressively large bouquet of flowers had arrived.

"Who are these from?" she asked, filled with curiosity
after saying good morning to Avery and inquiring how her
night had been.

"They're from your brother."

"*Brad?*" she marveled. *Maybe he has an ounce of empathy,
after all,* she thought with a stab of guilt for the way she'd
condemned him so thoroughly both to Finn and Avery.

"Of course not Brad! They're from your *other* brother.
Jamie."

"Really?" she said, pleased. "Can I look?"

Juliet peered at the card, whose message she found quite intriguing.

> *Horrified by what's happened.*
> *Here's to a speedy recovery.*
> *Much love, Jamie*

"Well, well…it looks as if you've had a secret admirer all this time," she teased.

"Not so secret," Avery replied with a slight, upward quirk of her lips. "I must have told you, didn't I, that Jamie and I talked briefly about going out in the early days of GatherGames?"

"Neither of you told me anything," she corrected flatly.

"Well, we mutually decided it wasn't the greatest idea…dipping our pens into office ink and all that." Avery shrugged. "But he's such a sweet guy, and sending flowers like this means a lot." She fell silent for a moment, and then asked, "Why in the world did you think Brad would send flowers? He had me escorted out of the office by the building's security guards when I told him I was quitting."

"Hope springs eternal, I guess," Juliet replied with a shrug of her own.

"That notion could get you in a lot of trouble. When are you going to realize that even though Brad's your brother, he doesn't give a damn about anybody else but Old Number One?"

"Score one for you in the 'Brutally Honesty Department.'" Avery immediately shot Juliet an apologetic look, but Juliet held up her hand. "No, you're right," she agreed with a sigh. "He's the perfect example of a self-absorbed Millennial-to-the-max."

"And a card-carrying member of our More-For-Me Generation."

"Weird, isn't it, that Jamie, he, and I were born only a few years apart, but are—"

"The two of you are completely opposite," interrupted Avery.

Juliet heaved another small sigh. "I just keep thinking that Brad'll—"

Avery interrupted again. "Stop drinking from the poison well, will you, Juliet? It *is* what it is with that guy. You've got both a really sweet brother and a skunk of a brother. It's time you accepted the truth. It happens in a lot of families."

Just then a figure appeared in the door, backlit by windows in the corridor. For a split second, Juliet thought it might be Finn Deschanel—but it wasn't.

"*Allo*! I'm Etienne," announced a young man of about Finn's height. "Time for your physical therapy again, *mademoiselle*."

Closer inspection of the person standing in the doorway revealed a tattoo on the man's burly neck and a gold earring piercing his lobe. He was wearing white pants and a white shirt with longish hair curling at his collar.

"If it's okay with you, Avery," Juliet proposed, "while you're working with Etienne, I'll check out of my hotel and go back to your apartment to see if I can get the heat issue sorted out."

"Good luck with that, but thanks," Avery replied, smiling weakly. "I wish I could instruct you, but I've forgotten exactly how I got it going the first time." Juliet could tell her friend was dreading the next hour, but all Avery added was a spunky, "Okay, *monsieur*...let's get this torture over with."

Juliet felt that by now, she must be digging ridges with her wheeled suitcase into the concrete ramp that led from the entrance of the American Hospital of Paris to the street that paralleled the massive institution. To her relief, the number 82 bus was pulled up at the curb, its open door welcoming her until she realized that she needed a pre-paid ticket to climb aboard. Her look of dismay must have filled the driver with pity, for he beckoned her to get on the bus, pointing to a map above her head that indicated she should get off near the *Musée d'Orsay*, whose back wall faced the street that she'd explained in her halting French was her destination.

Wearily, she pulled her suitcase onto the bus. She settled into one of the plastic seats and secured her bag between her knees to prevent it from rolling across the aisle. For a half hour, at least, she could relax until the next challenge of being an American in Paris presented itself.

With another stroke of luck, one of Avery's neighbors was just exiting the big, oak door at Number 7, *Rue de Lille*. After Juliet hailed him and explained her presence there, he disclosed that he and his wife were fellow Americans who lived with their baby son in one of the luxurious flats just below the frigid attic. Brian Parker, from New York City, worked for a business-consulting firm with an office in Paris. He pointed toward the stairs that led to the apartments above their heads.

"Actually, I had noticed that Avery hasn't been here in a while," he said, expressing his shock that she had been one of the victims in Friday's terrorist attacks. "Please give her our best and let us know if there's anything else we can do."

When she informed him of the heating problem, he immediately volunteered to help her when he got home that evening, "...if you haven't been rescued by the building's concierge by that time."

"Is there Wi-Fi in the building?" Juliet asked doubtfully, considering the building was probably constructed in the eighteenth century. If by some miracle there was, she could do some of her work remotely and perhaps buy an extra day or two to remain in Paris.

"Feel free to piggy-back off of ours," Parker offered and gave her the password. "We're just below Avery's place and she mentioned it reaches up there."

Within an hour of locating the concierge to seek help getting the heating system to work, Juliet had tidied up Avery's small space and made a list of needed provisions. Soon, she headed out on a shopping mission with Brian's advice as to grocery stores, the nearest *boulangerie* for bread and pastries, and the names of several bistros and cafés that he and his wife, Melanie, like to frequent.

Just as Finn had, Brian recommended *La Calèche*, right across the street, as a very nice spot for lunch or dinner. With a wave of his hand as he headed off for his day's work, he'd called, "Tell Philippe that I sent you. He especially caters to locals."

With directions in hand, Juliet finished her shopping chores without incident and stored her purchases upstairs. When she called Avery, however, the call went straight to voice mail. Figuring she was probably exhausted from her hour of physical therapy and sound asleep, Juliet quickly heated up and consumed a bowl of ready-made soup she'd bought earlier. Consulting her Paris Districts map book that neatly fit into her jacket pocket, she set off for the campus of *L'École des Beaux Arts*.

Despite her concern about Avery, she was wildly curious for a closer inspection of the institution where her great-great grandmother had attended architecture school. Thinking about the pioneering Amelia Hunter Bradshaw who had married James Thayer in 1907, Juliet's thoughts drifted to her own family. She felt a stab of sadness that no one from home had texted her back after she'd sent word she had landed safely in Paris. She paused on a street corner and checked her email. Her spirits lifted a notch when she scrolled across an earlier message from her dad and one of encouragement from Jamie. Nothing from her mother or Brad, of course.

A bitingly cold wind assaulted her ankles where she stood on *Rue Bonaparte*. She hurriedly approached a wrought iron gate placed in the institution's tall walls that enclosed a massive, stone-paved courtyard. She had checked online to confirm that *L'École des Beaux Arts* had re-opened its doors after Friday's attacks. She paused at the gate to take in the sight of the world's most prestigious establishment offering classes in all variety of the practical and fine arts. Bicycles and motorcycles were lined against one stonewall, an encouraging indication that things were slowly getting back to normal. Just inside the gate, a gaggle of expressionless armed guards stood beside a small table where her handbag was thoroughly searched—another visible sign that the fatal melee at the cartoonists' headquarters and the recent slaughter of so many innocent civilians less than a week earlier had prompted an all-out local response.

Once past the security checkpoint, she slowly surveyed the series of arched corridors stretching in all directions and searched for a sign that might indicate where the administration offices were located. Pausing at an open door down one hall, she absorbed the sight of a live, nude male model posing with one foot on a riser, the object of attention of some dozen art students in a drawing class. In another room, she saw students standing in front of individual easels working on landscapes that Juliet assumed had been previously initiated out-of-doors at various locations in Paris and its environs.

Riveted, Juliet realized she was holding her breath as she watched them paint. After some fifteen minutes, mesmerized by the scratching sound of pastel chalks some were using, as well as the pungent odor of linseed oil and paint other students employed, she asked *sotte voce* of a figure nearest the door for the location of a local art store where she could buy some sketching supplies.

"I speak English," replied a reed-thin young woman with dyed red, stringy hair and purple lipstick. She named a few art supply emporiums.

"Do you have the Paris Metro app on your phone?" she asked.

"No, but I'd like to," Juliet replied quickly, and proceeded to click onto the App Store and downloaded her informant's recommendation in a trice.

"*Bon!*" the student said approvingly. She took command of Juliet's phone and typed in the nearest metro stop to the school, followed by another, and brought up the names of the underground trains that would get Juliet where she wanted to go.

"Would you do that for the American Hospital in Neuilly?" Juliet asked. "My friend, who's a student here, was shot last Friday in the attacks and I want to know the quickest way to get there from here."

"*Mon Dieu!*" The young woman with the scarlet mane stared at her with alarm, her dark brown eyes lined with bold strokes of black eye pencil. "I heard today that there were several students from here who were injured or died," she said, handing Juliet's phone back to her after showing her the metro line from nearby *St. Germain-des-Pres* that ran to *Ponte de Neuilly*, a stop within easy walking distance of the American Hospital. "Is your friend going to make it?"

"Yes, but it may be a while before she can paint again." Juliet decided not to mention fellow student Jean-Pierre's critical condition. Then she repeated the question that had initiated their conversation: "Can you tell me what you think is the *best* art supply store around here?"

"Sennelier's," she answered emphatically. "It's just

around the corner...number three, *Quai Voltaire*. It's over a hundred years old. Cezanne purchased his supplies there!" she said proudly. "I buy everything in that store, but it's not cheap, which is why I mentioned the others when you asked. Sennelier's is by far the best, though."

Juliet thanked her and glanced at her watch. It was too late to talk to anyone in the school's administrative office, or to indulge in a shopping expedition for art supplies. Instead, she decided to head directly back to the hospital to see how Avery was doing. A half hour later, emerging from the metro, she proceeded down the *Boulevard du Chateau* to the American Hospital's now-familiar front entrance off *Victor Hugo* where she'd originally collided with Finn.

For several minutes, she remained outside watching a parade of visitors stream through the revolving door, wondering, despite her best resolve, whether Finn was in the building sitting vigil with Jean-Pierre's family—and what condition Avery's friend was in.

"Focus!" she said under her breath.

She was in Paris to tend to *her* friend. With renewed purpose, she strode toward the door, this time without her wheeled suitcase in tow.

CHAPTER 9

Juliet spent the next two days in Paris checking in with Avery between therapy sessions that dealt with both her physical and psychological issues. She did her best to cheer up her friend by smuggling in meals from her favorite bistros and visiting the huge department store, *Galleries Lafayette*, in search of a bottle of Avery's favorite perfume, along with a pretty nightgown to replace the unflattering hospital smock.

Meanwhile, Juliet struggled to keep the heating system in the attic apartment under control. It was either stifling or plunging into temperatures that were chilly-to-frigid by dawn's light. On the fifth day of Juliet's visit, Avery returned to her hospital room, exhausted from rehab, and slept for four hours, straight. After an hour waiting for her to wake up, Juliet slipped out of her room and took the metro to the stop nearest the *Quai Voltaire*. She soon found her way to Sennelier's art supply shop.

As she rounded the corner onto the street fronting the Seine near the *Pont du Carrousel,* a little gasp escaped her lips. Sennelier's storefront rose before her in all its turquoise and gold painted splendor. The colorful front facade dazzled the eye with tall windows crowded with a rainbow of wares: chalks, packages of pastels, tubes of oils, tins of watercolors, paint brushes, and a number of fanciful canvases showing the range of colors to be purchased within its walls.

To Juliet's great relief, the fourth-generation proprietor, Sophie Sennelier, assisted her with her purchases of an array of pencils, pastels, a small watercolor set, and a good-sized sketch book—all of which Juliet was able to fit in her tote bag as the two women spoke a combination of French and English.

That afternoon, after bringing lunch to Avery and watching her fall asleep, Juliet took her new art supplies to the green spaces of nearby *Bois de Boulogne* where she sketched for an hour and then made a side trip to see the iconic *Arc de Triomphe*. The next day she followed the same routine: she lunched with Avery in her hospital room and then found her way to *Parc Monceau*, an eighteenth-century gated green space surrounded by opulent mansions studded with *belle époque* monuments of prominent French writers and musicians. Everywhere she looked, there was one more breathtaking sight after another, and she could only imagine what the magnificent park would look like in the blush of spring. In contrast, the ubiquitous guards brandishing guns everywhere reminded her that the beauty of Paris had probably been altered forever.

Almost as a kind of protest, Juliet braved the crowds in the later afternoon and took the elevator to the top of the Eiffel Tower. Gazing down, she was startled to be able to spot Finn's barge floating serenely in the Seine on the river opposite.

She even ventured into the 10th *Arrondissement*, wanting—yet fearful—to pay her respects to a particular scene of the November attacks, *Le Petit Cambodge*. The air was biting when she walked out of the *Goncourt* metro stop. She was taken aback to see that the restaurant where Avery and Jean-Pierre had been shot was a modest neighborhood eatery literally across the street from the St. Louis Hospital. Avery had described the crush of ambulances crowding the entrance leading to the emergency ward, a jam-up that had prompted her to beg the drivers to take her to the American Hospital, instead.

Now, Juliet could only gaze at the restaurant's boarded-up windows and cordoned-off sidewalk that was piled high with bouquets of flowers, candles, and all manner of tributes to the diners and staff who had suffered such grievous losses. Parisians, bundled against the cold, approached in small groups to add to the offerings. Juliet stood frozen in place, her own arms filled with a bouquet of long-stemmed white roses that she'd bought at a flower shop en route. A well of emotion clogged her throat as thoughts filled her mind of Avery, pale in her bed, and Jean-Pierre, hooked to a ventilator in the sterile confines of the ICU. Then she considered the dead that were being buried this very day, and the other 368 wounded whose lives had been shattered on November 13th.

Why? Why! her heart cried out.

No answers came as she approached a spot to lay her flowery memorial beside the others. Her eyes blurred with tears, she slowly turned her back on the display and sought out the nearest park. Despite the November chill, sketching outdoors had the effect of calming Juliet's turbulent thoughts and the simmering fear whenever she walked on public streets or entered a shadowed metro station where terrorists might strike again.

On November 20th, the one-week anniversary of the attacks, Juliet called to speak to Jamie in person in the wake of a series of texts that grew increasingly insistent. On the phone, his voice conveyed his obvious anxiety to know specifics of Avery's condition.

"She's doing better each day," Juliet reported, adding, "and she's really touched that you've been sending flowers and gifts so often. The doctors have told her that eventually she'll be able to paint again and continue at *L'École*."

"That's such great news!" Jamie exclaimed. "Can she talk on the phone yet?"

'She's still pretty fragile…and the nurses say I'm the only person they'll let in for the moment. But seriously, bro, she did want me to tell you how much she appreciates everything you've had delivered to her hospital room."

"What about her parents? Have they come over?"

"I don't think they know anything." Juliet paused. "She didn't even want me to email them about what's happened."

"Really? That's crazy."

"That's Avery." Changing the subject, Juliet asked, "So how's work?"

"Same old same old," Jamie replied, his voice taking on an exasperated tone. "You better prepare yourself for a call from Brad any minute now, demanding to know when his design director is gonna return home. Your week is up, he said when I got to work today."

"Has he asked about how Avery's doing?" She already anticipated his answer.

"Not once."

After her call to Jamie, Juliet headed back to the hospital. Twenty feet from Avery's door she was flagged down by the friendly nurse she'd met on the ward the first day she arrived.

"I have some sad news…" the woman began.

Juliet sucked in a breath and shot a worried glance toward Room 203. "What's wrong? Is Avery okay?"

"No, no, it's not her." The nurse paused and placed her hand lightly on Juliet's arm, her expression melancholy. "It's her friend Jean-Pierre. He died about an hour ago."

"Oh, no!" wailed Juliet softly, her eyes instantly filling with tears.

"As you probably know, he was declared brain dead earlier this week and, this morning, his family gave permission to turn off the ventilator."

"Oh, dear God…"

The nurse nodded sympathetically, adding, "He slipped away a few hours afterward."

Wiping her cheeks with the back of her hand, Juliet murmured, "Does Avery know yet?"

A voice behind her said, "We were waiting for you to return to the hospital before we told her."

Juliet whirled in place. Finn Deschanel had been sitting unnoticed in a nearby chair, awaiting her arrival. His aunt, Claudine, was also there, although she had remained seated, her face drawn and hollowed-eyed, as if she hadn't been to sleep for days.

Glancing from one Deschanel to the other, Juliet was immediately consumed with anxiety, wondering aloud how Avery would react to this tragic turn of events.

"And the poor Grenelles," she added, her voice wavering. "They must be just devastated."

Nodding, Claudine slowly rose from her chair. "They still haven't left the ICU waiting room. They wanted to know if they could visit Avery and tell her about their son's passing themselves."

Juliet would never forget the scene of Jean-Pierre's parents and grandmother entering Avery's room and encircling her hospital bed shortly after Finn had walked in and taken the lead in breaking the news.

Avery remained silent, her hands convulsively clutching the turned-down sheet. When the Grenelle family came to stand near the head of the bed, Jean-Pierre's grandmother spoke slowly in French so Avery and Juliet would be sure to understand.

"We know you were a good friend to him as well," she began, her words etched in sorrow. "We're proud that he gave his life trying to save yours. It gives some meaning to the terrible way he died."

Avery shook her head from side to side, her lips twisted, her fists pounding the bedcovers. "But I'm to blame!" she cried. "I invited him to that restaurant because it was cheap as well as good. I insisted we come to this hospital because of the pile-up of ambulances at St. Louis." By this time, tears bathed her cheeks. "And because of all that, it probably meant he didn't get the help he needed quickly enough and—"

Finn stepped forward and interrupted in rapid English.

"There was nothing that could have been done," he insisted in a firm but gentle tone. "It could have happened at any restaurant in Paris. The doctors have told the family that Jean-Pierre received such fatal wounds when he was shot that he was virtually brain dead within seconds of the assault. It wouldn't have made any difference *what* hospital he was brought to." He gently placed a hand on her good shoulder, but his words sounded almost stern. "This is survivor's guilt talking, Avery," he said urgently. "If you truly want to help his family, let the Grenelles know you appreciate their coming here. Let them see you're grateful for the sacrifice Jean-Pierre made to save your life."

Juliet felt Avery's tortured glance seeking hers and she nodded encouragingly through her own tears. Avery shifted her gaze to Eloise Grenelle and sought her hand. In French she whispered, "Madam, I will never forget Jean-Pierre and how he saved my life." Her eyes beseeched Jean-Pierre's parents. "I will never forget how sweet your son was to me from my first day in class. I will never forget. *Never!*"

And then Avery covered her face with her hands, shoulders heaving, and began to cry deep, wrenching sobs while the rest of those in the room gathered close, arms around each others' waists, all with tears streaming from their eyes.

Except for Finn, Juliet noted. He was dry-eyed, but she could see the pain emanating in his expression like a heat shield reentering space.

The first one able to speak coherently was Claudine. After a rapid dialogue in French with her friend Eloise, she said in English to Finn, "I suggest you and Pierre go, now, to make arrangements for the funeral. Juliet and I, if she's agreeable, will accompany Jean-Pierre's mother and grandmother back to my apartment to make a meal."

Avery raised her head and Juliet knew instantly she couldn't leave her. Before she could voice her concern, Claudine moved closer to the bed.

"If I can get permission, Avery, do you think you feel well enough to spend an evening resting on my couch? My building has an elevator and we can take you by taxi and bring along a wheel chair to transport you back and forth."

Avery hesitated and then nodded. "I walked the length of a corridor today during PT," she said, reaching for a tissue to mop her eyes.

"You *did?*" Juliet said, amazed. Then she sobered, "But look, you've had a big shock. If you don't feel up to it, I'm happy to keep you company here, and—"

"I want to go!" Avery cried. "I want to be with you all."

Claudine rang for the nurse and insisted a call be made to Avery's doctor, wrangling permission for his patient to spend a few hours in the bosom of her late friend's family.

"The doctor thought it would be the best medicine," whispered the kindly nurse who'd remained in the room. "Especially since Ms. Evans was able to walk on her own today. A week or two more, and she'll be ready to go home and hopefully make a full recovery in six months' time."

Juliet felt her breath catch. *Six months... Who's going to take care of her when I leave?*

And leave fairly soon she knew she must, given Jamie's warning on the phone earlier today that Brad would soon demand she return to San Francisco—or else.

Juliet had never seen anything quite as glamorous as
Claudine Deschanel's apartment on *Rue Jacob*. Once past
the outsized carved wooden door that faced the street, the
entryway made her think she was entering a palace, with its
ivory marble statuary, Corinthian columns flush with large,
white stone block walls. Limestone flooring led to a brass
elevator that looked nothing so much as a giant birdcage
that rose at a stately speed to Claudine's third-floor
residence and opened into a black and white square-tiled
foyer.

"Welcome, my darlings," Claudine greeted them in a
hushed voice. She flung her arms wide displaying butterfly
silk sleeves set into a wildly colored floor-length caftan that
Juliet speculated might have been a Rudi Gernreich
original. Her fingers and wrists flashed with beautiful
jewelry, including an arresting emerald and diamond ring
that Juliet couldn't help but note with silent admiration.

The walls of Claudine's flat were painted a lush, butter
yellow with matching silk drapes that hung from twelve-
foot windows. Three crystal chandeliers dangled from a
mammoth molded ceiling overhead, the curved surface
replete with painted angels and cherubs gamboling across
a robin's egg blue sky.

Claudine, Eloise Grenelle, and Avery had departed
the hospital in the first taxi summoned, and by the time
Juliet, Jean-Pierre's mother, and sister Colette arrived,
Avery had been installed on a damask-covered Louis XVI
couch upholstered in the same sky blue shade as the ceiling.
A cream-colored cashmere throw was tucked over the
length of the patient's body and she appeared half asleep.

"Eloise is in the kitchen laying out the *charcuterie*,"
Claudine announced in a low voice, describing the array of
sliced meats and sausage, small, sweet pickles and radishes

that would tempt them all, once Finn and Pierre returned from finalizing funeral arrangements. She took their coats and then directed briskly, "Juliet, dear, I still could use help arranging the vegetable platter and slicing the baguettes and some cheese." She glanced at Avery, now deeply asleep.

By the time Finn and Pierre arrived everyone was back in the grand salon sipping cups of strong, black tea laced with lemon and honey, including Avery sitting up in a wheel chair brought from the hospital. Claudine, still clearly in charge, gathered the somber group around her elegant dining room table with its matching, highly polished mahogany chairs.

After the assembled ate their meal in near silence, she raised a glass of champagne like the ones that glittered at each place setting. "In French or English," she urged, "let us each relate a fond memory we have of darling Jean-Pierre…and raise a toast."

In grief-laced tones, Eloise spoke of her grandson's delight as a little boy visiting her on the barge and taking naps in the pilothouse before it was converted into an apartment as a way of supplementing her income after Jean-Pierre's grandfather died.

J-P's father also choked up when it was his turn to speak, describing his son's first attempts at drawing, noting that by six or seven years old, the parents knew for a certainty that he would one day become an accomplished artist.

"It's hard to believe he showed such talent at that age," he murmured in English for the benefit of the Americans present, "but what I tell you is true."

When all eyes turned to Pierre's wife, she merely shook her head and waved her hand in the air, unable to speak.

Finn paused and then raised his glass of sparkling water.

"Jean-Pierre possessed an almost instinctive empathy for people and the world around him." A wry smile formed on his lips. "He must have been informed something about who his grandmother's new tenant was on the barge. He always waved hello, and if he saw me sitting on deck, reading as I did most of last summer, he'd bring by a book he thought I might enjoy. And he *never* criticized my laboring French."

For a moment, a ripple of laughter relieved the mournful atmosphere that mantled the dining room.

Avery spoke next, telling once more of Jean-Pierre's befriending her at art school so "just like with Finn, he could improve his English and me my French, plus he truly had the desire to befriend people."

Glancing sideways, Juliet noticed tears once again beginning to fill Avery's eyes.

"He was eight years younger than I am," Avery related softly in French. "He was kind of like the little brother I always wanted...and now, because I treated him to dinner at that restaurant as a thank-you for all the nice things he'd done for me, he's—"

Juliet leaned over and gingerly rubbed her friend's good shoulder. "Avery, what has happened is nobody's fault but the terrorists!"

Finn rose abruptly from his chair, startling the assembled. "Yes, it's the terrorists," he said, his hands fisted at his sides, "but let's not forget the actions of certain, heartless opportunists, a bunch of blind followers, plus the technology and propaganda that so easily twists minds."

A silence fell, then, and before anyone could say anything else, Claudine asked quickly if Juliet would come to the kitchen with her to help her fetch the coffee.

"Yes, of course," she murmured, rising from her chair, but not before she felt a flush fanning across her cheeks.

All she could conclude was that Finn must truly harbor a deep-seated revulsion for the kind of violent videos her brother's company had developed and spread throughout the world, including, possibly, some of the world's terrorists. She had been knee-deep in that world, and he probably despised her for it.

Claudine suddenly barked another order: "Finn, you will please clear the table, and everyone else, finish your champagne."

Juliet stumbled into Claudine's white-tiled kitchen with its marbled-topped counters and enormous stove with six burners that once must have been commanded by a chef and an entire domestic staff. Neither she nor Finn spoke while she arranged delicate porcelain *demitasse* cups and saucers at the same time Finn made several trips in and out of the dining room, carrying the dishes, as commanded by their hostess. Juliet swallowed hard and concentrated on balancing a tray with the cups and a large, silver coffeepot, insisting on taking it without assistance into the dining room.

In the time they'd all left the hospital and gathered for their meal, Claudine had somehow obtained a large apple tart with a glaze that glistened under the light of the mammoth chandelier hanging above the long dining table. With practiced efficiency, she began to cut generous slices of the confection, topped with Chantilly cream. Avery only picked at the magnificent dessert with her fork and Juliet sensed it was time to take her back to the hospital before she keeled over from both physical and emotional exhaustion—feelings Juliet was experiencing herself.

Fifteen minutes later, Finn escorted the two women downstairs. He hailed a taxi, insisting he escort them back to Neuilly-sur-Seine to see Avery and her borrowed wheelchair safely to the hospital.

"But what about your MG?" Juliet protested.

"I'll come get it later. Let's get you both into this taxi."

His earlier remark about technology and those involved in it playing a role in the recent attacks continued to gnaw at Juliet and she wished he would let her handle Avery on her own. Once the patient was settled in the taxi and the chair tucked into the trunk, Juliet turned to Finn. "Look, we'll be fine. There's absolutely no need for you to come, too."

"I'm coming," he said shortly. "Get in. I'll ride in front with the driver."

Avery dozed while Juliet stared silently out the window during the drive back across Paris to the outskirts of the city. By this hour, the streets of Neuilly were deserted as the taxi chugged up the ramp and pulled to a stop in front of the hospital entrance. Finn gently took hold of Avery's good arm and eased her into the waiting wheelchair.

Juliet said, "I can take it from here." She nodded in the direction of the taxi, its motor still running. "Better grab the cab before it takes off."

"I'll see you home, too," he said.

She shook her head. "You've had an exhausting day. I'll get Avery upstairs and take the metro back to her apartment. No problem."

Finn seemed surprised at her suggestion. Without further comment, he walked them both into the hospital lobby, hailed an orderly to help, and then bid them goodnight. Juliet saw out of the corner of her eye that he'd retreated outside and stood by the taxi, watching. As Avery was wheeled toward the elevators with Juliet trailing behind, she sensed Finn's following stare on her back. It didn't take long before Avery was settled into bed, extracting from Juliet a promise to see if she could be released soon.

"Tell the nurses and doctors how well I did tonight,"

she said, her eyes drooping as soon as her head touched the pillow. "I want to get out of here."

And within minutes, Juliet could tell that Avery was fast asleep.

"Hey, Ms. California…want a lift?"

Juliet halted in her tracks just outside the hospital's revolving door, sending cold night air swirling about her ankles.

"Finn! What are you doing here? I thought—"

"You don't think I'd let you take the metro this late at night after the kind of day we both had?"

She peered at the taxi still parked at the curb. "The meter's been running all this time?" she asked, mildly horrified.

"Right, so get in," he commanded.

With Finn sitting beside her in the back seat, they rode along in silence for several blocks. Finn finally spoke first. "You were upset by what I said at Claudine's, weren't you? About the blame for what happened here being partly due to the actions of certain people and the technology they used?"

Juliet stared at Finn across the expanse of the cab's interior, silenced by the truth of his words. When she made no reply, he said, "I thought about it while you coolly said your goodbyes at Claudine's, and again, just now, and took Avery upstairs. I realized that you thought I was referring to you and everyone at your brother's company, didn't you?"

"Well, weren't you?" A well of emotion had begun to fill her chest.

"I was referring to defense contractors and their lobbyists. To politicians, who so easily vote to go to war. To *myself*. To everything I've been a part of. Everything our

Brave New World is now a part of. And yes," he admitted, "I was thinking of your brother, Brad."

Juliet continued to stare at Finn, her mind full of colliding thoughts about the choices she'd made and how earnestly the man sitting next to her was trying to tell the truth about himself. How the horror of the last days had exploded in everyone's lives.

All of it.

Finn gently reached across the space that separated them and took her hand, his touch instantly causing tears to rim her eyes as they had on and off all day since learning of Jean-Pierre's death.

"I waited for you because I wanted to see you safely home, Juliet. This whole thing has been horrible for everyone, including you. And I'm so sorry if you misunderstood my words at dinner. I meant myself," he repeated, "not you"

"Oh, Finn," she said, her voice sounding strangled even to her own ears. "There's no way to untangle all this. It's just…so…sad. It's so awful and heartbreaking. And I feel…I guess I feel this bereft because there doesn't seem any way to…to fix *any* of it."

"No one person can fix this." His thumb gently strafed the palm of her hand that he had continued to hold. "All we can try to do is fix ourselves in whatever ways are needed."

"But I guess I'm just like you and Avery," she said between gulps for air. "I feel *responsible*. What about the unintended consequences of everything I've done in the last five years? How could I have not predicted the ultimate outcome of millions of people—and especially the kids—playing ugly video war games that Brad and I and the rest of us produced? How could I not have spoken up more strongly in all those meetings I attended that the explicit packaging I'd designed was, itself, an incitement to violence and hatred? I reacted to what you said at Claudine's because I *do* feel guilty that the Thayer family made the act of killing humans a lucrative sporting event! There's an entire generation who are totally de-sensitized to what the real thing is actually like. They don't wear a uniform or serve their country. They don't see the carnage. They just play *games!*"

"You didn't do this all by yourself," he said, holding her hand more firmly.

"I know…but it all feels so…broken."

Juliet fought the great, heaving sobs welling up in her chest. The next thing she knew, Finn had pulled her against his chest and she was conscious of her tears spilling all over the front of his leather jacket.

"Ah, Juliet…"

After a few minutes, her shoulders still heaving, she drew away.

"I-I can't even blame *this* meltdown on jet-lag," she said, staring into her lap.

"Blame it on…everything." By this time, the taxi had come to a halt in front of Avery's flat. "C'mon. Let's get you home."

Home? Where was home? She fought another wave of emotion.

Meanwhile, Finn leaned back in his seat, ignoring the running meter.

"Look, Juliet, we have to step back and take in the big picture. At least, that's what I'm trying to do. What happened to Jean-Pierre and Avery are just two examples of the unintended consequences of a million tiny decisions we all made that nobody wants to think about, or take responsibility for. At least, *you and I* are considering what we, personally, brought to this chamber of horrors. You may find this hard to believe, but I have real confidence we can both determine from here on out the paths that work for us in this life. At least, that's my goal."

"I hope you're right," Juliet murmured, looking out the window at the forbidding door that guarded the entrance to Avery's garret at the top of the building.

Finn noticed her glance and rested his hand on the taxi's door handle.

"By the way..." He titled his head and squinted at her. "How're you doing with that damned heating system up there?"

Juliet rolled her eyes and prepared to get out of the taxi. "On a good day? *Comme si, comme ça.*"

"Well, that's not very encouraging."

"At night I think the heat switches off in the entire building."

"Probably only in the former maids' rooms and not in the rest of this swanky place," he wagered. "How cold, exactly, is it, would you say?"

Juliet hesitated. "Forty...forty-five degrees, maybe."

"*Merde!*" Continuing in French, he told the taxi driver, whose meter had been running for at least an hour since they'd left Claudine's, to wait right there. "The young lady has to go upstairs to get her things. Then, we're going back to *Rue Jacob* where my car is parked." To Juliet, he said, "You're sleeping on the barge, no arguments." He gave her a stern glance. "Now, go get your suitcase and I'll wait right here. I'd help you, but I don't want to lose this cab."

CHAPTER 10

A half an hour later, with the Eiffel Tower still glowing its patriotic lights, Finn and Juliet arrived back at *L'Étoile de Paris* bobbing peacefully on the Seine.

"You make up your bed," he suggested, handing her the sheets and blanket she'd so hastily folded the last time she had slept on Finn's barge, "and I'll brew us some tea."

"Won't that keep us awake?"

"Not this brand. Special stuff my shrink told me about... *Dormez Bien.*"

"'Sleep Well' tea?" she said with a laugh. "Sounds good to me!"

So much for her resolution to keep her distance from the dashing Major Deschanel. Within minutes they had each assumed their customary places on opposite ends of Finn's sofa and he began to ask her about life in San Francisco.

"You've never been there?" she asked, taking a sip of tea from her mug.

"Yes, when I was a kid. My father was stationed at Fort Ord on the Monterey Peninsula for a year, before the base was shut down. All I remember about your town is the fog and riding the cable cars, which I loved."

"Well, it's not always foggy," she said, defending her hometown with a smile. "Come visit in October, sometime, and you will definitely leave your heart in San Francisco. I think it's one of the most beautiful cities in the world. Like Paris," she added, gazing over her shoulder at the magnificence of the Eiffel Tower whose sparkling reflection on the river's wavy surface doubled her pleasure.

"Maybe I will," he said, smiling back at her. "Come visit sometime."

Juliet let his friendly words fill the pilothouse. She quickly glanced down at the mug full of tea she held in her hands. "My problem is, I've used whatever artistic skills I have living there as a commercial graphic designer, not as a painter. It's not what I want, but—like the rest of the world—I have to make a living." She looked up and met Finn's steady gaze, adding, "And as my brother Brad constantly points out, no one is lining up to buy my landscapes."

"Are they good?"

Juliet shrugged, oddly admiring the fact he'd asked such a blunt question.

"Not good enough...not yet. But I honestly think they could be if I just had the chance to do what Avery's done— come to Paris to get more advanced training. I've also heard about an art academy that's in southern France. Have you ever been to Lake Annecy, near the border with Switzerland? Someone at the art store here told me there's a great school down there, but I don't know much about it. Cezanne painted there, I heard."

"Haven't been to Lake Annecy, but you have that dreamy-eyed look," he said, a smile quirking at the corners of his mouth, "Better get with it, Juliet. None of us knows how much runway we have left."

Juliet stared back him. "Is that just a saying that pilots use, or are you...ill, or something?"

The thought of Finn having a terminal disease struck a strange chord of dismay in her. Was that why he was leading such a solitary existence?

He touched his forehead with a finger on his right hand. "PTSD, remember? When I first got here, I had some very dark thoughts about the top of that tower out there, a stupid idea that I seem to have shaken free of these last few months. But it got me to thinking. None of us knows how long we have in this life."

"Yeah...Jean-Pierre...a tragic case in point."

"Exactly. So, as I said, we'd better both get on it! Figure all this out so we have some runway to take off from and enjoy our lives, doing what matters."

"You're a pretty wise fellow, you know that?" Juliet murmured.

"Hard won wisdom," he replied. "Just like yours." He paused, and then said, "So why don't you?"

"Why don't I what?"

"Take a year or so off and come to Paris to paint? Or to paint better?"

Once again, Juliet stared at the mug of tea resting in her lap. "I can't for all the reasons I told you before...my obligation to see that Brad pays back the equity loan on the Bay View. The only way I can do it...is to help make the firm a continuing success so there's money to—"

Finn abruptly set his mug on the coffee table in front of the sofa. "How much money do you think will satisfy your brother Brad? What's the dollar figure he's set?"

His tough questions silenced her for a long moment. Finally she said, "I don't know. Probably he doesn't know, either."

"Look, Juliet..." He was staring at her intensely in a way that she found totally unnerving. "We all get to choose how to spend our time on this earth. Your father chose to give his son the money. Isn't it up to *him* to demand he be paid back? From what you've described, the GatherGames business is booming, big time, with or without you as design director. But without you, your brother will have to pay someone a higher salary than he's probably paying you—so no wonder he wants you back. And, what if he'll never declare how much money is enough? I gather those Silicon Valley guys rarely do."

Startled, Juliet turned over Finn's caustic words in her mind. Then, without warning, he leaned across the sofa and she thought for a moment he would take her hand again. Instead he appeared to change his mind and settled back against the sofa cushion.

"Juliet, no one can 'make' any of us do anything. Not the government. Not family. Not friends. We simply give in to the demands that others put on us—give them permission, in a sense—or, alternatively, we stand up for what we think is best."

Juliet nodded slowly and cracked a faint smile. "Well, Major, you've given me a lot to think about. But let us remember, you probably have a military pension, or the G.I. Bill or something supporting you, right?"

"That, and I've saved a bit of money," he acknowledged. "It's given me the luxury of about a year to consider what I want and need to do next. Like you, I've got to figure out what I want, and how to live it—and pay for it"

With a suddenness that Juliet remembered from her last stay on the barge, the lights of the tower performed their sparkly display and then switched off, plunging the opposite shore into utter darkness. She pointed to the brass ship's clock on the bookshelf. "Gad, we've been talking nonstop! But there's just one more thing I need to say and then let's hit the hay."

"No...hit the *rack*, as we say on board," he teased. "Fire away."

"I just can't get past the fact that my father put up the Bay View Hotel as collateral for Brad's company."

"It's a big asset," he acknowledged, "and worth a lot of money, I suppose."

"Dad risked our *home*," Julie exclaimed, "and the place my great, great grandparents built a hundred years ago after the utter devastation of the city. It's sheltered us for five generations! As far as I can see, Dad did it just to please and placate his son whom, I guess, my father thinks has outshined him. And Brad seems so indifferent as to how this might impact the rest of us if—somehow—his company goes down the drain in a future recession…or he overplays his hand, and loses the company to some venture capitalist who wants to eat his lunch."

"Does Brad live in the hotel like you do?" Finn asked.

Juliet nodded. "But to him, it's merely a roof over his head and a place to sleep. He has absolutely no warm or fuzzy feelings for family traditions or history. I feel so powerless about it all and it's kept me awake many a night since I found out about the equity loan."

"Well, you have my sympathies since I know what that's like—not being able to sleep, I mean—but maybe the tea we just drank and the boat's gentle movement will lull you into dreamland tonight," he kidded her.

Then, in a move that totally surprised her, Finn slid across the small sofa and kissed her gently on the forehead.

"Dormez bien, Mademoiselle Peintre en Plein Air."

She met his glance, only inches away.

"Your fledgling *plein air* landscape-artist-in-residence thanks you," she said softly.

"You're welcome." He briefly glanced down at her lips and then rose to stand at his full height. *"Bonne nuit."*

"Good night," she said, resigned that they both were doing the right thing to keep their distance. With a cheery smile, she pointed to the short ladder leading down to his stateroom. "I'll dash down there, if that's okay."

In minutes she'd brushed her teeth, used the toilet, donned her usual sleep uniform of black tights and a tee, and was back in the pilothouse. As soon as he saw her return, Finn immediately headed for the stateroom she'd just vacated.

"'Night," he repeated.

"*Dormez bien*, yourself," she called after him.

Rather to her surprise, she fell asleep almost as soon as she snuggled beneath the sheets and blankets swathing the couch. When she awoke in the early dawn's hour, her mind a whirl with the last days' events and conversations, she could see the light was on in Finn's stateroom below. Despite the soothing tea they'd both drunk, she wondered what—of all the problems he faced—had kept him awake?

Juliet managed to go back to sleep, awakened a few hours later by the sound of Finn entering the barge with his daily bag of freshly-baked croissants in hand, and promising coffee would be ready soon.

"Okay if I have a quick wash?" she asked as he poured ground coffee into his French *presse* coffeemaker.

"Absolutely. I left some towels on a stool right outside the shower cabinet."

With his back turned, she dashed down the few steps to his cabin below, grateful to feel warm water cascading down her body while fighting off the image of a naked Finn Deschanel occupying the same space every day.

Juliet, my girl... get a grip!

When she turned off the water, she heard Finn speaking on his mobile phone not ten feet from the curtain that separated the shower stall from the rest of his sleeping area.

"I want you to send the signed documents as soon as possible, okay? Tell her no more fucking around, *okay?*" His harsh voice sounded as if he was barely keeping his temper in check. As he headed back up to the salon above their heads, she heard him say, "Send everything to my aunt's address on *Rue Jacob*. I want this over with!" Then she heard him swear from the pilothouse, "*Merde!*" under his breath as he clicked off his phone.

Juliet quickly dressed in a pair of jeans and a navy cashmere sweater, glancing at the looming rain clouds outside the porthole over Finn's double bed. Emerging from his stateroom, she found him sitting on his end of the couch with his coffee and the newspaper. He looked up at her with a frown.

"I'm sorry you had to hear my phone conversation just now."

"I'm sorry, too," she said, advancing toward the sofa. "You sounded upset. I had turned off the shower, so I couldn't help but hear the last bit. Is everything okay?"

Finn hesitated. "It will be, once my divorce is final. The marriage has been over for more than two years, but the *t*'s are finally about to be crossed and the *i*'s dotted. At least I hope so."

"I'm so sorry."

"Yeah, a sorry mess pretty well covers it. It's been a bitch, but it's almost over, thank God." He looked at her over the rim of his coffee mug. "She's finally willing to deal with the legalities because she's getting married again."

"Wow."

"Not wow, but that's the way it is."

A long silence grew between them and Juliet told herself she should change the subject. But she didn't. "It must have been really hard for you both, with all your deployments to the Middle East..."

Finn shrugged and replied, "Actually, we got through that period reasonably well. The trouble began after I got shot down and then transferred to Nevada, flying drones, and we were living together again." He abruptly handed her a mug he'd set down next to his own. "Here's your coffee."

Case closed.

Just then there was a knock on the pilothouse door. Colette Grenelle stood outside imparting the news that J-

P's burial was scheduled to take place at eleven o'clock in the morning on Monday, November 23rd.

"My parents were able to buy a cremation niche in the Columbarium at *Père Lachaise* Cemetery," she announced proudly, referring to one of Paris's most prestigious burial grounds. To Juliet she explained, "Many famous artists are buried there...Balzac, Chopin, writers like Oscar Wilde, and many famous painters, including Delacroix."

"It is a great honor," Finn agreed for Colette's benefit. "Jean-Pierre's professor, Alain Devereux, helped Pierre and me arrange it."

While Finn and Colette continued to discuss the details of the upcoming ceremony, Juliet seized the moment to excuse herself, take her courage in hand, and walk out on Finn's deck into an overcast November morning to make an important phone call. If she wanted to stay in Paris for Jean-Pierre's funeral, it was time to contact Brad. She glanced at her watch and saw it was just after midnight in California. She crossed her fingers that she could merely leave a message giving the compelling reasons why she intended to extend her stay in France.

She listened as Brad's phone rang once, twice, and then, as if in answer to her prayers, the device went to voice mail. She quickly explained that the man who saved Avery's life by throwing his body over hers during the terrorist attacks was being buried the following week.

"I want to see Avery through this part of the trauma and then stay until she can return to her apartment and fend for herself, which should be within the next two weeks. I've got my computer with me, so send me any assignments and I can work from here. Love to everybody...and thanks. Bye."

There! Let him yell and scream.

Barely three minutes passed after she reentered the barge and accepted Finn's offer of a second cup of coffee before a text pinged on her phone. Juliet stared at the message and frowned.

"Not good?" Finn asked, turning to close the door behind Colette.

"It's from Brad." She showed him the text that read: *You are in breach.*

"In breach of what?" Finn asked.

"My employment contract. A minute ago I left a voice message saying I planned to stay for J-P's funeral and help Avery get settled in her apartment when they release her from the hospital. I offered to take on any assignment while I'm here."

"And that's the answer you got back from your *brother?*"

Juliet could tell he was genuinely shocked.

"Actually, it's a little better than I expected. He didn't pull a Donald Trump on me and text, 'You're fired!'"

"What a sweetheart."

Juliet heaved a shrug, took a gulp of her coffee, and then prepared to head back to the American Hospital to see how the patient fared this gloomy November morning.

"Now you have some idea what I'm dealing with," she replied, and headed out the pilothouse door.

"I'm thrilled they're letting you out of the hospital ahead of schedule, but it's really freezing in your apartment, Avery," Juliet warned. In actual fact, she was aghast Avery had persuaded her doctor to release her from the hospital so soon. "We don't want you coming back here with a case of pneumonia."

"I'm doing really well," Avery insisted, "and besides, all the hospitals in Paris are full of victims much sicker than I was. I think they're letting me go because they can take some transfers from over-taxed medical facilities nearer where the terrorists struck."

Avery was sitting on her bed, fully dressed, even having applied make-up that restored her to looking close to the healthy young woman she once had been—except that she still had her arm in its now-familiar sling.

"Maybe *you* should stay on Finn's barge and *I'll* sleep in your flat while I'm here," Juliet proposed, "—that is, if we can get some more blankets and maybe a plug-in electric space heater in that attic of yours."

"I want to go back to my apartment." The stubborn look on Avery's face was one Juliet remembered all too well from their days arguing over a design at work.

Juliet scanned Avery's discharge papers. She was being released from the hospital because she was without infection and ambulatory and—most importantly—her outing to Claudine's apartment "bore witness to her excellent progress." The other factors were that her pain meds were now taken by mouth and her American cousin, Juliet, had "vouched she would be available to look after her for the next critical ten days while the patient makes follow-up visits to her various doctors."

"I vouched no such thing!" Juliet declared, exasperated. "I'm telling you, the temperature was forty degrees, the few times I slept at your place."

"You and Finn just don't know the intimate secrets of the maid's room heating system," Avery replied, with a wave of her good hand.

"You told me you didn't remember how to work your heater, either! Even your neighbor, Brian Parker, couldn't figure out how to maintain a consistent temperature."

"That's because all the really posh apartments below the attic have been completely renovated with new thermostats. Don't worry, I'll get the concierge to teach me again how to make it work, and I have a friend I can stay with if it goes wonky."

"And just who is that?" Juliet demanded suspiciously. Only her painting professor had been in touch while Avery had been in the hospital. "This is no time to be a good sport. You need comfort and *rest*. You can't be moving up and down stairs and in, or in and out of a bunch of artists' crash pads!"

Avery snorted. "'Crash pads?' Are you kidding me? Every single one of my friends at *L'École* lives better than I do."

"And why *is* that?" Juliet demanded. "Seriously, Avery, you have the money to live a little better than you do. Should I look for another place for you while I'm here?"

"No need to fly into commando mode. I love the building I'm in, and, after all, you were the one who told me about number seven. There are rumors an apartment on a lower floor may soon be up for sale at the insider's price, so just cool your jets."

"But I'm worried about *now*," protested Juliet. "You have a long recovery ahead and I have to leave soon. How in the world are you—"

"I said, don't worry about me!" Avery interrupted, sounding genuinely irritated. "You enjoy the barge and the handsome Major Deschanel, and I'll revel in the peace and quiet of my own four walls. Do you have any idea how much I look forward to not having anyone wake me up every night—and that includes even you? And we'll see each other every day while you're here when we go to all my doctors' appointments. Now, let's blow this pop stand, can we? I don't want to be late to J-P's funeral."

CHAPTER 11

Following the somber ceremony interring Jean-Pierre Grenelle's ashes, the Grenelle family gathered at a cousin's home, while Finn, Claudine, Juliet, and Avery returned to Claudine's glamorous apartment, where she provided yet another wonderful meal of flavorful *cassoulet* that looked for all the world like something out of *Bon Appétit*.

"And let us not forget the wine," Finn said, topping off everyone's glasses except his own.

"An excellent choice, Patrick," Claudine complimented. "Thank you so much for bringing it today." She raised her glass. "Let us raise a farewell toast to dear Jean-Pierre...and may his passing be marked with our continued love of family and friends. Let us honor his memory by refusing to let what has happened bleed all the joy from our futures—and especially yours..." Her glance drifted in benediction from her two female guests to her nephew.

"Amen to that," echoed Finn.

Juliet and Avery locked glances. "To J-P," whispered Avery. She gazed at her hostess. "I will try not to let this bleed—as you put it—all the joy from my life, Claudine, but it's...so...*hard*."

"I know, *cherie*," Claudine replied somberly. "But, I have lived through the Vietnam era, remember—that was full of hate and violence and warring factions within and without America. And in my long life, I've learned we have a choice. As Abraham Lincoln once said—and trust me, I didn't know him personally," she joked, bringing a smile to Avery's lips, "'people are about as happy as they decide to be.' I've had a few major setbacks in my time, but I urge you to make up your mind to be happy instead of sad. Just *decide* and do it," she urged.

Avery said in a small voice, "But that feels so...impossible."

"Well, it's a different kind of battle," she said. "Sometimes we, too, must decide to decide to fight...but the fight is against the power of fear, violence, and hate. I've found in my life, anyway, the only answer is to love. That, and a sense of gratitude for the good things we *do* have in our lives. These, and kindness, are the only effective weapons we have."

Juliet's thoughts recalled Finn telling her, in answer to her question if Claudine had ever been married, that the man she'd loved—a friend of Finn's father—had been killed as a forward observer in the Vietnam War. Grief-stricken, Claudine had eventually fled to Paris, gotten a job at *Paris Vogue* in her early thirties, and never came home.

As they all raised their glasses in a second toast, they were startled by the sharp sound of a bell.

"Someone's downstairs," Claudine said with a puzzled look. "I'll just go see who it is and tell them to go away."

The remaining three sipped at their glasses in silence, glancing through the dining room door. Juliet imagined her companions were turning over in their minds Claudine's wise words, just as she was.

Just decide to be happy. No matter what. Happy, grateful, and kind... Those are some great concepts, but where can I find my better angels to help pull it off?

Claudine's voice and a deeper masculine one interrupted her reverie. All three guests turned in their chairs to behold a man now standing in the doorway. He was tall, with close-cropped salt-and-pepper hair, and dressed in a dark khaki military uniform with a rainbow of grosgrain ribbons pinned to his chest and reams of braid encrusted on the brim of his hat tucked under one arm.

"Hello, everyone," he said, staring directly at Finn.

"My apologies for barging in like this. I'm only in Paris for two days. A security conference with our allies, called because of the recent terrorist attacks. Believe me, I had *no* idea…"

His sentence trailed off as Finn slowly rose from his chair. Juliet spotted a trio of appliquéd stars gracing each of the visitor's shoulders. Then it dawned on her. Three-star General Andrew Deschanel had dropped by, unannounced, to pay a hurried courtesy call on his older sister, Claudine—and inadvertently discovered his son's city of refuge.

During the ensuing silence, Juliet gazed from one shocked expression to the next on the faces of the three Deschanels. After an awkward series of introductions—and before the general could say anything further to his son—Finn abruptly announced that he had to be on his way to drive Avery and Juliet home.

"Must you leave so quickly, son?" demanded the general in a tone that signaled Finn's answer should be in the negative.

"Ms. Evans, here," he said, his tone cool and controlled, "was one of the victims in the attacks, and has only just been released from the hospital. She's tired and needs to go home. We all do. We buried a friend today."

Claudine quickly interjected, "This afternoon, Andrew, the four of us attended the funeral of my friend Eloise's grandson, killed on the thirteenth." She looked steadily at her brother. "I'm sure you can understand that it's been a trying and emotional day. I hope you can stay the night. I'll go make up a bed in my spare room."

With a brief nod, as if the general had agreed to the strategic retreat of one of his platoons, he asked the only other man in the room, "Where will you be going, son? Can I catch up with you later?"

Finn met his father's glance, and after a long pause,

replied, "Actually, I'd have to say that I'm still in the process of figuring where I'll eventually go, and I'm not yet ready to discuss that with you. Good to see you, though, sir. Goodnight." He turned toward his aunt. "Goodnight, Claudine. Thank you for the fitting tribute to our friend Jean-Pierre."

Juliet could only nod her goodbyes to General Deschanel and her hostess while Finn swiftly ushered Avery and her through Claudine's elegant living room and out the front door.

Finn said very little as he assisted Juliet into the back bench of his MG, and then tucked the bear rug around Avery in the passenger seat. Once he'd parked in front of number seven, *Rue de Lille*, he silently carried Avery's small suitcase up the six flights of stairs. Meanwhile, it took nearly fifteen minutes for Juliet to slowly guide her friend up the winding staircase—resting on the landing of each flight—to her front door for the first time since she'd left her apartment for dinner at *Le Petit Cambodge*. Inside, Avery immediately sank on top of the quilt on her bed. As usual, the attic apartment was bordering on artic temperatures.

Hands on his hips, Finn shook his head. "Good for you, making it up here, Avery, but you can't stay in this attic. This place is an igloo."

Avery pulled herself up to a sitting position and announced, "My brain's finally free of those meds and I just remembered exactly what the trick is." She proceeded to explain the finer points of the French heating system to Finn, and sure enough, after a few minutes of her expert instruction, he managed to produce warm air blowing through the rusty radiator grill.

"I can't believe you got it to work!" exclaimed Juliet.

"You just have to have the touch and a smart instructor," Avery said with a smug smile in Finn's direction. "Now, go! The both of you."

Juliet pointed at the tiny refrigerator. "Damn it! We forgot to pick up some staples for you!" She turned in frustration toward Finn, who quickly volunteered to run down to a nearby *épicerie* to secure milk and eggs for Avery's breakfast the following morning. Before either woman could protest, he'd disappeared down the winding staircase outside the door, announcing he'd be right back.

With a shrug of acceptance, Juliet said, "While he's gone, let's get you settled into bed."

Avery nodded, her fatigue evident as she merely pointed to a hook on the back of the door where a nightgown hung. Juliet careful removed the cloth sling that protected Avery's shoulder and arm. After she assisted in removing her friend's clothes and put the gown over her head, Avery said, "I'm sure you detected the distinct chill in the air when Finn's father arrived."

"Hmmmm," Juliet responded noncommittally, gently reattaching Avery's shoulder sling.

"Finn didn't exactly look pleased to see his pater," she persisted.

"From what I gather," Juliet replied, only willing to divulge what was general knowledge about Finn, "I don't think the general was particularly pleased with Finn's recent decision to resign from the Air Force." She pulled the bedcovers aside while Avery slipped in between the sheets, adding, "Apparently, the Deschanels have been a military family for a zillion years."

"So Finn's break with family tradition didn't go down well?"

Juliet affected a shrug, not wanting to betray any further confidences that Finn had shared with her. "I'm sure it'll smooth out, eventually."

"You could see how shocked they all were to see each other. Even Claudine."

"Yeah…I guess." And then Juliet changed the subject

with a promise to return in the morning to escort her friend to her physical therapy session at a new location near her flat.

As her head sank against her pillow, Avery said with a teasing grin, "So, it's back to the barge? Lucky you."

"Yes, back to Finn's couch in the pilothouse," Juliet replied pointedly. "He's been great to let me stay there until I have to leave Paris."

Avery suddenly had a look of mild panic. "When's that? How long can you stay?" she demanded. "Is Brad giving you a hard time about being here?"

"Of course he is," Juliet said, forcing a smile, adding with as much reassurance as she could, "but I'm going to try to buy a little more time."

Avery glanced around her tiny living space. "Now I *do* wish I had rented a bigger apartment so you could stay with me! I figured I'd be the only one sleeping here because I was taking all those classes and—"

"Don't apologize! As you reminded me, I was the one who pushed you to find a place on this street. And besides, it's been fun staying on the barge."

"And hanging out with Major Gorgeous?"

"Avery!" Juliet was tempted to reveal Finn's marital status so as to put an end to her teasing. "I just met the guy, and besides, I supposedly have a boyfriend back home. Finn and I live on two different continents! We're the perfect example of two people who are majorly, geographically inappropriate for each other, so don't get goofy on me, or I'll think it *is* the meds. Try to get a good night's rest." She turned off the bedside light. "You'll need your strength for the PT session tomorrow."

"You've got to dump Jed Jarvis," Avery murmured, half asleep already. "He's such a rat, like all of them at GG, except Jamie..."

"No argument there."

Avery's eyes suddenly snapped opened. "Seriously? You're going to give that jerk the boot?"

"Promise. As soon as I get back. Now go to sleep."

Avery obediently shut her eyes once more and was breathing evenly by the time Finn's footsteps could be heard coming up the stairs.

Juliet held a finger to her lips, warning, "Shhh..." and beckoned him to stand quietly near the pint-sized refrigerator while she removed milk and eggs and bread from the plastic bag he held. Soon the items were lined up on the tiny shelves. The pair made a silent retreat and closed the door, tiptoeing down the stairs.

When they reached the bottom, Juliet turned to Finn. "Look," she said, "I saw from the expression on your face at Claudine's that you were kinda...upset to see your dad. Since you two might need to talk, maybe it would be better if I found a hotel."

Finn scowled down at her.

"If I meet with him at all—doubtful, at best—I don't want it to be on the barge."

"Why not?"

"I don't want him to know where I'm living," Finn replied with vehemence that startled her. "I want my privacy. I want to protect what I have and take the time that I need to...to sort everything out without him trying to dominate every single thing I do!"

He gave an angry yank to the heavy front door leading to the street. Juliet scrambled to keep up with his long strides as he led the way to the spot where he'd parked the MG. She reached out and put a restraining hand on his arm.

"Okay, okay, sir!" she exclaimed, trying to make a joke of the situation. Finn halted in his tracks and turned around to face her. Juliet spoke before he could. "As it happens, I'm perfectly happy to be your buffer zone to avoid sleeping on Avery's floor—if that's a service I can render. Thanks for letting the barge serve as my refuge as well."

She felt Finn's gaze studying her face. One corner of his mouth quirked upwards.

"You know what? I *like* you, Juliet Thayer. You are one, cool lady. Let's find you a *kir royale* and me a strong cup of coffee. We both need to warm up."

Juliet laughed and pointed directly across the street. Finn turned around and stared at a red awning with the letters spelling *La Calèche*.

"How about the café right over there?" she suggested.

The two of them sipped their respective beverages in companionable silence while late diners at *La Calèche* signaled for their bills and handed over their credit cards.

Finally, unable to completely file away the evening's earlier events, Juliet ventured, "You should have seen the look on your face when your father walked into Claudine's dining room. I gather you haven't seen the general in a while?"

To her surprise, Finn seemed almost eager to talk about the strained relationship. "We haven't exchanged a word or communicated in any way ever since I told him I'd decided to resign from the Air Force. He blew his stack, and hung up on me."

"And you didn't call back?"

Finn shook his head. "I didn't tell him I was heading for France, either." After taking a sip of his small cup of espresso, he added, "Claudine has faithfully kept my confidence, and I feel rotten that she's now in the uncomfortable position of having to refuse to tell her brother exactly where his son is living."

"Knowing Claudine a little bit, I can't help but wonder if she doesn't rather enjoy sparring with her brother. But you know," Juliet speculated, "he's got to have been worried about you, don't you think?"

She noted the now-familiar crease that appeared between Finn's startlingly blue eyes.

"Trust me, my father is more worried about the Deschanel family military legacy than anything else."

"But you've been in the service ever since you got out of the Air Force Academy. Doesn't that count for something with your father?"

"I served the nine years I owed the government in addition to the four years in the Air Force Academy and another two taking flight training. The fact I spent time in the Middle East desert, in rehab, and flying drones meant nothing to him. I'm a quitter."

"He's a soldier. Surely he knows the kinds of bad stuff you've been through."

"If he does, he's never said anything to me that showed the slightest empathy."

"Does your father know about your PTSD or where things stand with Kim... or about the divorce? Maybe *that's* got him concerned?"

Juliet realized full well that she was "fishing" but she couldn't seem to help herself. For reasons she didn't want to acknowledge, it was important to her to understand Finn's state of mind concerning his ruptured marriage.

Finn drained the miniature cup and carefully set it down in its small saucer. "By now, I expect Dad knows from Kim or her parents that the divorce will soon be final...though, believe me, he doesn't know the whole story."

"Which is...what?" she prompted, adding with a hint of chagrin for being so pushy, "That is, if you want to tell me."

Finn's expression hardened. "No, I don't, particularly."

"Sorry. I just thought—"

He cast her a look of mild apology. "Look, there's no need for you to be subjected to this little family drama of mine." He signaled for the check. "Let's head on back to the barge, okay? You've got to be back here to help Avery early tomorrow, and I...well, believe it or not, I've got a cooking class at ten."

"No!" Juliet exclaimed, glad Finn at least had tried to make amends for his abrupt shutting down of their conversation about his breach with his wife. "What is it this time? How to make the perfect *Crêpe Suzette*?"

"Naw..." he said, guiding her out the door of the bistro and into the dark, chilly street. "*Crêpes Suzettes* are for amateurs! I'm taking a class in how to cook duck in five different ways. *Canard a l'orange...paté de canard...canard fumé—*"

"I get it, I get it!" Juliet laughed. "It sounds fattening and delicious!"

Just at that moment, a car careened down the street with a man in the backseat hanging out the window, shouting and waving his fist over his head. As it turned the corner, a noise sounding like an explosion rent the air. Finn made a grab for Juliet's shoulders and pushed them both down beneath one of the empty sidewalk tables as he rolled to one side to absorb the impact of their fall.

"Oh, my God!" Juliet gasped, her back crushed against Finn's chest.

Just as quickly, the street returned to complete silence. The restaurant's proprietor suddenly appeared at the door, staring down the street, not noticing they were on the ground under one of his metal tables. Meanwhile, Juliet could hear Finn's ragged breathing as they remained motionless. The restaurant owner shrugged and disappeared back inside. Juliet remained absolutely still in Finn's arms, instinctively allowing whatever time he needed to calm down. After a few moments, he slowly stood up and then helped Juliet to her feet.

"Just a bunch of drunks," he pronounced on a long breath, "driving an old car that backfired, I guess. Sorry if I—"

"No! No! It absolutely sounded like gunfire," she agreed with a shiver. "I guess after November thirteenth, we're all going to have various versions of PTSD."

"You okay? I didn't crack a rib or anything tackling you like that?"

"I'm perfectly fine, but let's get out of here."

The drive back to the barge took less than fifteen minutes. Once out of the car, she kept her hands in her pockets as the two of them silently walked side by side along the quay toward the barge. Her cell phone suddenly emitted a ping, which caused her heart to speed up with the knowledge it was probably the start of the workday in San Francisco. Pulling it out of her pocket, she peeked at her message icon:

**Be back here by November 30
or you're fired.**

Finn held open the gate to the metal gangway that led to the deck of the barge.

"News from home?" he asked as she passed him into the pilothouse.

She showed him the text.

"From your brother, right?"

"Yeah…Brad The Bad."

"Why is it your job alone to keep the pressure on him to pay back your dad? Can't your other brother demand Brad cough up the cash?" Finn removed his leather jacket and hung it on one of the spokes of the barge's steering wheel. He reached for her coat and hung it on the spoke next to his.

"That's not the only reason I should go back."

Finn indicated the couch and they both sat down.

"You want to turn in your notice?" he said with a wry smile, surprising her in the next moment by reaching for her hand and giving it a squeeze. "If you did that, then you could come right back here and enroll at *L'École*."

"It's not just my job. I also have to…" She paused, mid-sentence. Why in the world did she feel compelled at this inconvenient moment to tell Finn about her relationship with Jed and how she had decided to end it as soon as she got home?

One decision has nothing to do with the other, she scolded herself.

"What else do you have to do when you're back in San Francisco?" he prompted after she'd failed to complete her previous sentence.

"Oh, nothing, really…I guess I'm just worried about how Avery will fare when I do leave. She looked panicked tonight when I told her I couldn't stay much longer."

"Well, I'll keep an eye on her for you," he volunteered. "And I'm sure Claudine will too. Little by little—as impossible as that seems after what's happened—life will return to the 'new normal.' The sun will come up tomorrow…and other poems."

Juliet was surprised to feel the oddest twinge of jealousy at the notion of Finn and Avery becoming close friends in her ensuing absence, a reaction that made her instantly ashamed. Finn had been separated from his wife for nearly two years…and was most likely as lonely as Avery must be—and eventually ready for a new relationship. Meanwhile, she'd be seven thousand miles away and living a totally different existence. If Finn and Avery found solace in each other's company, she should be happy for that.

She forced a smile, thanking Finn once more for being so kind to them both through their entire ordeal.

Manufacturing a yawn, she said, "Boy, am I bushed, aren't you? Time for beddy-bye, I'd say. Mind if I use the…uh…head?"

"Of course," he said gallantly. "Oh, and by the way," he called after her as she descended a few steps. "Ever been to Giverny?"

Juliet paused, mid-step and turned around.

"Not yet, but that's my dream, one day, to go there to paint in that garden where Monet did all those wonderful canvases of water lilies."

"So you *do* plan to come back?" Finn asked, adding, "because…maybe when you do, I'll have my life better sorted out."

Juliet paused to absorb his last words. Then she said, "Maybe I will, too," and scampered down the last two stairs into the barge's smallest room.

After a quick shower in Finn's minuscule stall, Juliet returned clad in her regulation nighttime attire. Finn was sitting in his leather chair, reading. He had made up the bed on his sofa while she was down below.

"Hey…that was very nice of you to do," she said, discretely slipping her bra and underpants back into her suitcase parked on the floor. There was something so intimate about having her personal affects tucked away in a man's lair.

Finn rose from his chair, preparing to head down below to his own bed. He glanced at his watch and then looked out the window at the Eiffel Tower, still lit in blue, white, and red lights. "I should think about sleeping up here sometime," he said, walking across the room to stand beside her. "The view's pretty spectacular, isn't it?"

"I'm going to miss this sight so much," she sighed.

"Are you?" He turned toward her slightly. "And I

think I'm going to miss your company."

They locked glances and then he bent down and brushed his lips on the top of her head as if she were a well-behaved child. Awkwardly, they exchanged faint smiles and chastely bid each other goodnight. Juliet slipped beneath the covers on the couch while she watched Finn turn off all the lights and pad down to his stateroom. She turned her gaze toward the blazing tower and watched it erupt into its nightly five-minute sparkle show before going utterly dark. The velvety blackness enfolded her and she concentrated on the lapping of the Seine against the hull. Even so, and tired as she felt, it took her nearly an hour to fall asleep.

CHAPTER 12

Just after dawn the next morning, Juliet awoke to the sound of her cell phone ringing. She made a lunge for it on the floor beside the sofa and saw that the caller ID announced her brother Jamie was trying to get in touch. Worried about waking Finn, she leapt out of bed, grabbed her coat from the spoke on the ship's wheel, and clumsily stepped halfway into her shoes as she croaked "Hello?"

Once outside on the deck, the skies were a pale crystal and the temperature bordered on frigid, but Juliet could see it was going to be a fine day.

"Jamie, do you know what time it is here?" she demanded with a laugh.

"Eight a.m.," he said confidently.

"Check again. It's barely seven. In the winter, Paris is eight hours behind California."

"Oops. Sorry, but I wanted to find out how Avery is doing. I've been watching CNN and it all looks so—"

Juliet interrupted. "She's out of the hospital, as of yesterday, which was a big surprise. I was able to take her to the funeral of the guy who saved her life by throwing his body over hers when the shooting started."

"What a horrible thing that must have been." A pause. "Was he her boyfriend?"

Jamie's last question had a definite edge to it.

"No. Just a friend and fellow artist. She'd taken him to dinner that night to thank him for helping her navigate art school. And anyway, what's it to you, bro?" She was more than convinced that Jamie continued to harbor a soft spot for Avery.

"I'm just glad to hear she's doing better, is all. And

how about you? What's it like in Paris, now?"

"It's absolutely freezing here," she noted cheerfully. "But the city's getting back to a strange kind of normal and the Parisians are amazing. Even after everything that's happened over here, they'll be damned if the terrorists will shut down their lives. People are back eating in cafés. They're going to work and riding the metro, but you see piles of flowers everywhere at various memorials, and it's...well...still kind of scary. At least for me. They caught all but one of the terrorists. He supposedly fled to Syria, but—"

"That's what I'm worried about," intervened Jamie. "Where *are* you, anyhow? Are you someplace relatively safe?"

Juliet turned to look into the salon through the pilothouse window. Finn was up, clad in a pair of running shorts he apparently slept in—at least when he had company. He also sported a faded Air Force T-shirt that completed his morning ensemble. He was standing at the desk, facing the two burners, making coffee. She saw a long, ridged scar that ran from the rim of his shorts down his left leg to below his knee.

"Don't worry about me," she replied, keeping her voice light. "Believe it or not, I'm under the full protection of a former Major of the United States Air Force. His landlady's grandson was the young man who got killed having dinner with Avery."

"What do you mean 'under the protection of'? What part of Paris are you in?"

"I'm on a river barge, of all things. Across from the Eiffel Tower. It's pretty fabulous, actually." She eyed the deck section of the boat near the stern. "If the weather were decent, I could set up an easel on board and paint the most incredible river scene."

"Wow...sounds great. But how did you end up there?"

"It's a long story that I'll tell you when I see you. And, yeah, if it weren't for what's happened, I'd be in seventh heaven."

Just then, Truffles, the black cat, rubbed her furry side against Juliet's leg. It felt warm and comforting.

"So it sounds like you've got things pretty well under control," Jamie said. "You'll be back, soon, though…right? Brad has been—"

"Honestly?" she cut in, a tight knot expanding in her chest as she remembered Brad's nasty text from the night before, "I don't want to hear about Brad right now. Avery is mourning the loss of her friend and is struggling, big time, with survivor's guilt. She has a long way to go until her shoulder and right arm are completely healed. She has physical therapy every other day and lives in an attic, a million steps to the top. She shouldn't be alone, and she won't let me contact her family. I'm needed here…at least for a while longer," she finished, unable to disguise her exasperation.

Brad should just sit on it! she thought angrily. It made her blood boil that people like him had absolutely no idea what was facing all the surviving victims and their circle of family and friends—nor did he apparently give a damn.

"Hey!" Jamie in response to her tirade. "I'm on your side, remember? He told me about the text he sent threatening to fire you if you didn't come back soon."

"Yeah…he's such a sweetheart." Her bitter tone surprised even her.

"What about this," Jamie proposed. "When you fix a date for coming home, I'll fly over there and keep an eye on Avery. We'll have locked down the new video and the entire editing department goes on hiatus for the Christmas holidays, plus I'm owed a ton of vacation days to boot. That way, you can return home by the end of the month and keep Brad from firing you, which he threatens to do every day to warn the rest of us that he won't brook any disloyalty."

"C'mon, Jamie...come clean. Do you have some special reason you're so concerned about Avery?"

There was a long pause on the other end of her cell phone, and for a moment, she thought they might have become disconnected.

"I really like her, Jules," Jamie said at length, "and I think Brad...well, I'm sure his ...uh...behavior is one of the reasons she bailed. I feel really bad about that. If she hadn't quit, she wouldn't have been in Paris and gotten shot."

"Brad's way of running GatherGames makes *me* want to quit, too, but her getting shot was one of life's random events, so we really can't blame Brad for every rotten thing that happens. But listen," Juliet said, hearing the urgency in her own voice, "that's a very generous offer you've made to come over to keep Avery company while she recuperates. In fact, I think it's the best option available to us, actually. Why don't we have a changing of the guard, then? It's going to be a while until Avery can decently fend for herself and seriously get back to her painting. In the meantime, our friend Finn can keep an eye on her until you can get to Paris."

"Ah...so it's 'Finn,' is it? How old is this Air Force major you're staying with on a barge in the middle of the Seine?"

"My age," she replied shortly. "Former helicopter rescue pilot."

Juliet omitted adding Finn had also flown drones— and was still a married man.

"An Air Force *pilot*, no less," Jamie teased.

"He was. He's out now and currently unemployed."

"What should I tell Jed?"

"Don't tell him anything!" she snapped. "My staying

here has been solely due to the fact that Avery's apartment was freezing until she moved back into it and could make the crazy French heating system work, and—"

"Okay, okay!" Jamie said, laughing. "Don't be so defensive! I'm sure you are totally behaving yourself."

"I am!" she retorted, and gave her brother a brief rundown of Finn's kindnesses to everyone involved in the tragedy of Avery and J-P. "He has some serious complications in his life, just like I do, so, trust me, there's absolutely been no hanky-panky between us."

"Sounds like a stand-up guy."

"He is."

Just then from inside the pilothouse, Finn held up a steaming mug of what Juliet assumed was coffee, pantomiming if she wanted him to bring it out to her.

"I've gotta go," she told Jamie. "I'll propose the idea to Avery of your coming over here and let you know her reaction as soon as I figure out when I have to leave. Bye for now, and thanks for checking up on me."

"Dad's been worried too, you know. I'll tell him you are safe and apparently in good hands, courtesy of the United States Air Force."

Just as when they were high school kids and he teased her about various boyfriends, Jamie couldn't resist ribbing her about her Paris host. Then, as he always did when they were away from each other, he said, "Bye, now, and love you."

"Love you too, bro."

Now that Avery was installed back in her own living space, Juliet was encouraged that her friend appeared to be slowly recovering the use of her wounded arm. When she arrived at Avery's that morning she was greeted by the sight of her sitting on a stool in front of her easel. The hand of her good arm held a brush and she was dabbing paint on a canvas she had apparently been working on before the attacks.

"Hey, there…" Avery said with a vague wave of her brush.

"Hey, there, yourself!" Juliet replied, giving her friend a thumbs-up.

"There's food in the 'fridge that the Parkers from downstairs brought up. Help yourself."

Sensing Avery was deep into her project, Juliet said, "I've already had my breakfast. I only just dropped by to say hi and see if you needed anything else. Finn wants to take me to see Giverny or the botanical gardens here in Paris. That okay with you?"

"Yeah, sure," Avery responded absently. "See you guys later for supper? I think I'm ready to go out 'cause I've got a serious case of cabin fever. My treat. I owe you both, big time."

Surprised Avery wanted to eat in a restaurant after the events at *Le Petit Cambodge*, Juliet said she'd make a reservation and dashed back out the door.

That morning Finn had, in fact, offered to take Juliet to see some sights she'd had on her Bucket List. Once back downstairs, however, she crossed the street over to *La Caléche* and made a phone call while she nursed a coffee at a table just inside the door. Next, she punched in Finn's number, reporting the startling news that Avery had started painting again.

"That's great! Can I take you both to dinner to celebrate?"

"That's so funny. Avery just said she had cabin fever and thought she was ready to eat in a restaurant again."

Then she told Finn that she had determined she could no longer put off going back to San Francisco and before she'd called him, she'd made a reservation to fly home.

There was a slight pause before he replied, "Well, you have to do what you have to do, I suppose." Then, "Look, I'll call *Bistro Belhara*. Is eight, tonight, okay?"

"Better make it for seven. Avery starts to poop out by quarter to nine. And she insists tonight's her treat. To thank us both for…well…everything, I guess."

"Got it. Are you still up to driving to Giverny or going to see the botanical gardens today?"

"I'd love to—but now that I think of it, how about we do that tomorrow or the next day? Since I'm flying home in a week, I've got some stuff on my To Do list I should accomplish before I leave. It probably makes more sense to run a few errands today and then I can meet you later at Avery's and go on to dinner."

"Works for me. I'll pick you both up at six-thirty. We can do one of the gardens tomorrow if you like."

Unlike Jed, whenever she ever needed to adjust a plan with him, Finn always seemed reasonable and accommodating.

"All that sounds perfect," she added gratefully. "You are a totally good egg, you know that?"

"My eggs can be a bit scrambled at times, but I'll take that as a compliment." He laughed. "See you tonight."

Juliet clicked off her phone, paid her bill, and then walked the few blocks to *L'École des Beaux Arts*. Once past the security check, she took courage in hand and sought out the administrative offices. There, she secured enrollment papers for classes the following year that specialized in landscape painting. Leaving the office, she walked into the vast courtyard dotted with students hurrying to and from classes. With the papers tucked in her tote bag, she gazed at the building where Avery was an art student and Juliet's great-great grandmother had come to study architecture so many decades before. She had no idea when—if ever—she'd make the break and come back to

Paris, but a slight shiver skittered down her spine at the notion that she might one day figure out a way to carry on the family's artistic tradition and study advanced landscape painting within these walls.

"*Yes!*" she exclaimed aloud, delighted by the thought. A young woman nearby turned around and stared at her curiously. Juliet offered a cheery wave. As she turned to leave the school, a sudden flood of doubt assailed her. She had been doing computer-generated graphics for so long...did she still know how to hold a paintbrush?

The *Bistrot Belhara* at 23 *Rue Duvivier* in the 8th *Arrondissement* turned out to be almost as small as Avery's flat, but famous for its classic French food "offering a Basque sensibility," according to an online description Juliet had checked. To begin their meal, Avery and Juliet ordered a *paté encroute* and swooned over its flaky, golden pastry filled with minced duck infused with a rich, red wine sauce. Finn ordered sweetbreads, crispy on the outside, moist inside, and plumped with tiny potatoes. The three of them then shared a *cassoulet* and thought it almost as good as the one Finn and Claudine had made. The trio concluded with rice pudding, "unlike anything I've ever eaten in the States," Juliet moaned, licking the back of her spoon.

For an hour, the three could almost forget the tragedy that had befallen Paris, yet Juliet sensed as they drank their espresso that Avery was becoming increasingly ill at ease. The room had filled up with diners, and Avery glanced from side to side in the small space, as if she felt the threat that something frightening could erupt at any moment.

"Shall we get the check?" Juliet asked with a bright smile.

Avery nodded and then plunged her hand into her handbag.

"But let's ask the waiter to take a picture of the three of us," she said. "I want to remember this night after Juliet has gone back to San Fran."

A passing waiter obliged, and Finn obediently put an arm around each of his fellow diners, adding in an off-hand way, "Now, no putting this on Facebook, remember."

"Don't worry," Avery said, her expression darkening. "You think I want anyone to see me with my arm in a sling? But shall I send you guys a copy?" Before they could answer, she typed Juliet's email address and asked for Finn's, sending the picture to them both with a tap of her finger.

Though Finn had made light of the moment, Juliet knew he was as serious as Avery was about not wanting the image to go beyond the three of them.

The man is hiding out from the world, Juliet considered silently, *and most specifically from his father and his almost-ex-wife back in Nevada. But why?*

When Avery excused herself to go to the ladies room, Finn reminded Juliet of his offer to drive her to see the painter Monet's gardens at Giverny before she left.

"I imagine the gardens are dormant, given the time of year, but you said how much you wanted to see it...and you should definitely see *Les Jardin des Plantes.*"

"They're the botanical gardens here in Paris?"

Finn nodded as Avery returned. Juliet asked her if she'd like to join the two of them on an outing the following day. Avery shook her head. She glanced apprehensively around the crowded restaurant and out the window facing the street.

"This was nice, tonight," she began, "but honestly? I don't think I'm quite ready to hang out among huge crowds. And besides, the next few days are jammed with all those doctors' appointments and my damned physical therapy." She turned to Juliet. "But you should definitely let Finn take you…"

"I'm here to keep you company and be of some help," Juliet protested. "If you'd rather not go, I'll just bag it and go with you to all the stuff you have to do."

Avery shook her head vehemently. "I'm to have to learn to manage on my own very soon, so let's both put our time to good use. You've sat in enough hospital rooms and stuffy doctors' offices to last a lifetime. Please! Go with Finn! I can hire Uber drivers to take me to see the doctors these last few days you're here. I want you to see more of Paris, if only to persuade you to come back soon! We'll have dinners together, so don't feel guilty."

In the end, Juliet decided to forgo traveling an hour outside Paris to Giverny, given that the next day dawned cold and wet.

"Then instead," Finn proposed that morning, "we could head for the botanical gardens here in Paris. There are a lot of glass greenhouses there, so they'll be plenty to see indoors, out of the damp and cold."

Due to the continuing inclement weather, Finn and Juliet decided that the greater part of valor was to leave the MG where it was parked near the barge and ride the metro from the nearby Passy station across the city. Juliet continued to find the sight of armed guards jarring as they emerged from the *Place Monge* station. Finn assured her it was just a short walk to *Les Jardin des Plantes* and the natural history museum next to it.

Striding briskly down *Rue Censier* toward one of the main entrances to the acres of growing plants and large greenhouses, Juliet pointed to a two-level spire clad in distinctive Moorish designs. "Wow… that's really tall. What is it?"

Finn hesitated before answering. "That's the *Mosquée de Paris*, the center of the city's Muslim community."

Juliet despised that her intake of breath was audible. She allowed her gaze to drift to the top of the ornate building where there was a small parapet.

"So there are Muslim calls to prayer, right here in the heart of Paris?"

"Yes. And there's also the Arab Institute, over there." He pointed off to his left. "It was founded thirty-five years ago by twenty Arab countries with the intention of fostering cultural links between the Arab world and the West. I've heard that there are ten centuries of incredible Islamic works of art in there."

"But you haven't been to see it yourself?"

It was Finn's turn to inhale deeply. "No. Not yet. But I hope one day I'll...be able to."

For some reasons she couldn't explain even to herself, she sought Finn's hand.

"Me, too. Someday. I have to fight the instinct to judge all Muslims by what happened here."

Finn turned to face her. "One of these days, we're going to have to accept our differences and stop trying to persuade the other side which religious sect and lifestyle is 'best'."

"And we'll have to get over our fear of each other when it's not warranted."

"Someday," Finn agreed soberly, and squeezed her hand before he released it.

The pair spent as much time as they could endure strolling through the cold, soggy gardens with little but bare branches in view, and then coping with the steamy temperatures of the numerous hothouses that stood throughout the acres of botanical gardens. After an hour, Juliet pointed to an exit sign in one of the largest of the glass structures.

Finn laughed. "Had enough horticulture for one day?"

She nodded, although when they emerged into the gardens once again, the sun was just breaking through the clouds overhead.

Juliet said with a laugh, "If you paint landscapes, you've got to learn to draw trees and flowers and so forth, but it would be much better to study such things in the spring."

Finn glanced at the plants nearby that were dripping with moisture. "Well, then...I hope that means you're planning a return trip?"

Juliet gave a little shrug. "Fingers crossed..."

"Since it looks like those clouds are moving east, how about we head for the Luxembourg Gardens where we can grab some food in the café and hope the weather improves even more?"

Juliet was embarrassed to admit how much more comfortable she felt once they had left the "Arab Quarter" and entered the Luxembourg Palace grounds that were surrounded by ancient gateways and criss-crossed with carefully laid out gravel pathways, precisely-trimmed trees and hedges, and sumptuous statuary.

"Do you suppose we'll all get to the point where we *can* understand and appreciate and respect our differences?" she asked.

"You mean between the Arab world and the West? God, I hope so...but I will never respect killing innocent people as a way of saying 'We're right.'"

"That goes for both sides, agreed?"

Finn pulled his eyes from the distant trees and regarded her for a moment. "Amen to that," he said. Then, he pointed the way down a hedge-lined gravel path towards an enormous fountain looming on their left.

By this time, the sun had fully emerged from behind large, puffy white clouds. Raindrops glistened on a long, double row of trees, prompting Juliet to try to imagine how magnificent the gardens must look when the thousands of plants and flower beds were in full bloom.

"You're right. I *have* to come back here in spring," she murmured as she absorbed the beauty of the peaceful haven in the heart of the city. "Do you mind?" she asked Finn, pulling her sketchpad from her tote bag to make a quick drawing of the de Medici Fountain where their wanderings had led.

"Of course not," he said. He pointed to a pair of metal chairs next to a stone rectangle that encased a pool of water. At its end stood an imposing columned fountain with gigantic classical metal sculptures, tinged green with time and moisture.

"You have the de Medici Fountain all to yourself today," he said. "It's got to be a good fifteen degrees warmer than yesterday, so I'm happy just to sit here and relax."

Juliet was surprised by how Finn's presence didn't unnerve her as she began to draw, even when he snapped a picture on his mobile phone of her hunched over her sketchpad. The statues, water features, and foliage began to blossom beneath her pencil, almost as if by their own accord. A wave of exhilaration came over her as each stark winter branch she created spread out on either side of the magnificent waterworks, the bareness beautiful in its own way, despite the leafless trees and empty urns. *Yes,* she thought, *I can still draw freehand—but can I paint?* That was still to be seen.

"We never got that coffee," Finn noted when Juliet snapped shut her sketching pad and filed it and her drawing implements into her tote bag. "How about ending our explorations at *Place St. Sulpice,* with a quick look into the church that took a century to build? There's another nice café there on the corner."

When Juliet caught her first glimpse of the double row of columns flanking the front of the magnificent *St. Sulpice,* she understood immediately why this was one of Finn's favorite churches in all of Paris. The winter chill increased a few degrees when they entered its shadowy depths, but her spirits were warmed by the votive candles nestled in red glass containers that glowed like garnets in every niche along the walls.

A sudden, loud chord rumbled deep from the bowels of an organ whose pipes took up an entire wall of the mammoth structure. The booming, reverberating sound rang out, followed by a skittering of expert fingers practicing for an upcoming service.

Without exchanging a word, Finn and Juliet moved toward a chapel on their right filled with a large rust and white-colored striated block of marble topped by life-sized, mournful angels weeping over a Madonna figure holding a dying man in her arms.

Finn nodded toward a clutch of long tapers. Handing one to Juliet and keeping a second for himself, they lit the wicks from the same flame on the offertory stand and placed the slender candles, side-by-side, into metal holders. Finn took her hand while they both gazed, mesmerized by the pair of golden lights dancing before their eyes.

"For Jean-Pierre and those who died November thirteenth," Finn murmured. "May they rest in peace."

"For Jean-Pierre, his family, dear Avery, and all of France," echoed Juliet. "May they—and the rest of us— find solace in the coming days."

For several minutes they stood silently holding hands before the flickering flames. Finn dropped a few coins into the donation box and stepped back, pointing to the walls on both sides of the chapel.

"Painted by Delacroix, pretty close to when he died," he whispered.

Both gigantic paintings were full of winged angels and mere mortals doing battle with all manner of slain foes.

"They're beautiful, but a little too violent for my mood right now. Can we get that cup of coffee?"

Finn led her from the church to a small café on the corner of the square where they ordered two *café crèmes* and a pastry to share while young men selling the cartoon publication *Charlie Hebdo* wove in and out of the small tables where they sat. Juliet felt her heart lurch slightly when Finn dug into his pocket for change and pointedly bought a copy of the very magazine that prompted the year's first terrorist attack against those involved in its publication. She glanced around nervously, but no one appeared to respond to his rather overt act of defiance.

"I think you are becoming an expat very much like your Aunt Claudine," she said under her breath.

"Good. At least I hope so. Can't let the bastards get you down."

With only half her coffee yet to drink, Juliet began to worry that she'd left Avery alone too long.

Finn quickly reminded her, "As she, herself, said to you at the restaurant the other night, she'll have to wrestle with her devils after you're gone, and so each of you giving the other some space while you're still here might be a good idea." He paused, and then added, "And besides, we're having a pretty good time together, wouldn't you say?"

Startled, she lowered her eyes to her coffee and nodded. "Yes, I'd say we are." She looked up to meet his gaze, "But I keep wondering. What particular devils are *you* currently wrestling with these days, Finn? I see your light on in the wee hours most nights."

Finn placed the magazine on the small table and gave a short laugh. "What are *you* doing awake, may I ask?"

"Well, I still think I get more sleep that you do. But

when I do wake up, you're always awake, too. I hope it's not because I'm staying on the barge."

Now it was Finn's turn to stare into his coffee cup. "Even when you're not there, it's a toss-up for me whether it's better to sleep or to stay awake."

"How do you mean?"

"Well, I told you about how this PTSD thing can bring on nightmares, and God knows, I'd rather not expose you to the uproar."

"Oh, Finn…please tell me you're not staying awake while I'm there to avoid having a bad dream?"

"Well…it's been on my mind," he admitted. "The other problem is that when I do fall asleep, sometimes I wake with a start at the slightest sound and—as you witnessed—I've been known to dive for cover, which isn't very convenient, since my bed down below is built-in and nailed into the floor. I can make an awful ruckus, hitting the deck."

Juliet realized he was trying to make light of his problems regarding sleep. She found herself strangely overcome by a fierce desire to offer something… anything…by way of comfort. However, before she could think what that might be, he cracked a rueful smile. "You'll be pleased to hear, though, that I actually think I'm making some progress. The good Doctor A has taught me deep breathing techniques and ways to switch away from certain reoccurring thoughts. Sometimes, I listen to classical music in my headphones all night, and I've even got a white noise machine I use. All kinds of high-tech stuff like that." He picked up his coffee cup and took a long draught. "I'm even part of a PTSD sleep study, no less," he added with mocking pride.

"That's great, Finn. I mean it," she said earnestly.

"Well, there's a vet who got his MD degree after he left the service and is now a professor at Harvard. He's been involved in some new studies."

"Like what?"

"Ones that show that—in addition to the psychological damage that results from witnessing harrowing events in combat—"

"You mean like being shot down in a rescue helicopter and seeing other soldiers die?" she asked pointedly.

"Yeah, traumatic stuff like that. This Harvard guy and his team are developing more sensitive magnetic resonance imaging—you know—MRI brain-scan machines that show there is more subtle, 'unseen' damage that is done by the *physical*, concussive sound blasts that explosions and crashes can cause."

"Wow…you mean that just hearing and being near an explosion, even if a soldier isn't hit by flying objects, can cause damage to the brain?"

"And not just to soldiers and airmen. Anyone who either gets his or her head hit, or is exposed to thunderous sounds may experience what the Harvard guy calls 'brain disconnects.' The latest theories are that the brain's neuron receptors become jolted and out of alignment, so to speak, and so the brain signals—the synapses—are no longer able to link properly between the receptors. And if that happens, the synapses can't make the rapid connections they do in normal brains. It could cause malfunctions of anything from memory, to motor skills, to areas of the brain that process the emotions."

"That's totally incredible!" exclaimed Juliet. "So there may be hard-to-detect but real damage to the *mechanics* of the brain that doctors couldn't measure before, and not just the flight-or-flight emotional reactions to reliving traumatic events?"

Finn's relieved expression told her he was grateful that she appeared to grasp the nuances of the new research.

"Exactly. Both emotional and organic issues may be

at work for some poor bastards…or in other people, just one type or the other. It's all about having the correct diagnosis and better brain scans."

"This is amazing! So PTSD can have both physical *as well as* emotional causes—and sometimes both? Do doctors and the Veterans Administration agree about the findings?"

"A few do, but for most—not yet. It's just starting to filter through the medical system," he said with a shrug. "Until recently, if the docs didn't see blood or something gross on a scan, the injury didn't exist and they wouldn't commit to treating it. All this new evidence indicates that maybe three to four hundred *thousand* troops that served in the Middle East may be having problems that haven't been correctly or completely diagnosed, but are caused by concussive events on the battlefield that are resulting in these 'brain disconnects.'"

"Well, I sure hope this new stuff takes some of the onus off the poor vet," she declared. "Nobody thinks a guy is cowardly if he has diabetes or high blood pressure."

"But real men don't get spooked by back-firing cars, remember? Trust me…it's highly embarrassing."

"Most people have never experienced the kinds of events that military folks like you have who've fought this fifteen-year war, so it's moot."

"You want to tell that to my father?" Finn said with a bitter laugh. "It's an easy bet that most of the generals are the last to want to know because the implications are huge—and would cost a lot of taxpayers' money to try to fix."

Juliet leaned into the small table, rattling their cups. "Look, Finn, you've shown a lot of courage, just admitting you have a problem, and even more guts, seeking help by way of going to the American Hospital. And, just so you know, if a nightmare makes you scream at night while I'm on board the barge—so be it. It is what it is." Then she grinned at him. "You don't scare me."

"You've been lucky so far."

"I kinda know what you're talking about when it comes to nightmares, though." She began to relate that her brother Jamie had admitted that merely *editing* video war games had begun to make it difficult for him to have a full night's sleep without the disruption of horrifying dreams.

"But is that really possible?" she wondered aloud. "Could just *seeing* violent images be causing his sleep problems?"

"Does he edit the sound, also?"

"Yep. And lots of it. And the sound effects are purposefully loud and scary."

"Well, who knows for sure, but it could be that the loud sounds assaulting his ears through his headphones, as well as the images, are affecting him. I'd love to talk to that brother of yours sometime. And so would my shrink, I bet."

"You may soon have a chance. He wants to spell me helping out with Avery and come to Paris during the holidays to look after her for a while." Juliet raised an eyebrow and continued, "It's pretty clear to me he likes her. *More* than likes her, in fact. He's called or texted me every day to find out how she is."

Finn grinned. "Well, that's nice to hear, and it will be good to know she'll have company over the holidays. They can be rough spent alone."

Juliet experienced a sense of unexpected relief to see that Finn didn't appear the slightest bit upset to learn that Jamie might be attracted to Avery. Not that she, Juliet, had any claim on the man, she reminded herself sternly. After all, she would soon be headed back to San Francisco with no idea when she might ever return to Paris.

What a depressing thought that *was…*

Juliet sat up straighter and silently vowed she would find a way to return to study art. And if Finn Deschanel was still on his barge as a newly-single man when she did find her way back, all the better...

She was startled by Finn's interrupting her train of thought.

"Juliet? Did you hear what I said? Be sure to tell your brother he's more than welcome to bunk with me when he gets here...that is, unless he and Avery will be—"

She laughed, mentally shaking herself out of her daydream. "I don't even know if Avery has any idea my brother has serious designs on her. But I'll be glad to tell Jamie that—at least when he first arrives in Paris—I can highly recommend *L'Étoile de Paris* as a great place to land!"

"Be sure to warn him about the nightmares, though."

Juliet met his glance and they were silent for a long moment. "I will let him know," she said finally, her heart aching for the generous-spirited Finn. "And believe me, he'll completely understand."

CHAPTER 13

The early evening skies were clear by the time Finn and Juliet walked from the café, up *Rue St. Père*, turning left on *Rue de Lille* and, fifty feet later, found themselves in front of the large wooden door at number seven. Juliet thanked him for a wonderful day of sightseeing and her first sustained chance at the Luxembourg Gardens to use her new sketchbook.

"I think I'll rustle up something for Avery's dinner on her one burner and then head back to your barge later, if that's okay? I only have a few more days here and—"

"Sounds like a good plan," he assured her. "I'll leave the door to the pilothouse open in case I've headed to bed, or if I go out to catch a movie or something."

For a split second, Juliet yearned to grab his hand and head for a movie, too. Something fun. Something to take her mind off everything that was weighing her down. A casual evening with this nice man who stood just inches away was exactly how she longed to spend the evening. She sighed inwardly. Duty called.

"Okay, then. I'll see you later," she said, leaning forward and impulsively kissing him on both cheeks, European style. She felt him linger a second with his lips returning the kiss on her left cheek before he leaned back and bid her goodbye.

"Give my best to Avery," he said, "and call me if you don't feel like riding the metro back to *Passy*. I can meet you half way...I can always use the exercise." His lips curled into a crooked grin and, with a wave, he turned and strode down the street in the direction of the Eiffel Tower.

Juliet reviewed the lovely hours she'd spent with Finn as she labored up the six flights of stairs to Avery's flat, but once inside, she immediately sprang into action.

"How does a dinner of scrambled eggs and sausage sound?" she offered after a quick survey of the contents of Avery's miniscule refrigerator.

"Given I have one burner, it has great appeal," Avery replied, leaning back on pillows Juliet had placed behind her after helping her move from the stool next to the wooden easel to her bed.

"How'd the painting go?" she asked.

"Not great."

"No? I'm sorry. Maybe it's too soon for you to stay seated for so long a time?"

"I just couldn't…get into it." Avery glanced at the canvas on her easel.

Juliet served their meager dinner on a small tray and held her own plate in her lap as the two ate their supper in companionable silence. After a few minutes describing the sights she'd seen at the botanical and Luxembourg gardens, Juliet brought up the idea of Jamie coming to Paris "…to keep you company over the holidays. He has time off since the editing department shuts down during the last two weeks in December."

To Juliet's relief, Avery was both touched and delighted at the prospect.

"I was already getting into a serious funk, knowing you'd be leaving soon," she said. "What did you have to do to bribe Jamie to give up his vacation?"

"He was the one who suggested it," Juliet said. "Spending Christmas over here with you was all *his* idea, and Finn said he could stay on his couch while he's here."

"Really? What sweethearts those two guys are."

Impulsively, Juliet said, "Jamie's been really worried about you, you know? Do you mind if I ask you if...you were ever attracted to him? I definitely think he is to you."

Avery stared at her hands folded in her lap. "Jamie?" She raised her head and met Juliet's gaze. "I might have been, if things had been different."

"Different how? You mean about working for the same company?"

"Yes, that...and other things."

"What other things?" Juliet asked, taking Avery's plate with her own and heading for the small sink under the eaves. Behind her she heard Avery inhale a deep breath.

"You really don't know, do you?"

Juliet placed their dirty plates in the sink with a clatter and turned around.

"Know *what*? What are you talking about?"

"That Brad and I...had a major disagreement about...well, about the design department and how things should be run in the company."

Juliet leaned back against the sink and rolled her eyes. "It no secret you two didn't agree on the direction we were going with the video war games, that's for darn sure."

"It was more than that."

"More? How more?"

Juliet wondered at Avery's long pause, followed by another inhaled breath.

"Brad repeatedly tried to jump on my bones. Big Time."

"Oh, shit! Really?" Juliet raised both hands as if warding off a blow. "Of course, really. Okay. Tell me. Everything."

"Well, you asked for it," Avery said, shaking her head in warning.

Juliet wiped her hands on a nearby dishtowel and took a seat at the end of the bed.

"Shoot."

In the next few minutes, Avery spoke in a cool, calm voice, describing that Brad had "put serious moves" on her not long after making her design director.

"As you probably noticed, he and I met outside the office a few times, always, I see now, under the guise of talking business, but really because he wanted me...to... basically...sleep with him whenever he asked."

"Oh, please! This is truly hideous!"

Avery was gazing into space with a faraway look as she recounted the details of a particular event that triggered her quitting GatherGames. "One evening when I was in the art department after everyone, including you, had gone home, he came in and wanted me to go to dinner to 'discuss a situation that needed to be resolved,' he said. He sounded so serious, I figured it must be something that was actually important, so I went. When I got in his car, he drove us to your hotel."

"What an absolute jerk!" Juliet groaned.

"He said he'd ordered up dinner from room service and once we were in his suite, he immediately tried to...well, no, *claimed* I wanted sex just as much as he did because I'd come upstairs with him. I protested that jumping into his turned-down bed with a chocolate on the pillow wasn't what I provided in the way of artistic services. He got mad and grabbed my arm."

"Oh lord! What did you do?"

"At that moment, I picked up one of the silver covers keeping our dinner hot and aimed it at his head—but my arm wasn't long enough—so I banged him hard on the shoulder. He didn't fall down, but at least he lost his grip on me and I ran out of the suite—straight into your *other* brother who was coming down the hall."

Juliet covered her face with her hands, moaning between her fingers. "Jamie lives two doors down the corridor from him. Did you tell him what happened?"

"No...but Jamie saw that I looked a complete wreck, and I was only a few feet from Brad's front door."

Juliet removed her hands from her eyes. "So you didn't tell anyone what had happened, and the next day you quit," she stated flatly.

Juliet remembered how Brad kept rubbing his shoulder that same day Avery announced her resignation. When she'd asked him about it, he said he'd hurt it playing squash. It was probably bruised black and blue from Avery's banging the domed food cover against him in her attempt to escape his clutches.

Juliet said, "Don't you imagine Jamie has a good idea why you left GatherGames, given you ran into him right afterward?"

Avery slipped lower on the pillows. Pursing her lips, she replied, "Probably, but I just left without ever speaking to him again." She suddenly rose up on her elbows, her eyes flashing. "However, you should know that I didn't walk out of that office until I negotiated a *very* generous severance package out of Herr Thayer, thank you very much!" She fell back against the pillows, spent. "Believe me, I was thinking of quitting long before all this happened, and in a weird way, I was relieved."

"And so you recommended me as your replacement to save any of the other women from risking harassment?"

Avery scowled at her across the bed, energized again by her anger. "You were totally ready to assume the job and deserved a promotion—*and* a raise—which I hope you got! And as I've said a million times, commercial graphic art isn't my thing. Video war games aren't my thing. The entire dot-com world wasn't my thing! I was drifting down the wrong path and I knew months before this happened that I should get out of there. Amazingly, my mini trust fund from my dad had recently kicked in—which was a total surprise, actually—and that, blessedly, gave me an ace up my sleeve when it came to playing hardball with Brad about my severance package."

"Good timing…" Juliet murmured. "And nice of your dad."

"Guilt," she said shortly. "But even before the dust up with Brad, I didn't do anything about leaving the company because, basically, I didn't want to abandon you and Jamie to that world…and I could see you both had many more ties to it than I did. Brad's stupid move gave me the kick in the butt I needed to get outta there." She shut her eyes, exhausted. "And now…how about *you* getting out of *here*? I'm wiped. See you *à demain*," she finished sleepily in French.

Juliet remained motionless at the bottom of Avery's bed for several minutes, staring out the gabled window over the frost-covered roofs of the city. *Who could have imagined that because of Brad's assault, my best friend would come to Paris and make a pal of Jean-Pierre, also studying portrait painting at L'École. Then, one night, out of nowhere, some guy with a Kalashnikov would rush into a little, neighborhood Cambodian restaurant and…*

Juliet's eyes filled with tears and she pressed her hand against her mouth to keep from making a sound that might wake Avery. It was just as Finn had said…*unintended consequences… actions… and reactions that no one could predict.*

No wonder visual images of traumatic events could repeat and repeat in the mind's eye. In her own head, a whirlwind of thoughts revolved around her elder brother physically coercing her best friend; of two art students being mowed down by strangers bursting through the door of a neighborhood restaurant; of Finn grabbing her to dive for cover at the sound of a car back-firing…

She watched Avery's breathing become deep and regular while she tried to absorb the impact of what Brad had done to the woman sleeping in this tiny garret in Paris. She considered the way that everything she and Avery were dealing with currently had flowed from that single event. But despite all that, she realized her dearest friend was in the right place, now, and doing the right thing.

Juliet glanced at Avery's easel, where a portrait of an intriguing man of middle years stared back at her. Some would judge his hair in need of a trim, but the strands strafing his collar and his direct gaze gave him an appealing, raffish look of an artist or writer. Avery's portrait depicted a person it would be interesting to get to know and Juliet marveled that Avery still had the guts to keep on keeping on, despite everything that had happened since she'd begun the canvas.

You inspire me, Avery Evans…and I'm just warning you, I might turn up back here sooner than you ever imagined.

Juliet carefully rose from Avery's bed so as not to awake her, knowing that at least two of the three Thayer siblings would dedicate themselves to helping her survive this nightmare, especially after learning the part their oldest brother had played. And then she silently padded down the six flights of stairs and let herself out of Avery's building. The streets were deserted and for a moment, she felt a stab of apprehension at the thought of walking to the metro alone. Should she call Finn? She pulled her cell phone out just as a taxi approached and she flagged it down with a wash of relief. Settling into the back seat as the red numbers of the meter flashed, her thoughts drifted to Finn. Would she have ever met him if she hadn't rushed to Avery's side? She reminded herself for the hundredth time that despite the attraction she had begun to sense they both had been feeling, he was still, technically, a married man, with a number of devils, as he called them, to wrestle in the coming months—and perhaps forever. And soon, she'd be six thousand miles away.

She was startled when the cab halted abruptly. Her mind had been wandering and she hadn't even noticed they'd crossed to the Right Bank. Through the taxi's window she spied *L'Étoile de Paris* below the spot on the road where the driver had pulled up to the curb. Across the water, the glowing Eiffel Tower beckoned her welcome.

"*Ici, Madam?*" he inquired gruffly.

It was late and Juliet imagined it must be unnerving to drive at night in a city where other terrorists might be contemplating new attacks. She hastened to assure the cab driver he'd stopped in the right place.

"*Oui, oui, monsieur. Merci beaucoup.*"

She handed him the euros noted on the meter, plus a few more to show her appreciation, and got out of the car. Lights were still on in the barge's pilothouse, and as she mounted the gangway, she caught sight of Finn in his leather chair, a book flat on his chest and his eyes closed. Peering more closely through the windows, she saw he'd already made up her bed on the sofa and turned down the covers.

What a kind and thoughtful guy he is...

Even though they'd known each other such a short time and under very bizarre circumstances, and they were just friends—or pretending to be—she had never experienced such consideration and care from any man in her life. What would it be like if she moved to Paris? What would it be like if the two of them—

She called an abrupt halt to such meanderings and tapped lightly on the door. In the next instant, Finn leapt to his feet, then sank to a crouch, his eyes darting frantically to the far corners of the cabin before they locked on her figure peering through the window at him from outside on the deck.

She watched him take a deep, steadying breath and then attempt to smile. He rose to his full height once more and crossed the stateroom to open the door.

"It's...you," he said. He briefly covered his eyes with his fingers and shook his head as if attempting to rid himself of whatever images were in his brain. "You're back."

"Yes, I'm back," she repeated in a deliberately casual tone, stepping over the threshold and gently closing the door behind her. In the silence that hung heavily between them, she draped her coat on a spoke of the boat's wheel next his jacket. Turning around, she asked, "How about I make us some of that Sleep Well tea you have? I sure could use a cup."

"Obviously, so could I." After a moment's pause, he made no effort to dismiss his odd reaction to someone attempting to enter his lair. He gestured toward the chair from which he'd leapt to his feet and said, as if he were angry with himself, "just when I thought it was safe to go back into the water...the shark bites again."

He crossed the pilothouse in the direction of his makeshift kitchen, brushing past her without meeting her gaze. "But, let me make the tea. Feel free to go below to get ready for bed."

Juliet remained standing where she was in the middle of the upper cabin, watching him pull out a brown, earthenware teapot and a tin of loose tea, realizing that he had a very big struggle ahead of him and would most likely think himself unfit for female company for a long time to come. She was startled to feel a pang of sympathy not only for herself—since she could no longer deny that she was very drawn to this man—but strangely, also for his wife Kim. Whatever had passed between them, the last few years must have been its own kind of nightmare.

The next day, Juliet found herself replaying the moment when Finn jumped up from his reading chair with a look of panic in his eyes. Adding his emotional state to her list of worries, she entered Avery's flat, determined to persuade her to let her own father know of his daughter's whereabouts and her continuing fragile condition. Juliet had brought her laptop with her and swiftly composed a draft email to him while Avery was brushing her teeth and choosing what to wear for the day.

"Here," Juliet announced a few minutes later, holding the computer screen in front of her friend. "Read this. I think you should send it...or something close to it. I'm leaving soon and your father should know what's happened to you. He's in New York and could get here much faster than I could if there was another emergency."

Avery's lips compressed while she absorbed the proposed message.

"I just gave him the facts," Juliet said, hoping Avery wouldn't be furious with her. "It only says that you've been living in Paris this last year; that you were shot in the terrorist attacks on November thirteenth, that you're recuperating well here at number seven, near the art school where you've been studying advanced portraiture. It's just basic information, Avery...nothing more. And he deserves to have it!"

Avery continued to stare at Juliet's composition until she leaned forward, and with her good hand, typed in, one letter at a time, her father's email address and savagely pushed the 'send' button.

"There! Are you satisfied?" she demanded, tight-lipped. "Fat lot of reaction you'll get. Now, can you help me on with these damn jeans?"

By the time Juliet had assisted Avery into her clothes, she heard a ping resounding from her computer.

"Well, well, what do you know?" Juliet chuckled,

trying to keep the "I told you so" out of her voice while peering at the screen. "Here's a reply from someone named Carolyn Bryson that your father is in China on a business trip 'with uncertain internet access,' she says, but that you will hear from him 'the very minute' she's back in contact with him and adds she's very distressed to hear what happened to you."

"Don't hold your breath about my dad," Avery said, turning away and rummaging with one hand in her sock drawer. "He always has employed very nice administrative assistants who eventually just respond 'sorry, period' to me in one form or another."

"Well, this Carolyn person adds, 'Your father had word that you were living in France and was very worried. I'm sure it will be a great relief to know you are safe and recovering—news I will tell him as soon as I am in touch.'"

"How would he know I was living in France?" Avery demanded.

"Maybe he was worried he hadn't heard from you in a year and called someone in San Francisco who knew you'd come over here? Then, when he heard about the Paris attacks, he mentioned to his assistant how concerned he was. This Ms. Bryson sounds great."

Avery remained silent for a moment, and then said, "Well, we shall see if I actually hear from the man himself."

Until she'd been shot, Avery had made it a practice never to discuss her parents, other than in a few biting comments over the years, leaving Juliet to conclude that her friend had been disappointed by her mother and father any number of times in the past.

"Okay, then," Juliet said with deliberate cheer, "let's leave it alone and see what happens. Meanwhile, which doc is it today?"

Silently, Juliet told herself she could only hope that the dramatic events in Paris would be enough to prompt

Stephen Evans to reach out to his injured daughter who suffered from more than just physical wounds to her arm and shoulder. Meanwhile, Avery pointed to her winter coat draped over a chair, along with piles of clothes she hadn't managed to put away.

"No doctor appointments today, thank God. Today I want to put on that coat, walk to school, and sit in on one of my portrait painting classes."

Juliet reacted first with pleasure that Avery was making efforts to put her life back together. Then came a wave of worry.

"Are you sure you're ready to do this? I mean, revisiting *L'École* so soon after—" She fumbled for words that avoided mentioning Jean-Pierre Grenelle. "You haven't seen anybody from there yet and you've only been able to sit up for short periods of time."

"As you said yourself, Juliet, you'll be leaving soon and I have to face it all on my own at some point. Why not today, when you'll be right there beside me?"

CHAPTER 14

L'École des Beaux Arts was an easy walk from the flat, but Juliet hailed a taxi as soon as she and Avery emerged on *Rue de Lille*.

"Save your strength for climbing that first flight of stairs at school," she advised.

Upon their arrival, their handbags, per usual, were searched and then they slowly ascended the wide cement stairway at the entrance, making their way down a corridor to an open door, forty feet away. Juliet described her earlier trip to explore where her forebear earned her certificate in architecture at the close of the nineteenth century. As they drew closer, they could hear a male voice lecturing in French on the shading of faces on a canvas to create a subject's realistic bone structure. And then they arrived at the threshold where some dozen students stood by their easels, listening intently to their professor, a tall man of middle years in a white, cotton, paint-spattered smock. He stood commandingly in front of the class making quick marks with a pencil on a canvas with the faintest outline of a human head.

Avery motioned to Juliet that they should remain outside the door and to listen to the instructor's directions as the class drew to a close at the end of the hour. Juliet glanced at the high ceiling above her head and heard the murmur of other classes that were also in session in this wing of the school. Suddenly, it struck her that she was probably standing at the very spot Julia Thayer, née Bradshaw, had passed by many times, more than a hundred years before. She was no longer conscious of the students inside the classroom asking questions of their professor.

Her mind filled with what it must have been like to be a bona fide student here a century ago. A swarm of resolutions buzzed in her head.

I must study here! I must take landscape painting classes. I must do the art I am meant to create...

"C'mon, Juliet!" Avery whispered hoarsely. "Class is over."

Startled from her reverie, she followed Avery into a large room that smelled pungently of turpentine. The space was littered with a raft of easels and various half-finished portraits leaning against them. A table stood against one wall with brushes soaking in large jars and paint-encrusted rags piled in one corner.

"Avery! *Ah, Cherie! Regardez, tout le monde!* Avery *est revenue pour nous!*"

Yes, thought Juliet with silent thanks, Avery had, indeed, come back to "everyone" in the portrait class—a miracle, given what had happened to Jean-Pierre, as the teacher sorrowfully explained to his class.

The new arrivals were soon surrounded by students who had also known J-P, as he was being referred to in rapid French by several offering their condolences and pressing Avery for information about what had happened that horrible night.

Juliet watched with alarm as Avery struggled to keep her emotions in check, which she managed to do until the last of her classmates departed. Within seconds, she collapsed in tears against Juliet's shoulder. "I'm s-sorry, but seeing everyone was like reliving it all over again!"

"Oh, sweetie," Juliet replied, stroking her back, "that was what I was afraid of." She gazed at the class instructor who looked strangely familiar. In a flash of recognition, she remembered the portrait Avery had been working on all week. It must be of Alain Devereux, her professor and the man who was the first person to send Avery flowers at the hospital with a card that asked when he could come see her.

Avery sank onto a stool near an easel, her head shaking from side to side. "While everyone was asking me questions," she said, wiping her eyes with the back of the hand not restrained by her shoulder sling, "all I could think about was J-P standing up from the table at the restaurant when the shooting started... throwing me to the floor... covering my body with his. His friends, here, will never see him again, and—"

Juliet sent Avery's teacher a look of desperation. The tall, lanky man swiftly strode to her side. Every aspect of his demeanor was one of deep concern and sympathy and Juliet instantly took a liking to him. He put a gentle arm around Avery's good shoulder and in English said, "I am so happy to see you, *cherie*. It was brave of you to visit us here so soon. When you said you were coming, I had hoped it wouldn't be too much for you, so soon after..." He floundered an instant. "So soon after your terrible injuries."

So *Professeur* Devereux had been speaking by phone to Avery recently, Juliet noted silently, observing that Alain's arm remained around her friend's shoulder.

"Maybe you're right," replied Avery. "Maybe coming here so soon wasn't such a good idea." She inhaled a few deep breaths to try to regain her composure. Meanwhile, Juliet introduced herself to Alain and suggested that she and Avery head back to the flat.

"But I want to be able to come here!" Avery cried. "Painting is the only thing that means my world will go on after...after—"

Alain stepped back and took his student's chin gently in his hand. "Of course you should start painting again. But rather than here, with all your memories so fresh, why not work at my atelier? You can come there, even if I'm here teaching. If you find it too difficult to be where Jean-Pierre used to be—perhaps you'll feel more yourself working in my studio. We can have lunch. We can have dinner. I will give you instruction, just as I would here, until you feel better. Would you like that?"

Avery's tears had stopped and she met Alain's glance with the most vulnerable expression Juliet had ever witnessed on her friend's face. "Would you allow that, Alain? Would you let me work in your private studio?"

He nodded with a broad smile to confirm his invitation.

Avery turned to Juliet. "You know, don't you," she said with obvious pride, "that Alain Devereux is one of the finest portrait painters working in France today? He's painted everyone who's anyone in Paris and has just been given a commission from a current cabinet minister, haven't you?" she declared, turning back to her instructor.

Devereux shrugged and merely said, "*Oui.*"

Juliet repressed a smile. Was Avery smitten with her painting instructor? Had they been seeing each other outside of class before she was felled by the terrorist attack? Then she thought about her brother Jamie and wondered if his playing "rescue ranger," as her mother had accused her of doing when she flew to Paris, was such a great idea after all? Given the signals she'd seen exchanged between Avery and Alain, she certainly didn't want Jamie to have his heart broken.

Hey…let them figure it all out!

After all, Avery said she liked the idea of having company for the holidays. Maybe Alain Devereux is a married man, she thought, relieved, and was just being kind.

Just like Finn…

Juliet cast a friendly smile in Alain's direction as Avery clutched his arm with her free hand. Her eyes darted around the classroom as if she were picturing Jean-Pierre at one of the easels. Juliet could see another wave of sadness had her in its grip.

To Alain Avery declared, "I absolutely hate that Juliet's going back to San Francisco." Her shaking voice showed the difficulty she still had controlling her emotions.

Meanwhile, a ping on Juliet's phone announced a message. It was from Finn.

> **Since you've set the date for your departure, can I take you and Avery to Le Bistro de Paris tonight? It's only a few blocks from her flat.**

Juliet waved her phone in the air. "That's from my landlord," she joked, hoping to cheer up Avery. "Let me just call him. I'll be right back."

She trotted down the corridor, anxious to be out of earshot. Finn answered on the first ring. After they exchanged greetings and Juliet thanked him for his invitation to dinner, she described Avery's emotional state after having seen her classmates at art school for the first time since the shootings and the death of Jean-Pierre.

"I'll ask her about dinner, but she's had a real setback, I think. Frankly, I don't think she's up to going out again tonight."

"Well...okay. I understand."

"But I'm really glad you called," she hastened to add, "because I need to talk to you. We don't have to have dinner, or anything, but could you possibly meet me—now—for coffee or something?"

"Absolutely. What's up?"

"I need to ask you about...well... *PTSD*. From what just happened here at the art school, I think Avery is showing some serious signs and—"

"Of course," Finn interrupted. "Why don't you take

Avery back to her apartment and I'll pick you up in half an hour?" He paused. "How about I take you to a street that's already decorated to the max for Christmas…and with the most wonderful pastries you ever tasted? It's bound to cheer us both up and you can take a treat back to the patient. Sugar helps, I've found."

She knew he was joking, of course, but his response soothed her somehow. A few minutes later, Alain walked the two women to the front of the school and saw them safely into a taxi for the short ride back to number seven. Once upstairs, Avery waved away Juliet's help and wiggled out of her jeans on her own.

"Let me help you with your sweater," Juliet insisted.

"Okay," Avery grumbled, "but I've almost figured out the trick to do it on my own, Ms. Busy Body."

A weary Avery allowed Juliet to pull back the covers so she could climb into bed.

"Have a nap," urged Juliet. "I'll bring you back something for supper."

"Don't," Avery murmured. "I just want to sleep. I'll see you tomorrow."

Would she sleep, Juliet wondered, or wake with nightmares? Was Avery starting to "isolate," or did she simply need some time alone? Juliet couldn't wait to put her questions to Finn.

Thankfully, he was waiting at the curb in his MG when Juliet trudged downstairs and they quickly drove across the Seine to the Right Bank and onwards to the *Rue Rambuteau* in the 3rd *Arrondissement*.

"First we go to *Pain du Sucre*, if you don't mind," he said, his eyes scanning for a place to park. "It's a great bakery and I am on a mission."

Juliet looked down the straight little street that stood chock-a-block with pastry shops and small cafés on both sides. Pine Christmas garlands studded with rosy apples stretched above several windows jammed with every imaginable culinary temptation.

"Mmmm…" Juliet moaned. "Forget dinner. Let's just gorge on macaroons and chocolate éclairs."

Finn spotted a car pulling out and he swiftly guided the little MG to take its spot.

"This place is already a zoo, but I promised Claudine I'd put in an order for her annual *buche de Noël* that she serves at her Christmas Eve party."

"They must be something special if you have to sign up a month ahead of time. A *buche de Noël* is one of those chocolate cakes that looks like a Yule log, right?"

"Trust me, they're so special that after December fifth, it'll be chef-versus-chef battling it out on this street trying to get their orders honored," he declared with a mock grim expression. "C'mon. Follow me!"

The narrow thoroughfare was noisy and crowded as they made their way to *Pain du Sucre*, a storefront aglow with tiny lights and packed solid with shoppers. After waiting in line for fifteen minutes before Finn could place his order for pick-up on December 24th, he also purchased a small apple tart, glazed golden with caramelized sugar syrup on its top and perched on a platform of pastry so flaky, the sales woman took over a minute to carefully ease it into a box. As Finn waited for his change, he suggested they pick up a spinach quiche next door.

"We can take our booty back to the barge and you can give me the details of what you think may be going on with Avery."

Grateful for Finn's plan, Juliet nodded, and within ten minutes, they were parked near the quay that led down to the boat. Finn heated the quiche briefly in his toaster oven and served it with a small green salad.

"I wish I had a real oven, but I've learned to live without one," he said with a laugh, pointing to the small, electric appliance.

"This salad dressing is delicious!" Juliet enthused, her mouth full of the first forkful of lettuce and arugula from her plate.

"I just learned to make it this week," he disclosed with a smug smile. 'You like?"

"I *definitely* like. Do you share your recipes?"

"Only with people *I* like..." He gave her a steady glance across the sofa where they had taken up their usual positions, plates on laps. "I'll text it to you later."

Juliet felt her cheeks flush but kept her eyes on her plate and kept chewing.

After a moment's silence, Finn proposed, "And now I want to watch your face when you tuck into this spinach-and-egg confection."

Juliet inserted her fork into the quiche and tasted her first bite, allowing her tongue to roll over the spinach laced with more *crème fraiche* than she wanted to think about. Savoring the wonderful mix of flavors, including a dash of nutmeg, she rolled her eyes in appreciation.

"Oh...my...goodness," she breathed. "There's quiche, and then there's *this* quiche! It's heavenly."

Finn refilled her glass with liquid rubies. "And the wine? I bought you a bottle of a great Bordeaux—at least I remember it being pretty incredible."

"It's fabulous." She took a swallow and smiled at him. "Are you trying to get me drunk?"

"Maybe a little... I could tell on the phone how upset you were."

When they had finished their meal, he rose to brew two espressos while she carried their plates to the sink with its straight-on view of the Eiffel Tower. She could no longer deny that she would dearly miss not only the good food, but also the incredible surroundings and the wonderful sense of warmth and compatibility she'd experienced on Finn's barge.

"Here you go," he said, pouring the steaming brew from his glass coffee pot into demitasse cups. "I know it's sacrilegious, but want some hot milk?"

She nodded, and then took a sip of the coffee and closed her eyes, savoring its delicious taste and aroma.

"Ah...but wait!" he chided her. "You must have a bite of this first!" He fed her a forkful of the apple confection he'd called *tarte tartin* with a dollop of whipped cream.

Obediently, she chewed and swallowed and then slowly shook her head.

"You know, don't you," she murmured, "that you're driving me crazy? How am I going to eat all my meals at my desk after this?"

Finn raised an eyebrow and then surprised her by removing her coffee cup from her hand. He set it on the counter near his coffeepot and leaned toward her. When their lips met, Juliet imagined she tasted deliciously of apple and cinnamon and sweet cream, just as he did.

"I want you to promise me you'll never eat at your desk again," he said softly, "unless it's a truffle or two that I air express from *Pain du Sucre*..."

"Or," she murmured, "just send me a *tarte tartin*..."

Their kiss deepened and Finn's arms pulled her against the length of him. Juliet's mind flew in all directions, mostly with flashes of Jed, and then Kim's pretty face in the family photo at the Air Force Academy on Finn's graduation day. But finally, everything faded in the wake of Finn's nuzzling her ear and then cupping her face in his hands to return to kissing her, producing electric sensations from their two bodies pressed hard against each other.

"Do you have any idea how luscious you are?" he muttered, "And I don't just mean how you taste."

His arms lowered and his hands slid below her waist, pressing her derriere firmly so her pelvis melded with his own, his long legs pressing against hers so tightly, she could feel his arousal.

"Oh, Finn…are we being crazy? I'm leaving and you're mar—"

"I know!" he said, his tone fierce, pulling back to look her in the eye. "Not very honorable of me, but I couldn't fight it anymore."

"Whatever 'it' is, that makes two of us," she acknowledged while willing herself to move half a step away. She reached out and laid a hand lightly on each of his broad shoulders, thrusting out her lower lip in a mock scowl. "All what's going through my head right now is how I dread going home, and how I just want to curl up and—"

Finn mirrored her actions, taking hold of her shoulders as well. Stopping her words, he leaned forward and brushed his lips against hers once more.

"I just want to curl up with *you*—and I should tell you, you must be part of my 'cure' because I haven't felt like this in about four years."

She glanced down at his waistline, unable to repress a knowing smile. "Feel like what?" she said with mock innocence.

He pulled her roughly to him once more. "Like *this*," he said emphatically, pressing her close so she had no doubt as to what he meant. Then he held her more gently and sprinkled tiny kisses on the top of her head before he took a step back. "But I suppose you're right about keeping our cool."

Regretting her own step back before she took it, Juliet nodded her agreement.

"You suppose right, flyboy," she said with a shaky laugh. "I'm not sure I've *ever* felt quite like this, but we each have got very complicated lives right now, agreed?"

"That would be an understatement." He dropped his

hands by his sides. "I am probably the definition of 'not fit for combat duty.'"

"By that do you mean having a close connection with someone of the female persuasion?"

"I don't trust myself," he said in a low voice. "I feel so much better, now, but I don't know if I'm truly coming out of the tunnel. Until I do know, I don't want to make your life even more complicated."

"Ditto," she said with a sad smile. "My tunnel is this damn situation with my family and my job." She reached out and squeezed both his hands, wishing silently she could draw him back into the embrace that had felt so wonderful. Instead she let go and said, "Hey! We're doing the right thing, aren't we? And besides, we're supposed to be talking about Avery. I saw so clearly today what a very tenuous state she's in and you're the only person I know who probably understands what she's going through."

Finn nodded, and Juliet knew that the moment of crossing the Rubicon had passed. They would remain on opposite shores. They would not fall into each other's arms tonight and let the consequences be damned because the consequences were about as serious as they could get. She knew it and so did Finn.

"Let's go back to the couch," he proposed. "You, on your end. Me, on mine."

"All right, but first I'm going to get ready for bed, okay?"

"Tights and all?" he asked with mock solemnity. "No frilly French nighty to drive me out of my mind?"

"No nighty…just my chastity tights. Seems like a good idea, under the circumstances."

"It probably is."

Juliet noted his tight jaw, but a wry smile had just begun to appear on his normally clean-shaven face that, by this hour, had a very sexy shadow along his chin.

"Be right back," Juliet said, with a hint of regret, and headed down below to change.

As the evening wore on, Finn gazed across the sofa and wondered at the rush of feelings prompted by the woman sitting three feet from him, her legs curled under the blanket that would cover her while she slept—alone—aboard the barge one last night.

There was no denying the truth: Juliet Thayer had crashed into his life at a moment of tragedy and grief and he would sorely miss her company when she left. There had to be more than just the family business pulling her home when her best friend obviously needed her help for a few weeks longer. *There must be a guy in San Francisco. No woman as attractive, accomplished or loyal as she is would be without men stumbling all over themselves to be with her.*

While she described the symptoms she'd witnessed with Avery earlier that day at art school, Finn felt his breath catch and his gut churn at the thought of Juliet seriously involved with someone in her hometown. But, in fact, it was all very, *very* complicated. If he didn't see things through with Kim and didn't know, for certain, that he was no longer a danger to anyone—a danger to lovely, honest, talented Juliet—he might spoil everything in the long run.

I guess when you really care about someone's welfare more than just your own, you're flying at a higher altitude, Finn, my boy.

It was probably a good thing that Juliet was going back to San Francisco. It would be nothing but push-pull until he'd got the divorce papers signed and finally concluded his relationship with his soon-to-be-ex-wife.

Juliet's next question roused him from his wandering thoughts.

"So, now that I've described what happened today in her painting class, do you think it's a good or bad idea if

Avery tries to work at her teacher's studio every day? What if even *that* sets off her anxiety, like what happened today in the classroom? Maybe I should make her find someone like your shrink who can help her deal with her version of PTSD—if you think that's what's really going on here?"

"You and I aren't the docs," Finn reminded her, doing his best to concentrate on the subject at hand. "First of all, she needs a definite diagnosis, and I'm happy to introduce her to Dr. Abel at the American Hospital."

"Is he experienced in all varieties of post trauma? I mean, Avery wasn't in a war, like you were."

"Doctor Sonja Abel is a 'she,'" Finn corrected Juliet, "and in my humble opinion, what happened at *Le Petit Cambodge* was very like what happened to us in places like Fallujah. You'd be sitting somewhere, supposedly safe, and wham! An AK47 or Kalashnikov would suddenly go off and the guy on your right was dead or dying."

Juliet nodded somberly. "At least, for starters, let's try to get her to your doctor."

Finn agreed, adding, "If you want, I'll set it up and take her as soon as I can get her an appointment. Dr. Abel has been in touch with these Harvard guys I told you about that were former vets and now are doctors and professors. Their latest research shows pretty conclusively that for some, it's not only the emotional trauma that does damage when you experience tough stuff, but also that the brain itself can be physically damaged even by just the tremendous force of the *sound* waves coming from the blast itself. Avery was exposed to many bursts of fire, shot at close range."

"But what is it, again, that actually gets damaged if it's only loud sound wave blasts," Juliet asked skeptically, "and not actual physical wounds to the head?"

"Not to get too technical," he said, wiggling the fingers of both hands an inch apart, "remember I told you about the parts of the brain that exchange messages...the neuron receptors?" Juliet nodded, staring at his large hands. "Well, imagine those neuron receptors are the tips of my fingers, here, and the sound blasts push them out of alignment. The synapses—the energy signals telling the brain what to do that whip back and forth in the space that exists between the neuron receptors—can't get the messages to transfer from one receptor to the other. The normal linkages don't match up...don't connect...*because* of this misalignment."

"So Avery's problems may not just be a fight-or-flight reaction due to fear of bad things about to happen again? Things might have *physically* got shaken up in her head?"

"Possibly. This stuff is all very new. The more sensitive MRI machines that the researchers at Harvard developed can see subtle changes in the way the neuron receptors in the brain are misaligned or disconnected in people who experienced the concussive force of explosions and their resulting sounds—even if the bomb didn't hit them."

"What are the signs in a person when the...ah...synapses don't snap correctly?"

"Well...sleep problems, and being startled by the wrong stuff, like what happened when we came out of the café that night—"

"Or when I merely opened the pilothouse door that night?"

"Exactly. Then there's the big, obvious stuff, like horrible headaches, and memory loss and getting spooked when a room fills up with too many people. Of course, there's the big, *big* stuff like not remembering when the Vice-President gave you a Silver Star or something. But there's also stupid, annoying things, like suddenly having no idea how to count your change at Burger King, or how, soon after your injuries, to turn on a tricky heat valve in your Paris apartment, and so forth."

"Wow…" Juliet murmured.

Finn nodded. "Yeah…it's a lot to take in, but Dr. Abel is up on it all. Hopefully, with time and work on Avery's part, she'll be able to overcome a lot of what's troubling her in the aftermath of the attacks. Sometimes nerves repair themselves…slowly, for sure." He met Juliet's worried gaze from across the sofa. "And there may be drugs that can be designed to block the wrong signals getting through, or help restore the good signals between neuron receptors. We know the brain has amazing plasticity," he added, with an encouraging smile. "And sometimes it's thought the neurons can forage new pathways around the damage. Dr. Abel told me that for some people, good experiences teach their brains to respond in a different fashion than in the bad, old, post-trauma way."

"You mean, kind of carve new pathways, new connections?"

"You are one, smart lady," he said with a smile. "But yeah. For me, it's probably going to mean a combination of cures. At least, let's hope that turns out to be true."

Was he trying too hard to convince her that he'd eventually be okay?

"Well, at least, the drug companies are working on it, aren't they?" she asked.

Finn hesitated. "So far, Big Pharma has been slow to risk money on developing new drugs for this type of brain injury, but Dr. Abel swears that the guys who pioneered these theories won't give up till they do."

Juliet looked away.

Does she think I'm probably a hopeless case? Not worth keeping in touch with, except when it comes to Avery?

Maybe he was.

She rose from the sofa, hands on hips and pointed to the door to the stateroom and bathroom below the salon.

"Stay right here, will you? I drank a lot of coffee," she said apologetically, "And I have a couple of more questions to ask you before we call it a night."

CHAPTER 15

Juliet came up the wooden stairs after her trip to the head and resumed her position on the couch while Finn had remained in his corner.

"I was just wondering," she said, settling her back against the cushions and pulling the blanket over her legs. "What generally sets off a person with PTSD? I mean, obviously, that car backfiring that night on the street *sounded* like gunfire—and even I had the instinct to duck—but Avery only started to get wiggy when she was in that restaurant as it began to fill up with customers. At *L'École*, she began to shake when her classmates crowded around, wanting to know the details of what happened to J-P."

"My guess is those were scenes that mirrored the moment the shooters entered the crowded restaurant and opened fire. Her brain went right back to relive that moment."

Juliet nodded slowly. "If you don't mind telling me," she asked, titling her head to one side, "what other kinds of things can set *you* off, for instance?"

She saw that Finn took a deep breath and appeared to come to some conclusion. In a low voice, he began to describe the triggers that still had the power to affect him.

"Loud, unexpected noises, mostly, which I trace back to the blast when my helicopter was hit. I had a busted up leg, of course, that hurt like hell. Later—probably because my head got pounded in the crash—I developed ice-pick-in-the-brain headaches for a year, which finally went away."

"But you got past a lot of that, and were even able to go to Nevada to fly drones, so why did you suddenly retreat to Paris?"

A long pause became total silence between them. Finn looked over his shoulder, toward the stairs leading down to his stateroom, appearing for all the world to Juliet as if he wanted to bolt. Instead, he slowly turned his head back and met her troubled gaze.

"After a year, I pretty much recovered from the physical damage as far as the VA doctors were concerned, but…then I entered those unmarked trailers in the American desert and shook hands with the devil."

"What do you mean?"

"The very first week I was there I had my first drone kill."

"And…?" she asked, careful to keep her tone neutral.

"And…just as I released the Hellfire missile on what were termed 'high value targets', a little boy came chasing after his dog who had run around the corner of the compound."

"Oh, no…" she whispered.

"Once you push the button, the missile takes fifty-five seconds to reach its target. The drones taking off in the Middle East have mounted cameras on the unmanned plane. Our monitor screens in Nevada showed everything that happened in the target area."

"Oh…God…" she moaned.

"I sat there in that cushy leather chair, knowing that in a few more seconds that six-year-old kid would be blown to particles so small, no one could identify him."

"Finn…" Juliet said, her throat tight.

"Then I watched on that damn screen as the child's mother, who was a block away, came screaming and crying down the street when she saw her house had been flattened and was burning white hot. We saw her arrive on the scene and dive into the ashes, searing her hands and arms, frantically trying to find her little son."

"Oh, Jesus…" Juliet murmured, her eyes filled with tears.

Finn continued to lock glances. "Right then, our shift was over and the next team walked into the trailer. I went back to my house at the base where Kim happened to have invited people over for a barbeque that night. She was annoyed that I was late. She wanted me to cook hotdogs on the grill and pass out the beer."

"And you weren't allowed to say anything about what had happened that day? You couldn't tell her you'd just blown up a—?"

"You got it," he interrupted harshly. His own eyes were moist. "I watched the charcoal burning white hot beneath that meat…and I think I lost my soul that day."

Juliet reached across the sofa and seized his nearest hand that felt cold as a cadaver's.

"I know it's not much comfort, Finn, but I am so, so sorry you had to go through something like that."

"I'm not the only one who went through it."

Finn abruptly withdrew his hand and rose from the couch to cross over to the windows, staring at the mirror image of the Eiffel Tower glistening in the river below it.

"Did you ever finally tell your wife about this? About what happened that day, and how it made you feel afterward?"

His eyes remained glued to the tower reflection as he shook his head. "By that time, after those tours of duty and the months in the hospital, and then flying unmanned combat drones on high target missions…I didn't really understand what was happening to me physically or emotionally. I just kept going to work and doing what I was told. I was numb, I guess. Everything was so macho on the Creech airbase that, when my symptoms got worse and I had new ones, I knew nobody really gave a damn. And besides, I just…well…withdrew. And then Kim—"

"What new symptoms?" Juliet cut in.

Finn looked at her over his shoulder. "I was irritable. I had these flashes of anger over little stuff. And...I was depressed. Some mornings I could hardly get out of bed, put on my uniform, and go back into those trailers. Some guys could just shrug it off. 'Hey...fewer rag heads to kill our men,' and they'd laugh. It's the new kind of warfare—since nobody wants the draft to come back and the politicians fear voter backlash when there are casualties that come with the boots-on-the-ground way of fighting," he said with bitter sarcasm. "But none of those justifications worked for me. I started to worry about the enemy getting hold of our weapons systems and using drones on *us*. I was pretty crazy, there, for a while."

"It's a Pandora's box, isn't it?" she said barely above a whisper. "The North Koreans or some other rogue state someday could target downtown San Francisco with a drone..."

Finn nodded. "The more I thought about what I was doing, the more I just felt like a weakling and a jerk. So when my commitment was finally up, I didn't tell anyone, but I quit. I just walked out of those trailers, put in my resignation, and waited for the paperwork to come through. Once it did, I got on a plane, and never looked back."

"You just left? What about Kim? Didn't you at least explain to her what you were going through?"

Finn cast her an odd look and said curtly, "It would have made absolutely no difference."

Juliet reared back on the couch. "You didn't tell her? Ever?" she asked, incredulous. "About the missile killing that little boy and his dog? About your worries about drones hitting America one day?"

"I obeyed orders and kept my word to keep my mouth shut."

"Screw orders!" Juliet fumed. "This was your life!

Your family! How do you know you couldn't have worked through your problems in your marriage if Kim understood what was torturing you? How fair was that to her not to tell her?"

"It would have made no difference!"

"You'll never know, will you?" Juliet shot back.

By this moment, Finn was obviously angry, too, over their exchange. Suddenly, she was not only shocked, but also worried that their heated conversation might set off serious emotional fireworks. In as dispassionate a tone as she could manage she said, "Look, I can see that talking about this upsets you. I-I'm sorry if I overstepped the boundaries, but since you told me about the drone strike and that little boy—"

Finn took a step toward the sofa and she felt herself flinch. However, his expression was contrite. 'Juliet… I'm sorry for being so testy, just now. The truth is, my wife basically left the marriage first. I guess it's still a pretty raw spot, on top of all the other stuff I was dealing with. It's no excuse for my rudeness just now, but maybe it explains it."

Juliet relaxed her grip on the blanket that covered her legs. "Well, I can certainly understand that you both were obviously dealing with some very tough circumstances, but not to tell her anything.…"

When Juliet left her sentence dangling, Finn shot her a speculative look.

"As it happens, the 'circumstances,' as you so politely phrase it, were excruciating…but that's enough about me." He glanced at the brass ship's clock on the nearby shelf. "It's getting late, but first, I want you to tell *me* something. Who did you leave in San Francisco? You're a very intelligent, talented, lovely-looking woman. Is anybody waiting for you when you get home?"

Startled by this U-turn in their conversation, Juliet bit her lip and didn't answer right away. Finally she said, "I have what I guess you'd could call a 'boyfriend' back home—which sounds pretty lame when one is thirty-six."

Finn cocked an eyebrow. "What's his name?"

"Jed Jarvis."

"A serious boyfriend?"

"My mother hopes so," she joked, adding, "and I supposed the betting money among family and friends is we'd get engaged at some point. He's a whiz at designing and programming software, though, and I've been dating him officially for about a year." She offered Finn a steady gaze. "And since I've been in Paris, I know now that I don't want to be in a relationship with him anymore."

She was inordinately pleased to see Finn's shoulders relax slightly.

"Want to tell me why you feel that way?"

"Actually I do," she said, holding his glance. "He's not the kind of guy who pays much attention to anything but himself. He isn't the sort who has your back, you know what I mean? I can't count on him for much of anything, and frankly, I've kinda been the same way with him. We never have real conversations. Not even close to the ones you and I have had since I've been here. I never tell him how I feel or what's really going on with me, because—frankly—I don't think he's very interested. And he can be clueless and thoughtless and—"

"So why has it taken you a year to figure this out?" Finn demanded.

Juliet felt strangely elated that Finn was showing the telltale signs of jealousy just hearing about Jed. Then, she was ashamed and reminded herself Finn was still married to a woman who had no idea of the agony he'd been through—because he hadn't told her.

"Look, I know it sounds ridiculous," she allowed, feeling lost in a sea of contradictory emotions, "but Jed's been my eldest brother's friend since grade school. When

I hit thirty-five, last year, he came on to me at the big birthday party my parents held for me at the hotel. I... we...just sort of drifted together after that night. I should have seen right away we're not right for each other, but I was swamped with work once Avery left for Paris, and he was...well, *enmeshed*, I suppose is a good word, with our family and my brother's company. He was a convenient escort, I guess I'd call him—a fact which doesn't cast me in a very attractive light."

"And your parents are in favor of this...match?"

Juliet scoffed. "My mother is in favor of *any* match. She doesn't seem to want a spinster daughter on her hands who still lives in the family hotel. Getting away from San Francisco as I have, I can see everything much more clearly. I'm a creative type. Jed's one of the techies in our company. We see everything differently. He's the one who developed the specific encryption software original to *Sky Slaughter* and he's going to make millions off it, along with my elder brother."

"This Jed guy sounds like a good catch to me," Finn declared. "Lifetime security. A friend of the family. That would certainly be very convenient."

Juliet felt her pulse speed up and was cut to the quick by Finn's mocking judgment. "You don't know me if you think I'm a person who'd back a horse merely because I think he'll pay off across the finish line."

Finn gave a brief shake of his head, as if angry with himself.

"Apologies again. I don't even know the guy and already I don't like him, but that was a stupid crack. It's sounds to me as if you just floated into the deal with Jed, pretty much like I did with Kim."

Mollified by this, Juliet replied, "Since November thirteenth, making a fortune in violent video war games seems pretty obscene to me. I can't do it for much longer, or be with a guy like that just to keep my family off my back about my 'future.'"

"And your father? What does he say?"

"He says nothing. He hardly ever takes on my mother once she has an *idée fixe*. I can see, now, it was purely wishful thinking to hope my dad would side with me if I said I didn't want to be with Jed anymore."

Finn shot Juliet a hard look. "Why is it you're only just now recognizing all this?"

"I'm only just admitting it to myself, and now I want to do something about it. As my Grandmother Thayer once said to me, 'Darling, *nothing* in pants is sometimes preferable to *something* in pants.'"

"Present company excluded, I hope?"

Juliet stared at him blankly.

"That's a joke."

Embarrassed by the thought that, perhaps, Finn thought he was the reason she had come to the conclusion to dump her boyfriend, she took her courage in hand and spoke her mind anyway. "Present company definitely *ex*cluded. But, seriously, Finn, knowing what I know, now that I've been to Paris since the attacks, it makes me literally sick to my stomach to have been any part of the video war game industry. Maybe it's fine for other people. Maybe it doesn't warp young minds like I think it does. And I'm sure there are 'good' games and 'positive' electronic games. Maybe they teach dexterity and motor skill—or whatever! But the truth, for me, anyhow, is that I realize how much I hate games, period. I can't go back to that life …not after what Avery and the Grenelles and all Parisians have gone through, to say nothing of the relatives of the 9/11 victims."

Finn crossed to the couch and stood gazing down at her. "And so, like me…all paths of self-awareness led to Paris?"

She cast him a sad smile. "One way or another—or so it seems for the two Americans on board this vessel. And, in one sense, I'm grateful to have gained some perspective having come here, although I *so* wish it hadn't been at the expense of Jean-Pierre and Avery."

Finn took another step closer to the sofa and startled her by bending down and once again cupping her face in his hands. She wondered if he was feeling the same jolt of electricity she did each time they made physical contact. His blue eyes seemed almost black and all she longed for was to stay with him aboard *L'Étoile*, study landscape painting, and set out on a new path leaving all her worry and troubles behind.

This time his kiss was brief. Seconds later, he stood straight and stated flatly, "But despite these ah-ha moments, you've decided to head back to San Francisco, am I right?"

A shocking sense of desolation filled her chest. "Yes. I have to go back. I can't believe that my plane leaves in less than twenty-four hours. I don't want to go, but—"

"Then don't." Finn's response overrode her own. "I don't want you to go, either."

Juliet looked up at him from the couch, stunned to hear these words. He held out his two hands, pulling her to her feet. The blanket that had been covering her legs fell on the floor between them. She made no resistance when he pulled her into his arms once more, their bodies aligned, their lips inches apart.

"It's so strange the way our paths crossed," she whispered, "and no matter what happens, I don't think I'll ever be the same after coming here."

"Then stay."

It almost sounded like a command. He leaned down and kissed her with such renewed intensity, she felt as if he were imprinting himself upon her so that if she did leave, she would never forget this moment. She felt a crooked grin creasing his lips, but she could only break their kiss and shake her head in a kind of despair.

"Oh, God, Finn…why do we have to live six thousand miles apart?"

"Didn't Bogie say to Ingrid Bergman, 'We'll always have Paris?'"

He was teasing but his voice was hoarse and his breathing sounded ragged around the edges.

"I hate that line in Casablanca!" She leaned in and now it was she who was kissing him. She despised how weepy she felt. Finally, she pulled back once again. "They both were so noble…so self-sacrificing. I couldn't *stand* that scene when they said goodbye!"

"I wanted more for them, didn't you?"

She couldn't believe the tears that had started to blur her vision.

"You and I can't have more. Not right now. Not with the mess we're both in."

And with her stark statement, reality came back with a crash. She wiped her eyes with the back of her fingers. "Listen," she said, holding tight to his hands as if willing him to understand her next words, "I love what I feel with you tonight when we kiss, and what I feel whenever we sit in the corners of that couch, but what impacts everything for both of us is that we happened to have met at exactly the wrong moment."

"No, don't say that! We can just take this a step at a time."

"How are we going to do that?" she demanded. "I leave tomorrow!"

He shot her a sly grin. "Maybe a perfectly reasonable next step is to forget being so noble and head down the ladder to my stateroom. Then, the *next* step is cancelling your flight and—"

Juliet shook her head vehemently. "No more jokes. And it's not just that you're still a married man," she explained urgently. "For me, what's weighing against just about everything is what's going to come crashing down in San Francisco. My family's entire financial net worth is enmeshed in this world of war games. All our assets of the last five generations—my dad's savings…the hotel my ancestors built—*everything* we have is now tied up in this stupid joint enterprise. I don't want to be a part of Brad's crazy empire anymore—and that definitely includes his right hand man, Jed Jarvis. I can see that, but Finn," she implored for his understanding, "I can't just plunge into a major life change and move to Paris in a flash. I have to go back home and figure out how to untangle myself from everything and hopefully help my parents get untangled if there's any way to do that."

She pulled Finn's hands upward and laid her cheek against the back of this fingers, silently praying that he would accept the complexity of the issues confronting the two of them. After a few moments, she released his hands and continued in a low voice. "I can't even legally sell my company stock, yet. I can't just abandon my mother and father at their age—even though persuading them that they should bail out of Brad's company is probably an impossible task. Even so, I have to give it one more shot. I have to figure this out, Finn, or at least try to…and I have to return home to do it. The heck of it is, I don't have a clue where to begin or how to make any of this happen."

Finn remained silent during this long explanation. Then he pulled her against his body, wrapped his arms around her shoulders, and just held her. The strength and warmth of his embrace told her that he did, indeed, understand their dilemma.

Juliet pointed to the stairs that led down to his stateroom. "But just so you know, I would like nothing better than to dive into that double bed of yours and—"

She felt herself flushing. When had she ever been so honest with a man, especially a man to whom she now realized she was attracted on so many levels?

"And do what in that bed?" he murmured into her ear. "'Fess up, so we'll know what we're missing."

"Make love with you. One, wonderful night in Paris."

Finn reached for her hand and laid her palm against his cheek. Gazing down at her, he bestowed a smile weighted with sadness and regret…and even a ray of hope.

"Maybe there'll be more than one, wonderful night if you go back to San Francisco tomorrow to do what you feel you need to do, and *then* come back. I see, now, how it all makes a kind of upside-down sense, and our sleeping together tonight doesn't. I get it, but what a loss."

"Don't I know it!" She melted against his chest again and tucked her head under his chin.

"Well, isn't this nice?" he murmured. "My consolation prize?"

"Best I can do, under the circumstances," she mumbled into his neck. "But please be clear about one thing: I think you are truly something else, flyboy."

"Maybe, one day, I'll be able to prove it to you, but there's no question. You've got some hard choices ahead, just like I have."

Puzzled, she asked, "Haven't you already made those tough decisions? You left the military and now you're living here."

"No…" he said with a slight shake of his head, "I haven't made all of my decisions. Not yet."

"But, you've cut off all ties with your family."

"I cut them while I figure out the future for myself…and while I try to get past the worst of this PTSD stuff. That is, if I can."

Juliet took a step back, her arms still wrapped around

his waist. "So you might...well...you might mend some fences, in the end?" she asked, thinking of Kim. Her heart clutched at the possibility.

Finn looked away. "I'm at a point in my life when I don't think it's smart to make any predictions, so I won't. There are too many loose ends that still need tying up.'"

The mood between them had suddenly shifted and Juliet felt a distance had bloomed in the silence that filled the pilothouse. What did he mean "loose ends?" Something other than the divorce? But what? She sensed he was holding back on something and was struck by the unhappy thought that it was probably a huge blessing that she was heading back to San Francisco before she got in too deep with this enigmatic man. Major Finn Deschanel had dark corners in his life she knew nothing about, places he was obviously not willing to share with her—unless poked and prompted. Not until she'd finally pulled it out of him had he even admitted the very crucial fact that he had a wife back home—however estranged they might be.

Composing herself as if she were leading a contentious meeting in the conference room at the office, she took a step back and heaved a small shrug. "It looks like we both have a lot of cleanup to do on these littered paths of ours..."

"I'd have to say, yes, we do," he agreed, his tone equally neutral.

She gestured toward her suitcase on the floor beside the sofa.

"Well, I still have to pack and then I'd better get to bed."

Finn glanced toward his stateroom below deck. His expression had become a peculiar mix of unhappiness and concern.

"Right. But before you end this conversation with that light-and-polite look on your face...can you promise me one thing?" His voice was gentle, now, and it stopped her cold.

"What? Promise what?"

"That there won't be a permanent moratorium on kissing you?"

Her lips formed into a prim line. "Obviously there should be," she retorted, meeting his glance.

Ignoring her last words, Finn closed the space separating them and pulled her into his arms again. Before Juliet knew what was happening, he kissed her until she could barely breathe. To her surprise, and despite the intensity of feeling behind his unexpected actions, she felt no fear, no sense that he had turned into some raging madman. Rather, it seemed clear to her that he was trying to express to her in a way his words could not that he was drawn to her as seriously as she was to him, and that he hugely regretted the confounded complications that stood in their way. Her body responded, even though she couldn't find words to express the uneasy feeling she had that he hadn't disclosed everything that was troubling him.

As if he could sense she was disturbed, he murmured in her hair, "I'm so sorry my life is such a mess."

"Well, if it's any consolation, my life's a mess, too. And this—right now—is getting dangerous."

"For me, too."

"You're married, Finn. You and Kim share a long history. Facts are facts."

"Which fact are you talking about?"

She stepped away. "That isn't funny!"

Finn stood with his hands by his sides. "I'm sorry. Again. You're right. None of it's a joke. We probably *should* declare a moratorium. I couldn't think of anything else to say because...just now, I wanted to scoop you up and carry you down to my stateroom like a cave man heading for the hills."

She heaved a sigh of finality. "Well, we can't do that."

He gave a short laugh. "Good call. At least one of us is keeping our heads."

And within seconds, he disappeared from the main cabin, firmly shutting the teak door between his stateroom and the pilothouse above.

CHAPTER 16

When Juliet awoke the next morning, the door to Finn's stateroom was open and his bed was made in the empty room. By the time she'd dressed and closed her suitcase for the final time, he'd returned with his usual supply of croissants and immediately set to making them coffee.

"Thanks," she said, taking a mug from his hand, seeking its warmth while trying to ignore heaviness in her chest. They both knew she was on a countdown to her departure later that afternoon. "I'll just finish this and then I'd better get going. I want to spend my last day here having a quiet lunch at Avery's and then I'll head for the airport."

"Please tell her that I've got her on my radar screen," Finn said, "and to expect a call from me if she's willing to see Dr. Abel."

"I'll feel her out about it and text you before I take off." Juliet took a last sip of her coffee. "And thank you so much, Finn...for everything."

"You're welcome."

During this polite exchange, Truffles, the cat, suddenly popped through an open window above the desk and provided a diversion from the difficulty of making conversation until it was time for Juliet to leave. When, finally, she rose from the sofa, Finn did too, retrieving her mug and a plate sprinkled with the last, flaky crumbs of her croissant. They stared at each other for a long moment, neither making a move.

"The holidays will be upon us full force before you know it," he offered, breeching the awkwardness that neither of them knew how to say goodbye. "Don't forget to tell Jamie that he's welcome to the couch here for as long as he needs it."

Touched by this kindness, Juliet could only nod her thanks. Finn put the mug and plate on the coffee table. Another long pause stretched between them before she stood on tiptoe, leaned forward, and brushed both Finn's cheeks with a feathery kiss, European style, as she'd often seen his Aunt Claudine bestow on her nephew upon departure.

"Merry Christmas...early, Major."

"And a good holiday for you, too, *Mademoiselle* Juliet. I'll think of you during midnight mass with my aunt at Notre Dame. It's about the only time she goes to church."

She offered him a faint smile of regret. "And I'll do the same for you at Grace Cathedral on Nob Hill. It's Episcopal. I hope that counts."

Without either of them saying a final goodbye, Finn carried her suitcase down the gangway.

"Are you sure you don't want me to drive you to Avery's? I could swing by later and take you to the airport."

He pointed in the direction where the MG was parked on the street above the quay. A breeze ruffled the water between the barge and the cobbled walkway, and Juliet lost her resolve to make this a casual farewell.

"Let's not make this any harder than it already is." She touched the tips of two fingers against her mouth and pressed them to his lips in benediction. "*Au revoir*, flyboy."

She grabbed the handle of her wheeled bag and marched up the incline with quick, purposeful strides, feeling Finn's gaze riveted on her back all the way. When she reached the road above *L'Étoile de Paris'* mooring spot, Juliet almost felt as if a magnet was attempting to pull her back to the spot where Finn now stood on the deck of the barge near the door to the pilothouse. She hailed a passing taxi and while she waited for the driver to stow her luggage in the trunk, she allowed herself to turn, raise her hand, and offer a last wave. In return, Finn put his right hand over his heart and then waved back.

Her mind spun in circles wondering what Finn had actually meant when he'd said that he couldn't make any predictions about whether he'd "mend fences" with members of his family. Did he mean he and Kim might give their marriage another chance? Then she relived the moment when he'd put his hand over his heart and bid her farewell. Confusion, followed by exasperation, succeeded by a pang of sadness to be leaving suddenly made her throat ache.

Yes, it was a good thing she was departing France this day. Just like Finn, she couldn't make any predictions what the future might hold.

Juliet's plane landed at San Francisco after an uneventful eleven-hour flight. She was relieved to see the text from Jamie as soon as she turned on her phone.

Waiting curbside outside Air France baggage.

She had barely given him a hug when he exclaimed, "Did you hear about San Bernardino?"

"What about San Bernardino?"

Juliet was totally mystified about his naming a California city some three hundred and fifty miles to the south of San Francisco.

"Another terrorist attack," he reported as he pulled onto the freeway. "It happened while you were in the air. Some jihadist converts shot a bunch of people at a Christmas party there."

Juliet's heart felt as if it had rotated in her chest and

she felt clammy all over. She'd just left Finn and Avery and *this* had happened?

"Oh, God, no!" she moaned, praying that Finn had called immediately to set up an appointment with his doctor since Avery had reluctantly agreed during their last lunch that she'd go to "talk once," she'd said, with his PTSD shrink.

It was the first week in December.

Merry Christmas, America, she thought, a sense of despair grabbing hold.

"Turn on the news," she commanded, pointing at the car radio.

"It's all terrible," Jamie replied. "I was listening all the way down here. The reports just kept repeating themselves. And before we get home, I need to warn you that Brad is demanding you return to work even before you unpack your bags."

"Nice," she said with her usual edge of sarcasm when it came to interactions with her elder brother, "though his ordering me around before I even walk into work is no surprise."

"We've got trouble. Big time. He and Jed have both been requested to meet with the FBI about the encryption we use in our video war game software."

"And that doesn't surprise me either."

"So far, Brad's put them off and called the lawyers."

She turned to face her brother who was gripping the wheel of the family SUV.

"Jamie, after what I just experienced in France in the aftermath of the terrorist attacks there, we are all entering a 'New Normal.' And believe it or not, I've actually come over to thinking that in the wrong hands—either by the terrorists or an authoritarian government—encryption can certainly result in really bad stuff, but it's also the public's *last* protection of privacy and freedom."

"Wow...when did you come to *this* conclusion?"

"I talked to somebody who's really informed on the subject," she said obliquely.

"Your Air Force Major?" Juliet heard the skepticism in his voice.

"My Air Force Major was so repulsed by drone warfare that he resigned from the service after fifteen years as a career officer. Don't assume he's some knee-jerk military-industrial-complex cheerleader."

"Okay, okay! No need to be so touchy about it," he said with a grin.

Juliet shot him an exasperated look. Then she said, "You and I both agree that encrypted communication is crucial in matters of banking and business and all sorts of electronic interchanges—including the government's— that demand security to function. But trust me, bro, this is going to get very headachy for Brad, for you and me, for the company—and especially for Mom and Dad. Being in the video war game business has enmeshed our family into all sorts of crap that, in my fervent opinion, we shouldn't be party to."

"Brad already went on record with the guy on the phone from the Feds. He told him that he would refuse to provide any "back door" help to authorities—even with a court order. Apparently there are some six hundred and nineteen companies like ours who have invented their own brand of encryption, including cell phone apps like 'What's App' and 'Telegram' —all with billions of patrons."

"Yeah, and a small percentage might be terrorists," she affirmed. "In Paris, the authorities theorized the shooters used 'What's App' to send un-decodable messages, world wide, when they planned their attacks. But just because someone can reach into a drawer for a knife and stab people doesn't mean the government should claim the right to access to *everybody's* kitchen's knives...especially without a warrant."

"Brad says everybody in the industry is on the Federal hot seat and he and a lot of other companies are taking a stand in the name of 'freedom.'"

"Oh, spare me our brother's platitudes," she retorted. "He doesn't care about anything other than selling *Sky Slaughter*. But for sure, it's not at all a simple debate," she added while absorbing the sight of the TransAmerica pyramid as they headed for the Bay View Hotel on Nob Hill. "Do the Feds think encrypted messaging was involved in San Bernardino?"

"The issue there is the Feds want to get access to the security codes to the attackers' cell phones to find out if there may be other associates or family involved in carrying out the attack."

Juliet wondered aloud, "Who would ever have thought *our* family would be drawn into any of this? Doesn't it feel sometimes that our monthly paychecks are blood money?"

"Same as," Jamie replied glumly.

Juliet found herself obsessing about how Finn may have reacted when he heard the news about San Bernardino? How bad a setback to his or Avery's recovery might this be?

Interrupting her anxious speculations, Jamie said, "Well, Brad figures that the heat will be mostly on companies that invented the messaging services used on smart phones. They'll probably leave the smaller gaming companies alone—at least for now."

"That's probably true," she agreed, "but my main concern, now, is how Avery is going to react to this latest news. She's not in great emotional shape, Jamie. Nobody is who was caught up in those horrendous attacks." Her thoughts immediately recalled the night in Paris when the car backfired—and Finn's instant reaction to duck for cover.

She studied her younger brother's profile that was so like their father's, along with his kind heart and mild manner. Both men had an approach to life that couldn't have been more different than Brad's, but she'd never understood why the contrasts between the three Thayer men were so stark. Meanwhile, Jamie signaled a turn and headed up the steep hill that led to the hotel's underground garage.

"I told Brad two days ago that I can't stomach editing war game videos anymore," he announced, not taking his eyes off the road. "I told him I wanted to quit."

"Oh, boy. I bet that went over well. But good for you! I feel the same way."

"Well, that was before the FBI called. This morning he practically went postal, yelling about what he'd do if *anyone* left the company at this 'crucial juncture.'"

"Well, until things cool down, just claim you're due all that vacation time and go to Paris anyway. Get outta Dodge. Avery's thrilled you're coming over for Christmas. Given these latest attacks, it's really important that someone is with her right now."

"That's all I could think about as soon as I heard the news," Jamie said. "And what a relief she wasn't wounded in the arm she paints with."

Juliet glanced at him closely. "So you really do care about Avery, more than just as a friend and former colleague." It was a statement, not a question.

Jamie looked embarrassed. "I always liked her, but we both decided that it wasn't such a great idea to…ah…mix business with pleasure, given Brad's strange attitude toward her from the moment she joined the company."

"Yeah, he always acted like he either wanted to jump on her bones, or fire her."

She glanced over to gauge Jamie's reaction to her last

words. Did he know—or just guess—what had happened in Brad's rooms at the hotel?

But all he said was, "Yeah, those two were oil and water."

The car nosed into the underground garage and pulled into a designated parking place for hotel staff.

"Forget all that for the moment," Juliet said. "What's important right now is that we have to figure out a way to get Mom and Dad out of the financial bind they've put themselves in by granting Brad the ten-million-dollar equity loan against the hotel. The sooner the hotel is out of jeopardy and their retirement money is safe, the sooner you and I can make our escape."

Juliet was startled when her brother banged on the steering wheel.

"That was *Dad's* decision to risk the hotel to help his favorite son," Jamie shouted with a bitterness Juliet realized must have long been simmering. "It's his to lose."

"Well, it's ours to lose, too, remember."

"I don't care about that anymore," Jamie declared, his green-gray eyes flashing with pent-up anger.

"Well, *I* care about the hotel. And what about Mother?" Juliet protested. "God knows, she's always taken Brad's side on just about everything, but think about their age and the fact they've worked all their lives to keep the place going."

"Mother's even more to blame," insisted Jamie, unmoved. "She pushed Dad to risk everything on the Golden Boy...so it's on both their shoulders, seems to me. I can't let their stupidity and favoritism rule my life forever!"

Juliet was taken aback to hear such uncharacteristic vehemence uttered by her younger sibling. She reached over to touch his sleeve.

"Hey, Jamie...believe me, I'm so sorry you've had to

hold the fort like you did while I was gone. I'm sure it was no fun."

"It's not just that. I'm tired of the whole deal and have been for a long, long time." His face was flushed and he looked more serious than she'd ever seen him. "I just want out, Jules, and to hell with my so-called legacy! I can always find work lots of places as a video editor. Brad and our parents have risked it all without a qualm or a thought for our future welfare, so why should I care? Let them be slaves to it!"

"But you and I—not Brad—will be slaves to taking care of them one day, with or without the funds to do it." She put a hand on his sleeve. "But believe me, I hear you."

"Well, you'd better hear this, Juliet! If Mom and Dad continue to side with Brad on every single thing like they always have, I'm done. No parental care-taking for this guy."

Juliet could plainly see that her younger brother was at an emotional breaking point. To change the direction of their heated conversation, she quickly told him about Finn's offer of a place to stay in Paris over the holidays.

"Whatever else you decide to do," she said, hoping to calm the waters, "why not definitely take some time off, and do it soon? It's the perfect moment, given production shuts down over the holidays."

Jamie inhaled a deep breath and nodded. "I've already bought my ticket to France. I'm leaving December eighteenth, and your friend's offer of a bed is great." He looked at her sheepishly. "I don't know if Avery will welcome me beyond hanging out at a Paris café or something."

"Given that she was shot *in* a café and her friend was killed there," Juliet reminded him, "you can help her by just being a friend and escorting her to doctors' appointments and to her professor's painting studio whenever she wants to go." She looked at her brother steadily. "This *is* a caretaking job, not a time to make any serious romantic moves on her. Do you think you can do that?"

"I'll do whatever you say," he said with a look of chagrin. "I'm sorry. It's been pretty shitty while you've been gone. I need to get away from all this for a while."

This was the moment she realized that she had to bring up another explosive subject concerning their elder brother. "OK, so now listen... Avery told me why she quit GatherGames so abruptly. She also said she expected that you understood her reasons as well."

In the driver's seat, Jamie turned in her direction again, his face losing its color. Another car pulled into the underground garage and parked nearby, but they ignored it.

"I've had my suspicions about Avery's abrupt departure, but I didn't know for sure," Jamie said. "Brad tried to get her to go to bed with him, didn't he?"

"Basically, he tried to assault her sexually and threatened career repercussions if she didn't go along with it."

"What a—"

This time, it was a restraining hand she laid on Jamie's sleeve. "Tell me why you assumed that he'd made some sort of pass at her?"

"That night, I saw how upset she was rushing down the hall, away from Brad's room," he said, seething. "Then, two days later, she was gone. I figured he'd done something unsavory, but do you actually think it rose to the level of sexual assault? In a court of law, I mean? After all, she went to his apartment..."

"Damn it, Jamie!" Juliet shrieked, "when will you men understand sexual harassment, as well as assault, are *crimes*, not a case of 'maybe if she hadn't just gone into his hotel room?' Her boss *lives* in a hotel. She thought it was a legitimate meeting! When he put the moves on her, she hit him with a silver dome from room service!"

"Jesus! Really? What's happened to that guy?" he wondered aloud. "Brad used to kid me mercilessly when we were younger, but now he's just turned into a nasty s.o.b."

"Look, he's the eldest son...the little prince of Nob Hill." Juliet tried to keep her tone light and her own bitterness at bay. "I guess he felt from an early age he was superior to us two and entitled to whatever he wanted because our parents did nothing to disabuse him of that opinion. Mother pampered him and coddled him, and told him what a genius he was. I think he just got used to bullying everyone to get his way—and succeeded ninety percent of the time."

"Well, that's for sure," Jamie agreed. "Over the years, Dad and Mom didn't do much to curb his 'I am the King' attitude. For one thing, Dad's kinda in awe, I think, given his eldest son made a couple of million dollars before he hit thirty-five."

Juliet gave a short laugh. "Well, you've got to admit that The Big Bro was pretty close to a genius in school...and a champion athlete and all that. No one ever really restrained him about anything, or said he couldn't have or do virtually whatever he wanted. No wonder he became 'Mr. Unbridled Entitlement.'"

"Well, I'm here to tell you," Jamie said grimly, "he won't be entitled to *my* services for very much longer. As soon as I can figure out what's next for me, I'm outta here. Permanently."

Juliet continued to stare at her younger brother across the passenger seat in the darkened garage. "I'm out, too," she declared softly, "as soon as we sort out this family mess. I'm going back to Paris to study and paint."

"That's great," Jamie said, "but neither of us had better announce our future plans too loudly right now. The other thing I need to tell you before you see anyone else in the family is that rumors are all over the place that a couple of the venture capitalists on our board are tired of dealing with Brad's thinking he's emperor-of-the-world. Word is, the VCs are nosing around for a buyer so they can sell GG and make back their investment sooner, rather than later. They've apparently lost confidence in him as a CEO. Too many reports filed with our Human Resources department about his abusive management style."

"Good!" Juliet replied. "If the company is taken over, the venture capitalists will settle out and Dad will get back his investment." She patted her brother on the shoulder. "Hopefully, you and I will get our payday by then and we can cash in the stock we were granted when this whole thing began."

"Except that Brad told me to my face just this morning that, given the threat of a takeover, he won't tolerate anyone in the family rocking the boat by hinting we're thinking of siding with dissident members of the board. He mentioned specifically that he'd do something terrible if any of us tried to sell our stock."

"Why does *none* of this surprise me?" Juliet groaned, opening the car door. "Well, we can't sell, anyway, until we pass the five-year threshold next July."

Jamie got out on his side and extracted Juliet's luggage from the trunk. He set it on the garage's concrete floor.

"We're painted into a corner, you and I," he said. "That is, unless we're willing to leave with nothing."

"Not necessarily," Juliet said thoughtfully as she grabbed her shoulder bag while Jamie seized the handle of her suitcase. "What *if* the VCs make a takeover move soon?"

"How would that help us?" Jamie demanded as they walked toward the back entrance to the hotel, their voices echoing in the underground garage.

Juliet smiled as he held the door open for her. "Well,

VCs who want control of the company might make the principal stockholders, including us, an offer we won't want to refuse."

"What kind of offer?"

"Give us cash *now,* equal to what we'd get if we sold our shares in July."

Jamie frowned, worry lines creasing his forehead. "I honestly think Brad would put a hit out on us if we accepted something like that. Besides, Dad and Mom would have to vote in favor of the takeover, too."

"But a buyout at a good price would save their bacon!" Juliet protested, pushing the button on the service elevator that she and Jamie had used since childhood to travel between the floors of the family hotel.

"Mom would consider it a betrayal of her darling boy," replied Jamie, "and it would, actually, be just that. They'd have to choose between getting their investment back versus allowing Brad to maintain control of the company he's running."

"And will ruin, before he's through," Juliet said. Then she groaned as the elevator doors opened, "Oh, lord…this is all just horrible. So many things could go sidewise in situations like these. I'll never get back to Paris at this rate."

"Yes you will," Jamie insisted, his eyes suddenly brighter.

The pair entered the empty elevator and Jamie pushed the button for the floor where the Thayer family siblings had their collection of rooms.

"How so?"

"I just thought of something!" he said. "What if some of us key employees actually did let a few things be known quietly to several select, trustworthy members of the board of directors without Brad ever hearing of it?"

"Like what?"

"Like the fact that, because of mean old Brad and his

lousy leadership style, key people like us want to leave our jobs. The 'vulture' capitalists waiting in the wings would hear about it from dissident board members and that might conceivably prompt them to move faster to buy the company. Mom and Dad wouldn't really have a choice except to sell to the new guys, or lose the hotel…and Brad would get a big payday, too, though his ego would be trashed. No harm, no foul."

As the elevator came to a stop at their floor, Juliet clapped her hands. "Brilliant! Or at least it's an idea definitely worth thinking about."

Jamie nodded, putting his hand in the door to prevent it from closing on them.

"Because, if there were a takeover," he said, "you and I could then make a claim of 'management change of control'—which the fine print of our contract says is a reason for our stock deal and our options to accelerate in terms of when we could sell, and we would be able to unload them faster."

"This is true?" she said, surprised.

"Yep. I've been studying each paragraph of the contract I signed when the company was founded—without reading it carefully five years ago, may I add."

"Same here, I'm embarrassed to admit."

"Yeah," Jamie said with a short laugh, "you and I are both key players in some regard—since we've been around since the beginning—but we're definitely chopped liver, given our relatively small number of shares compared to Brad's."

She held up her arms, hands crossed at the wrist as if they were roped together. "Well, all I have to say is—please, God, let someone buy GatherGames and liberate us from this bondage. I long for the day when I don't feel like an arms dealer!"

Jamie laughed at her feeble joke. They both realized,

now, that they had to find a way to set free at least four of the five Thayers of Nob Hill.

Juliet ignored Brad's edict and spent the first hour in San Francisco unpacking. As expected, she was summoned by text to show up at Brad's office "a.s.a.p." She'd been relieved to learn that Jed had been dispatched to China on a mission to secure a better deal for the printing of their new packaging materials—and thus she'd been spared that confrontation.

As she walked down the corridor in the former warehouse south of Market Street, she thought about the day, six months earlier, when Brad had offered her Avery's job as graphic design director, along with the title of "Chief Branding Officer."

Surprised and undeniably flattered by her taskmaster brother's seeming confidence in her ability, a small voice in her head had warned that Brad never did anything that wasn't first and foremost in his own interest.

"Branding Officer, no less," Avery had noted dryly, having predicted that Brad would recruit his sister to replace her. "Behold the 'Golden Coffin' of permanent servitude."

The observation had proven all too accurate after Juliet asked Brad for time to think about the promotion.

"Yes or no? I don't have time to screw around on this."

"I need a day," she'd insisted. "I'm driving Avery to the airport."

"So Avery's off to Paris to paint portraits? Really?" he mocked. "She'll be back with her tail between her legs in less than a year. And by the way," he added with a nasty edge to his voice, "I'd had it, big time, with that bitch's pretentious crap about the so-called creative credo. We're creating stuff right here!"

"Yeah…" Juliet had retorted, incensed by his derogatory language, "we're replicating life in a tribal war zone and teaching juveniles to think killing is *fun*."

"Hey, it pays your bills and then some, little sis," he'd shot back. "And like Dad said, working for me, you can still dabble in art and be practical at the same time. Create those little watercolors of yours on the weekends, why don't you?"

"What weekends?" she'd countered, annoyed by the disdain Brad so clearly had for anyone who preferred art above commerce. "I've worked every single Saturday since I came here."

"Then be a Sunday painter!"

"Very funny."

"So, what's your answer about the job?" he'd insisted that watershed day. " I got a meeting in five minutes about the IPO!" She noticed the sweat circles beneath the short sleeves of his ubiquitous black T-shirt that stretched tightly across his chest to emphasize his cyclist's six-pack abs. Making a public offering by registering a formerly private company on the New York Stock Exchange was tricky business, Juliet knew, and clearly Brad, in a word, was sweating it. Employee stability was a key factor, and Avery's departure had been a blow.

"My answer is 'maybe,'" Juliet had said, wanting to heighten his stress level as he had hers. "I'll tell you tomorrow."

Juliet remembered the scowl that had spread across her brother's face. "I don't *have* to offer you this promotion, you know. I'm only doing it out of family loyalty."

"You're doing it because Avery Evans quit and you know I'm tempted to do the same thing." She'd gestured vaguely toward the jumble of cubicles beyond the walls of Brad's office that were filled with twenty-somethings who had a habit of sleeping under their desks when work was intense. "You work people this hard, Brad, you eventually break them," she'd warned him. "And besides, commercial graphic design and branding have nothing to do with why I went to art school."

"Well, I don't see many folks lining up to buy your landscapes, or Avery's portraits, either. At least your family was willing to bail you out after graduation."

"You didn't 'bail' me out! I put my work on hold because you and Dad *begged* Avery and me to help when you started this electronic sweatshop. Just like you arm-twisted Jamie out of that video editing job at Pixar Studios."

"Another great *artiste* gone to the Dark Side."

Brad could be withering when anyone wouldn't do his bidding. During this remembered conversation half a year ago, Juliet had honestly felt relieved she had no sharp weapon close at hand during their so-called job interview.

"Jamie has given you nothing but his professional best," Juliet had hotly defended their younger sibling, "and Avery and I've produced a great look for this company, brother mine. Check your latest sales reports."

"'Great,' you say?" Brad said, arching an eyebrow at an angle he knew was guaranteed to get a rise out of her. "Sales tripled only because I deep-sixed everything but the *Sky Slaughter* series. Let's just call what you two did around here 'okay'...*okay?*"

Juliet had summoned every ounce of energy not to blow her stack. In the calmest tones she could muster she'd replied, "You know, don't you, that insulting your baby sister like you have my entire life is not going to get you what you want this time, Mr. Bully Boy? Do you need me as design director, or not?"

Brad had seemed to understand, that day, that he was skating on thin ice and raised his hands in pseudo surrender.

"Okay, okay! I'm just saying that maybe a little gratitude is in order here. Thanks to *Slaughter* sales quadrupling what we made the previous year, Jamie bought a sailboat and you were able to pay off your school debt, remember? Going forward, you'll be making a lot more money than most women in tech, believe me!"

"Oh, so I'm a gender charity case, am I?"

Trust Brad to allude to the debt she'd racked up going to Art Center of Pasadena instead of to a 'real school' like Stanford, as her mother had argued fiercely. But Juliet had held firm and offered to pay her parents back as an enticement to let her have her way—and she'd kept her word. That day in Brad's office, right after Avery had bailed, Juliet nearly walked out in her wake. Looking back, if it hadn't been for her parents' perilous financial situation, she would have.

"C'mon, lighten up!" her brother had cajoled as their bickering wound down. "I'm just saying you and Jamie—and Avery Evans, for that matter—have had a very good ride here the last couple of years, considering we started in the hotel's garage. So, okay…do we have a deal?"

Juliet had been proud of her salary demands to Brad that day.

"Add an additional fifty thousand dollars to my salary as design director *and* Chief Branding Officer, along with seventy-five thousand additional stock options that vest in two years—and I might consider it," she'd said.

"Okay. The salary bump, plus *sixty*-five thousand options that vest in four years," Brad had countered. "That's my final offer."

"*Two* years vesting and the salary bump, or no go," she'd insisted, "and I'll take the sixty-five thousand stock options."

Her brother had hesitated a few seconds before reluctantly agreeing to her terms. "But you have to swear not to tell anyone I gave in to this extortion."

She could see that he, too, was fighting hard to keep his cool. Theirs was just another of his typical, bare-knuckles negotiations about money— and they'd played the game to a draw.

"I'll keep our deal confidential," she'd promised.

"Well, okay then," he'd confirmed, churlish in his acceptance. "I'll give you sixty-five thousand additional stock options out of *mine*."

"That vest in two years," she'd repeated firmly. She put on her no-hard-feelings smile. "I'll send you an email to confirm the details of this discussion. And thanks."

"You're not welcome."

"Hey, bro…with a million-plus shares in your own account, you'll hardly noticed the difference," she'd replied and exited his office before he could renege on their deal.

Given the vagaries of start-ups, fickle investors, and Wall Street's demands, she knew full well that the company could suddenly go sideways and the extra options to buy more stock at a cheaper price wouldn't be worth the paper they were printed on.

The subsequent angry exchanges over the packaging for the *Sky Slaughter* video series had convinced her in the months that followed that her brother had promoted her last spring not because he had faith in her abilities, but merely to deter her from deserting him at a crucial moment before the public stock offering went into effect.

And here they were at another such moment. GatherGames was traded on the stock exchange, now, and Juliet was under even fewer illusions about her job security, especially hearing from Jamie how the "vulture capitalists" were circling for a possible take-over bid. Even the

Founder could get the boot if the VCs or the company's directors ordered it. It was "The Dot-Com Way," and far from the artistic life she'd ever imagined for herself.

She inhaled a deep breath and paused a moment outside Brad's door to gather her wits—and her courage. Everything Jamie had related earlier on the ride in from the airport was spinning around in her brain, along with the knowledge of her eldest brother's despicable behavior toward Avery in his private suite at the Bay View. Her thoughts drifted to Finn's honorable self-restraint her last night in Paris when both of them wanted nothing more that to fall into his double bed. Forcing such distracting reminiscences from her mind, she tapped Brad's door. A voice on the other side growled, "Come in!"

"Lafayette, I am here," Juliet announced, hoping to set a jovial tone for their upcoming conversation.

Brad glanced up and saw who was at the threshold. His thin lips suddenly bloomed into a broad smile that looked as if it belonged to someone else. "Well, hello there!"

Trim in his uniform black T-shirt and equally dark chinos, he swiftly rose from his glass-topped desk that supported a large-screen Mac computer but was bare of anything else. "Welcome home! I'm so glad to hear that poor Avery's on the mend."

He bolted from behind the desk to give her a peck on the cheek, adding, "I've really missed you—and all the good work you've done for this place."

Perhaps, she thought, as he gestured for her to sit in a chair opposite his desk, she was hallucinating—or—her brother's looming fear of getting the boot as CEO had waved a magic wand and turned Bradshaw Thayer IV into "Mr. Nice" overnight.

How long that would last was anybody's guess.

CHAPTER 17

Avery stared at the plaque affixed to the door reading *DR. SONJA ABEL, MD – Psychiatry*. The office was down a long corridor in a wing of the American Hospital that she'd never seen before, and Finn could tell she dreaded walking over the threshold.

"I'm sorry I've dragged you all the way here," she said, her voice tight. "But I really don't think I need to do this, Finn. Why can't I just paint my way out of this? *You* know," she added with a weak smile, "my own special brand of occupational therapy."

"Well, one reason is," Finn said, turning the doorknob, "you can't even bear to pick up a brush because you've told me all you see are pools of blood on your blank canvas." He pushed open the door. "Believe me, I know something of what you're going through and I can only say that Dr. A has helped me get past some of this stuff."

Once Finn had steeled himself enough to share with Avery, as he had with Juliet, some of his own post-traumatic problems, he'd managed to get her this far. Now, he was determined to deliver her to Dr. Abel as he'd promised Juliet. After that, it was up to Avery herself to commit to treatment—or not.

"C'mon, kiddo. We two are going to lick this thing," he said with an assurance he didn't feel. He addressed the receptionist. "This is Avery Evans. She's here to see Dr. Abel at two o'clock."

Brad's attempts to display ingratiating behavior to his staff and younger siblings endured less than a week. While

Juliet had been in Europe, a majority of board members insisted the CEO attend anger management sessions. Despite this edict, the more that the news was filled with the specifics of how the home-grown jihadists in San Bernardino planned and executed the assault on local government employees, the more insistent were Brad's calls for "action" drawings depicting video characters getting blown up by drones.

"The guy acts as if home-grown terrorist attacks are a good marketing ploy for his damn war game products!" Juliet complained bitterly to Jamie prior to a scheduled design discussion a few days after returning home. At Brad's direction, her staff had produced illustrations depicting roadside explosions in front of a small desert village with bodies of ISIS fighters tossed in the air and wounded on the ground, with a few camels killed for good measure.

During the meeting itself, Brad pointed to drawings posted on one wall in the conference room. "Bor-ing!" he declared. "That stinks! So does that...and *that*! What's wrong with you people? We need action! ISIS body *parts* flying through the air," he fumed in front of the art department's entire staff. "*SS 2* is due to launch and ship in two months' time," he said, referring to *Sky Slaughter – Death in the Desert,* the next video war game in the proposed series "and just look at the insipid dreck you're giving me!" He glared at his sister, wagging a finger a foot from her face. "Where are the incoming Hellfires? A U.S. drone overhead? The videos show blood and guts," he shouted, slamming his fist on the conference room table, "and the images on the box have to be the same! That's what *sells* this product, you idiots! If you don't produce more of what I asked for on the packaging, you're nuked, *got* it?"

And then he stomped out of the room, leaving his audience to stare at his retreating back in stunned silence.

The night before Jamie's departure to Paris, Brad abruptly organized a family dinner held in a small, private dining room at the Bay View. After the waiters served coffee and dessert and retreated into a catering kitchen nearby, the five Thayers were left sitting uneasily around the linen-clad table. The room's pale pink silk draperies kissed the rich, off-white carpeting and complimented the ashes-of-roses hue of the brocaded walls. Opulent Christmas decorations of genuine pine garlands and golden pears, entwined with forest green and gold French ribbons, graced the top of large, gilt-framed mirrors that hung at both ends of the intimate space reserved for special family occasions.

Brad tapped a silver knife on his wine glass, asking for everyone's attention.

"I know you've all heard scuttlebutt, but I called you here to tell you in person that, yes, I spoke again with the FBI and officially refused to cooperate or reveal anything about our encryption system. I also have private intelligence that certain VCs on our board are looking for a buyer—or buyers—to mount a hostile takeover bid against us. I'm sure it's no surprise that I'm organizing a full-fledged battle to fight it—and I expect all of you to help in this effort."

He glanced around the table, but Juliet, like the rest of her family, was staring at generous servings of chocolate lava cake, its hot, glistening cocoa filling oozing across gold-rimmed porcelain plates.

In the deafening silence Brad declared, "C'mon! Sales are booming. We've all worked too hard to let them take this away from us!"

"Us?" scoffed Jamie, looking up. "You mean, *you*. In my view, selling GatherGames when everything is on a high would make Dad and Mom whole, as far as the Bay View's equity loan is concerned. Juliet and I could cash in our stock much earlier and make individual career plans, which we both want to do."

Before Brad could give voice to the glare he cast in the direction of his younger brother for such insubordination, Juliet jumped in to support Jamie's show of bravery.

"Look, Brad," she began, "let's consider events from several practical perspectives. A takeover at a good price would give Mother and Dad some peace of mind for their retirement years. You'd have plenty of money to start another company, and we could all say 'this chapter is closed, and thank you very much,' and then be on to the *next* chapter, whatever that's going to be for each of us. As far as I'm concerned, buying us out sounds great to me!"

Brad turned from staring at Jamie with fire in his eye, to looking as if he were going to toss his silver dinner knife into his sister's chest. She'd never seen him so livid.

"I should fire you right here for your disloyalty!" he said, his voice low and menacing, "and the only reason I'm not is I want you to completely redesign the lousy packaging you've done!"

The senior Bradshaw Thayer sitting at the head of the table held up both hands as if to ward off his son's fury. He spoke in a tone that surprised Juliet with its firmness. "Now, son, don't say anything you'd regret. I'm a member of the Board of Directors too, remember, and you and I need to talk about this calmly and rationally. Your sister and brother are only speaking their minds."

"Shut up, Dad!" he ground out between clenched teeth. "You may be on the board, but you know *nothing* about how these takeover raids go down. I want all of your complete support and if you don't give it to me, I'll make certain none of you come out of this whole. I want—"

Jamie pounded a fist on the table. "Don't you dare talk to Dad like that! He knows plenty about your business, and so do Juliet and I! He and Mom signed an equity loan that puts this hotel and their entire future at risk, so you'd better damn well listen to him and listen to *us*, you narcissistic—"

Just then, their mother jumped to her feet, rattling their dessert plates and wine goblets. Her lipstick red wool suit offered a nod to the upcoming holiday season, but her helmet of hair, recently coiffed in the hotel salon, framed a face flush with anger. Her vermillion lipstick stretched into a single grim line as she brought down the handle of her own silver knife loudly on the table, gaining the attention of everyone.

"Stop this squabbling right *now!*" she demanded.

Juliet waited, wondering if this time, at last, her mother would refrain from automatically siding with her Perfect Boy, and, instead, see the wisdom of plotting an exit strategy from GatherGames that would insure her own and her husband's future, along with that of the rest of the family. Mildred Thayer's audience sank back into their pale pink upholstered dining room chairs, looking at her expectantly to see which side she would favor.

They didn't have long to wait.

One of the few female engineering students in college before she joined her husband's architectural firm many years before, she wagged an agitated forefinger at Brad, senior, seated at the other end of the table.

"You all should be ashamed of yourselves—and especially *you*," she scolded her husband, "for not circling the wagons to support this family's enterprise." Her sweeping gaze included the rest of the assembled. "This is a challenge, certainly, but Brad understands the electronic video game business far better than any of you!" She turned on Juliet and Jamie. "He and his team know a lot more about these unholy moves made by the greedy VCs than either your father or I do, and unquestionably more than *you* two!" She glared at her younger adult children. "We can't let them humiliate Brad junior this way! We are going to support him one-hundred percent, do you hear me? One-hundred percent!" she repeated.

Juliet looked at her father who didn't say another word. He simply lowered his eyes to stare at his untouched dessert. And she realized, as never before, that her mother would always run the show within her parents' marriage—and the family as a whole.

Hearing no opposition, Mildred Thayer resumed her seat and continued in a calmer tone of voice, "I agree wholeheartedly with Brad that the VCs on and off the board are vultures, and now that the company is earning big profits, they want to own it all, and would probably depose Brad as CEO, once they gained total control."

"That's because they think he's a *lousy* CEO, and *I* agree!" Jamie spoke up.

This time, Mildred slammed the palm of her hand on the table. "I vote 'no' on the takeover bid, and I expect the rest of you to do the same!"

Again silence.

Unable to stand it any longer, Juliet jumped up from her chair, her fists balled at her sides. "Forget the issue of who controls GatherGames! The world is changing, Mother. The Paris attacks—and now San Bernardino—should tell us that sending out these violent videos that make shooting people just a *game* is a terrible business for this family to be in! Has it ever occurred to you that there may come a day when whackos in some other country that doesn't like us sends killer drones over San Francisco—and all because they saw how to do it in products our company produces? Maybe the VCs on our board want to get their money out before the industry itself takes a hit. Or maybe, as you say, the takeover boys think they can make many *more* millions producing garbage-loads of this horrible crap! Either way, I don't care! I want out."

"Your bottom line will care if I boot you out right

now!" Brad shouted.

"Then do it, so I don't have to witness what happens around here when the FBI makes life miserable for companies like ours. Why can't you see that the VCs' wanting to take us over is a blessing in disguise for this family, to say nothing of restoring its honor?"

"Honor?" Brad spat. "Oh puh-leese, stop being such a damn drama queen, Juliet!"

Her mother joined in. "Exactly. There's no real evidence to support anything you've just said, so sit down!"

"You don't think so?" Juliet turned to face her mother. "Well, what if the Feds get a legal warrant? What if the investors on the board get nervous as these terrorist attacks keep happening and the money guys want to pull out of being in this business? What if the tide turns with public opinion about the shit we're selling to the universe and—"

"Oh, give it a rest!" Brad intervened. "You always see the dark side."

Mildred Thayer looked to her son for support. "And if the Feds put out a warrant, you'll refuse it, won't you Brad? All of Silicon Valley feels that way, so you'll have lots of support." Mildred waved a dismissive hand in her daughter's direction. "Ultimately, the F.B.I. will go after the big boys like Fox Interactive and Hasbro, not small-fry companies like ours."

For her part, Juliet could feel her blood pressure rise in its usual fashion. She was desperate to leave the room before she railed against her father for his silence, along with her mother and elder brother for the smug smiles that now creased their lips.

"Can't you see what a bigger issue this is?" she implored.

"The issue is so much bigger than what *you're* talking about," Brad said, his tone dripping with disdain. "I suppose you don't give a damn about everyone's right to privacy. A couple of terrorists using encryption is the price of American freedom."

"Believe it or not, I happen to agree with you on encryption, although I wouldn't phrase it that way. But it's total bullshit when it comes to *your* reasons for taking this stand!" Juliet lowered her voice, her teeth clenched. "You just want to keep raking in the cash producing violent video games to prove to everyone what a genius you believe you are! But, let's *do* talk about a genuine 'bigger issue.'"

She looked directly at her father who presented the classic picture of a deer in the headlights. "What about the quaint notion of the *moral* issue involved here, Dad? What about your being part of a company like GatherGames— you, a man who supposedly builds things, not tears them down? Our gaming products teach children to think killing other human beings is *entertaining*! A fun sport. And now it's part of the violence and carnage happening all around the world—"

"Oh, now, here it comes," Brad interrupted, "Juliet on her soap box."

Juliet glared at him. "Maybe you wouldn't blather on about the 'price of freedom' in defense of your sickening video war games if you could have seen what the terrorists in Paris did to take away the freedom—permanently—of the innocent people who were killed, to say nothing of horribly wounding hundreds of others, including Avery Evans." She searched the faces of each of her family members in turn, her glance coming to rest on her father as tears of frustration and disappointment filled her eyes.

With an underlying sense of despair she mocked, "So, Dad...it's okay with you that we, the hallowed Thayer family of San Francisco, USA, play a part in what happened to blameless people like Avery who got mowed down by guys with Kalashnikovs and AK-47s, maybe even *inspired* by some of the products we produce? Don't you see, Dad?" Juliet pleaded, willing her father not to look away. "This has nothing to do with encryption. We produce images that celebrate *slaughtering* other human beings! You and I and Jamie have a role in this horror show, just as much as Mother and Brad! We're all making big bucks out of it, which makes us co-conspirators. *All of us*, and we'd better start to face it!"

"Young lady—" her mother began, but Juliet cut her off with bitter sarcasm directed at her father.

"Daddy, think about the Thayer family's brand of blood-and-guts as you drink your champagne and eat your roast beef this holiday. Think about the business our family is in as you celebrate *Christmas* at Grace Cathedral! You know: 'Peace on Earth, Goodwill Towards Men?'"

She turned to address her mother, whose scowl had never altered from the moment her daughter had begun her tirade. Juliet wondered if they'd ever speak again, but the volcano erupting inside her couldn't be stopped. "And when you hold your little holiday brunch with your bridge buddies this year, *Mrs.* Thayer, think about the roadside bombs our video games glorify." She balled her monogrammed linen napkin into her fist. "What a bunch of hypocrites we all are, myself included!"

Juliet looked across the table at her brother Jamie, lowering her voice. "I'll drive you to the airport tomorrow morning. I can't stand to be in this room another second!"

She rose from her chair, threw her napkin on the table, and walked out of the private dining room.

The next morning, Jamie volunteered to take the wheel to drive to San Francisco International, down the peninsula to San Bruno, south of the city. As he nosed their black SUV up the ramp to exit the hotel, he said, "Hey…you were pretty dramatic last night."

It was just past six in the morning. The clear December skies formed a big, blue square as they headed out of the underground garage and up Jackson Street, turning left on Jones. These several hours later, Juliet had started to feel remorseful that she had let her temper hijack her emotions at dinner the previous evening.

"I know," she acknowledged glumly. "Like our sainted mother and elder brother are so fond of pointing out, I'm the family's notorious 'drama queen.'"

"Well, you had plenty of provocation. You said what had to be said. Pretty damn well, I might add."

"Thanks, but I'm sorry I lost it like that. It's just that I couldn't believe how Dad made one tiny attempt to get Brad to look at the family's situation from a viewpoint other than his own selfish one, and then Daddy folded his tent the second he got the slightest opposition from Golden Boy and Mom."

"And you expected something different to happen?" Jamie headed down the steep hill toward the 101 Freeway and the airport. "And, incidentally, get ready," he warned. "Brad didn't actually fire you—which I knew he wouldn't in front of Mom and Dad because he needs to maintain a united front—but he's going to use the stock owed us to keep us tied to the company as long as he wants."

"That's what I just don't get," complained Juliet. "All that money in the balance—to say nothing of the fact that poor Dad will probably lose control of the hotel if the game company goes sideways at some point—and he just lets Mom and Brad roll over us all."

"Check and checkmate!" Jamie replied with a shrug.

"Did you ever beat Brad in a game of chess?" Before Juliet could answer, he pronounced, "No. Neither did I."

Juliet said glumly, "Basically, as long as we want the money we've worked for these five years, you and I will be slaves to the 'company store,' and Brad knows it." She stared out the window at the stream of holiday traffic ahead of their car as they entered the freeway. "I am so ready to forget what's owed me for the work I've done, quit right now, and get on that plane today with you!"

"No!" Jamie insisted with startling vehemence. "I've switched sides about this."

"What?" Juliet said, alarmed.

Jamie shot her a grin. "After what you said last night, I see we can't give up yet. Your job, while I'm away, is to locate a killer lawyer not associated with GatherGames or the family and try to find out the true meaning of every, single sentence of fine print in our contracts regarding our stock. There might be something in there that would give us some leverage in negotiating an exit strategy, along with the dissenters on our board. Who knows what might happen if it got around to some of the board members that you and I were willing to join them in offering to sell our stock to any outside folks interested in acquiring GG? And if we can't get that deal, by next July—if I read our contracts correctly—we have every right to sell the family shares we each have and also exercise a portion of our options to buy more stock at the old price. At the very least we should get some independent legal advice about all this."

"Engaging our own lawyer would be considered family treason of the first order," Juliet noted, "but I hear you, and it might be the only way out of this nightmare. A fight with the VCs to the death on Brad's side could ruin everything for Dad—as well as us."

Jamie nodded in agreement. "Maybe Pa would finally

accept that sleeping with the enemy is the only way to get back his investment—or lose it all. For us, it's finding a way of bailing out of this horrible industry with at least some of the money we earned."

"Of course, if we join the dissident members of the board, we'd be putting Dad smack in the middle of a family feud," she warned morosely.

"When are you going to face it, Juliet?" Jamie demanded, moving into the right lane in order to take the exit into the airport. "He's Brad's father, as well as ours, and he did very little to come to our defense in this last go-around."

"Well, for sure he is the Man in the Middle. That's got to be hard."

"Look!" Jamie's exasperation was now boiling over. "Bradshaw Thayer, the Third, is a sweet guy and a pretty good architect, but he's weak. He'd sacrifice his nearest and dearest to avoid facing a conflict. Which means that even though we're worried about him—and, by the way, he'll worry about you and me as well—he's more than likely to allow us to get sold down the river by Brad or the VCs. Our father would do virtually *anything* to avoid having to grapple with our dear Mother-the-Engineer, a lady who crushed his balls long before we were born."

Juliet banged the back of her head against the car's leather headrest. "God Almighty, you just nailed it. This is absolutely awful!"

"Just go find us the right attorney, okay?"

Juliet nodded. "Okay, 'cause we're the only ones who will look out for our interests."

"Number one of which is to get out of the electronic war game business, agreed?"

Juliet nodded again as Jamie brought the car to a halt in front of the airport terminal.

"Not only do I want to get out of GatherGames, I'm

going to donate a big chunk of anything I end up with to some anti-bullying nonprofit that I'm going to track down!"

"Well, speaking of bullies... I've been meaning to ask you," he said. "When are you officially going to dump Jed Jarvis?" Juliet had earlier disclosed to her brother her plans to break it off with her supposed boyfriend. "That guy is no pal of ours, Juliet, and he'll side with Brad at every opportunity."

"He only got back from China yesterday when I saw him briefly at the office." She felt like such a wimp, because she could have dealt with this particular issue then and there. "If you must know, we haven't been together since before I went to Paris."

"Does he know you plan to give him the boot?"

"I didn't think it was decent to announce it in an email, or even on the phone." Silently, she was forced to admit to herself that she dreaded telling Jed to his face that it was over between them. Maybe she was more like her father than she realized?

"I never liked the guy," Jamie said as a security cop was walking in their direction while their car sat at the terminal's curb. "Jed used to get on my case all the time when I was a kid, just like Brad did."

"Well, here's the thing," she assured her brother, a sudden vision of Finn sitting across his couch from her on the *L'Étoile de Paris*. "Deleting that particular relationship is the next 'To Do' on my Christmas list."

Jamie raised his hand in a fist bump, which Juliet matched with a laugh. And with that, both of them got out of the car and met at the trunk. He handed her the keys.

"Well then, Happy Holidays, Sis," he said, giving her a hug before pulling his suitcase out of the back. "And thanks for putting me in touch with your friend Finn. I'll give him and Avery your very best."

Wishing for all the world that she could deliver that message in person, she summoned a smile and said, "Roger that. Merry Christmas, sweetheart. Travel safe."

CHAPTER 18

On Christmas Eve, Claudine Deschanel and her group of friends and family were among the hundreds of parishioners to emerge from Notre Dame with snow falling in a thin veil, dusting the ground as well the iron fencing marking the perimeter of the vast grounds. Finn stared up at the soaring spires that pierced scudding clouds overhead, certain that there would be even more snow by morning. His thoughts drifted like the icy flakes to a remembered vision of Nob Hill he'd seen as a boy, some 6000 miles away from where he walked in Paris this night. He wondered if Juliet would think of him at her local church service in San Francisco. He'd certainly found himself thinking of her as the solemn organ music reverberated against the cavernous cathedral's arched rafters.

To his right, Avery and Jamie Thayer walked side-by-side, their boots leaving a trail of slushy footprints. Finn had found Jamie to be a courteous houseguest on the barge, and from everything he'd observed thus far, the video editor and Avery appeared to be enjoying each other's company. This was a great relief to Finn, as he'd been vaguely worried that Avery, in her fragile state, might misinterpret his own genuine concern for her wellbeing as something…romantic. There were times when she seemed very needy—an emotional state that, from Juliet's descriptions, was not her friend's ordinary way of behaving. Her sole dependency on him regarding her diagnosed PTSD could have developed into a situation that would have made them both highly uncomfortable. He was grateful that Jamie had arrived at just the right moment.

The best news, as he reported to Juliet in their regular email exchanges, was that Avery's sessions with Dr. Abel also seemed to have helped bolster her psychological wellbeing. Fortunately, her left hand, arm, and shoulder had been unaffected by her injuries the night of the massacre, and with each day that she painted at her professor's private studio, she'd begun to recover some degree of normalcy in her life. In fact, Finn noticed that Avery currently spent more daylight hours at Professor Devereux's *atelier* than she did at her own flat, which was a good sign, he figured. He'd told Juliet that week that he imagined in a month or so, Avery might even be ready to return to her formal classes at art school.

As their little group reached the street, the wind picked up. Snow began to fall more heavily, coating the massive cathedral's outstretched flying buttresses with a mantel of white.

"Ah, there's a taxi!" Claudine exclaimed, startling him from his wandering thoughts. She pointed a gloved hand at a vehicle heading in a direction that would take them to her flat on the Left Bank. Finn already had his hand up and, as soon as the cab drew to the curb, they all piled into it and he gave the driver his aunt's address. Claudine had earlier proposed that they come to her apartment for midnight supper this Christmas Eve, a meal that she and her nephew had spent the day preparing. From his position in the front seat, Finn listened to the three backseat passengers' friendly chatter and felt gratified that Avery appeared to be taking his advice to guard against the instinct to "isolate...and call it self-preservation."

"I've had to fight shying away from other people all the time," he'd confessed to her recently, "but the good Doctor A urges me to keep in touch with those I know wish me well."

After he'd said that to Avery, the first image that had

come into his head was a vision of Juliet. Her understanding and empathy had been obvious from the start, and she'd even seemed to accept his confession that he was very attracted to her, even if she felt uncertain if he were "fit for duty" in a new relationship. She'd appeared immediately to grasp the issues and repercussions associated with his having PTSD and had been supportive of his need to understand the whys and wherefores of his failed marriage to Kim.

Why was it so hard for him to admit to Juliet the underlying reasons his marriage to Kim had blown up? *One thing is for sure—I can't totally blame everything that had happened on PTSD,* he thought with a stab of guilt. *God Almighty…why does life have to be so complicated?*

His meandering thoughts came to an abrupt halt when the taxi drew up to Claudine's front door.

"Ah, good!" declared his aunt. "Here we are."

"I'll get this," Jamie insisted, quickly handing their driver some cash. "I'm finally getting the hang of these euros."

Once the group arrived inside the door to Claudine's flat, Jamie suggested they call Juliet—San Francisco being eight hours behind Paris time—and wish her an early Merry Christmas.

Avery glanced at her watch and clapped her hands with delight. "Yes. It's just past midnight here, so it's officially Christmas—in Paris, at least. Oh, how I miss that girl!"

"This is the first Christmas I haven't celebrated the holiday with her," Jamie said, handing over his cell phone. "Go on, Avery…you call her. She'll be thrilled to hear your voice."

As for Finn, he felt a deep pang of regret that he wasn't spending his *first* Christmas with Jamie's sister—and wondered at the strangeness of it all. When it was his turn to say hello to Juliet, he immediately sensed that she might be the one feeling depressed. Turning his back on the group at Claudine's, he took a few paces toward the apartment's foyer for privacy's sake and asked in a low voice if everything was all right.

"Actually? No...it's not. In fact, it's pretty grim around here," she said. "There's a big power struggle going on at work—and at home, too. I dread meeting everyone at church tonight, and then at my parents' suite tomorrow morning to supposedly celebrate Christmas Day."

"Trouble in a family business has gotta be tough." Finn wished again they weren't across the world from each other. "I'm really sorry you're going through something like this, Juliet. I'm sure it only feels worse since it's Christmastime."

Silence rang in his ear. She finally spoke, an audible catch in her throat. "It *is* the worst! You cannot know how much I wish I was in Paris with you all."

"So do I, *mademoiselle*...so do I."

"Tonight I'm going to walk down Taylor Street on Nob Hill with my family for evening service at Grace Cathedral. It's usually so beautiful there on Christmas Eve, but it all feels so hypocritical. This year is horribly different with Jamie away and...all the other stuff going on."

"Your brother is a great guy, and he seems to be enjoying himself, but I'm sure you miss not having him there for Christmas."

"I do." Her melancholy palpable, she said barely above a whisper, "I miss you, too, Finn."

"Same here. In fact, I'll double that."

In a small voice she promised, "Shall I light a candle in your honor at Grace Cathedral later tonight?"

"I just did the same thing for you at Notre Dame." He hoped the truth of this would cheer her a bit.

"You did?" He was startled to hear tears edging her

words. "Oh, Finn…that means…a lot. Thank you so much!"

"Well, I'll thank you in advance for returning the favor…and I'll picture you there in San Francisco, asking for forgiveness of my sins," he said with a wry smile she could not see.

"Oh, please, Finn…," she murmured, "You're no sinner. Just look at the glass house I'm living in right now. No one is speaking to each other these days and we're still about to release the most grisly video war game ever, yet…off we Thayers will go to church tonight."

In a rush she told him about the coming release of GatherGames' *Sky Slaughter 2: Drones in the Desert*, and described a series of heated arguments she'd had with Brad over the violence depicted in every aspect of the latest war game, its packaging, and especially its promotion.

"I tried to make him tone it all down, but I've lost every battle. The hell of it is, now that I'm back home and know the details of what's going on around here, I *can't* quit until the struggle for control of the company is settled. My father and mother don't agree on anything that's going on, and I feel so guilty about what I'm doing at work, and the money I'm making, and I can barely drag myself to office every day." She paused and then said, "Why am I burdening you with this? There's nothing you can do and you probably think I'm—"

"Look, Juliet," Finn cut in. "That's exactly how I felt before I resigned my Air Force commission. Believe me, I feel for you and I can tell that you are trying your very best to figure it all out. No one can tell you what to do, and certainly not yours truly. Just know this, though," he said, wishing he could reach through the phone and take her in his arms to offer comfort for the misery she was clearly going through, "I have full confidence you'll find your way through this tangle…and out the other side."

He could tell Juliet was covering the microphone on her mobile so he wouldn't hear her crying.

Finally she whispered, "Thanks for that. You're really a wonderful guy, you know that?"

"Why, thank you, ma'am," he said, wishing for the hundredth time that the two were in the same time zone.

"I've done one good thing, however," she said.

"Just one?" he teased, thinking of her many kindnesses to Avery—and to himself. "And what is that?"

"I am officially no longer thought of as Jed Jarvis's girlfriend."

Finn felt an unexpected rush of relief that hit him right in the gut. "Ah-ha. Glad to hear it. Was it hard?" he couldn't resist asking.

"So easy, it was kind of indicative of our entire relationship. Our discussion turned out to be a sort of 'Frankly, Scarlett, I-don't-think-he-gives-a-damn' experience."

Finn roared with laughter, followed by her muffled voice telling someone she would meet them in the hotel lobby in a couple of hours.

"You gotta go, right?" he confirmed.

"Not for a little while yet," she assured him. "But there's something else I want you to know. Remember what I said when I first met you: that I'd never cast the first stone at you?"

"Yes."

"Well, it's truer than ever, given our latest video. I had to go to the final screening this week and the images haunt me night and day. All I can think of is that you lived it all for real."

Finn replied in a manner he hoped she'd interpret as humor, "Hey, you're a girl. You females are a superior species and your brains are wired to want to protect what you love, not destroy it."

"Is that ever true," she murmured. "Please tell

everyone in Paris I miss them so much and that I'm sending all my Christmas love…and especially to you, too, flyboy."

"Thank you. The same back. And by the way, it's already Christmas in Paris so may yours—when it officially arrives—turn out better than you fear."

"And enjoy yours, you lucky duck. Bye," she said, her voice barely audible and with a wistfulness that made his throat tighten—and then she clicked off.

When Finn awoke a few hours later, he saw a message and a photo on his cell phone featuring a close up of a glowing, ruby-red votive candle sitting on an altar in a side chapel of Grace Cathedral. Below the picture was a text from Juliet.

> **Dearest Finn:**
> **Here's your very own candle, lighted in your name.**
> **Merry Christmas, cher monsieur…"**

The following day, Juliet knocked on the door of her parents' suite hoping the traditional Thayer family breakfast on Christmas morning would be as uneventful as the church service they'd attended the previous evening. She'd managed to sit at the far end of one pew and avoided all but the most perfunctory conversation with the rest of the family. Afterward, her parents and she walked the four blocks down Taylor Street to the Bay View while Brad wandered off to a friend's Christmas Eve party. Her hope was that her brother would have had his fair share of potent eggnog and would sleep in, giving the morning meal a pass.

A few moments after her knock, her father's voice rang out, "Come in!"

She entered the beautifully appointed rooms facing San Francisco Bay and exchanged air-kisses and "Merry Christmas" with her parents. Sage green satin draperies and a matching collection of loveseats and chairs positioned around a marble fireplace gave the family quarters the turn-of-the-century *beaux arts* elegance that Juliet had known at the Bay View all through her childhood. In one corner stood a small, stylishly decorated Christmas tree installed, as it was each year, by the hotel's decorator.

"No Brad, yet?" she asked in what she hoped was a cheerful, nonjudgmental tone.

Her mother sent her a look that bordered on a scowl. "He just called. He's running late, putting out a number of fires, he told me. On Christmas, mind you!" She raised her index finger and pointed it in Juliet's direction. "I hope you haven't been discussing anything with other employees about the…ah…issues regarding the unpleasantness going on right now."

"Frankly, I have no idea what's going on 'right now,' other than getting yelled at by my sainted brother at every turn."

"Now, Juliet…Mildred," her father stepped in. "Can't we *not* talk about business for at least this one day in the year?"

Her mother tossed her head and walked over to a sideboard that had to be a hundred years old, but whose mahogany had been painted a pale sage to match the drapes. She poured herself a glass of orange juice. "Well, at least without Jamie here," she said over her shoulder, "we don't have to listen to you and him whining in stereo."

Juliet shot a look at her father who returned a sympathetic gaze but remained silent. With a sigh, she reached into a colorful shopping bag she'd brought with her and placed three presents under the tree.

"Coffee, pet?" her father asked her, and Juliet could

tell he was doing his best to try to smooth things over.

"Absolutely," she responded and crossed to the cart brought up by room service before her arrival. She was cheered to see the hotel's famous popovers—crisp and warm—nestled on a linen napkin in a silver bowl, along with soft, sweet butter and raspberry jam.

Twenty minutes later, after everyone had poured a second cup of coffee, Juliet's father glanced at his watch. "Well, it's obviously taking Brad longer than he thought. Luncheon will be served downstairs at one, so why don't we start to open our presents?"

He reached for a small box from under the tree. Juliet immediately recognized the familiar wrappings that identified the package having come from Gumps, the venerable department store that had prospered in downtown San Francisco ever since gold and silver were discovered in California in the mid-nineteenth century.

"Dad?" Juliet breathed. "What naughty thing have you done?"

"It's for you...from your mother and me."

Her mother merely cocked an eyebrow and remained silent as Juliet untied the silk bow. Inside was a small, jade dolphin on a delicate gold chain.

"Oh...it's beautiful!" Juliet breathed. "I love it!"

She had first seen the creatures as a little girl when a pod swam just offshore on a warm day near Baker Beach.

"I still have the dolphins you drew when you were seven, framed in my office downstairs," her father said with a chuckle. 'I knew, then, you'd be an artist or architect someday."

Juliet smiled at the memory. A few days after her excitement over the sighting, she'd created her first seascape on a piece of paper she'd found on her father's slanted drawing board. She'd used his colored pencils to draw several of the mammals arching above the water.

"Here, help me put this on," she said, turning toward her mother to fasten the clasp. "Thank you so much," she said over her shoulder as her mother attached one end of the fine gold chain to the other.

"Don't thank me. Your father picked it out."

"I meant thanks for helping me put it on."

Will we never understand each other, she wondered bleakly?

Mildred Thayer was as protective as a mother grizzly over anything and everything that concerned her firstborn, yet Juliet had always felt that she had disapproved of practically everything her daughter ever said or did. Juliet cast a questioning glance at her father, who quickly looked down at his coffee cup. Then a strange thought occurred to her. Was her mother actually jealous that her dad had picked out such a piece of lovely, sentimental jewelry for his daughter? Juliet couldn't deny she had always played the role of "Daddy's girl," but, after all, she *was* the only female of the three siblings. No one could deny that she and her father had many things in common, including a love of art and design. Why did her mother seem to take offense at his slightest gesture of affection?

With an inward sigh—and for something to do to fill the silence in the room—she walked over to the sparkling tree. A package the size of a wall calendar leaned against a lower branch and had her name on the tag.

"Who's this from?" she wondered aloud.

"It arrived yesterday," her mother said from the upholstered chair that was pulled up near the crackling fire. "It came from Paris," she added, her voice edged with— *what*, wondered Juliet? *Anger? More disapproval?* "It had Avery Evan's name on the outside packaging."

Given the strained relationship between Brad and his former employee, Juliet figured it might be wise to unwrap the present before her brother arrived and then discreetly put it into the large shopping bag she'd brought with her.

She ran her finger under the silver paper.

"Oh!" she exclaimed, as she pushed aside the wrapping to reveal an oil portrait.

It was an amazing, close up likeness of Finn Deschanel standing on the deck outside the barge's pilothouse with the Eiffel Tower looming across the river over his left shoulder. Avery had perfectly captured the unusually dark blue shade of his eyes, much bluer, even, than the sky that surrounded his head. Her breath caught as she absorbed Finn's sharply defined, high cheekbones and strong jaw...yet Avery had portrayed the exact vulnerability around his mouth she clearly recalled. She couldn't stop staring at the lips that had kissed her so passionately the night before she flew back to San Francisco. Attached was a card in Avery's handwriting.

> *Something tells me this belongs to you.*
> *Your flyboy has been the best friend a*
> *PTSD survivor could have. I think it's fair*
> *to say we both miss you madly.*
> *Merry Christmas and come back in the spring.*
> *Love, A*

By this time, her father was peering over her shoulder at the painting.

"Why, that's first rate work," he praised, adding, "and don't you think it's a good sign that Avery is able to paint again?"

"This portrait proves to me that Avery *wants* to paint again," Juliet replied. She sought her father's glance. "She was horribly traumatized by what happened when her friend died—"

"Yes, yes...we've heard all that before," Mildred interrupted. "No need to bring up such depressing things on Christmas, for pity's sake!"

Juliet's father had continued to inspect the portrait, and then seized the card and looked at his daughter with a sly grin. "So, I can see by the flight jacket that this is the former Air Force pilot you met that Jamie said he'd be staying with in France. Handsome young man, if Avery's work is true-to-life. What sort of aircraft did he fly?"

"Rescue helicopters in the Middle East," she said, noting how her mother was now paying close attention to their conversation, "and then—after he got shot down—he piloted unmanned drones."

"Is he a friend of Avery's?" Mildred asked, her eyes narrowing.

"Actually, I met him first," she disclosed reluctantly, "at the American Hospital where Avery was taken, along with her friend who died—and who happened to be the grandson of my friend Finn's landlady.

"Ah…so I gather this pilot is the source of your opinions about the dangers of using drones in warfare… and private encryption used by civilians?" Mildred said sharply. She looked at her husband. "Not surprising, is it? Most military men are against others demanding their civil rights of free expression."

Juliet shook her head in frustration. "Major Finn Deschanel actually thinks encryption is necessary in today's world, but he quit the military rather than to continue flying drones, Mother, so I doubt you know *what* his opinions are."

"I can certainly guess!" she shot back. "We all know that the U.S. government uses encryption. But it's no secret they wouldn't want anyone to gain a back door into *their* version of this secret coding."

"The difference there is—they're trying to protect this country, not train America's youth to be electronic killing machines just for fun and profit!" Juliet felt her ire starting to rise as it always did in these discussions.

Mildred, too, was starting to get upset.

"You're sounding like a broken record! Brad reviews

all the research data and there's very little that says video war games make kids any more aggressive than playing football does."

"That sounds suspiciously like the arguments the tobacco industry used—'there's no absolute proof that cigarettes, alone, cause cancer.'"

"Look, gals," the senior Brad intervened, pretending to play the lighthearted mediator, "This is one of those discussions that turns out to be kinda like Pandora's Box. Once it's opened, all sorts of devilish beasts can fly out. It's Christmas! Can't we call a moratorium on this discussion— at least just for today?"

Her mother smiled as if she'd won the skirmish.

"You're right, for once." She flashed him a manufactured smile. Then she turned to Juliet, pointing at the portrait in her lap. "I suggest you put that away. I don't want you to use Avery's gift to rile up Brad by saying Jamie went to Paris to see to her welfare. He considers Avery Evans disloyal in the extreme."

"I'm sure Brad already has figured out that if Jamie went to Paris in the dead of winter, he'd surely see Avery in the wake of the Paris attacks."

Silently she speculated on what her mother would think if she knew her precious elder son had sexually accosted Avery in this very hotel. Juliet struggled to keep from bursting out with this defense of her friend, so, instead, she took pains to neatly wrap Avery's portrait of Finn in its silvery paper and slip it into her Christmas carry-bag.

Just as she'd stowed the present behind one of the upholstered chairs near the fireplace, brother Brad, along with Jed Jarvis, walked into the room without knocking. "Hey, Dad...Mom," he said as he and Jed advanced into the room. "Merry Christmas," he added perfunctorily He looked at his sister and then looked away, as if dismissing her very presence.

Brad senior glanced briefly at Juliet and said to his son, "Just one thing today, all right? No family spats."

"Oh, no!" Jed joked, punching Brad in the arm. "Did I miss another Thayer family argument? Juliet is so entertaining when she gets red in the face."

"Merry Christmas to you, too, Jed," she snapped.

"That's a *joke*, Juliet," he replied, pursing his lips. "You're so touchy these days." He leaned toward her ear and whispered, "PMS a problem this week?"

Juliet reared back in her chair and stared at the long, lanky figure in a black T-shirt matching the one Brad always wore.

"Cut it out, Jed," she warned in a low voice, "or you can leave right now."

How in the world had she ever considered this guy a boyfriend or, worse yet, slept with him? It was a question about which she owed it to herself to spend some time seriously considering since at that moment, she could hardly stand the sight of him.

Meanwhile, an uncomfortable silence filled the room. Juliet recognized that it was her own damn fault Jed had come to the annual Thayer family brunch. Since no one in the room knew she'd officially broken up with Brad's oldest buddy, he'd obviously been extended his usual invitation to join them Christmas morning.

Glancing at Jed, now, she recalled how hugely relieved she'd been when he hadn't shown the slightest concern or dismay over her recent actions to end their relationship. Even so, given Jed's behavior just now, she could see that he was, indeed, upset by her rejection, mostly due to pure pride and not any great sense of loss, she imagined. She seriously doubted that he'd even admitted to anyone— including Brad—that she'd dumped him. But why hadn't *she* let her parents know?

She knew the answer before it had formed in her

mind. She was chicken. She had used the excuse of it's being the holidays and the current family turmoil with the family business to avoid telling them. The main reason, she knew—if she were brutally honest with herself—was that she'd been afraid to face even more of her mother's wrath.

When will I simply not care if my mother approves of me or not, she wondered bleakly.

She glanced again at Jed. A look of feigned, injured innocence had spread across his face. Then, he merely shrugged, as if Juliet's existence was of no consequence. He and Brad moved to the sideboard where, instead of orange juice, Jed poured himself a generous cup of the family's traditional champagne-laced punch.

He leaned toward Brad and said just loud enough for Juliet to hear, "I have to hand it to you, buddy…I'm amazed how you can deal with Debbie Downer twenty-four-seven."

Juliet reached behind her chair, grabbed the edge of the wrapped portrait of Finn, and rose to her feet. *I have to get out of here, or I am going to start to scream!* She forced a smile and addressed the assembled group. "Continue opening presents, everyone. I'm just going to take my loot to my room. Be back in a bit," she added, and before anyone could stop her, she made her escape.

CHAPTER 19

"Avery, the portrait of Finn is fantastic!" Juliet declared into the wavy Skype image of her friend that appeared on her laptop. "I'm so happy you're painting so wonderfully again."

"It's the first new one I started since...well, you know," she said with a wan smile. "I wanted to thank both you and Finn for all you've done to help me."

"So Finn's shrink was a good thing?"

"Helping both of us, I think. That doc really knows her stuff. She worked for the VA before she joined the American Hospital, here. Among several things we do in our sessions, she's basically showing me how to retrain my brain and consciously choose to think something else when bad stuff comes up. It doesn't always work, mind you, as Finn has probably told you, but I'm definitely getting better."

"Does he know you sent me the portrait of him?" Juliet asked casually.

On her laptop's screen Avery's smile grew wide and she chuckled. "Of course! I thought I'd better get his permission before I gave it to you. His only worry is that you wouldn't know what to do with it."

Juliet held her laptop's pinpoint camera in the direction of the portrait so Avery could see it was in her room.

"Well, I love it! I'm going to hang it today on my wall, right over there," she gestured. "Tell Finn I'm thrilled to have it, will you please?"

"Here, tell him yourself. It started snowing like mad last night so we all decided to stay over at Claudine's after midnight mass at Notre Dame. Now Jamie and I and my art professor are at Finn's barge for supper. Here, let me hand my cell phone to him."

Juliet had been so concentrated on Avery's face on the screen that she hadn't noticed the background, which she now saw was the wood and glass windows identifying the pilothouse interior on *L'Étoile de Paris*.

Finn's handsome face and distinctive deep voice suddenly filled her screen, a replica of the portrait she still held in her hand.

"Hi…Merry Christmas again," he said. "Or I should say *Joyeux Noël*."

"And the same to you."

He cast her an apologetic look. "Hold on just a sec, will you? I'm cooking something on one of my burners. Let me turn it down while we talk." He turned away to fiddle with the controls and soon turned back to her.

"What are you making?" she asked.

"I'm hoping I've mastered *Coquilles St. Jacques*."

"Oooh, fresh scallops dripping in that wonderful cheesy white wine sauce?"

"Lots of white wine called for so, I figured how bad could it be?" Then he added, "The good Doctor A says booze cooked in food is okay…all the intoxicants are gone."

Juliet laughed. "The taste without the one-two punch. Clever you!" Then she asked, "You even have the shells to serve them in?"

Juliet told him about one of the Bay View's chef specialties, that of making sea scallops presented in large shells and cooked in a Napa Valley *sauvignon blanc*.

"Borrowed the shells from Aunt Claudine. The lady worked for *Vogue* for thirty years, don't forget. She possesses every specialty serving item known to the culinary world."

"It sounds like you're all having fun," she said, unable to keep the wistful tone from her voice. "Wish I could say the same."

Finn frowned and paused. "Hey, what's wrong? More family squabbles?"

"That, plus Jed was just being a son-of-a-gun this morning. I'm glad Jamie is missing all the nastiness, but man, do I wish I were over there with you all."

"*I* wish you were right beside me, helping dish out the chow."

She laughed. "Chow? You need a much more elegant turn of phrase for the French cuisine you're creating."

"Speaking of which, hold on again." He walked toward his right where the sink and burners were embedded in the desktop. "I'm turning this baby off. There!" She could clearly see the Eiffel Tower out his window. "Okay, what gives with that ex-boyfriend of yours?"

"Oh, I don't want to put a damper on your day, there," she hastened to say, trying to wind up their conversation on a positive note. "I'll tell you sometime when your scallops aren't bubbling. Enjoy your feast, but you'd better let me speak to my baby brother before I sign off."

"Okay," he replied and she could hear the reluctance in his voice, "but I mean it, Juliet. I *really* wish you were here with us."

"Thank you for that…and the sentiment is mutual, believe me. At least I have Avery's wonderful portrait of you for company in my rooms."

"It felt a little weird when she showed it to me, saying it was her Christmas present to you. I thought maybe you won't want it, or won't have a place to hang it."

"I love it, Finn," she assured him. "See that wall behind my desk over there?" She pointed behind and to her right. "It's going right there as soon as I can get a hammer and nail."

Finn's relieved expression filled the screen. "Turns out Avery sneaked a photo of me and worked from that for a week. Now, I want her to do one of *you*. I've commissioned her, in fact." Before Juliet could react to this startling news, he said, "I gave her that great picture I took of you sketching the de Medici Fountain at the Luxembourg Gardens that day. Uh oh. Here's Jamie. Bye, now."

Sensing her call was interrupting the party, Juliet briefly told Jamie how she'd just literally fled the family scene.

"Brad hasn't softened his position one iota since you've been gone. He's demanding our total loyalty in the coming fight with the VCs. Wants everyone to sign some sort of document, but I haven't seen what it says, yet."

"Holy crap. The guy is paranoid."

"Maybe not. The rumblings are getting louder about a potential takeover. I can tell Brad knows that there are folks who wouldn't necessarily fight a change of control."

"What does the lawyer say about *our* position?"

"He's still looking into it at the rate of six-hundred-and-seventy-five-bucks-an-hour."

"Wow. Well, let me know what you find out, as I'd really like to never come home." Then Jamie amended, "For a while, at least."

"I hear ya. Sounds like you're having fun, right?"

Jamie's voice lowered and he turned his back to the others who were sipping drinks and eating some sort of hors d'oeuvre. "Like you, I love Paris, but I've got some close competition here, I think."

"With Avery? Really?"

"Really," he repeated in an even lower voice.

"Who?" *Please not Finn,* she thought suddenly.

She saw her brother cup his hand over the phone's speaker. "A Frenchman. Alain somebody. He's standing right behind me. He's Avery's art teacher where she studies. He *eez ver-ry char-mant*, you know what I'm saying?"

Juliet glimpsed the elbow and shoulder of an additional male figure in the background. She could see the furrows between Jamie's eyebrows. She smiled back at him with as much cheer as she could muster.

"Look, bro…you're pretty damn charming yourself, so don't give up. Alain's been great to Avery since the attacks, that's all. Meanwhile, say hello to the Eiffel Tower, will you?"

Jamie turned his head to look out the windows facing the river. "Ah…so you know this view pretty well, do you?" His grin looked comically distorted on her screen.

"Only as a very well-behaved guest." Then she added, "I miss that view. A lot."

In the way that Jamie could always read her like a book, he said, "Does Jed know how you feel about the view?"

"He knows I finally told him to get lost."

"Well, now…that *is* a nice Christmas present," chortled her brother.

Juliet laughed too. "Merry Christmas, Jamie. Give my love to everyone there."

It had begun to rain hard by the time Juliet reached the lawyer's office on Battery Street on a cold January afternoon, two days after New Year's. Edward Adelman, of Adelman and Marx, was a specialist, she'd learned, about stock options in start-up companies that had gone public on the New York Stock Exchange. Adelman was also skilled in coordinating hostile takeovers—or fighting them. Whatever his clients hired him to do.

The advocate, celebrated among his peers for his lean-and-mean approach to the law, reached for her dripping raincoat and hung it on the back of his office door. If he weren't in his custom suit and tie, Juliet speculated he was most likely one of San Francisco's "Spandex Warriors." These were the sinewy professional men in their mid-thirties and forties seen hunched over six-thousand-dollar road bikes as they crossed the Golden Gate Bridge most weekends and toiled up Mount Tamalpais in Marin County on the other side of the Bay. Juliet judged the man was fit, buffed, and only mildly arrogant.

Deeply conscious of the clock ticking at $675 an hour, she swiftly broached the reason for wanting this face-to-face meeting following a brief conversation by phone.

"So, Mr. Adelman—"

"Edward...please," he said with a practiced smile as he indicated a chair opposite his office desk and closed the door.

"Edward," she corrected herself, ignoring a sixth sense that he might be coming on to her. "So, from our initial phone call, it sounds as if you're saying that my younger brother and our parents and my own best chance for receiving the most advantageous payout to exercise our company stock options would occur *if* there is a change-of-control within the company?"

Adelman nodded, adding "And in the case of you and James, this would be especially true if you two elect—or are asked—to terminate your employment at GatherGames as the new owners take control."

"Got it," Juliet said.

"Under those circumstances you would—or *I* would, actually—bargain for an immediate payout of your stock and for an acceleration of your options granted to you to purchase more stock at the price when the company was founded. All this would be in exchange for a fast exit—which would then, of course, leave your brother Bradshaw without some important family allies and bolster your position with the take-over contingent even more strongly."

"Whoa…" Juliet said on a long breath. "That's pretty radical. Is it the only way to get my parents, Jamie, and me out of this thing in one piece?"

The hotshot lawyer nodded once more, a self-satisfied smile quirking the corners of his mouth. Then his expression grew serious. "This is a guts ball game," he warned. "In the legal world, we call it '*negotiated* accelerated vesting' caused by an 'ownership change of control,' coupled to the termination of you and your brother as employees—with all events orchestrated to happen at the same time. It's a pretty neat hat trick, but we've managed it in a number of hostile takeover situations like yours."

"In other words, the dissident investors on our board of directors, or someone they choose, take over—and Jamie and I and our parents band together for a certain price that the new owners are willing to pay us immediately, in return for surrendering our roles at work, our stock, the options, and votes—and all this takes place at the same time?"

"Correct."

"And what about my parents' ten-million-dollar equity loan on the hotel granted GatherGames when the company concentrated solely on video war games?"

Adelman smiled, clearly enjoying his role as the maestro of this mischief.

"As I pointed out earlier, all these transactions would have to be negotiated almost simultaneously with the new management. Paying off the equity loan against the Bay View Hotel would be part of the overall deal."

"It does sound tricky."

"It certainly can be…but that's why you hire someone like me."

"At your hourly rate…which I calculate is about

$11.25 a minute," Juliet said baldly, "tricky is as tricky does, I suppose."

Edward Adelman blinked as his lips settled into a straight line that reminded her faintly of Jed whenever she'd disagreed with something he'd said.

"Actually, you'll be paying me about nineteen cents a *second* to pull off this particular trick."

"If you actually do pull it off, it'll certainly be worth it," she replied. "But if it doesn't work, my parents could lose everything, we could end up with pennies on the dollars of our five-year investment and nobody in the family speaking to each other."

She allowed her words to hang in the air. Adelman cocked his head and cast her a steady look, as if accustomed to hearing the veiled complaint that the firm's fees were outrageous, even by San Francisco standards— and with no guarantee of a happy outcome.

No point in beating around the bush, she thought. "So what do you calculate are our chances of success?"

"You all have a fair amount of clout in this situation, given the shares of stock you own outright, along with the hefty number of stock options that you, your younger brother, and your parents have been granted as founding employees and investors. It's probably very worth your while to initiate such bold moves so you can cash in the options as well as the stock long before the ten-year expiration date."

"Ten years?" she moaned. "I thought it was two! Isn't that the deal I signed?"

"In certain instances, yes, it's a ten-year wait. You can sell the family-held stock at five years, which occurs in July of this year." He glanced at the sheaf of papers on his desk, adding, "Bradshaw Junior's granting you those additional stock options when you became design director last year might not have been legal without the normal, longer waiting period, but I'll negotiate all issues at the same time, seeking an immediate payout of everything from the new owners. It's been done in other cases."

Juliet was aghast that she'd known so little about the papers she'd signed. She silently chastised herself for not consulting her own lawyer long before this. When the company had been formed, she'd signed her name on whatever her father or Brad put in front of her, assuming that they both had her best interests at heart.

She'd been only half right.

Edward said, "From the contracts you showed me, your father signed the same deal, as did your brother James. The reason for the usual ten-year delay to exercise and sell *all* your stock options is to grant the company stability. However, when founding members do cash out at a given date, they reap the rewards for having worked since Day One."

"But what if my parents don't want to do what Jamie and I want to do?" she asked with a worried frown. "What then?"

Her mother's blind loyalty to her eldest son was a huge obstacle to overcome, along with her proven ability to control her husband on this subject.

"In that scenario, if you authorize me to, I will do my best to secure a favorable settlement of these questions for just you—and your brother James, too, if he so desires. We'd still propose to those taking over the company an accelerated vesting in such a way to reduce your tax liability."

Juliet tapped the pile of papers sitting on the highly polished desk. "Jamie and I will pay whatever tax is due because we want out immediately if there's a change of control. Expect to hear from us if we decide to exercise this plan."

"Of course," he murmured. "I understand. As you

said on the phone, this is just an exploratory meeting today."

She glanced at the wall behind Adelman's head and noted a Stanford diploma, wondering, with a sharp intake of breath, if the ice-in-his-veins attorney was in college at the same time Brad was. She pointed above his head. "I see you went to the same university my brothers did. Just to confirm...my coming to see you and the matters we've discussed won't leave this room, correct?"

"Of course not," he responded, clearly offended by such a suggestion. "Our firm promises absolute confidentiality."

"San Francisco's a small town," she reminded him.

"And we are a firm that obeys the strict rules of the California Bar Association."

"Glad to hear it," she replied, offering him her sweetest smile. "Did you know my brother Brad when you were there?"

"I certainly knew who he was. So do most of the Stanford grads in town, I suspect. Champion long-distance runner, *summa cum laude*, then biz school star, and all that."

"That's why I asked," she said, her glance locked on his.

The attorney looked down at the file folders on his desk and said, "Well, rest assured, nothing that transpired in this room leaves this room."

Juliet glanced at her watch. She'd been there two minutes shy of an hour.

"Excellent. Well, tick-tock. The hour's not quite up and it's time for me to go."

Edward Adelman rose from his executive chair and retrieved her raincoat from the hook behind his door. He helped her put it on and escorted her to the reception area, nodding a greeting to a colleague who was just then emerging from another office. As attorney and client approached the elevators, Juliet noted the young associate wore perfectly pleated, navy trousers, a sky blue and pressed dress shirt—no tie—but with the sleeves rolled halfway up, revealing the deeply tanned forearms of a weekend athlete.

"Hey, Eddie. Up for a game of squash tonight?" he called to her attorney.

"Can't, Gavin. Gotta a ton of work. Maybe on the weekend?"

The other lawyer shot Juliet an appreciative glance before he raised his hand, cocked his thumb over two extended fingers, and feigned shooting at Adelman. "Gotcha. We've gotta plan, buddy."

Still smiling, he winked in Juliet's direction.

What an ass… That could just as easily have been Jed Jarvis sauntering down the hall, she thought.

The elevator arrived. "Good to have met you in person, Ms. Thayer," Adelman assured her, holding his palm against the door to allow her to step inside.

Juliet smiled her thanks. "I'll be in touch when my brother James and I—and my parents—have a chance to confer and then come to some decision about what we want to do next. It may be a while, but you'll hear from me either way."

"If the rumors of a take-over get any louder, don't wait too long. Timing is everything in these matters."

"Quite a juggling act," she agreed tersely. Then she added, "Thanks again."

After the meeting with her attorney, Juliet felt matters in her life had suddenly gone far beyond mere juggling. She was now engaged in a high-wire act, balancing a high-pressure job she despised with operating in sleuth mode to try to stay on top of the constant maneuverings of

GatherGames' wrangling board members. Rumors were rife that companies like Nintendo, Rock Star, Valve, and Sony Computer Entertainment were all sniffing around, aware of the possibility that the company's restless principal investors might be interested in doing a merger or encouraging a takeover bid.

Two days after Juliet's meeting with Adelman, the attorney gave her the good news that he had all the rules and regulations at his fingertips and was ready to "execute" whenever she felt it appropriate to "pull the trigger" on negotiating a total buyout. Juliet had taken his call in the empty ladies room at work and then had immediately called France.

"Okay, then," Jamie said. "But I think, for the moment, we should just sit tight and keep our mouths shut and our ears to the ground."

"But if this takeover kicks in," she whispered hoarsely, repeating the lawyer's warning over the phone, "we *cannot* hesitate. At that point I'll give Mom and Dad the same information the lawyer gave us. It's up to them to decide what they want to do."

"Good work, Sis. I'll see you soon."

"How's it going with Avery?"

"Tell you when I get home. Bye, now."

CHAPTER 20

Jamie arrived in San Francisco from Paris a few days after Juliet's conference with her attorney. Both siblings reluctantly soldiered on at work, informing each other of various office rumors floating down the halls.

On a surprisingly balmy evening in March, the pair sat at an outside table at Poggio, their favorite restaurant across the Golden Gate Bridge in the little maritime town of Sausalito. Tourists meandered along the streets, window-shopping and licking their over-sized ice cream cones, while, in the distance, a deep horn blast announced the departure of a local ferry to San Francisco.

Jamie took a sip of his wine and grimaced.

"What?" Juliet demanded.

"I was just thinking. Once I finally get free from everything—unlike you, who'll be heading for Paris—I don't actually know what my next move is."

"Editing feature films at Pixar?" she asked hopefully.

"That train already left the station, I'm afraid."

"How about Paris, yourself?"

"I'm pretty sure that's a non-starter."

"You mean, with Avery?"

Jamie glumly disclosed that Avery had told him she felt she was not "fit for any relationship other than friendship" while she was going through physical and psychological rehab. Remembering that Finn had said something similar, Juliet reached a sympathetic hand across the linen-clad table.

"And then there's that art teacher guy, Alain," he reminded her.

Juliet had been startled to see that Avery's art teacher

had joined her on Christmas Eve. *Was he just a good friend and mentor, or more than that?* Until Juliet knew for sure, she wouldn't offer an opinion on that subject, but replied, only, "If I were you, I wouldn't give up just yet about Avery. I imagine she's simply speaking the truth about where she is emotionally in the wake of the trauma she's experienced. From my reading about PTSD, it's going to take her some time to work her way though what's happened to her."

Jamie cast a sideways glance. "Finn told me he's dealt with similar issues because of his time in the Middle East and getting shot down and all."

Juliet leaned back in her chair. "He told you about that?" she murmured, guessing that Finn did *not* tell her brother much about his stint as a drone pilot. Finn's specific duties were most probably still top secret stuff, and she suspected that he had revealed to her the death of the little boy caught in the crossfire only because the two of them felt an emotional closeness in the raw aftermath of the Paris attacks last November.

Jamie nodded. "Yeah, he told me about his helicopter going down in Afghanistan and how the concussive force of the crash rattled his head pretty good." Her brother smiled at her across the table. "Finn's a great guy. I think he likes you a lot."

Juliet could feel a flush moving up her neck into her checks.

"I like him a lot, too, but wouldn't you say that at the moment, we're both geographically unsuitable, plus a few other outstanding issues?"

Like the small detail that he's still married to Kim...

Jamie said, "At the moment, I'd say yes. But down the road?" Her brother cocked an eyebrow. "When you go back to Paris to study at *L'École* like our great-great granny," he grinned, "who the heck knows what might happen?"

Finn's hands were filled with his latest purchases from an open-air street market when Aunt Claudine opened the door to her apartment and greeted him on the threshold. He had barely put his packages down on her gleaming Carrera marble countertops when she handed him a letter stamped with a U.S. Government address on the envelope.

He ripped it open, his eyes swiftly scanning the first paragraph.

"Holy…shit…" he breathed.

Claudine leaned over his shoulder. "What is it?"

"It's from someone in our Embassy here in Paris who is also attached to the European Command. He's asking to schedule an appointment concerning an 'Allied Joint Task Force for European Security being set up in the wake of the Paris attacks.' One part of the plan is to use small drones to survey vulnerable infrastructure."

"So?" Claudine said skeptically. "How does that concern you?" She squinted at the letter a few moments longer and sighed. "Do I see the hand of my dear brother in this latest development?"

"I think that's a big, fat 'yes.'"

Claudine offered a Gallic shrug. "Well, strange as this may sound, coming from *moi,*" she said, studying the next few paragraphs along with her nephew, "never say 'no' until you know what they're offering." She poured herself a glass of white wine from a bottle sitting on an ornate silver tray in the center of the kitchen island. "You're looking for a new path," she said, gesturing with her glass. "Civilian security instead of combat operations might employ your skills in a way you'd be helping, not hurting people. At least find out what they want."

"I dunno," Finn murmured, still staring at the letter. "It might appear to be a civilian job, but…"

He didn't finish his sentence. Even so, he decided to follow his aunt's often-sage advice and at the very least find out what he was being offered.

Finn parked the MG near the *Place de La Concorde* and walked the rest of the way to the U.S. Embassy. Within minutes of sitting down with a clean-cut man in his mid-thirties that Finn would swear had been a former—or current—U.S. Marine, his host pointed to a fairly thick file on his desk.

"We're considering you for a post to head up the American sector of a joint domestic drone surveillance operation of potential terrorist targets all over Europe. The NATO countries would each be represented, led by experienced former drone operators like yourself who would pilot small craft over everything from nuclear power plants, to dams, to miles of railroad tracks, looking for suspicious activity."

Finn strove to keep his face expressionless, but his mind was spinning like a roulette wheel in Monte Carlo. Did he want to remain permanently in Europe? As Claudine had suggested, was this a way to use his obvious skills in a non-combat fashion? How would he feel with a joystick in his hands again? He studied the man his instincts told him was a member of the C.I.A., cloaked as a U.S. Embassy attaché. If that were true, what else would be expected of such "surveillance" employees?

Meanwhile, the officer explained that Finn would work with his French counterparts in Paris and Brussels under the auspices of the NATO pact.

"We'd train you to fly the small, commercial drones that would cover critical infrastructure in the designated countries." When Finn didn't reply, the embassy official cocked his head to one side and said, "It looks as if you might have more questions."

"I do. What's in the fine print? Am I a civilian drone contractor or a full-fledged member of the Agency?"

His interviewer gave a short laugh. "We'd consider you a hybrid."

"Half civilian...half C.I.A.? Isn't that like being a little bit pregnant?"

The attaché looked at him steadily across his desk. "To do this job, you'd have to re-enlist in the Air Force, still at your rank of Major. You'd serve as our representative on the joint task force—a convenient way to keep this from appearing to be an overt C.I.A. operation."

"But that's what it is, right?"

The man, whose gabardine suit was a tad tight around the shoulders where a leather holster and pistol might be tucked under his armpit, merely smiled. Finn smiled back and said pleasantly, "Lots to consider here." He rose from his chair, offering to shake the interviewer's hand. "I'll give it some serious thought,"

Truth was, if the business was truly a civilian effort, he might be genuinely interested as a way to use the considerable skills he'd acquired over the years to help stay a step ahead of the bad dudes. But this smacked of his father's typical manipulations. It obviously greatly galled his parent to have a son interrupt the long line of Deschanels in the highest realms of the military. The General must have thought the non-combat use of drones might entice him back into the service. Finn vowed silently that there was no way he would bow to Andrew Deschanel's bidding merely to restore the high-ranking military man's belief in family continuity—which was probably what all this was about.

Finn headed for the door without making any

commitment beyond promising that he'd be back in touch with his answer. When he returned to the MG, he rolled down its ancient top, glad for the sunny skies, even if the temperature couldn't exactly be called a spring day. His gaze took in the budding cherry trees along the road as he turned over in his mind the information he'd just learned at the embassy. *So the powers-that-be wanted to keep an eye in the sky on governmental and civilian facilities throughout Europe.* Finn smiled at his windshield. This intelligence had just given him an idea…

"I'll be gone over the Easter holiday," Juliet announced in a staff meeting that included her two deputy designers, along with Brad and his administrative assistant. "It'll be less than a week."

"What!" her brother exclaimed. "Why?"

"Because we've sent off the *Drones in the Desert* packaging designs to the production department. I need a break and so does my team."

The color images on the prototype boxes were so bloody and horrifying that she couldn't even stand to have them sit on top of her desk anymore. She looked at her assistants. "Feel free to take the long weekend over Good Friday and Easter. You guys all deserve it." To her brother she said, "These folks have worked tremendously hard."

"What if we have to fix or adjust something?" Brad challenged with an angry edge to his voice.

"The project's locked and loaded. You make any changes now, and it'll cost you a fortune," Juliet answered calmly. "And besides, you personally signed off on every single aspect of the next release. Don't tell me you want to add to the body count on the box at *this* late date?"

Brad remained silent, glowering at his end of the conference table. He was just being his usual controlling jerk self, she realized, feeling pleased she had called his bluff. Her mind shifted to the lovely invitation from Finn sitting in her email inbox inviting her for Easter Sunday, March 27th. He'd also added a rather intriguing postscript.

Besides hoping you'll return to L'Étoile de Paris to see this city in the spring, I want your opinion on something I can only speak to you about in person.

She forced herself to concentrate on the business at hand. Brad still had a frown on his face, but he hadn't actually forbidden her to take a few of the many vacation days owed her after so many years of intense work. Her excitement about her upcoming trip began to bubble in her chest and she could hardly keep a broad smile off her face.

"Well, if that's all we have to discuss, troops," Juliet said, closing her laptop, "thanks to everyone for the endless hours you've given to this latest project. I'm truly grateful for all your efforts. Brad?"

Her brother didn't even bother offering her design team a word of appreciation or bid farewell to those in the meeting. Instead, he rose from his outsized leather "CEO throne," jerked his head in the direction of his assistant, and strode out of the conference room without a backward glance.

Juliet would have been embarrassed if anyone in her family could see that she was almost completely packed on the Tuesday before her Thursday evening flight from San Francisco to Paris. It was just after midnight when she closed her carry-on suitcase, leaving her large tote bag open for last minute items. She heard her cell phone ping with the familiar alert sign from her BBC News app. Hoping it was nothing more than a candidate declaiming whether

Britain should stay or leave the European Union in the debate for the upcoming Brexit referendum, she reached for her phone and clicked on Messages.

Suicide bombings at Brussels Airport

"Oh, dear God, *no!*" she exclaimed to her empty bedroom and raced to her TV.

CNN was the first with more news about an 8 a.m. attack at the airport in Zaventem, Brussels. Juliet remained sitting cross-legged at the end of her bed, glued to the broadcast for the next hour. She was horrified when word was announced of a third explosion, also in Brussels, set off in a metro station, killing some twenty people.

What must Finn and Avery be feeling to hear this news? Wouldn't this latest horror in nearby Brussels be an enormous psychological setback for them? It certainly felt that way to her.

The hotel phone in her room rang. It was Jamie.

"Are you watching TV?" he asked. "Hundreds wounded or killed, they say."

"I can't imagine what it's like to be hearing this in Paris."

"That's exactly what I was thinking," Jamie agreed. I don't think you're going to have a very enjoyable weekend over there, Sis."

Juliet glanced at her packed suitcase and her travel tote, ready for her to grab it and walk out the door. Suddenly, she wondered if more attacks were planned for other European airports—DeGaulle, for instance. She shuddered. If she was scared, how did the French feel right now? She couldn't allow her fear of experiencing the horror of another attack keep her from what every instinct told her to do: go to Paris. If travelers like her cowered at home, the terrorists would win.

"These are scary times, that's for sure," she murmured into the phone, "but I'm going. In fact, if I can get an earlier flight out tomorrow, will you take me to the airport?"

"Of course."

"And don't tell anyone before I get out of here, okay? I don't want to argue about it. I'll just go. We're all caught up at work, thank heavens. Leaving a day early won't jeopardize anything here and maybe my presence in Paris can help."

"Let me know when you want to meet me in the garage."

"You're the best," she declared.

She replaced the receiver as she continued to stare, mesmerized, by the shocking images of explosions going off and blood on the floor inside the check-in area of the Brussels Airport. An endless loop of graphic video showed emergency responders rushing to get some three hundred wounded to hospitals throughout the Belgian city. Minutes melted into hours, but still she couldn't take her eyes of the screen. Should she call Avery or Finn, or just get on a plane? After contacting the airline to substitute her Thursday flight for one that would leave the next day at noon, she decided not to call Paris only to be bravely told by Avery and Finn that she shouldn't make the trip just now. She was just going to grab the first plane out and *go*!

With that heavy decision made, she fell back on the bed, exhausted, and slipped into a fretful sleep.

Juliet's anxiety and exhaustion weren't helped by the twelve-hour trip across continental America and the Atlantic Ocean, nor by the increased security she met at De Gaulle Airport when her flight landed. When she finally emerged from the arrivals terminal, with helicopters once again flying overhead, she felt tense and jumpy as she waited in line for twenty minutes before securing a taxi to

Rue de Lille. Upon her arrival there, she was dismayed when no one answered the bell at Avery's flat, nor responded to her text. She was about to leave when the street door opened and Avery's neighbor, Brian Parker—well turned out in an impeccably tailored pinstripe suit and silk tie—strode across the threshold, obviously on his way to work.

"Why, hello!" he greeted her. "You've come back. Brave woman."

Juliet explained her worry about her friend in the wake of the most recent attacks in Brussels.

Parker shook his head. "This perpetual anxiety everyone here feels has become really unnerving."

In response to Juliet's question as to her friend's whereabouts, he offered, "Maybe Avery's gone to stay with a friend, although my wife has told her that she has an open invitation to sleep in our spare room, if she's on edge. Actually," he added, with a thoughtful look, "I haven't seen much of her lately. I think my wife mentioned to me a few days ago that Avery's been spending her time painting in some guy's studio. She doesn't answer her phone or text?"

Juliet shook her head and heaved a sigh. "She's probably got her phone turned off. She does it all the time when she's working. Is it okay if I leave her a note on her door upstairs? I gave her back my key."

Parker smiled his agreement and allowed her in while he continued on his way. She sprinted up the six flights, scribbled a note on the back of her airplane boarding pass and wedged it halfway under the door.

Surprise! I'm a day early. I'm heading for Finn's. Call me!

Back downstairs, she retrieved her wheeled weekender bag from the corner where she'd left it in the building's foyer. Once outside, she hailed another taxi and directed it to cross the nearest bridge over to the Right Bank. She happily pictured the surprise on Finn's face when she'd knocked on his door. As she tramped down the cobblestone ramp that led to the quay where the barges were moored, her heart quickened and she felt a goofy smile spread across her lips. In her haste to see Finn, she left her suitcase at the bottom of the gangway and ran up the incline. She reached the deck and looked through the plate glass window over the door to the pilothouse—and stopped dead in her tracks.

On one end of the couch facing the coffee table laden with a plate of croissants, a coffee pot, and a mug, a slender woman perched on the corner of the sofa that Juliet had once claimed as her own. She had caramel-colored hair, a pretty face, and a buxom figure that matched that of the woman clad in a lavender sundress in the family photo sitting on a nearby shelf. This day, Finn's wife, Kimberly Deschanel, was wearing a velour running suit—or was it pajamas?

For a split second, Juliet thought she would pitch off the boat into the Seine. Her breath came in short gasps and she wondered seriously if she were about to black out. Grabbing for the stout wires strung between the metal guard posts protruding from the boat's gunnels, she steadied herself, but not before a blind fury filled her chest and she almost let out a scream. She had arrived twenty-four hours ahead of schedule. Finn would never expect that his wife and his incipient girlfriend would run into each other. The tableau of the two of them, chatting over coffee and croissants at this early hour, burnt itself in Juliet's fevered brain.

Just then, Finn looked up, and his expression, first of recognition, and then of consternation, told her everything she needed to know. She whirled in place and tore down the gangway, its clanging sound alerting everyone onboard to her presence even if Finn hadn't already spied her through the window. She heard him call her name from the now-opened door to the pilothouse, but she ignored him, grabbing her suitcase and sprinting like an Olympian up the ramp and back onto the street. She swiftly cut across Pompidou Bridge and mounted a cement staircase, mindless of her thumping bag or her aching arms, in her effort to reach an escalator that took her even higher to the platform at the Passy metro station and a train—any train—that would get her away from the scene she'd just witnessed.

That's what you get for wanting to 'surprise' a guy you don't know very well!

Not know him very well? Make that not know him at all...

Still trying to catch her breath and calm her pulse, Juliet again felt she might faint. She stumbled onto an arriving train whose destination she didn't even know and, for another ten minutes, she merely sat in her seat, not caring where the car was headed. When her breathing finally returned to near normal, she pulled out her cell phone and punched up her Paris Metro app. The gods were with her. The train she'd jumped on so blindly was one where she could transfer at Montparnasse to the Number 12, a line that would eventually let her off very close to *Rue de Lille*. There, she would sit at the café across the street and wait for Avery to return home, however long it took.

She shut down her phone as the train pulled to a stop and she entered the busy station. She was barely aware of military-clad police with their war weapons guarding passengers making their way to various platforms. Reaching her final destination, she emerged into brilliant sunshine. She'd almost forgotten the attacks in Brussels—the very reason she'd jumped on an earlier plane and flown all night to offer her sympathy and support for two of the people she most cared about in the world.

Juliet was shocked to realize that her heart actually hurt. She had been kidding herself that she was in control of how she felt about Finn Deschanel. Whatever his problems were... whatever battles he still had to fight... whatever ties he obviously still had with his wife, Juliet knew now, with a dread that rivaled anything she'd ever felt before, that she had fallen in love with him. She'd been denying herself that deep knowledge, not committing her whole heart, she thought, until it seemed certain that he was feeling himself again and "ready" for a life with her. But the truth was, she *had* committed her heart, and now it felt bruised and broken.

What a pathetic, obtuse creature I am...

What else could she surmise beside the fact that Finn had come to the conclusion since their time together before Christmas that he could work it out with his wife? While Juliet sat at a small table on the sidewalk at *La Calèche* waiting for Avery to appear, her thoughts swung wildly between sorrow and fury and finally an attempt at acceptance.

If she truly cared for his welfare—she should be happy for him, right? Finn and Kim had had a life together before he'd been shot down...and long before he'd flown drones or met her. It was a *good* thing, wasn't it, if a couple could reconcile the issues that had torn them apart and live, again, in peace and love?

She couldn't kid herself, though...she also felt angry. If life had so abruptly changed for Finn, he should have had the decency to tell her not to come for Easter. It would take time for her to feel anything but a crushing sense of betrayal. All he would have had to do was take ten seconds to send her a text. It would have seemed cruel, but at least she wouldn't be sitting in a café feeling like an abandoned child!

The big wooden entrance door to Avery's flat across the street swam before her eyes. She brushed away tears with the back of her hand and drank a huge gulp of her coffee, its heat burning a path down her constricted throat.

I will do it, she vowed silently. She would do her very best to release Finn with love and gratitude for the way in which merely knowing him had shown her that she deserved better than a relationship with someone as self-centered as Jed Jarvis. She would one day be truly happy for Finn. She swore she would!

CHAPTER 21

Juliet was on her second cappuccino when she spotted Avery walking arm-in-arm with a tall, lanky figure she quickly identified as art instructor Alain Devereux. She watched, dumbfounded, as Avery turned her head with a smile and pressed her cheek against Alain's jacketed shoulder as he kissed the top of her head.

They were obviously a couple. A couple in love.

What an idiot I've been to think I can just barge in on lives that seem to be proceeding most happily and independently without me!

However, in the next instant, Avery recognized Juliet sitting outside the café.

"Oh my God! Jules!" she squealed from across the street. "I thought you were coming Friday morning! Did I get it wrong?" She smiled at Alain. "Wouldn't be the first time."

She kissed Alain goodbye and told him in her vastly improved French that she'd call him as soon as Juliet got settled in. For his part, the artist seemed to take this unscheduled change of plans in stride, bowed a polite farewell to Juliet from across the street, and reversed course. Juliet paid her bill and dragged herself and her suitcase toward the big wooden entrance at Number 7.

Upstairs, Avery had barely shut the door to her tiny garret before Juliet sank onto the end of the unmade bed and burst into tears. "How could I have been so stupid," she berated herself, "to fly six thousand miles on the assumption that Finn Deschanel would simply be waiting for me to walk in the door? And how could, my *best* friend not be honest about the obvious liaison with Alain Devereux?"

Bewildered, Avery took a seat beside Juliet on the bed.

"What in the world has happened to prompt all of this?"

"Well, f-for one thing," Juliet stuttered between hiccups, "you kinda, sorta forgot to tell me that you and Alain were more than just student and teacher before I sent my poor, love-sick brother over here to take my place as Ace Rescue Ranger!"

"That's not fair!" protested Avery. "You never told *me* that Jamie was so smitten before he came over. I let him down as gently as I could." Her gaze narrowed. "But this is not just about Alain and me, is it? I've never seen you cry like this. Have you seen Finn, yet?"

The fight went out of Juliet just as quickly as it had risen in her chest.

"An hour ago, I found Finn with another woman," she related miserably, adding, "his *wife*."

Avery glared at Juliet accusingly.

"Well, well…didn't you kinda, sorta forget to tell me the guy you've obviously fallen in love with was a married man?"

"They've lived apart for more than a year," Juliet defended herself. "I was there on the barge when he told his lawyer on the phone to finalize his divorce!" She glared at Avery. "Did you know anything about Kim Deschanel coming to Paris?"

Avery remained silent, and Juliet could almost see the wheels rotating in her head.

"You *knew*?" Juliet cried. Even to her own ears, her question was a wail.

"No, I didn't know! I had absolutely no inkling Finn has been seeing anyone, let alone his wife, but the fact that you are so upset by this tells me that the man means a lot to you—and that's the part you concealed, probably even to yourself!"

"I did," Juliet said, in a barely audible voice. "I kept telling myself I liked him a lot but that for many reasons, we were a geographical impossibility. Then I unwrapped your portrait of him standing next to the pilothouse and I realized how much I missed him and had totally fallen in love and thought maybe he had too when he invited me for Easter. When I heard about the Brussels attacks I went into a panic about how you two would react and hopped on the first plane out of San Francisco. But when I arrived today and Finn was onboard the barge eating breakfast with his wife on the sofa, all cozy and warm, exactly where I used to sit—I think I went...kind of berserk."

Juliet couldn't continue speaking and in the next instant, despised herself for dissolving into tears once more.

"Oh, baby, I am so sorry." Avery handed her a slightly soiled tea towel to dry her eyes. Although Avery no longer wore a sling to protect her right arm, she gingerly wrapped her left arm around Juliet's trembling shoulders. "If it makes you feel any better," she said softly, "I'm also in love with a very married man."

"Oh, God, Av, really?" Juliet moaned, turning to look at her. "Alain's also married? And we're supposed to be smart women! Why would you go and do something like that? At least I thought mine was heading for a divorce. Did you go into all this, knowing he was married?"

Avery heaved a shrug. "Yes... but we're in France, remember? Alain's been married for ages. His kids are grown. He and his wife lead totally separate lives. I don't even care he's married."

"What! Why not?"

"No, I mean it," insisted Avery. "Alain and Dominique are Catholic, so they'll never divorce. All but one of their kids lives on their own. Nobody raises any eyebrows that we're together. He and I are both artists," she added, as if that justified everything. "We each need our solitude, but we enjoy the times when we're together. And besides, it suits me not to be too entangled." She winked. "More my style, you know what I mean?"

"But what about children? We're thirty-six! Don't you want to have any?"

Avery shook her head, realizing she was about to speak heresy. "Actually? No. I don't want to be a parent. My portraits are all the children I want in my life. But *you!*" She gave Juliet's shoulders a gentle squeeze. "You're a completely different case altogether—more's the pity."

Finn found himself pacing back and forth in front of the door leading from the pilothouse to the deck. He hadn't believed his eyes when he'd seen Juliet standing at the top of his gangway and watched her register that there was another woman on board. *Did she realize it was my soon-to-be-ex-wife? Or did she think it was someone else? That I'm a two-timing—*

"Finn!" Kim exclaimed, bringing the chaos swirling around in his head to an abrupt halt. "Who was that, just now?"

"A...person who knows Madame Grenelle next door. She apparently decided it was too early to call here and left."

It wasn't a lie, but not exactly the entire truth, was it?

Kim said from the sofa, "Well, look...I came all this way! Can't we at least talk about all this?"

"Talk about what? My lawyer has kept me up to date. You could have just express-mailed the divorce papers to my aunt and I'd have signed them."

Finn took the legal-size manila envelope from her hands.

"I just wanted to be sure you received them," she

replied, not holding his glance. "I'm supposed to get married in June and the divorce obviously needs to be finalized before then."

"Obviously," he repeated, walking toward the desk, looking for a pen. "But you might have called first."

"I called Claudine."

"Yes, I know. She immediately rang me, which is the only reason I gave her the go-ahead to give you this address so we could get this over with." He looked over his shoulder. "But nobody told you to come over at seven a.m."

"I-I wanted to be sure to catch you at home."

"Well, I'd very much appreciate it if you keep it to yourself where I'm living."

"Your father knows you're here in Paris," she said, with a defensive shrug of her shoulders. "He was the one who told me how to get in touch with his sister."

"But why track me down?" he demanded. "Our lawyers were to handle everything. That was our agreement."

"*Your* agreement, you mean. You'd already cleared out of Nevada completely when I was informed there'd be no more direct communication between us."

Finn turned around and looked at her with a steady gaze. "And you know why that was, don't you?"

He felt himself begin to plot the fastest way to sign the papers and get Kim off the barge so he could do some tracking down of his own. Avery Evans's place would be his first stop.

"Yes, I know why you've refused to speak to me all this time." Kim rose from the sofa to peer over his shoulder at the desk. "Guilty as charged. But before you sign, I feel there are a few things we need to discuss—in person. The General had just been here—at Claudine's, he said—when I talked to him about…well…about the proceedings between you and me. He was quite upset to hear you'd filed for divorce. He and I agreed that the best thing was to put me in touch with Claudine so she could—"

"And my aunt," he overrode her sentence, "respects my privacy. She first asked my permission to let you know this address. I just didn't think you'd show up before breakfast," he repeated, gazing stonily at the woman he'd married right out of the Air Force Academy. "Really, Kim. There's nothing to discuss. Let's just both sign the papers and be done with it."

"But I don't want you to sign!" Kim cried, her voice escalating to a near wail.

Dumbfounded by this declaration, Finn stared at the bride he had escorted under a forest of swords on the steps of the U.S. Air Force Academy in what seemed, now, another lifetime.

"But you just said you're getting married in June!" he declared, exasperated. He bent over the desk silently cursing the fact he couldn't locate a pen. By the time he finally found one wedged next to his toaster, he was alarmed to see that Kim's eyes were brimming with tears.

"I know, I know," she said, barely above a whisper, "but—"

"But what?" He whirled to face her fully, pen in hand. "You left the marriage by having an affair, remember? Which means you left *me*. You had a baby with another flyer, *remember*?"

"But I still love *you*!" she cried. "I've always loved you, and I wanted us to have a baby so much! But you were so angry at everything…so distant and remote. You cut off any real communication with me even before your last tour in Afghanistan—and then, when you got home after rehab, you barely talked to me and hardly ever slept with me!"

She began to cry, her face buried in her hands. Scenes of his returning to their house on the Nevada air base and shutting the door to the spare room drifted through his mind. He'd had nothing to say to her during those horrible months when he didn't tell anyone what the drone job was like—not that she would have been able to understand what he'd experienced after his helicopter was shot down or the hell he endured in those unmarked trailers. What had happened to their marriage was nobody's fault—and yet, if he were brutally honest with himself—it was both of their responsibilities.

He reached out and gently touched her shoulder. "You're right, you know," he allowed in a softer voice. "At times I acted like a complete bastard. A *sick* bastard, by the way, but neither of us knew how sick I was."

Kim's hands fell from her face and she looked at him hopefully through her tears. "But you're better now, right? Claudine told me you were, and now that I'm here, I can see that." She reached out and seized the hand not holding the pen. "Please, Finn...let's not do this! Can't we figure this out? I...I still love you!"

Finn gently pulled his hand from hers and set the pen on the desk.

"Kim...we are way past a reboot—"

"Please, *please* Finn!"

She was begging, now, and it made him want to sink through the deck to escape her entreaties. He walked back to his leather chair where he had felt reasonably secure when she'd been sitting on his sofa.

Kim followed him, pleading, "I know what I did was terrible and I've paid a huge price, but can't you please try to understand—"

"I do understand," he intervened, reaching for a calm he didn't feel. "I completely get how lonely it was for you during those deployments, and how I drove you crazy when I got back, still in such terrible shape after the four guys I'd tried to rescue died in the crash. And then I flew the drones. But there's too much that's happened since you and Pete… had a child together. You took a different path. So did I."

"How were you so sure it was Pete's son and not yours?" she challenged with a tilt of her chin.

"My gut told me…plus a couple of DNA tests."

"You tested *whose* DNA?" Kim demanded, her voice rising.

"Yours, mine, and…the baby's."

"How?" she challenged him, skepticism dripping from that single word. She crossed back to the sofa and flounced down. "How did you get my son's DNA? You didn't even want me to tell you his name!"

"When I first got out the hospital and we were stationed at Creech—"

Interrupting, she said, "You were at your absolute worst, then."

Finn nodded. "Very true. I didn't know what was happening to me then, but I just knew I couldn't deal with anything but going to work and coming home and trying to sleep. And you said in the middle of all that, that you were pregnant." He shook his head. "Well, given how we were with each other by then, it seemed very unlikely."

"I was trying to live a normal life!" she protested. "I *tried* to get you to make love to me. I couldn't figure out what the hell was going on with you, and Pete was so…."

Finn nodded again. "It was pure crap for all three of us, I know. And that afternoon we had that barbeque at the house and Pete was there…. don't ask me how, but I knew instantly when I saw you two together that you and he had had an affair and that the baby you were carrying probably wasn't going to be mine."

"And you never said a word!" Kim accused. "And by the way," she added, with a steely glint in her eye, "everyone said you were a total shit for leaving a pregnant woman in her eighth month. You just walked out without warning—boom!—and moved into the bachelor officers' quarters on the base. It was humiliating!"

"You'd left the marriage first by having the affair with Pete," he repeated without emotion, as if just stating a simple fact. "I stayed at the BOQ until I was certain that the baby wasn't mine."

This time Kim shouted her demand. "*How*, God dammit? How did you know for sure?"

"Just to be sure my intuition was right, one day on my lunch hour, after you'd brought the baby home, I waited down the street until I saw you leave the house with him. Then I just jimmied the broken window frame at the back, walked in through the kitchen into the bathroom, and took some hair out of your hairbrushes."

"And then…?"

"I had the hair samples tested, along with my own." He gave her a hard look. "Turns out, my instincts were a hundred percent correct."

"So that's when you left the country and didn't tell anyone where you'd gone—or why?"

"That's right. I'd put in my resignation a few months before and the final paperwork came through the week before DNA tests came back. After that, it all seemed a sign that it was time to get outta Dodge." He spread his arms wide. "So, here I sit."

"There you sit," Kim echoed, the anger drained from her features and her eyes so full of sadness, it nearly undid him.

His tone softening, he said, "Look, Kim, I—"

"I don't want to marry Pete."

Her expression told him that she thought her startling declaration might shift things between them.

"Then don't marry him," he said in an even tone.

"But I want to be with *you*!"

Finn shook his head. "We two are long past that as a

possibility."

"Why? Why can't we—"

"It's not just about your baby," he interrupted. "It's *us*. We're not right together. We never were, but we persuaded ourselves otherwise. Us, together, won't work."

"Please, Finn!"

He held up his hands, a silent gesture for her to listen to him. More gently he said, "I want you to know how sorry I am for the way I walked away without explaining what was going on with me. We're pretty different people and we didn't find that out soon enough to prevent this train wreck."

"What do you mean?" Tears began to spill over her eyelids and stream down her cheeks.

"We like such different things and each of us sees life through a completely different lens."

"But that's not true!" She was getting angry again. "You *used* to like what I liked when you were at the Academy. You liked sneaking into my bed, didn't you? You liked fucking me."

Finn tried to repress a smile at the memory of hot, young lust. "And you liked it too. We were nineteen and full of raging hormones. But we're totally different people, now, and I'm guessing we always were, but we just didn't see it back then. Meanwhile, we've gone down very different roads and finally gotten to know ourselves better." He waved at his crammed bookshelf. "I like simple stuff. I like reading…and cooking—can you believe it? And I like living in a small place like this. You like hanging out with lots of friends and thinking about a new, bigger house and all the things you want to put in it. And children," he added. "You wanted kids and I knew for sure I wasn't fit to be a father back then—"

"But now? Do you want kids now?" she demanded.

"Some day, I hope…but, no…not now."

"Not with me, you mean. Not after—"

Finn didn't answer as the truth bloomed between them.

Kim inhaled deeply and Finn guessed she would toss one more Hail Mary pass at him. In a tiny voice she ventured, "But we're both military brats. That's something we share… along with a lot of family history, and—"

"But I'm a military brat who loves exploring new places," he intervened, "and you…well, moving around so much has made you want to burrow in your nest and never move again, which I totally understand. You hated it when we transferred to Nevada, and wanted nothing so much as to go back to Colorado and live next door to your parents, which makes perfect sense, now that they're retired. But *I* don't want to be in Colorado or D.C. where my dad is based. In fact, now that my mother has died, I hope I can avoid my father as much as possible from here on out."

Kim was calmer now and looked at him steadily. "He cares about you, you know."

"In some ways, yes, I think that's true. And it's not that I don't care about him and my sister, Maureen. I do. A lot. The problem is, I have a dad who just wants me to do exactly what he did…be the next General Deschanel. I know, now, that's not the life I want, not the life I *ever* wanted—now that I think of it—but I was too much of a coward to tell him to his face. And Maureen…well, my sister has married into the military, too, and thinks I'm just weird for the way I feel about the wars our country has been fighting for fifteen years. Truth is, none of us Deschanels hardly knows each other. Not really."

"Oh, Patrick…" Kim said, and Finn realized the brutal truth of his words had finally hit their intended mark.

He slowly rose from his chair and crossed to the sofa. He leaned down and took hold of her left hand. Major Pete

Dexter's diamond engagement ring winked back at him.

"Kim, I am truly sorry for the pain I've caused you. I went into radio silence for most of our marriage and that wasn't fair to you at all. My only excuse is that, for most of the time we were married, I was experiencing some strange form of modern day shellshock. When I got back from the Middle East it became a lot worse flying drones. For sure, I owed it to you to tell you what was going on with me and how nothing in my life fit before, during, or after I joined the Air Force. As I said, the truth is that I was too much of a coward to come clean with what I was feeling back then. Nothing was making sense, but I want you to know that none of that was your fault."

"But, then, if you know, now, that you were going through something strange, why can't you—"

"Because I can't," he said simply. "I can't back-track and fix it *with* you, or *for* you, or for *us*, and for that I am truly sorry. I'm going to sign these documents today, and I hope you will too. I want you to have a happy life, Kim. It just can't be with me."

Finn returned to the desk where he'd left the pen, along with the legal documents awaiting their signatures.

Behind him, Kim stated flatly, "There must be somebody else. You've met someone, right? Some little French number who—"

Finn looked over his shoulder. "Trust me, no little 'French number' is going to walk in here."

He was lucky Kim had not dwelled on the sight of Juliet storming down the gangway. Then his gut cramped at the memory of her stricken expression when she saw he was with another woman eating croissants before ten a.m. How could she know that Kim had waited for him on the quay until he returned from his morning trek to the *boulangerie*? Oddly, though, with Kim now standing next to him at the desk, Finn felt a wave of compassion for what the last years had put both of them through.

"C'mon," he said with a genuine smile. "Let's do this right...and please know that my signing these documents isn't about French girls or my dad. It's about facing the truths between you and me and wishing each other well from here on out."

There was a long pause and then Kim gave the tiniest shrug of accord.

Finn said, "Let's have a decent end to this so we can both move forward and find some peace." He bumped his fist gently against her chin. "And may I say, I admire you for the gutsy thing you did today."

"What was that?" she asked, subdued.

"To come all the way to see me and force me to hash this through with you. I think we've done that pretty well, don't you?"

"I didn't win you back," Kim said with a stubborn, sideways glance he remembered so well when she didn't get her way.

He held up the pen. "You gave it your all, so be proud of that. Let's do this nice and dignified. I'll go first."

And with that, he bent down and signed "Patrick Finley Deschanel" at all the spots indicated with red post-it tags.

Once again, tears had begun to stream down Kim's cheeks while she waited next to him for her turn. He handed her his pen with a faint smile of encouragement. After a long moment's hesitation, she, too, bent over the documents and wrote her signature on the lines next to his.

He carefully slid the papers into the legal envelope they'd arrived in and walked Kim to the door of the barge. They stared mutely at each other with the swish of the Seine flowing swiftly with spring rain that had coursed from the Loire Valley and was headed to the sea. Finn opened the door to the deck and a cool breeze rippled through the pilothouse. Kim remained stationary, and then looked back at the large manila envelope containing the divorce documents sitting on his desk. Finn gently seized both her shoulders with hands that had piloted aircraft high in the sky and bent to kiss her lightly on each cheek, European style.

"All the best, Kim. Truly."

The woman he had known since before he'd turned twelve gazed at him wordlessly, her eyes still moist, and then she walked through the door he held open for her. He stood rooted to the salon's teak decking, listening to her footsteps treading on the metal gangway and then fading into silence.

Lost in thought, he felt, rather than heard, his cell phone vibrating in his back pants pocket. He pulled it out and saw a text had just arrived from Avery Evans.

> **Juliet's here, a day early, worried how the Brussels attacks were affecting us. Oh, and by the way, don't bother coming over here. She never wants to see you again. Can you guess why?**

Finn felt his breath catch. He glanced out the windows where tourists, strolling along the quay, often peered into his lair. Above the embankment wall near the bridge, he spotted Kim waving frantically at a taxi that screeched to a stop, allowing her to jump inside. Ducking his head to look at his cell phone once more, he tapped on the miniature keyboard.

> **Juliet stopped here first, but I had a visitor so she left before we could talk.**

He waited, his eyes glued to the cell phone's small screen.

> **Yep, and she sure didn't like what she saw.**

Finn threw back his head and closed his eyes in frustration. Quickly he typed:

**Tell her it's not at all
what it probably looked like.**

A long pause followed and Finn could tell there must be a discussion going on between the two women on *Rue de Lille*. Then came Avery's reply.

**Apparently those are the exact,
same words Jed Jarvis used one time...**

He stared unhappily at the small screen. All he could think of was the mantra he'd learned at Air Force damage control school when an emergency was in progress: *Contain...Control...Repair...*

Without answering Avery's latest text, he grabbed his leather jacket and bolted out of the barge at a dead run.

CHAPTER 22

Juliet knew she should be angry when a buzzer in Avery's attic apartment sounded not twenty minutes after Finn's last text, but all she could do was dash into the tiny bathroom, run a comb through her hair, and refresh her lipstick.

"Didn't I tell you?" Avery chuckled, looking at her watch. "He beat my prediction by ten minutes. I'll vamoose over to Alain's."

Before Juliet could answer, there was a pounding on the door. Finn must have taken the six flights, two steps at a time.

"Com—ing," Avery sang out sweetly. She shook her index finger at Juliet, whispering, "Now you be nice! Let him say whatever he's going to say before you jump down his throat."

"Why are you cutting the guy so much slack?" Juliet demanded hoarsely.

"Because, whether you believe me or not, I'm certain there's going to be a reasonable explanation," Avery answered, *sotto voce*. "He's crazy about you, kiddo, and he's old enough to know that a roll in the hay with another lady would screw everything up on the eve of your return to Paris."

"Guys do stupid stuff like that all the time!" Juliet hissed.

Avery reached for the doorknob. "Don't I know it?" she replied in a normal voice, "but not this guy. Hi, Finn."

"Talking about me behind the door?" he said, looking past Avery to directly meet Juliet's glare.

"Yep. And she's all yours. I'm just on my way out."

"No, you don't have to leave," Finn replied, striding into the room. "I want to take Juliet directly to Angelina's so I can tell her what she *didn't* see."

"Oh, yum!" Avery exclaimed. "And great location for a peace conference, I might add." She turned toward Juliet. "Forget tea. Angelina's tearoom should be called 'the chocolate room!' The inside is gorgeously *belle époque* and more than a hundred years old. Coco Chanel and Proust and the cream of Parisian aristocracy dined there since the day it opened. You'll love it!" She winked at Finn. "The secret recipe for their hot chocolate, alone, should win her over."

Finn took a hold of the handle of Juliet's suitcase and said, "That's what I'm hoping."

Juliet pointed to her luggage. "Not so fast. I'm not going with you to the barge later, if that's what you think. Leave that here!"

Avery winked at Finn a second time, but said with a straight face, "Well, you're not staying here tonight, Juliet. I'm expecting company later and it's *not* you, pal."

Juliet remained stonily silent while Finn piloted the MG across the *Pont Royal* to the Right Bank, heading eventually for the *Rue de Rivoli*, beyond the Louvre, and parking within view of the green expanse of the Tuilleries gardens. After he had locked the car, she reluctantly allowed him to take her arm and guide her into the tearoom's grand entrance past shelves chock-full of all manner of luxury food items, including tins of Angelina's famous African chocolate. They were soon escorted to a remote corner of a large, cream-colored room resplendent with floor-to-ceiling framed mirrors, soaring arches between dining areas, dark leather chairs studded with brass tacks, and round, intimate, marble-topped tables filled with well-dressed patrons willing to pay a king's ransom for a cup of cocoa.

"*Merci, Madame*," Finn said with a nod to the chic hostess clad in the perfect little black dress that Juliet reckoned all French women had in their closets.

Finn stood behind her to help push in her seat before he took his own. He waved away the menu when a waiter, looking smart in his black tuxedo and brilliant white starched shirt, appeared to take their order. "Do you have the Mont-Blanc pastry today?" he asked in French.

"But of course," the waiter answered in perfect English.

Finn cocked an eyebrow and smiled across the table. "It combines meringue, light whipped cream, and the tiniest threads of chocolate-chestnut paste forming a half sphere—a fantastic confection they've been making here since nineteen-oh-three."

"Fine," she said shortly. Her stomach was in such a knot that she doubted she would eat a bite when this paragon of pastries was delivered to their tiny table.

"And a pot of your African cocoa, please, and two cups," Finn directed. When the waiter retreated he said to her, "Please give me your hand."

"No," she refused, aware she probably sounded like a petulant teen. "Just give it to me straight, Finn. Why was your wife sitting on your sofa this morning, and why didn't you warn me when I said 'yes' to your invitation to come over for Easter?"

"Because my soon-to-be-ex-wife didn't warn *me* she had flown to Paris to personally deliver divorce documents for me to sign."

"So it *was* Kim Deschanel!" She threw her napkin on the table. "And did you bid each other a fond farewell the night before you actually signed to end your marriage? Was that why she was sitting in the pilothouse in her—*whatever* she was wearing—so early in the morning?"

Finn reared back with a startled expression. "You thought that the sports outfit she was wearing were *pajamas?*" he declared with a note of amazement in his voice. "You're jealous?"

"Given what it looked like, why wouldn't I be? And believe me, it doesn't feel good!"

"Of course it doesn't," Finn agreed hastily. He slowly shook his head. "You have no idea what an insane day this has been so far."

"I'm sure," she replied curtly. "It has for me, too. I jumped on the first flight I could get out of San Francisco because I figured the Brussels attacks might have thrown both you and Avery for a loop, and here we are, about to have a ten dollar cup of cocoa. Looks to me as if you're both doing just fine."

"No, we're not, or at least, we *weren't*," Finn countered, his expression sobering. "I called Avery the minute I heard what had happened in Brussels. She'd already fled to Alain's."

"What about you?" Juliet asked warily. "And what about the Grenelles?"

"Madame Grenelle, as you can imagine, was also totally undone by the latest attack. While you were in the air, I was on her side of the boat with her son, Pierre, while we three relived J-P's death all over again. In fact, I spent the first eight hours after the news broke trying to calm everybody down, including myself."

Juliet murmured. "It had to bring everything back…"

Finn nodded. "As a matter of fact, I got the first appointment I could with Doctor A, late yesterday afternoon. We talked through it and we both agreed that we're probably going to see a lot more of these horrible events as time goes on. She gave me some ideas how to cope better when—" He paused and inhaled deeply. "It's just—"

A wave of emotion spread across his face.

"What?" she asked softly.

Finn took another deep breath. "Stuff like the Brussels attacks and what happened in San Bernardino make me feel I'm...well...alone in the foxhole again. That first night, I started to shake so bad, I got in the shower and just stood under the hot water for twenty minutes until I could get my body under control."

"Oh, Finn..." She nodded sadly. "I got the shakes, too, when we landed at DeGaulle and I stepped off the plane. Not as bad as you described, but my entire body felt on full alert the whole time I waited in the passport control line."

He reached for her hand that had been toying with a silver spoon on the table in front of her. This time she didn't pull away.

"I'm just so damned glad to see you," he told her, lowering his voice, "and I'm really sorry your arrival in Paris was the exact opposite of what I wanted it to be. You've got to believe me that I wasn't happy when Kim turned up at my door just after seven o'clock in the morning, but as it turned out, we finally got to sort through the last couple of years about why the wheels came off our relationship."

Finn then related the events that had taken place on the barge that Juliet had only briefly witnessed through the pilothouse window. She hardly noticed when their order arrived, nor could she savor the smooth, subtle taste of the chestnut paste or the glorious sweetness of the meringue. With emotions roiling, she mindlessly sipped her hot chocolate while Finn filled her in on the painful disclosures that DNA tests revealed that a baby Kim had given birth to two years earlier was the result of an affair with a fellow flyer. He also described the relief he felt when he and Kim both signed the documents, now in his possession, that would officially end their marriage once his lawyer filed the papers with the American court.

"So Kim had tried to pass off this Pete person's baby as *yours*?" she asked, unable to disguise her shock. "No wonder you left Nevada as soon as you could."

"Well, to be fair, I was a pretty volatile guy at that point. Kim was scared to admit the truth—that she'd fallen into bed with Pete whenever she felt lonely or angry at me, and therefore, she wasn't certain whose baby it was. Obviously, she was full of guilt for having had an affair that had continued even after I got back from the Middle East." Finn hesitated. "And now, it turns out, she really doesn't want to marry the guy."

"Oh, great! When can we expect her next visit?"

"She won't be coming to Paris any time soon because it's finished between us."

"For you, maybe, but probably not Kim..."

Juliet felt a familiar lump expand in her throat. How could she believe him? How could she believe any guy? In the brief year she'd been with Jed, she was certain he'd stepped out on her a few times and cooked up some convincing lies to cover his tracks.

Finn reached out and gently skimmed the back of two fingers along Juliet's jawline. She could feel her heartbeat slow down and an unexpected sensation of comfort washed over her.

"After today, Kim knows, for sure, that chapter is closed," he said. "I don't want to upset you when I say this, but in a strange way, I'm actually glad she came. How often do you get to put a genuine period at the end of a sentence like I did this morning?"

"But are you sure it's the end?" The tightness in Juliet's throat made her words sound choked. "You two shared so much family history and military tradition, to say nothing of personal heartache and pain. And you admit you were a bear to live with back then. Now that she knows what misery you were going through, it must make a huge difference for her. *I'd* forgive you for leaving, if I were in her place."

"You are such a sweetheart…"

"No, I'm not." For some reason, she felt strangely compelled to mount Kim's defense. "She's told you she doesn't want to marry the other guy, so perhaps you could forgive her, too, and learn to love that poor, innocent baby." Juliet felt tears prick her eyes. "People can knit back their relationship if the link between them is strong enough."

Finn seized her hand and wouldn't allow her to look away. A voice at the back of Juliet's head told her she'd spoken in Kim's behalf, just then, as a way of protecting herself from the possibility that Finn might one day have second thoughts.

"That's just it, Juliet," he insisted. "I don't think Kim and I *ever* had a strong, emotional connection, other than we were both military brats and had a common family history. In the words of that Parisian ex-pat, Gertrude Stein, 'there was no *there* there' between us—ever. Not the way I feel right now when I know you're still mad at me and I'd do whatever it takes to make it right between us!"

As they stared at each other across the tiny table, Juliet wanted desperately to believe him. Yet, the vision of Kim sitting on the sofa Juliet had all but claimed as her own was impossible to push from her memory. A wave of exhaustion invaded her entire body brought about by the stress of the Brussels attacks, along with flying six thousand miles across the globe, the thunderous shock of seeing Finn and Kim inside the barge, then hauling her suitcase up six flights of stairs and crying her eyes out in Avery's flat.

"Oh, Finn, I don't know..." She looked down at their hands still clasped together, aware she sounded as tired as she felt. "Maybe you should just let everything settle down before you and I...well...before we even consider—" Her sentence dangled because she had no idea how to finish it. She withdrew her hand into her lap. Finally, she said, "You both have been through so much. I think you need to take time to assess everything."

"You're right," he agreed. "She and I have been through a lot, but we're coming out the other side—or at least I am. And I'm tired of 'assessing.' It's been two years since I slept with her, or anyone else for that matter—poor, pathetic bastard that I was! You'll never know how completely relieved I felt when Kim signed those legal documents this morning. And by the way," he added, "I'm more than a little pissed that you'd think I was such a rat that I'd sleep with some other woman two days before you were due to arrive here."

"Not just any woman...sleep with your *wife*!"

"May I repeat? She hasn't been that in any real sense for close to two years."

"Still..."

"Still, nothing! I did *not* sleep with her..." Juliet knew he was trying desperately to convince her. "I'm not Jed Jarvis—or any other rotten man you may have had in your life previous to me." A faint grin creased his lips. "You're sitting across from an officer and a gentleman, remember?"

Juliet felt the first smile of the day begin to crease the corners of her mouth.

"Well, thank heavens for that."

Finn's look of tender vulnerability at this partial reprieve unraveled her previous resolve to book the next plane out of Charles De Gaulle.

"Finish your chocolate," he urged her gently, "and let's get going. I want to show you something, and then I'm going to make you a wonderful dinner."

Juliet shook her head. "I'm totally stuffed with cocoa and meringue and about to keel over from jet lag."

"Okay, then," he countered. "How about we make a couple of quick stops for supplies while you snooze in the MG? When we get back to the barge, you can take a long nap while I do my thing on two burners. We can eat at midnight, if you want."

Juliet could only offer a groggy nod while Finn paid their bill, the cost of which she didn't even want to venture a guess.

By the time the MG pulled up to *La Pâtisserie des Rêves* at Number 93, *Rue du Bac,* not far from Claudine Deschanel's elegant apartment on *Rue Jacob*, Juliet was sound asleep in the passenger seat of the car. The bear rug she remembered from her first ride in Finn's car had been replaced by a lighter-weight green and navy tartan throw that covered her from neck to toe. Finn had scrunched up his jacket to cushion her head against the car window. She'd been barely conscious of the several stops they'd made at a butcher that specialized in duck brought to Paris directly from the countryside; at the cheese monger favored by his aunt where white cheddar with black truffles could be had; and at a wine store where Finn purchased a bottle of her favorite brand of champagne.

Eventually, the lack of the car's forward motion for a longer length of time roused Juliet from her stupor. She raised her head and gazed through heavily lidded eyes at a gleaming store window filled with large glass bell jars protecting colorful cakes of every description and oversized chocolate Easter bunnies sporting jaunty satin bows tied around their necks. Figuring that this was the destination Finn had wanted her to see in all its Easter finery, she rolled down the window, instantly spotting his broad back at the far end of the shop where he was paying for purchases that were being packed in white and pink boxes so elegantly fashioned that they could have served as gifts themselves.

Watching from afar, she absorbed the sight of the tall, former pilot balancing several rosy colored packages in his arms as he exited the shop and strode toward his car that took up only half a parking space on the street. Juliet reached to open the door so he could store his booty on the bench seat behind her and on top of her small suitcase.

"*Bonjour* from the Easter Bunny," Finn said with a grin. "I hope you like fruit tarts and more chocolate."

"I love both, but I thought you were going to cook."

"I am, but I haven't finished my pastry course at *Le Cordon Bleu*, so I thought I'd expose you to the masters of the art—*Monsieurs* Thierry and Conticini—who own a series of these shops, but I like this one the best."

He stowed the last of his purchases and soon they were driving along streets with trees whose branches burst with the pink and white blooms of spring that reminded Juliet of the beautiful boxes in the backseat.

"Good lord, it's all so gorgeous," she murmured, gazing through the window at an outdoor café whose sandstone walls were dripping with arching bowers of lush, lavender wisteria.

"The view from the barge is completely different now from the one you saw in the dead of winter," he said, signaling a turn. "As you can see, the cherry blossoms, wisteria and daffodils have exploded all over the city." Finn found his customary parking place on the street above the quay. "And something else has happened since you left that I'd like your opinion about."

"Really?" she asked, filled with curiosity. "What?"

"I'll tell you while I'm making our dinner. That is, if you can stay awake."

By this time, thanks to her nap in the car, Juliet was feeling a bit more herself and did her duty setting plates and cutlery on the small table-for-two positioned next to windows on the side of the pilothouse that faced the Eiffel Tower. Within forty-five minutes, Finn had produced a mouth-watering duck with orange sauce served on perfectly cooked wild rice laced with mushrooms sautéed in cognac, along with steamed asparagus on the side. Outside their window, the tower cast a golden glow on the Seine, the colored lights of the French flag having been replaced by its customary, clear sparkling bulbs.

"As a gal who has grown up in a five-star hotel with a noted chef on staff," Juliet managed to say with her mouth full, "this is totally fabulous!"

"You're not just saying that to be polite after you heard me cursing my sticky pan?" Finn asked, and she realized he wanted an honest answer.

"No. Everything is cooked perfectly and the flavors blend brilliantly. It's first class, Major. Maybe you have a future career as a chef? Ever consider it?"

Finn settled back in his chair and shook his head. "I know enough about *haute cuisine* by now to be certain that the restaurant business is a lot harder than it may appear. No, my interest in food will remain amateur status, but the subject of career choices is actually what I want to get your opinion about."

"Me?" she asked, startled.

"Yep, you. I've been offered a job as one of several managers of a joint European operation that would fly small, commercial drones in sensitive areas as part of a coordinated security strategy."

"Really? Here in France?"

She didn't want to sound disappointed that Finn

might be making plans to remain in Europe long term. Given the mess facing GatherGames in San Francisco and the distance between there and Paris, any idea that she could stay in France longer than a weekend, or that she and Finn had any hope for a genuine future together suddenly looked—given this job offer—slim-to-none. Forced to face the reality of their situation, she mentally lectured herself to abandon the notion that had begun to thrum in the back of her brain about how this highly romantic night might end. She glanced at the couch nearby and resolved to sleep there for the few days she'd be in Paris before heading home.

In the silence that followed Finn's announcement of the drone security project he gazed at her intently as if to measure her reaction to his news.

"Well, tell me this," she said in what she hoped was a neutral tone of voice. "How does the job offer strike *you*? Would flying drones—even civilian ones—here in France bring up any…ah…bad memories?"

"I wondered the same thing and talked it over with Doctor A. She recommended I pay a visit to a drone training school at the Saint Jacques Airport in Rennes and see what it felt like."

"How far outside Paris is that?" she asked, trying to keep her demeanor friendly and interested.

"It's in the middle of Brittany. About two hundred miles from here. I was given a chance to test fly one of the prototypes the operation plans to use."

"And? How did it go?"

Finn cracked a grin. "At first, I'll admit, I was a bit spooked, but believe it or not, it turned out to be fun. These little spider-like machines have great, high-resolution video cameras attached to them and they're able to survey everything from cracks in a dam to railroad tracks with switches pointing in the wrong direction."

"So, you think you'll do it?" Juliet lowered her eyes to avoid his piercing stare while she carefully cut another slice off the orange-glazed duck breast.

"Turns out there are a few speed bumps connected with the offer."

She looked up. "Such as what?"

"I'd have to rejoin the Air Force."

Juliet set down her knife with a clatter. "Why? I thought it was a European joint governmental project to keep civilians safe, not a U.S. military operation."

"That's just the issue," he said, pushing a forkful of rice across his plate. "Its purpose is to protect civilians, but…"

Finn didn't complete his sentence, so Juliet did it for him. "But it's being made to look as if it were completely a civilian operation, right?"

Finn merely offered a shrug.

Juliet placed her fork on the side of her plate with a grimace. "You mean it's our C.I.A. and other European intelligence agencies in charge," she declared. "A military deal, right?"

"You did not hear me say that."

"But once you're in the Air Force again, they could send you anywhere and ask you to do anything, right?"

"Man, do I love your brain," he said admiringly. "I was pretty sure I was going to tell them 'no' this week, but I wanted to get your take, first."

Flattered to hear this, Juliet finished chewing the delectable morsel in her mouth and then said, "Well, at least you found out you could still operate a drone without—"

"Running screaming from the controls?" he joked with a flash of black humor. "Yes, that was worth the entire process of looking into the possibility of accepting the job. I also learned that, believe it or not, France is far ahead of the USA in putting forth sensible regulations for civilian use of commercial drones."

"Really? Ahead of us? I see drones being used now in news reports and stuff," she insisted. "You know, overhead shots of wildfires burning out of control in the mountains in California. And there was a big story just before I flew over here that showed medicines being delivered by small drones in remote parts of Appalachia. And, doesn't Amazon plan to start delivering packages with the gizmos eventually?"

"Exactly, although I think the Amazon project is some ways off, but there are a million ways to combine small-scale drone flights with all sorts of commercial enterprises. The problem in the States is the Congress and the FAA have been slow to set forth the regs to license commercial operators."

"Well, they better start soon before one of those things runs into a jetliner."

"Amen, but I learned a Congressional committee is fast-tracking it now. So get this," he said with a laugh. "I've been thinking of going back to school to learn as much as I can about the various applications there might be for commercial drone pilots. Then I'll figure out if there's a part of this industry in the U.S. that would be a good fit for me."

"There's a school you can go to for this?" she marveled.

"Yep…kinda like *L'École des Beaux Arts* for commercial drone operations here in France. There's even a course for people who are already pilots of winged and blade aircraft. They grant a certificate and everything. Then, if I come back to the States, I'll have a leg up and get certified locally wherever I end up. It might be nice to ply my skills for purposes I can actually stomach *and* make some money to support myself at the same time. My vacation budget is beginning to wear thin after a year in Paris, even living cheaply in the stern of a barge."

Juliet smiled across the table, slightly giddy for both of them that Finn had begun to find a path that made use of his highly skilled training, but also could prepare him for a profession in the States that resonated with him, and of which he could be proud.

"I think that's a terrific plan! I'm really excited for you."

"Well, thanks," he said, his blue eyes dazzling. "That makes me excited that *you're* excited." He looked across the table at her steadily. "Maybe you could quit that job that's driving you crazy and go to art school in Paris this year? It'd be great to be students together before we both hit the perils of middle age." He made a sweeping gesture that included his end of the barge. "And you'll always have cheap digs in the shadow of the Eiffel Tower."

Juliet was brought up short. Was Finn inviting her to move to France, partly on his account? The entire idea sounded totally impractical...and wonderful. But all she said was, "Me? Move to France, now, to study at *L'École*? That's always been my dream, but it's just not in the cards at the moment."

As if he hadn't heard her last words he said, "You could enroll, even part time, at *L'École*...or take the landscape painting course at Giverny...or sign up for a semester or two in that school in the South of France you told me about."

"You mean in Annecy?"

Juliet was amazed and touched to realize he'd actually given considerable thought to ways she could navigate a path from commercial graphics to fine arts.

"Right! That's the place...at the base of the French Alps. Where Cezanne painted, didn't you tell me one time? I could hone my drone skills and meet you on weekends here on the barge in Paris, or wherever. We could have a blast for a year or so until we were both ready for prime time in our new professions."

"Oh, Finn, that would be so great," she replied, hearing the wistful note in her response while her heart was hammering in her chest. Unless she was completely fanaticizing, Finn was actually asking her to be part of his life. But now she had to tell him about what her lawyer had texted her just before they'd sat down to dinner...

CHAPTER 23

Before Finn could beat the drum for her to pick up and leave San Francisco, Juliet somberly related the latest and intensifying rumors of a takeover at her family's company and her efforts to liberate enough privately-owned stock to retire the equity loan against the Bay View and give herself a cushion to live on while she went back to art school.

"My lawyer just texted me that it may take a few months, or even a year, but if Jamie and I can pull that off, it would actually make it possible for me to move to France to study landscape painting in a serious way, just like Avery's doing with portraiture."

Finn took a slow sip of his Perrier and topped off her glass of *Veuve Clicquot*. With its pinpoint bubbles and clean, dry taste, it had become her favorite bubbly, and she hadn't said 'no' to his refilling her glass all evening.

He raised his flute that glowed against the backdrop of the Eiffel Tower looming out their window, tracer lights now twinkling to mark the hour of ten o'clock. "Earlier you said I should take time to let everything that's happened to me this last year 'settle in,' wasn't that how you put it?"

"That's right." She wondered where this conversation was headed. "You have to do what you have to do, and as you can see, I need time to work with my lawyer to exit GatherGames with what's fairly owed to me, to Jamie, and to my parents."

Finn smiled briefly. "Well, here's to us. With any luck, it looks as if the timing within the next year might eventually line up for both of us. We're each on a path, with plenty to do and explore, but these trails seem pretty parallel—even if we're commuting between San Francisco and here. Nothing rushed, mind you," he assured her, sensing her vague alarm at the weighty implication of his words for both of them. "It sort of reminds me of that old Sinatra tune."

Juliet felt her eyes crinkle and a broad smile spread across her face. Her father had collected every song Sinatra had ever recorded. She could even sing it on key.

"*Let's take it nice and easy...it's gonna be so easy...*"

She halted, embarrassed to croon the next lyric, but Finn did it for her.

"*For us to fall in love...*"

"It's a great Alan Bergman melody," she murmured.

"Always loved that tune. Maybe it could be our theme song?"

In the highly charged silence that followed, Finn gently brushed the cool surface of his water-filled champagne flute against her flushed cheek.

"Oooh, that feels so nice," she whispered.

"And how nice it could be just to relax and enjoy ourselves and see where it all leads."

"But what if it takes me a year to untangle everything? What if it takes more?"

Finn smiled. "We'll save our frequent flyer miles and go back and forth as often as we can until we can live together in the same place."

"Nice and easy," she repeated with a little giggle.

"But we'll have to have faith in each other, though, Juliet," Finn warned. His rakish smile had given way to a serious expression. "For a while, at least, we'll be living on two continents taking care of business in our respective bailiwicks, so we'll have to trust that we both have similar goals *and* each other's best interest at heart. No screwing around, either of us."

"I know," she agreed with a sigh. "It's a pretty tricky setup, especially since you've been there and done that." He looked puzzled. "You and Kim living in two different places during your military service." She nodded toward the sofa where they both remembered Kim had sat earlier this day. "That didn't work out so well, did it?"

"You mean being separated a lot? No, it didn't, but it's you and me, this time," he said, his voice husky with emotion. "And in case you're wondering, I am quite enamored with you, Ms. Thayer. It'd be easy to fall in love with you. Fact is…if I'm really being honest, I'd have to say I already have."

Their gazes locked and she felt an electric charge skitter down her spine.

"I've been fighting that same feeling ever since my plane touched down at De Gaulle. Maybe before," she admitted, thinking of her tearful conversation with Avery and the way her heart lurched on Christmas Day at the sight of Finn's portrait.

"Fighting falling in love with me, are you?" he teased. "Why, I'm highly offended to hear that." Juliet could see he was faintly mocking but also serious. "*Wanting* to fall in love would sound a lot nicer."

"Come on, Finn! Let's face it. We've got a complicated situation here, and it's all been kinda crazy, you know? You and I literally bumped into each other in front of the American Hospital on that terrible day and now, after everything that's happened in the meantime, here we are…"

Finn rose to his full height and offered her a hand. "Yes, here we are. And aren't I a lucky guy?"

Juliet pushed back her chair and in one, continuous movement that signaled a decision in itself, she rose from the seat straight into his arms.

"We're both lucky…" she murmured, their noses

nearly touching, "I always think things are hopeless, but then, here you plot a flight plan I would never even have thought of. No wonder they promoted you to Major."

Finn ducked his head, his lips grazing her neck, inhaling her scent. 'Come fly with me tonight," he urged in her ear. "It's all I've been able to think about since I knew you were coming over for Easter."

She tilted her head back to stare into eyes so blue they were nearly black. "Are you sure that's such a good idea?"

Finn framed her face in steady hands that had flown aircraft to the far corners of the globe. "Oh, yes, baby. I'm absolutely sure this is a *very* good idea."

The sunny skies of a perfect Easter morning streamed through the porthole above the bed. Juliet swam to consciousness, deliciously aware of Finn's tall frame spooning hers, his lips nibbling her left shoulder while another part of his anatomy signaled he'd awakened before she had. *No more tights and a T-shirt for me*, she considered sleepily, *and no more running shorts for Finn.*

"Hey, baby…you awake?"

"Mmmmm…" was all she could manage.

"Does that mean you're sleepy or hungry?"

The last two mornings, Finn and she had risen together to walk to the bakery to lay claim to hot croissants, fresh out of the oven.

"Both." She turned over to face him. "But thank you for not leaving me alone in bed, even to get croissants." She brushed her fingers against the stubble on his cheek.

"Wouldn't be anywhere else." He held her hand against his face, his glance steady. "You are one fabulous co-pilot, you know that?"

Juliet actually felt a blush creep up her throat. She had been amazed how they hadn't slept a wink their first night together, but for some reason, each morning since, she'd felt exhilarated and bursting with energy despite the scant rest they'd gotten the subsequent nights. She suddenly flashed on all the mornings she'd awakened to find Jed had departed without even a goodbye to play an early game of tennis or head to the office before she did. What he did do was leave clothes on the floor, sometimes with a note that said, "Throw these in the wash for me, will you?" with no please or thank you.

She burrowed her head under Finn's chin, scattering kisses along his collar bone and then commenced playfully nipping his chest, deliberately moving lower in a path calculated to command his entire attention.

"Uh-oh...are you taking over the controls?"

"Watch me," she mumbled against the soft, vulnerable place where his thigh joined his pelvis.

Three days earlier, when they had removed each other's clothing, but before they fell onto the bed, he had pointed to the long, searing scar that incised the entire length of his left thigh where bullets had pierced his leg when the helicopter crashed, killing four soldiers on board. She had shocked even herself when she sank to her knees beside the bed built into the barge's bulkhead. She'd smothered the puckered flesh with kisses, wordlessly showing him she accepted everything he had endured, everything he might have thought ugly about himself. And when, just before dawn, he had cried out in his sleep and was covered with sweat, she held him against her nakedness, murmuring that she was here, she was real, and that the nightmare he'd been having was over.

"Shhh, sweetheart...we're on *L'Étoile*...floating on the Seine in the shadow of our beautiful tower."

"Oh, God! The guys...my guys...they were—"

"I know, I know," she crooned, pressing her cheek against his. "It seems so real, but it's *not*! You're here on the boat…with me. Juliet. The dream's not real. *I'm* real. We're both here and we're safe."

Finn's breathing had eventually slowed and he fell back to sleep, not stirring until she felt his body cradling her in the same protective way she had embraced his.

Now, giving the gift of pleasuring him this third morning they'd spent together was a gift to herself as well. When they finally rose from the rumpled bed, they showered together in the tiny cubicle just off the stateroom's stern.

Turning off the water, Finn said, "I probably scared the be-Jesus out of you last night. I'm so sorry—"

"Hey, you'd warned me about the nightmares." She brushed a kiss against his damp shoulder. "So when I realized what was happening, I wasn't scared. Just sad that these dreams still happen to you sometimes. Once you realized where you were, you went right back to sleep."

"You…well…you helped a lot."

"Just being here with you helps me a lot, too, Finn," she replied soberly. "It's been pretty grim in San Francisco. Here in Paris it feels…well, as if life can be very good."

"Good."

Toweling each other off, Finn glanced at the clock. "No croissants today, I'm afraid. We're due at Claudine's for Easter lunch in half an hour."

"And I still have to pack," she moaned, "but at least, that way, we can stay with her as long as we can before you take me to the airport."

Finn grabbed Juliet and pulled her hard against him as their towels unraveled from around their waists. "I hate that you're going back so soon," he said gruffly.

"Me too. But, welcome to the official flight plan you and I have agreed to, remember? Are you still certain this bi-continental deal is going to work for you?" She was worried, suddenly, what his answer might be.

"Yes, I'm certain." He scrutinized her face, his brow furrowed. "But how about you, standing here, bare-assed, in the light of day? How do *you* feel about it? What's it like for you, sleeping with a semi-dormant volcano?"

"Ain't going to be easy, flyboy, but I am all in."

Claudine had the long table in her elegant dining room already set with antique French linens, silver, and crystal by the time Finn, Juliet, Avery, and Alain met for Easter lunch.

"*Voilà!*" she said gaily, as Finn placed her highly touted *Jambon de Paris* on the crowded table. On the platter was a slow-cooked ham that not only retained a large percentage of its moisture but also absorbed the flavors of the herbal ingredients in which it was basted. Nearby were bowls of freshly steamed asparagus, tiny garden peas, and *pommes dauphine.* The crisp potato puffs were Claudine's specialty, made by mixing mashed potatoes with a savory puff pastry, forming the mixture into dumpling shapes, and then deep-frying them.

"These are the most fabulous tater-tots in the universe!" Avery declared, holding one up on her fork.

The assembled company soon fell to eating and chatting until, from the depths of Juliet's handbag, the sound of her cell phone interrupted the friendly banter. Claudine shot a mildly disapproving look as her guest jumped up to rummage in the bottom of her purse to turn off the insistent ringing. One glimpse at the screen, however, and Juliet dashed out of the room with an apologetic, "It's Jamie…"

She pushed the answer button—"Hi, Jamie. What's up?"

"You're flying home today, right?"

"Yes," she answered, her heart giving a flutter of alarm as she glanced at her watch. "It's the middle of the night where you are. What's going on?"

"There's an emergency meeting of the GG board late Monday afternoon, which will be tomorrow by the time you get back. Brad just announced that the takeover challenge from the Silicon boys in a rival game business is imminent and he wants all hands on deck."

"Of course he does," Juliet replied grimly. "Did you tell him that you and I and the parents want a separate deal if there's a buyout? Have you contacted our lawyers?"

In the silence that followed, Juliet felt Jamie's reluctance to answer her questions. Finally he said, "It's all happened so quickly and it's the Easter weekend, Jules!"

"The perfect time to stage a coup," she replied, keeping her voice steady. "At least leave a message for Edward Adelman right away, will you? Tell him what's going on and that I'm on my way home. In fact, I'm leaving for the airport in an hour."

"Thank God," Jamie said with a sigh of relief. "Brad's a crazy person right now."

"No doubt." She could imagine how a bully like her brother would react to having his power and prestige challenged by guys he'd probably gone to Stanford with, or maybe even had beaten at squash. "And I guess you're right not to say anything to Brad, yet, about our demands. Let's play our cards close to our vest until we know what's really going on."

Juliet returned to the table, attempting to present her normal demeanor, but Finn seemed to sense immediately she was upset. He looked at her across the table with a questioning glance.

"A bit of a glitch at home," she explained shortly, standing behind her dining room chair. She took note of her watch and addressed Finn. "I'll tell you about it in the car and you can tell the others later, if you want." She forced a smile at her companions so as not to spoil the jovial atmosphere that had prevailed before her phone had rung. "I think I just have time to sample some of those wonderful confections Claudine ordered from *La Patisserie des Rêves*. Then, sadly, I have to head for the airport." She looked directly at Finn, adding, "I hate to break up such a lovely party so I'm fine if it's easier to just help me find a taxi downstairs."

"Not a chance, *mademoiselle*," he replied. "First we have our dessert and coffee. Then we head for De Gaulle. I'll get you there in plenty of time."

That's my guy! Juliet thought with a profound sense of relief.

The takeover fight for GatherGames was bruising and the participants played as rough as was possible within the law.

"Or maybe just outside the law," Jamie grumbled when Juliet and he met with their lawyer after it was all over.

Brad had browbeaten the majority of the board, along with his parents, to hang tough with him, and had managed to get the weakest company director to resign. Within a few hours, he had replaced him with a fraternity brother who'd been born with a silver spoon in his mouth and brought some twelve million additional dollars into their coffers.

"The stockholders are satisfied we have acted in their interest by fighting off the takeover bid," Brad said smugly to a reporter from the *Wall Street Journal*. "And *I'm* satisfied the company is poised to be even more successful than ever, given the confidence shown by the latest investments into our firm, along with the initial, highly successful launch of *Sky Slaughter 1*. Even better, *SS2: Drones in the Desert* will be out momentarily, which is probably why these vultures tried to take us over to cash in on all our hard work."

And that was that. Problem solved.

"Except," noted Juliet bitterly to Edward Adelman and Jamie, seated at the glass-top table in the law firm's conference room, "practically everyone who works at GG hates the boss. In addition, our parents are still out their ten-million-dollar equity loan they took on the Bay View when they funded the company's expansion into war-game videos. The Golden Boy's won the battle, but the war isn't over. There are too many employees who hate Brad's guts and a lot of wanna-be investors are still circling."

Adelman looked from sister to brother and gave a shrug acknowledging defeat. "Unless your parents, themselves, take issue with Brad and demand they be repaid..." he focused a steady gaze in Juliet's direction, "for now, at least, you've returned to the status quo."

"*Merde!*" she hissed between her teeth, thinking of their lawyer's bill to come.

Jamie complained, "Brad's now demanding that none of us sell any of the family stock granted us at GG's founding, even though in two months, according to the rules of the company now listed on the stock exchange, we'll have the perfect right to do so." He looked across the law firm's conference table at his sister. "But unless we want to start World War Three at home, you and I are stuck—at least for the foreseeable future."

Juliet leaned back in the luxurious leather seat and frowned. Finn's proposal that she quit her job to join him in France was spinning in her thoughts. She looked at Jamie and said, "Well, we'll just have to weigh 'peace at any price' with our own needs and wishes, won't we? Meanwhile, we don't sign anything."

Adelman nodded. "Exactly. Keep me posted, and I'm happy to help if the landscape at GG alters in some significant way."

Juliet rose, pushed back the heavy leather chair and stowed a clutch of legal papers into her tote bag.

"I'll see you out," Adelman said, confirming their meeting was at an end. He ushered his gloomy clients through the glass door, across the reception area, and in the direction of a bank of elevators. Just then, Juliet noticed the young lawyer whom she remembered from the last time she was in the firm's office chatting with the pretty receptionist as they passed by. As Juliet came within three feet of him, she felt him cast her the same head-to-toe appraising gaze as on her last visit.

"Hey there, Eddie," he called out to Adelman. He graced Juliet with a knowing smile as if bestowing on her the gift of his appreciation for how she looked. "How's it going?"

"Hi there," the senior partner replied pleasantly and kept walking Juliet and Jamie toward the elevator doors.

The attention conferred on her just then made Juliet miss Finn Deschanel more than she ever imagined. How had she ever thought these kind of slick operators held any charm or attraction for her? She glanced up at a clock hung above the elevator doors. It was the middle of the night in France. Finn probably was in Rennes, sleeping in a cheap motel while taking the first of his small-scale drone classes to earn his commercial certification. He was already deeply launched into his part of their bargain.

How in the world am I going to advance my own?

The next day, Juliet was relieved to hear a deep, familiar voice on the other end of her phone.

"Hey there! I just called to say that you are now speaking to a guy who passed the first level of written exams—allowed to be given in English, thank God—and flew five drone exercises without mishap!"

Juliet rose from the stool next to her drafting table in the art department and dashed out the office door, heading down the hall to the ladies' room where she'd have some privacy. "Finn, that's fabulous, but of course you'd pass everything. You could probably be teaching the course."

"Some of it," he admitted. By this time, she'd slipped into one of the stalls of the empty bathroom and shut the door. "Trust me, though," he added, "I'm learning a lot about the ins and outs of flying these little guys into very small spaces, as opposed to operating a full-sized, winged aircraft. And by the way," he chortled, "the C.I.A. guy at the U.S. Embassy has finally given up trying to persuade me to reconsider his offer. He probably figured I wouldn't refuse it, given that a three-star general has obviously been breathing down his neck."

"Well, that's a relief," she replied, wishing that—likewise—her brother Brad would lay off his constant barrage of arm-twisting to get Jamie and her to sign a pledge that they wouldn't sell any of their stock until he gave the okay.

"As a matter of fact," Finn continued, "my status as a former, full-fledged military drone pilot has made me something of a celebrity at school. I might well end up teaching some courses here when I finally get certified."

"It sounds as if you're loving every minute of the training." Juliet smiled into the phone, hoping there was no detectable note of wistfulness. "And the great thing is, you're doing what you love, but on your own terms."

"*Exactement!*" he said, his French accent flawless. "But

what about you, sweetheart? You don't sound so hot. Tell me what's going on."

Finn's sensitivity to her moods, even across a distance of six thousand miles, never ceased to amaze her. She explained Brad's latest attempts to legally box her into long-term servitude if she wanted to emerge with the money she was owed.

"You didn't sign, did you?"

"No, of course not, but I can't seem to find a way out of this maze," she moaned, "and I'm so afraid that Jamie might cave, just to shut Brad up."

"If you don't sign, Jamie probably won't, either, don't you imagine?"

"That's what I'm hoping...but do you think I should just sell my stock on July first and say to hell with the rest of what I have coming? Or should I try one more time to persuade my parents that we have every right to recoup our investments...theirs in actual money, and mine and Jamie's in profits due us for five years of hard labor?"

"It's a tough choice, for sure."

"I miss you so much," she said in a rush, a lump suddenly swelling in her throat. "All I dream about is coming to Paris, but if I just up and sell the portion of stock I could legally liquidate in July, and my mother and father turn on me—which I'm sure my mother, at least, might—I'll basically be losing my family. For sure, they'll say I've betrayed the honor of the Thayers, along with my older brother..."

They both knew the doomsday scenario she'd sketched for him several times already. There was a long pause on the other end of the phone.

Exasperated, she said, "Well, what do *you* think I should do?"

Finn inhaled a deep breath. "Hear this, Juliet," he said, his voice low. "I miss you too. Much, much more than I even expected to, if you want to know…but I can't tell you what to do. I want you to return to Paris only if and when you feel it's in your best interests. Otherwise, you'll be just as miserable here as you are in San Francisco. Only *you* can decide whether to cut your losses and be happy in that decision—and come to Paris to study—or, stay and fight it out there in San Francisco to secure a better financial future. Either way, you have to be willing to take the possible consequences. But if you stay and fight and you don't achieve what you want—can you then be willing to walk away and feel okay about it?"

"Oh, Finn…it sounds so impossible when you put my choices like that."

"It's not impossible," he said in a surprisingly gentle tone of voice that was somehow soothing to her ears. "It's just hard. It's hard to choose between doing what others want you to do and doing what feels right for yourself. Believe me, I know."

"But *neither* choice feels right!"

"Then it sounds like you are not ready to decide, and that's okay, too."

"Really?"

"Really. And if you're worried I'm impatient with you, I'm not." His word's flooded her with relief. "I'm pretty content doing my thing over here, although let me tell you, I very much miss your being not in residence on the barge."

"You are such a sweetheart," she said with a sigh.

"A horny sweetheart, for sure…but thanks for the compliment."

Just then, someone entered the ladies room. Juliet immediately unlatched the stall door, smiled at the newcomer, and headed for the exit.

"I've gotta ring off, now," she said to Finn hurriedly. "I'm due in a meeting, but I'll keep you posted on this."

"You're in the ladies room, right?" Finn said with a chuckle. "Okay then. Text me a goodnight kiss later, will you?"

"Will do," Juliet said in a cheery, officious tone for the benefit of the young woman who worked in the coding department and was heading for the empty stall.

CHAPTER 24

Everyone in the art department had left their desks for the day this final evening in March as a finger of fog moved in through the Golden Gate Straits, rendering Alcatraz and Angel islands in the middle of the Bay invisible. Juliet, her coat in hand, was just about to walk out the door to meet Jamie for dinner at the Tadich Grill on California Street near their offices south of Market Street. Without warning, Brad's close-cropped blond head suddenly appeared in the doorway.

"Can I see you in my office?" he said, his voice crisp and businesslike.

Juliet glanced up at the clock.

"I'm due for dinner in fifteen minutes. How about first thing tomorrow?"

"You're meeting Jamie," he stated flatly. "He can wait. This won't."

How does he know who I'm having dinner with? Her heart thrummed in her chest, but she merely heaved a small shrug and attempted to appear calm as she slung her tote bag over her shoulder. She followed him down the hallway to his corner office with its seismic reinforcing iron beams that cross-crossed the brick wall of a former shirt factory. Twin girders also framed his stainless steel and glass-topped desk. She thought of her architect ancestress who would have been pleased to see how San Francisco had retrofitted many of its nineteenth-century buildings in case another temblor struck like the devastating one in 1906.

"Take a seat," Brad commanded, pointing to a chair that faced his desk. When both had settled, he shoved a solitary sheet of paper filled with single-spaced lawyereeze. "Please sign this," he instructed, adding, "I won't ask again."

Juliet skimmed the three terse paragraphs that basically promised that she would never sell any of her stock until given permission by her brother, the CEO, to do so. She looked at him and pushed the paper back in his direction.

"Are you kidding me, Brad?"

He scowled at her. "No. I'm not."

"I don't think this is even legal, but let me check with my lawyer," she said, doing her best to control her temper while buying time to try to figure out what was going on.

"No lawyers. Just sign." A skimpy inch of his blond hair fell across his damp forehead beaded with a sheen of perspiration despite the coolness of the evening air.

"And if I won't?"

"Then you're fired. As of the minute you walk out that door."

Juliet almost felt as if she were an actress onstage, playing out a dramatic scene that was a crucial turning point in the plot. Brad was staring at her, his eyes narrowed and his lips as thin as two elastic bands stretched near to breaking. She had a premonition that they were about to have an argument that had been bubbling on both their parts from the time he'd tampered with the training wheels on her bicycle when she was six. That day, he'd hidden the wheels so she couldn't ride in a section of the hotel's underground garage set aside for the three Thayer children to play in.

"You'd fire me if I don't sign?" she scoffed. "That's a pretty well-worn threat of yours."

Her words were convincingly calm and controlled, although it was obvious to her that Brad had become so agitated throughout the takeover fight—and clearly still was—that he just might follow through and can her this time.

He picked up the pen from his desk with his right hand while glancing at his Rolex watch on his left wrist. "I'll give you exactly one minute."

"Did Jamie sign?" she demanded.

From her brother's expression she could tell that Jamie must have left before Brad could put the same strong-arm tactics on him. Brad had probably learned from some co-worker that their brother had already departed to meet his sister for dinner somewhere.

"He'll sign." Brad glanced at his watch again. "Thirty seconds."

In a move that stunned even her, Juliet grabbed the pen from his hand and threw it with all her force across the office. It bounced off one of the iron girders with a ping.

"Gimme a break, Brad!" she declared, her voice starting to shake. "This is *my* stock we're talking about, here. I earned it and I'll sell it when I damn well want to! NO, I won't sign this agreement. What the hell is driving you to be such an asshole?" Brad actually looked shocked that she had the temerity to talk to him like she was, which added fuel to her fury. "I actually want to know why you act like such a prick all the time, not only to Jamie and me, but to ninety-nine percent of your staff?"

"You'll be sorry," Brad ground out between clenched teeth.

Juliet stared at her mother's favorite child and slowly shook her head. He was her brother...her flesh and blood...from the same set of parents. What had made him so different from Jamie and her? What had brought them to this moment after all their years of rivalry and Brad's casual cruelty to both his younger siblings for as long as she could remember? Why did he believe so strongly that he was entitled to the best of everything, to the first of everything, to whatever he wanted, even if he had to crush blood relatives who got in his way? What had given him such a belief about himself that nobody else mattered?

At length she said, "I know I'll be sorry. You've always tried to make sure of that if I stood in the way of anything you wanted. But let's not talk about me and what will happen between us after today." She waved her arm in a wide arc to include his high-tech office surroundings. "What I want to know is why is winning and being number one and pounding the opposition to dust so much more important than anything else in the world to you, including your own parents' welfare—the folks who raised you and paid for your education and loaned you ten million dollars to expand this enterprise?"

Brad looked startled by this sudden switch of topic. Juliet took advantage of his silence. "Okay, so you beat back a takeover bid this time." She lowered her voice almost conversationally and leaned over his desk, her elbows crooked and both palms pressing against the glass surface that felt cold on her skin. "Do you even realize that you are a *very* disliked personality around here? There will come a time when you *won't* win. When you won't have a single friend to back you up because you've lost your power and can't do anything for your hangers-on and they'll drop you from a dizzy height—splat! When you're not the Golden Boy anymore and Mother can't be your defender because she's old or dead. Then you will sit in a soulless room like this and wonder what the hell happened to you."

Brad simply stared at her, offering no response. She doubted anyone had ever called him out like she just had. She rose from her chair and gathered her belongings, her mind spinning with the implications of the words she'd laid before him as if they were Scrabble tiles on the smooth surface of his desk and maybe she'd finally won a round, for once. This was probably the end of any relationship she could hope to have with her brother who had also been her employer and the source of her income for five years.

"I'm leaving, now," she said, adding, "for good."

Brad finally spoke up. "I'll sue you! My lawyers will tie you up so tight that whatever stock you sell will go for attorneys' fees."

She affected a shrug, fairly certain there wasn't much a person could be sued for if she already was legally allowed to sell a portion of her stock as of July first of this year.

"Sue away," she offered. She zipped open her tote bag and showed him its contents. "See? I'm only taking my personal affects...make-up, hairbrush, wallet. I bought my own cell phone, but I'll leave you my laptop with everything intact. It's on my drafting table. All the files, including the computer-generated designs, are in the company system on my desktop computer, as well as those of the rest of the staff. I'll email you all the passwords. You own everything, Brad," she assured him, "the branding, the production specs, the invoices of everything ordered and paid for by the art department. And just as Avery did, I'm leaving every single thing I've ever done for you as an artist and designer and supervisor. It's all yours, Mr. Sexual Predator."

Brad's eyes widened with alarm as Juliet said, "Yes...I know all about that, too, so to avoid any mess, Avery and I would both suggest you don't summon your attack dogs."

Her brother jumped to his feet, but before he could sputter a word, she overrode him. "And if you're worrying I'll go work for one of your competitors, have no fear," she pledged, turning to leave. "I will never, ever have anything to do with video war-game production for the rest of my life." She flashed him a smile. "And that's an agreement I *will* sign—if you insist—so you truly have nothing to sue me over."

"You can't do this!" he shouted.

"Oh, yes I can," she said, calmness unlike anything

she'd ever experienced settling over her. "And just think…once again, you totally got your way. You are now the master of all you possess. But remember one, important thing…" She slid the zipper closed on her bag in a single, swift movement. "You don't actually own people in this world, Brad. Not Avery, not Jamie—and you certainly don't own *me!*"

And then she walked out of his office and headed for the Tadich Grill.

Even though Juliet was seriously late for her date to meet Jamie for dinner, she decided to walk the distance from the office building to the restaurant. As she strode down the darkened sidewalk through an eerie mist swirling through the canyons of downtown San Francisco, she felt shaky, yet strong. Brave—and also afraid for her future. But she felt *free*. Free from the fear of Bradshaw Thayer IV's bullying that had cast a shadow over her life for as long as she could remember. She was free to go. Free to sell some of her stock in a few months in order to finance a year in France. Free to choose her own path and practice the art she yearned to create. If she couldn't make a living doing that, she was free to take the time to find a new path, just like Finn was doing. With her talents and abilities, she could always find something to do that would sustain her. She was amazed by the thought that she no longer had to drink from the poisoned well that had been her life at GatherGames under her brother's intimidating domination and her mother's cool detachment. She might never understand why Brad had become who he was, she realized, but she knew, thanks to meeting Patrick Finley Deschanel, that all strong men were not like her brother whose narcissism had been a toxic force her entire life.

As she caught sight of the restaurant, she suddenly had a vision of her unsuspecting parents having a quiet supper of their own this night, as they so often did, at a little round table set into a bay window in the family suite. They would be dismayed when they learned what had just transpired between their two eldest children. Juliet had tried to act as her parents' guardians, but her mother had consistently taken Brad's side in all things for reasons she had never truly comprehended. As for her father, he'd caved in at every stage.

In a sudden flash of insight she realized that she was powerless to change that well-worn dynamic and she couldn't fix any of them. It was up to them to act in their own interest—and if they chose not to, it was not her responsibility anymore.

Nobody owes me the keys to the hotel. I had the joy of living there all these years and that's enough.

She was free.

As she entered the door to the Tadich Grill, a strange lightness swept through her, as if a warm, spring breeze from the budding green vineyards to the north had wafted through this old brick building, lifting her spirits with its gentle force. The *maître d'*, who had hosted the Thayer family here for many years, greeted her warmly and led her to her brother's table.

"Well, it's about time, kiddo," Jamie chastised her, rising from his seat in their favorite sequestered booth. "You're forty minutes late."

"I have a very good excuse which I'll tell you about in a minute, but first I need a drink."

She still felt deeply unsettled by her run-in with Brad, but also—and strangely—euphoric. Considering what had just transpired, euphoria was the last thing she had expected. She was in crisis, wasn't she? Why did it seem as if the weight of the world had been lifted from her shoulders? She turned her attention to the waiter. "A bottle of *Veuve Clicquot*, if you have it, John. And two glasses. We're celebrating."

"Of course, miss," he replied, cheerful in the knowledge that the bill for the sparkling wine, alone, would be substantial, and so would his tip.

"What are we celebrating?" Jamie demanded doubtfully. "I have four messages from Brad on my phone that I let go straight to voice mail."

"Trust me, you won't want to listen to them." She glanced at her surroundings. "Just give me a moment, will you? I have to go to the ladies' room and I'll be right back by the time the champagne arrives." And before Jamie could question her further, she headed for the rear of the restaurant.

She loved the Tadich Grill. It was reputedly San Francisco's oldest continuously operated eatery, founded, in its original incarnation, in 1849 in the wake of the Gold Rush. Its current California Street location near Battery in the Financial District attracted a wide spectrum of stockbrokers, dot-comers, hedge fund managers, politicians, "old" San Franciscans like her parents—and tourists, of course.

On the right, a bar almost the same length as the building itself stretched from the front door to back. Per usual, the stools were fully occupied with diners, as was the row of tables on the left. Starched white tablecloths, each sporting a bowl of fresh lemon wedges, were on every table. The aroma of fresh filet of sole simmering in butter and breadcrumbs, a dish for which the Tadich Grill was justly celebrated, poured out of the kitchen in the rear of the restaurant. Alternating with the small, square tables in the main room and built into the high-gloss, wood-paneled walls on the left were alcoves with booths like the one Jamie and she were assigned that were large enough for up to six patrons. Additional dark wood paneling with large mirrors covered the walls illuminated by Art Deco brass and milk-glass light fixtures that hung from the high ceiling.

It was an admittedly noisy restaurant, but if your name was Thayer, or that of other recognized San Francisco families like the Aliotos, the Feinsteins, or the deYoungs, a smaller number than six patrons would be granted one of the exclusive, bigger booths. Within the roomy cubicles cordoned off with individual curtains, private conversations could take place away from the cheerful babble in the main eating hall.

By the time she returned to her seat after washing up, the waiter stood at the ready to pour from the bottle of her favorite French champagne. Once he departed and Juliet raised her glass in a mystery toast, Jamie demanded, "Okay. What gives? Did Finn ask you to marry him long distance?"

Startled by this, Juliet burst out laughing. "No, but almost as good. Brad just fired me...or I quit. I'm not quite sure which one it was, but I am g-o-n-e, *gone!*"

"He fired you from your *job?*"

Juliet laughed again at the dumbfounded expression on Jamie's face.

"Yep! Even called Security to escort me out of the building, just like he did when Avery quit. He acted like a jackass, per usual, and I got mad, and without blinking an eye, he did a 'Donald Trump.'"

"Why did you fall for the bait? I thought we were playing it cool until—"

"There was nothing cool about Brad's dragging me into his office tonight and practically putting a gun to my head if I didn't sign an agreement not to sell any stock until he said I could." She was no longer smiling. "He tried to find you first to force you to sign, too, but you'd already left." She looked at him sharply. "And don't you do it!"

She spent the next twenty minutes sipping champagne and giving chapter and verse of everything that had happened in their brother's office that evening.

"Holy shit…what am I supposed to do now?" Jamie fell silent for a moment and then said more quietly, "I want to quit, too. Or get fired," he amended. "Doesn't the company have to pay us severance if it gives us the old heave-ho?"

"You bet I'm going to fight for some severance, and I don't blame you for wanting to leave," Juliet sympathized. "It's a snake pit, all right, but your leaving GG at the same time as I do may not be our best move, ultimately. We're going to need you on the inside for as long as you can stand it. I smell a big, fat rat at work in all of this. Somehow Brad knew, or suspected that you and I were planning an exit strategy so we could sell the preferred family stock at the company's five-year mark and make our escape. What happened tonight was a power play he tried to pull to stop us."

"But how would he know what we've been discussing?" Jamie wondered. "Didn't you say our lawyer promised absolute anonymity?"

Juliet nodded. "Yes. It's a big ethics thing with those firms. I'll have to go through the exit process with GG's Human Resources department, so maybe I can find out a few clues about all this."

"Good luck with that. They work for Brad, remember."

"But they also have to advise me of the SEC rules and my rights regarding the stock I own outright. I'm guessing I've pretty much lost my stock options after tonight's fight. I doubt, now, he'd graciously grant me an acceleration so I could exercise them as an investment—which our lawyer told me earlier he *could*—if Brad were a nicer guy."

"Which—guess what—he isn't."

"Even so," she continued, "I'll still have the family stock I own. Maybe there's no need for you to quit and give up on your options yet. If my hunch is right, there may be a way, down the road, for you and Mom and Dad to exercise yours and acquire more stock at a good price. You've just got to hang in and do what *you* told *me*: keep your ear to the ground and your powder dry while we wait to see if there's another takeover bid."

"You think there might be another one?" Jamie groaned. "Honestly, I don't think I can go through that again. Dad, either."

"It won't happen right away," she predicted, "but from everything I hear in the art department and in ladies' room on occasion, those vulture capitalists are still circling—which is why Brad is so paranoid about our selling our family stock in July. To him, it's nothing but a vote of 'no confidence' and a slap in his face, especially if *you* quit, now that I've been fired. You can use staying as leverage and refuse to sign anything!"

"He is such a jerk," Jamie muttered with disgust.

"Well, his legendary failure as a leader is the company's soft underbelly. Every kid in America may be playing *Sky Slaughter*, but from the rumors still floating around, somebody even bigger than the last group has great incentive to go in for the kill." She clinked her glass against her brother's as their waiter appeared with two aromatic plates of filet of sole doused in butter, lemon, and capers, with pasta on the side. "Here's to you and me getting out of this deal alive and in decent financial shape."

"What are the parents going to say when they find out Brad fired his own highly talented, hardworking, and competent sister?" demanded Jamie with a scowl.

Juliet smiled fondly at him across the table. "Thank you for saying that. As a matter of fact, Mom and Dad's reaction to all this will be very, very interesting. I'm betting, though, it won't be any different than it's always been. Brad can do no wrong."

Just then, Jamie's cell phone emitted a ping. He glanced down and heaved a sigh.

"Brad again. This time it's a text." He paused, reading, and then banged his head against the booth's paneled wall in a show of frustration.

Juliet couldn't contain her curiosity. "What's he saying now?"

Jamie read aloud from the small screen.

High High Priority! FBI interviews tomorrow re encryption issues. All staff at office by 6 a.m.

"Brad's going to give instructions to everyone on how to *lie* to the Feds?"

"Who knows," Jamie replied glumly.

Juliet dug her phone out of her tote. It was silent. No little red dot to indicate a message. No summons for her. Apparently, she had departed from GatherGames at precisely the right moment.

CHAPTER 25

As soon as Juliet calculated it was nearing daybreak in Paris, she had twenty-four-hour room service bring up tea and toast at midnight, her time, and sat in her suite's small sitting room to make a call to France.

"He canned you, huh? What an idiot!" Finn said after she'd told him the latest news.

"But what about the FBI appearing on our doorstep today?" she pressed.

"They're probably talking to a lot of companies in your industry."

"How far do you think they can pressure Brad about creating a 'back door' to GG's encryption software so they could read messages if warranted?"

"It's a big question whether deciphering encrypted messages that have already been exchanged can even be done, technically, except—maybe—by the world's most talented hackers. The degree of pressure by the FBI probably depends on whether any of the terrorists in all these various attacks around the world employed your company's particular encryption software in their communications. It's pretty clear the Paris thugs used the app called *WhatsApp*... but maybe the Feds are onto some other uses of encryption somewhere in the world that might point to GatherGames."

"Sheesh...this is getting serious."

"Well," Finn judged, "just remember—cyphers and codes and encrypted messages go back to General Washington and the American Revolution. These days, there are more than six hundred American companies with their own version of encryption software out there, so the

Feds are probably just covering all the bases. Odds are, the ones the FBI are after aren't your company's."

"Not *my* company, anymore, thank goodness," Juliet reminded him. "I keep lecturing myself that my parents' financial fate is in their own hands, but I can't help but worry about how this is going to affect them at this stage of their lives if anything blows up about this. Maybe it could tank the stock. We could lose the hotel!"

"Remember we talked about this?" Finn chided. "Your parents always had a choice, and so do you—and you've made it, or rather, it was made *for* you by Brad."

"Yes, but—"

"No, 'yes buts,'" he scolded. "Basically, you just got fired by your own brother, remember? What did your mother and father say when you told them Brad booted you out of the company you helped to found, and for no just cause, other than you wanted—maybe—to sell some stock when it becomes perfectly legal to do so?"

Juliet hesitated, hating the answer she would have to give concerning the conversation with her parents after she got home from the restaurant. "My mother said I was wrong not to do whatever Brad said since 'he was under a tremendous amount of pressure and deserved absolute loyalty from us all,'" she quoted.

"And your dad?"

She paused. "He just listened and didn't say a word."

"That was it?"

Juliet could hear the disappointment in Finn's voice.

"Well, after telling them what had happened with Brad and that the FBI was arriving, he squeezed my shoulder— I guess in sympathy—as I left their suite."

"You tell *me* something, then," Finn said. Juliet could imagine him sitting in his leather reading chair, gazing out the pilothouse window at the Eiffel Tower as the sun rose over the Seine, his cell phone pressed to his ear. "Why are you so loyal to those who haven't shown much interest in your welfare in all of this?"

Emotion clogged her throat and she suddenly found she couldn't speak. Finally, she whispered into the phone, "I don't know…it's just…they're my *family*."

Silence reigned between them.

"Tough stuff, this family business," Finn offered. "Gives a person something to ponder, though, doesn't it? But don't think I don't sympathize, sweetheart."

It was his tone—not his words—that soothed her soul.

"I know you do," she answered, her voice choked. Despite his expression of empathy, however, Juliet somehow felt he might also be frustrated at her lack of moxie to do anything but complain about the situation. Bleakly, she wondered how come she could never get mad at her dad, even though his silence so often let her down?

"So, what's next?" Finn asked.

What was next? She'd been so completely tied up in the drama of unfolding events that she hadn't had time to even think about it. It was the first of April… *April Fool's Day*, she thought wryly.

April in Paris!

Her father loved the Frank Sinatra version of that great song…

A quick rush of excitement ran through her. In early May, a summer session at *L'École* would commence that was especially designed for visitors from abroad. In June, there was also a week's workshop she could take at Art Colony Giverny where enrolled students were allowed to paint in Monet's garden two hours prior and three hours after the public was allowed in. There were also classes in watercolor in the "style of the Impressionists" at the art school in the lake city of Annecy, south of Lyon.

What was next? France!

"You still there, Juliet?"

"Yes, I'm here… I'm thinking."

"About…?"

Finn's voice sounded teasing, as if he anticipated what she was going to say and that he'd be pleased by her announcement.

"I'm coming to France."

"Fan…tastic! For how long?"

"I'm going to commit to stay at least six months to enroll in as many landscape painting courses in both oil and watercolor as I can squeeze into seven days a week."

"Excellent plan!" he complimented her, adding as if it were the most obvious thing in the world, "And you know you have a bunk with me. I'm not even in Paris half the time since the school has me flying drones all over France as part of my training, so I don't think I'd get on your nerves too much."

But would I get on yours? she wondered.

Some instinct told her it would be risky for both of them if she simply flew to Paris and moved in with Finn, given that there was so much still to learn about each other. For Finn's part, studying commercial drone aviation wasn't the only thing he had to work on—there was still the whole PTSD situation. His suddenly having a permanent, live-in woman in his life before he might be ready to take such a step could be disastrous. It could also very well be heartbreaking for her, since Juliet couldn't deny that Finn Deschanel was a very important factor in her yearning to study painting in France. What if it didn't work out between them…?

By this time, her intuition was practically yelling at her that if she were serious about switching from commercial art to fine art to make her living at the ripe old age of thirty-six, such a career change had to be her first priority. She also knew without question that serious focus and attention had to be paid while she took on the challenge of becoming an expatriate artist in a foreign country. If she and Finn were eventually to be together, their evolving relationship must be on a separate tract from their professional endeavors—and treated as such.

"You are the kindest, most generous person I know, you know that?" she began. "And I am so touched you'd invite me to share the barge, but let's remember 'our song.' *Nice 'n Easy does it every time*, right?"

"Are you saying you don't want to live with me?"

"I'm saying I'd love to live with you full time, but not yet."

"C'mon, Juliet, is that the real reason you won't move in with me?" The warmth had disappeared from his voice. "Or is it because you think I wouldn't be able to handle—"

She interrupted him. "I don't actually know if you *or* I could handle such a big step, given all the upheavals in our lives right now. I just think we should try to ease into all these transitions, which are huge for both of us right now, don't you agree?"

There was a long pause on the other end of the line. Finally, she heard him sigh. "You're right. They're huge life changes. I'm warning you, though, rentals in Paris are horrendous. I hope you've got some serious money saved."

Relief flooded Juliet as she realized that she'd been holding her breath as to his reaction to her rejection of his offer to live together right off the bat.

"Things are definitely lining up, Finn," she said, enthusiasm beginning to bubble inside. "Avery just emailed me yesterday that she's moving into Alain's studio to sleep as well as paint and was giving the landlord notice next month about the *Rue de Lille* flat. I'm sure if I told her right away that I wanted to take it over for a while, she'd let me. It's good weather, now, so I won't freeze, and it's right around the corner from *L'École*, which will make life so convenient for taking my classes…and," she added, hoping this compromise would sit well with Finn, "it's affordable and it's less than two miles away from your barge. It might be the perfect, intermediate step for us."

She waited for his response, which came after a few moments' hesitation.

"You know, you on *Rue de Lille* is the next best thing to your being full-time on the boat," allowed Finn, and from the warmth that had returned to his tone, she knew she had struck upon a workable solution. They could be close, and yet independent as they took time to explore what it was like to be together. "How soon can you get here?"

She smiled at the sound of Finn's voice, gruff and pleasingly impatient.

"Within a week?"

She had no idea how she could arrange things so quickly, but she couldn't wait to leave for Paris.

"Tell me the date as soon as you have your flight booked and I'll rearrange my classes to meet you at De Gaulle. You'll stay with me the first night, though, right? Two or three nights, maybe? I could even take you to Rennes to see my crazy flight school."

Juliet felt a familiar flutter of excitement spread through her midsection, along with a sense of enormous gratitude that Finn Deschanel was a man who could be counted on…a man of his word. He was that sort of 'Stand And Deliver' guy that could fly aircraft in formation and not screw up. He would show up when he said he would, and would never disappoint unless something bigger than he was got in the way.

Something horrendous like the aftermath of being shot down flying a helicopter and watching four buddies die…or returning home to a wife, pregnant by another man…

As for Juliet, there was a very good chance her mother

would never speak to her again when she announced she was leaving San Francisco. Yes, indeed, they both needed time to heal their own wounds. More certain than ever that their proposed living arrangements were wise for now, she finally said, "Of course I'll stay with you when I arrive. Are you kidding? I get all hot and bothered, just thinking about it."

"I can't wait either, sweetheart. Really."

Juliet felt a surge of joy. "You're probably going to have a terrible time kicking me off that barge."

With the phone in one hand, she walked to her closet and pulled out a large suitcase wedged in the back that she probably hadn't used in five years. She dragged the heavy luggage across the room as Finn said, "Are you sure you won't forget all this sensible 'transition' stuff and just move in with me?"

She leaned down and located the suitcase's industrial-sized zipper that would open the bag. "Well, I gotta admit, your offer's pretty tempting, but, truly, don't you think it's important we try to do this the right way?"

She waited a beat, and then came his answer. "Yes, I do, but man, have I been fanaticizing about you on this boat."

She flashed on the moment he had stood before her, naked by his bed, the scar etched down the length of his outer left thigh, visible in all its vulnerability.

"I have a few fantasies of my own," she confessed. "Tell Truffles to move over! Juliet's coming to town."

His laughter filled her ear and she could imagine his wide grin and ink-blue eyes creased at the corners.

"Oh, by the way," he added, and by the tone of his voice, Juliet realized he was trying to sound casual. "The divorce is final. Just got all the stamped paperwork two days ago. I am officially *not* married. After two, long years in legal limbo, there's no more 'technical' anything. I am well and truly a single man once more."

It certainly does feel as if the stars were lining up for us.

"Congratulations—or, as we say out here in the West—cool beans, flyboy. I'm going to hang up now. Gotta start packing."

Juliet's preparations to depart from her hometown soon became a blur of frantic activity, first to confirm with Avery that she could take over her lease on *Rue de Lille*; then to pack the rest of her things and send them separately to France, care of Finn on his barge, including her paint supplies and the winter clothes she'd need later. She waited to go downstairs to inform her father of her plans until she knew her mother had left for her bridge luncheon. Juliet was banking on her father telling her mother about her plans, so that the explosion sure to follow would erupt without her having to be a witness.

She took the service elevator all the way to the basement and walked along a cement corridor to a door at the far end of the hotel's east wall. The underground area instantly brought to mind their family's lore about the founding couple of the Bay View. James and Amelia Thayer had actually lived in this subterranean space while the six floors of the hotel were being constructed above their heads in the year following the cataclysmic 1906 earthquake and firestorm that obliterated 400 city blocks. Knocking softly at the door of her father's wood-paneled office, where he kept tabs on the hotel's day-to-day operations, she waited for his friendly, "Come in!" and swiftly entered his lair before anyone else knew she was there.

"Well, this is a nice surprise," he said, smiling and glancing over the reading glasses resting halfway down his nose. And then with a look of irony, added, "But, of course, you are now a lady of unexpected leisure and can call on dear old Dad in the middle of the day. Good to see you, pet. How're you doing?"

He gestured for her to take a seat opposite his desk. In one corner of the room stood a large leather chair, not unlike the one taking up space on Finn's barge. Her father's version had files stacked high upon it, along with rolled-up drawings from his "other job" as a practicing architect who only took on small commissions these days.

"My being unexpectedly a lady of leisure is the reason I'm here, Daddy," she said, getting right to the point. "I've just bought a one-way ticket to Paris. I leave tomorrow night. I'm going to take at least six months off and go to France to do a concentrated study of landscape painting." Then she added, "And by the way, I officially broke up with Jed just before Christmas. I should have told you earlier."

Her father remained silent and she could see he was mulling over her multiple announcements and probably wondering how the rest of the family would receive Juliet's declaration of independence. Then he said quietly, "I understand. Jed's been a good friend of Brad's, but I never thought he was the right match for you. And as for painting landscapes, I'm glad you're going to give it a try. It's what you always wanted to do, isn't it? You were very loyal to put aside your own plans to help your brother launch the company."

"Brad sort of forgot that part," she said archly. "Did he tell you he wanted me to sign an agreement that I could never sell my stock until he gave permission?" Bradshaw Thayer III's startled expression telegraphed the fact that this was the first he'd heard any of this news. "What did he say to you was the reason he fired me?" she demanded.

"He just said your work wasn't up to par lately and he had to replace you."

"And did you believe that?"

"No."

"Did Mother?"

Her father shifted his weight on his executive chair and glanced over to a pile of file folders on his desk as if he were suddenly anxious to get back to work. Without looking at her he said, "Well, as usual, she didn't take issue with anything Brad said on the subject."

"Did *you?*" She stared at him steadily until he reluctantly pulled his eyes away from the papers to meet her gaze.

"I knew you'd been doing an excellent job on projects not to your taste or sensibilities, so I didn't have to discuss it with either of them."

"Did you defend me, or at least ask questions?" she demanded again.

His chin sunk to his chest and he heaved a sigh. "Brad won that round."

"As usual." It was a biting, bitter comment, but at the moment, she didn't give a flying fig. "You let him win *every* round." She felt her head begin to throb. "So does Mother." She paused and then asked a question that had been rolling around in her brain since she was six years old. "Will you please tell me why Mildred Thayer thinks her Golden Boy can do no wrong? *Ever?* Even when you know, and I know, and Jamie knows, and the entire staff at GatherGames knows that he behaves like a narcissistic shit in almost every aspect of his thirty-nine-year-old life—and no one ever calls him on it!"

"Isn't that a little harsh?"

"No. As a matter of fact, I think it's quite an accurate description of how things go down around here. Just ask anyone—except Mother, whose darling first-born son can do or say any outrageous thing and she's just fine with it!"

Juliet's father was silent for a long moment. Then, as

if he'd come to a decision, he said quietly, "Your brother Brad was *not* her first-born son."

Juliet's lips parted with surprise. She stared at her father for several long seconds. "What? What do you mean, 'not her first-born?' I don't understand."

"I know, but perhaps it's time you should." He shifted his gaze to the window, avoiding her open-mouthed gaze. "I wish we had shared the truth with you kids long ago. If we had, perhaps we might have prevented this unhealthy dynamic between your mother and Brad from dominating our lives."

Her mind flew to a million scenarios. "What are you saying, Dad? Is Brad not your child, too?"

"Oh, he's my son, all right. My *second* son. Our first child was born while I was in the Army Corps of Engineers during the Vietnam War."

"And what happened to him?" Juliet asked, shocked to learn she had yet another brother.

Her father pointed to a photo of the entire family in a silver frame on a corner of his desk. "Before you three kids were born, Mildred and I had a son, but the thing of it was, Millie and I weren't married when he was conceived."

Juliet reared back on her chair, but all she managed to utter on a long breath was, "Wow."

"Your mother learned she was pregnant after I'd shipped out, which was a huge crisis for both families. Remember, now, it was in the late sixties, and Millie's family, the Churches, was just as prominent a clan in San Francisco as the Thayers."

"Mother has reminded me of that often enough."

As her father's revelations began to sink in, Juliet couldn't get over the fact that her snobbish mother had actually gotten knocked up, despite the introduction of the birth control pill at that time.

"Well, Mildred wrote to me right away, of course,"

continued her father, "but there I was…in the jungle in Southeast Asia. Not much I could do about it."

"Were you engaged at least?" Her father shook his head, and she pressed on, "Would you have married her if she *hadn't* gotten pregnant?"

She was shaken to her core by her father's lack of an immediate answer. She watched him closely while he struggled to summon a response.

"Since we're being honest here, today," he replied, finally, "I think I would have to say 'no.' I wouldn't have chosen her for my wife. At the time, I didn't think we were well suited, despite the fact we were both interested in architecture and our families were delirious about our supposed courtship before I joined the service." He heaved a sigh. "I don't want to in any way disparage your mother, but I knew in my gut she wasn't the right one for me when I took her out the first few times at the urging of my parents." He gave a small shrug. "This was why I enlisted in the service so I wouldn't have to stick around and get pressured into marriage. I shipped out and figured it was all behind me."

"Except for one little problem," Juliet said, her voice hard. "You'd slept with her without using birth control. So, obviously, it wasn't 'all behind you' because here you are, married to her with three more children. What happened to the baby? Did Mother put it up for adoption?"

A look of deep sadness invaded her father's still handsome features. "To save face, Millie went to stay with an aunt in Arizona until the baby was due. Her dad pulled some strings with the then Governor and got me an emergency leave to be flown back to San Francisco for a long weekend. We met at the downtown Civic Center, got married by a judge my father knew, and I was on the first plane back to Asia."

"You just gave in? And let them fly you across an

ocean to get married to someone you weren't in love with?"

"Well, the pressure from all sides was pretty intense." A familiar, defensive tone laced his words. "But yes, I gave in, as you call it. It became the pattern for my life. I was back in the jungle twenty-four hours later."

"And Mother and the baby?" Juliet asked, stunned by everything he'd revealed.

"After the ceremony at City Hall, she immediately returned to Scottsdale with a nice notice in the *San Francisco Chronicle* that we'd been married in a "'small, romantic ceremony', and that the bride had returned to Arizona to continue her studies in engineering while her husband finished his obligation to the U.S. Army Corps of Engineers. Turns out, two months earlier, she'd contracted the measles from a kid in her aunt's neighborhood. She carried the baby to nearly full term, but he was born dead. A blessing, I suppose, as I was told he had major birth defects."

"Oh, God…how awful."

"I never saw him, of course. He's buried in a desert cemetery somewhere. After another year in Vietnam, I came back."

"That must have been some homecoming," murmured Juliet.

"For a time, your mother and I were joined by the sorrow of losing that child. Mildred had, by then, earned her engineering degree, which was quite an accomplishment back then. We moved in here," he said, making a vague gesture to the hotel that rose above their heads, "and we both pretended that it would somehow all work out between us. A year later, we had Bradshaw, and Millie named him after me—again."

"She named *both* baby boys Bradshaw Thayer?" Juliet exclaimed, astonished.

"That's what she put on the grave marker, she said. Only this time, naming a son Bradshaw Thayer the Fourth served as a constant reminder to me of what a bad guy I'd been skipping out to fight a war I didn't believe in, just to escape getting engaged."

"So the Brad I know *was* her Golden Boy," Juliet mused. "Her redemption…and her revenge."

Her father arched an eyebrow, and then nodded in agreement. "And he was the Bradshaw Thayer that she far preferred over me. She was determined to mold him into a man of action…a man who never gave in and was successful in everything he attempted. She coached him and coddled him and told him every second how wonderful and perfect and brilliant he was, and that he was entitled—in a way I certainly wasn't—to every ounce of her love."

It was Juliet's turn to be silent, a million thoughts colliding in her brain. At length, she noted glumly, "So it seems that what happened with the two baby Brads guaranteed that there wouldn't be enough affection left over for Jamie or me."

"That's not completely true," her father countered. "Your mother wanted more children. Demanded them, in fact. She said I owed her at least that."

"She needed a *shrink*, not more kids," Juliet shot back, hearing the anger in her own voice as she remembered the seminal incident when Brad vandalized her bike when they were kids. "She never once sided with either Jamie or me whenever Brad did something mean or even cruel to us, and she *never* reprimanded him."

"I know that, pet," her father said. "It pains me enormously to say this, but she turned your older brother into a kind of monster…and I let her do it."

"You were part of it, for sure. But then, why didn't you ever stick up for us?"

"I hated the constant bickering and conflict and before long, I became one of those 'peace at any price' guys…a complete coward in the face of the force of nature your mother became once she was a partner in our business and the hotel. Brad replaced the little boy she lost, and she never got past blaming me for everything that had happened to us when I rejected her, joined the Army, and lit out from San Francisco—in that order."

"Well, she'd wanted to marry you!" Juliet protested. "She must have loved you. Didn't she worry about your safety? You were fighting for your country ten thousand miles away and could have been killed!"

"None of that seemed to matter to her much. As I said, we weren't well suited. She and her family supported the Vietnam War…and I sure didn't, especially after I got over there and saw what it was like. She liked the social scene in the city. I didn't. All those things. Looking back, we were two young kids driven by forces neither of us understood."

"Jeez, Dad!" It was one thing to wonder if your parents were ever truly in love, but it was quite another to hear from a reliable source that they weren't, *ever.*

Just then she flashed on Finn's description of his wandering into a marriage with Kim right after he'd graduated from the Air Force Academy, a marriage that he knew, from the outset, had little chance of success, given how unalike they were.

"You were in your twenties," she mused aloud. "You were probably just 'in lust,' not in love."

"We weren't even that, really," he admitted. "We knew each other. Our families knew each other. Everyone but me thought that it was a 'suitable match.' The night she got pregnant was the result of too many tequila shooters at Trader Vic's after a deb party—drinks that she paid for, as I recall."

"Well, hell, Dad," Juliet protested, "then Mother was just as responsible as you were for getting pregnant!"

"Ha! People didn't think that way back then." His short laugh was bitter and laced with palpable regret. "The next morning she said, rather gaily, that she didn't really care if she got pregnant…that we could 'always just get married—which is what everyone expects us to do,' is I think how she put it. I could tell she was getting panicky that, at her age, so many young men were going to war, or to Canada to avoid the Vietnam draft. I got the distinct feeling that she considered me a good enough catch, given that I was wearing trousers, heterosexual, close to her age and education, and from a prominent San Francisco family. And if *she* was panicky, *I* was scared out of my skull by what she'd said. That same day she offhandedly mentioned marriage, I went straight down to the recruiting office and signed up, thinking I might be sent somewhere stateside to shore up levees in Louisiana or something."

"You didn't enlist soon enough though, right? Your fate was already sealed."

"What happened afterward was a deep, dark secret, except to our four parents. Not one of them ever spoke another word about it. To stay sane, I tried to forget the sequence of events and just get on with my life—until now, when I've told you the story."

"And why *have* you told me?" demanded Juliet. "And why in the world did you stick with each other all these years?"

He gestured in the direction of the floors that soared above their heads.

"Thayers don't divorce. The stakes are too high, especially in the age of big corporations trying to take over small luxury hotels like ours. But be that as it may, I told you all this today because I knew how hurt you were by Brad's firing you and I wanted you to realize that your mother's and Brad's attitude toward you and Jamie has absolutely nothing to do with either of you. You are both wonderful people and I'm proud to be your father. And just for the record, I, too, wanted more children."

"As a buffer between you two?" Juliet was startled by how totally incensed she was by everything she'd heard. "As a handy distraction from how unhappy you were?"

"Well, you were the best distraction a father could ask for," he gently teased her.

For some reason, his answer made Juliet even more furious. "You both *used* us!" she accused. "You used Jamie and me for your own purposes and that feels pretty rotten, come to think of it."

Her father's stricken look made her instantly regret her brutal honesty. He had never hurt her. Her hand flew to the jade dolphin necklace she was wearing. All her growing up years, he had somehow let her know he loved her.

"Perhaps we did use you kids, in part, but I had enjoyed being one of four siblings, myself, and I wanted more children, period. I was so happy when you and Jamie were born." His voice broke. "You two were my salvation, just as Brad was Mildred's."

"Well, at least it's good to hear Jamie and I were wanted children and not just two more accidents after another few nights of tequila shooters."

"Believe me," her father replied with his first show of anger, "I saw the look in your eyes the other day when your mother didn't show an ounce of sympathy when you told us that your own brother had fired you after the stellar job you'd done, taking over when Avery left. I wanted to soothe, if I could, some of the wounds I saw each time she sided with Brad when she should have stood up for you."

"So, why didn't you speak up long before this?" Juliet asked, unable to let him off the hook from her deep sense of hurt. "*I* came downstairs to see *you*, today, not the other way around. Why didn't you stand up for me when you heard what Brad had done? Why don't you ever stand up for James...or for yourself? And for God's sake, why haven't you put some pressure on Brad to pay back the money you and Mother loaned him against this hotel, because, frankly, I'm tired of championing your cause."

"I know you are, sweetie, and I'm here to tell you, you don't have to anymore."

"But *you* have to!" she insisted. "Or you and mother could be in a world of financial hurt if something goes sideways with GatherGames—as it could, given the constant takeover rumors and this stuff with the FBI and the encryption controversy."

"I don't really think this FBI thing will amount to much."

"That's not the point!"

Her father's ensuing silence was as frustrating as the browbeaten demeanor he seemed habitually to wear like a second skin.

"The hotel's part of Jamie's and my life, too, you know," she pleaded. "If you won't fight for it for yourself and all the Bradshaw Thayers that came before—and might come after—don't lose it for *us*!"

Her father's tormented expression told her he was, in fact, very worried about the equity loan on the hotel used as an investment in GatherGames. "I hear you," he said with a heavy sigh. "I've spent a lifetime of accommodating everyone else, but I-I...just don't know if I can—"

Just then, the door flew open with no knock preceding the person who suddenly filled the threshold. Mildred Thayer, dressed like a social doyenne on the cover of the *Nob Hill Gazette*, was her usual chic self in a pale pink St. John woolen suit and matching leather pumps. Her shoulder-length dyed brown hair had been coiffed and sprayed, per usual, in the hotel's hair salon. She strode into her husband's private office and stood beside the desk, her arms akimbo, her hands plastered on her hips as if she were ready to do battle.

"Ah, Millie…how was your bridge game?" her husband asked politely.

"Oh, don't be stupid, Brad," she retorted. "Don't try to pretend you and Juliet, here, are having an innocent little chat." She turned toward her daughter. "Jamie just told me that you're leaving for France tomorrow night for six months. You might have done the courtesy of letting your mother know!"

CHAPTER 26

Juliet rose from her chair and turned to face her mother, wondering what it would have been like to carry a child for nine months, only to bury it in the sand? Summoning a nonchalance she didn't feel, she said, "You were deep into your bridge game, but you were next on my list to tell about my plans to go to Paris."

"How very kind of you," Mildred said, sarcasm dripping from every syllable. "Second on your list, was I?"

"Since Brad canned me so unceremoniously, I've had a lot of decisions to make, Mother, and not much time to make them." Juliet struggled to keep any defensive tone out of her voice. "In a funny way, the lousy thing he's done has given me an opportunity to do what *I* want, for a change, and I'm going to grab it."

"He said he had to let you go because you weren't paying attention to your work, and now I can see why," accused Mildred.

"That's absolute bullshit, but I'm not surprised you swallowed his lie, like always."

"Juliet Morgan Thayer, watch your language!"

"As a matter of fact," Juliet replied, a strange calm coming over her as it had when she'd finally told Brad what she thought of him two days earlier, "I paid *very* close attention to my work. I did everything he asked and more. Frankly, Mother, all I feel now is relief that I don't have to be a part of that violent dreck he's launching into the universe. I've got some money saved and I'm going to get serious about landscape painting. And yes, I'll be gone at least six months."

As a peace offering in honor of the dead brother she

never knew and the heartbreak her mother had endured at his loss, she made an impulsive proposal.

"Maybe you and Dad will come over and visit me while I'm there? Both of you are pretty good sketch artists yourselves. Come take some classes with me, why don't you?"

She reached out and lightly touched the nubby wool sleeve of her mother's fifteen-hundred-dollar suit. In the back of her mind, she wondered why she still hoped that Mildred Thayer would—just once—see a situation from her daughter's point of view.

Her mother's arms fell rigidly by her sides. "Paris will be a waste of your time and money," she declared in a tone that cut Juliet to the quick. "It's quite unlikely you're talented enough ever to make a living as an artist. Brad said your work 'lacked originality.' He said—"

"It doesn't matter what he said," Juliet broke in to put a stop to her mother's insults. "Who knows if I can make a living? I'm taking off because I want to spend six months in France away from *here*. Good or rotten, I'm going to paint landscapes, which is what I always wanted to do since the moment I went to art school. We can both probably agree that my bowing out of things right now is a very good idea. At least I'm not on the list of employees the FBI wants to interview today."

Mildred took a deep breath and reached for the back of a chair to steady herself. For the first time in Juliet's life, she saw a vulnerability there, a fear that perhaps her mother's eldest son had put them all in jeopardy.

"It's probably for the best that Brad and I won't be in such close proximity for a while," Juliet offered wryly.

Still gripping the chair back, her mother murmured, "It's just it's...it's all so sudden, your going to Paris, and the FBI grilling Brad—"

Mildred halted, mid-sentence, and touched her

forehead as if she had a headache coming on. For the briefest moment, Juliet caught a glimpse of what her mother would look like as an old lady. As for Juliet, a tiny but utterly unexpected fizz of happiness began to fill her chest. She was bound for *Paris*! Far away from the toxic Thayer family stew.

"Getting fired is definitely not the end of the world for me at all," Juliet assured both her parents. "I can't wait to launch into whatever is going to be next for me."

"I think studying in Paris is the perfect thing for you right now," her father said with a pointed look toward his wife. He gestured in the direction of the drawing of three porpoises Juliet had done years before that still hung in its frame behind his desk. "I saw your talent even back then."

Her mother's glance also landed on the framed picture. Her expression as she gazed at it in silence telegraphed to Juliet a deep sadness she'd never seen in her before. In the next moment, Juliet felt a strange, miraculous kind of liberation from the perpetual sense she'd had her entire life that her mother didn't care a whit about her only daughter's welfare. Mildred Thayer did care about Jamie and her on some level, Juliet realized after the revelations her father had just made. The problem was, the poor woman had never dealt with her own devils of grief, loss, and anger, nor had she taken responsibility for her role in how her life and that of her eldest living son had unfolded, in part due to the older woman's unhealthy behavior.

Juliet could see now that Brad the Fourth had been a bizarre sort of life raft bolstering her mother's own sense of self-worth. As her father had said, her mother's championing of Brad against all others had very little to do with any of Juliet's or Jamie's perceived shortcomings. Juliet had learned this day that she had allowed her mother's negative actions to shadow her entire life—

needlessly, it would seem. Well, *no more.*

As for her eldest brother, what youngster like Brad wouldn't have turned into an entitled little brat with all that praise and unadulterated adulation beamed his way? In a strange sense, Juliet thought with surprise, she and Jamie were lucky not to have been the "Favorite Child."

And as far as her father was concerned, she had seen this day that he was a loving but flawed man who had yet to stand up for what he wanted, or for what he knew his other children needed. Maybe he would, someday, but Juliet silently cautioned herself that she shouldn't count on it—and it wasn't up to her to try to make it happen.

Yes, she could always hope, but it was best to keep her expectations low.

At that moment, her father rose from his chair, calling a halt to Juliet's musings. For the first time, she noted how thin his hair had become on top of his head, and that his upper back was slightly curved, now, with a hint of scoliosis that ran on the Thayer side of the family. Despite his ruggedly handsome profile that must have dazzled the debutantes of his day, he looked all of his sixty-five years as he stepped out from behind the desk and stood next to his wife of four decades.

"Well, bon voyage and all good luck, Juliet, darling," he said with forced heartiness. "I think it's going to be a wonderful adventure for our girl, don't you, Millie? It was something we both would have loved to do a million years ago, don't you think?"

To Juliet's shock, her mother responded softly, "I always wanted to study in Paris like your many-times-great grandmother who built this pile." She gave a defeated little shrug of her shoulders. "But, it was not to be. And now, with all those terrorists in France…"

"What about the ones in San Bernardino?" Juliet reminded her gently. She reached out and squeezed her mother's hand. "We can't stop living life, Mother. If we do, they win."

Mildred gave her daughter's hand the tiniest squeeze back. "Well, maybe we'll think about coming for a visit mid-August when the fog is so thick around here, it feels like the dead of winter."

Juliet was taken by surprise by her mother's near-positive response. For the first time in at least two decades, she threw her arms around her shoulders and gave her a hug. Her mother remained stationary, her back rigid, her arms stiff in their pink sleeves. Mildred raised her chin and said primly, "I hope, at least, that you've helped your replacement prepare to take over your job in the art department. It's not fair to leave poor Brad stranded."

Juliet almost laughed. "Your darling son had an *armed* guard escort me from the building. He can damn well solve his own graphic design problems."

"That can't be true..." her mother murmured. "You're exaggerating, as usual."

In that instant, Juliet realized not to expect a leopard ever to change its spots. "Ask the guard," she said with a shrug. "His name tag said 'J. Rodriguez.'"

Mildred appeared taken aback at this news. As for Juliet, she didn't want bad feelings to be the last memory of saying goodbye to her parents for six months—or longer. She leaned over and gave her father the same hug she'd offered her mother. The two embraced for a long moment.

"Bye, Daddy," she said softly. "I'm taking over Avery's apartment at number seven *Rue de Lille* where Great-Great Grandmother Amelia lived when she went to *L'École*...so the Thayer family tradition continues. Please, both of you come for a visit."

"I hope to. I'm very proud of you, pet." She could see his eyes were moist. "Travel safe, you hear?"

She glanced at her mother. "By the way...just so you both know, my lawyer tells me that any of us can sell our family-owned shares of GG stock, or any portion of it, as of July 1, but I'll let you know before I do anything."

"Juliet!" her mother exclaimed. "If you sell yours, that would be very disloyal!"

"A trait that seems to run in the Thayer family, I'm afraid. Love you both. Bye, now. Take good care of each other, you two."

On the day of Juliet's flight, she literally raced through the hallway to catch the elevator downstairs to the Bay View's underground garage to meet Jamie who'd volunteered to drive her to the airport. They had barely headed for the freeway when she related the bombshell that their father had dropped on her when she'd gone to his office to say goodbye. She also passed along her theories why Brad's attitude and behaviors were so different from his siblings.

"Holy crap! They had a baby boy that Mother named Brad before they had *Brad?* This is pretty heavy stuff."

"No kidding. Once our Brad appeared, Mother's behavior became the classic recipe for creating a full-blown narcissist. I got the feeling that even *she* knows that, now."

"I guess we should be thankful we were third and fourth in the birth order," Jamie said with a shake of his head.

"That's exactly how I felt! But it's nice to know one thing," she said with a grin, "It certainly t'ain't our fault that the GatherGames CEO is such a total creep toward us and everyone who works for him."

"You almost make it sound as if it's not Brad's fault, either, given the continuous 'atta boy' brainwashing he received from Mother that he could do no wrong."

"I don't know whose fault it was, but it seems to me that once a person passes age thirty-five, the decisions he or she makes about how to behave in this world are pretty much under their control—and it's time to stop blaming anyone else. In my opinion—which, of course, nobody's asking—Brad still has a lot to answer for." Juliet shifted her weight in the passenger seat to look out the windshield and declared, "But moving on, I want to tell you something else."

"Spare me, if it's another keg of dynamite like the last one.

"No, no…it's all about me!"

"Uh-oh. Not another sibling with an 'I-am-the-Greatest' complex."

Juliet burst out laughing, relieved to see Jamie had recovered his sense of humor.

"Last night, while I began to pack, I had a great idea. I've decided I'm going to blog about my efforts to become a landscape artist as an ex-pat in France. I stayed up half the night designing a landing page to bolt onto my old JulietThayerArtist website. Problem is, I ran out of time, so I need you to update my original site and then electronically hook up the blog page to it while I'm flying today. That way, it'll be up and running as soon as I get to France."

"You *were* a busy bee," Jamie noted mildly, putting on the car's signal to take Highway 101 south to the airport.

"Well, will you? Do the back room stuff for me, I mean?" she persisted eagerly. "I've sent you a link with all the IDs and passwords."

"Sure," Jamie agreed. "Sounds great, and this way, I can keep close tabs on you, kiddo. Back door web access, and all that, unlike GG and the FBI. And by the way, I think the Feds were just fishing last week. I don't think our particular encryption system turned up in their investigations."

"Well that's a relief."

"So, what are you calling this online diary of yours?"

"'France Unafraid,'" she replied proudly. "Besides my leaping into the unknown, I also want to blog about what France turns out to be like in the wake of the terrorist attacks. From what I've seen so far, the French continue to refuse to give up their way of life. They're still sitting outside in cafés... traveling in the metro and by train...strolling along the riverfront. I think people outside France would be interested to know things like that, don't you? I'm going to mainly create my own images and take photos myself. I want to *illustrate* this story, rather than just write about it."

Jamie glanced across the front passenger seat. "That's the sister I remember—an idea-a-minute-gal." Despite his show of enthusiasm, Juliet detected the sad note in his voice.

"Don't think I'm not going to miss you, big time, Jamie," she said.

"And I'll miss you, Sis. You're abandoning me to the crazy people, you know."

"You have an open invitation to visit any time."

He gave a small shake of his head. "Avery's going to be living with that Alain guy. It might be...ah...kinda icky if I came over."

"Yep, she's already moved into his studio, but— nevertheless—I will be highly insulted if that's the reason you use not to come over to spend some time with me."

"And Finn Deschanel? You haven't told me what the state of affairs—pardon my pun—is in that department."

Juliet hesitated, then acknowledged, "I'm crazy about the guy."

"Not too surprising. He's good news," Jamie concurred.

"But he's got major personal and professional To Do

lists right now, and so have I. We've agreed to live separately and to be together when it works for both of us."

Jamie flashed her a skeptical look, prompting Juliet to suppress a smile. "My, my...how sensible that all sounds," he said with a straight face.

"Yeah..." she agreed. "We'll see how long *that* lasts."

Finn glanced at his watch every other minute, waiting among the expectant crowd at De Gaulle Airport. Other restless people milled outside the big doors where international passengers emerged singly or in clusters of friends and relatives. Some travelers pulled trim carryon bags behind them, and others pushed huge carts of luggage that could supply the needs of a small village. Finn felt his pulse speed up at the sight of security personnel dotted around the hall holding assault rifles against their chests. He willed himself to take a couple of deep breaths and focus his thoughts on the woman who would soon be walking through the Arrivals door.

Scanning the crowds for his first glimpse of Juliet, he speculated that she would have far more baggage this trip than her previous visits, given that she planned to stay at least six months, which was the permitted length of a visitor's visa to France. If she could secure status as a bona fide student, like he had when he signed up for commercial drone training, perhaps she could stay longer without applying for permanent resident status.

He couldn't deny he'd been nervous about this new direction their relationship had suddenly taken when Juliet called him to announce her brother had fired her. The next day, he had voiced to the good Doctor A an odd, free-floating sense of apprehension that had assailed him the second he'd hung up the phone.

"Don't get me wrong," he tried to explain. "I'm really excited she's coming, but I'm…worried."

"It's a big step for you," Dr. Abel agreed. She leaned forward, and with her usual empathy urged him to tell her, "What concerns you most?"

"That I'll have…well, you know…flashbacks, or screaming nightmares, or eventually just get cold feet about it all and hurt her by wanting to retreat into my cave."

"That's certainly been known to happen in cases like yours," she agreed, "but you've said, haven't you, that most of the things that troubled you when you and I first started working together have diminished a lot?"

"Quitting the booze, along with the opioids the VA prescribed definitely helped. But that's what bothers me," he protested. "What I'm feeling now is the opposite of the macho man I was on the phone with her, counting the minutes till this very gorgeous lady lands in my life again."

"Well," she said with a wry smile, "you tried that white knuckle macho stuff before you decided to come here for help. How did it work for you?"

"It stunk. Trying to pretend nothing was wrong made PTSD symptoms worse."

"Could the thing that you're dealing with now just be a little bit of ordinary stage fright? You haven't been with a woman on a consistent basis in a long time."

"More than two years," Finn admitted. "Even a couple of years before that, everything was out of whack."

"But didn't you tell me Juliet is taking over her friend's flat?"

"Right," he'd said, admitting that, in fact, *he'd* been the one who said he wanted her to live with him on the barge. "She felt it was best for us each to have our own place—at least at first. So why am I feeling so…so…suddenly bummed about all this and questioning myself on the eve of Juliet's arrival?"

"What's the first thought that comes to mind right now?" she challenged.

"What if it won't work out?"

"I'd call this a case of 'mini-PTSD,' Dr. Abel said with a small laugh. "Your first marriage failed, and perhaps a part of you doesn't want to risk failing again, plus…," she twiddled her pen between her fingers, "you are in the middle of establishing a new career for yourself that involves flying drones, which I'm betting remains a somewhat loaded enterprise for you. You're doing well on all fronts, Finn," she assured him, "but you've got a lot on your plate. Maybe the idea of being with someone fulltime—even someone as terrific as you've described Juliet Thayer—is creating anxiety that you won't do either venture well—unless you concentrate on one or the other."

Finn had felt a huge sense of relief that his therapist identified so accurately these strange feelings he'd been having. "That sounds exactly right," he said, nodding. "I could fail at both."

"So, isn't it lucky that Juliet appears intuitively to understand that her coming to France is a big change for both of you and wants her own space, too?" Then Dr. Abel added encouragingly, "My clinical opinion? Given how things are arranged between you, I think you'll both do just fine."

"She's a pretty fabulous woman," he agreed. "I just don't want to do something dumb that ruins everything."

"Call me night or day if you feel you're in a bind," Doctor Abel said in her customary, forthright style. "You're a courageous man and you've proved that over and over. As far as this relationship with Juliet Thayer, I'd say, why not go for it?"

Why not go for it? he repeated to himself silently.

After that session with the doc, Finn could feel the

anxiety slowly dissipating and now, he couldn't wait to see Juliet again, to hold her in his arms, and to—

Just then, he spotted her coming through the double doors. She was dressed in tight jeans, knee-high boots, and a starched white collared shirt, with a long, pale blue cashmere scarf looped around her neck to ward off, she'd told him once, the plane's air-conditioning on long flights. Her shoulder-length auburn hair looked almost red as she walked beneath the overhead lighting fixtures that illuminated the reception area. Even after a twelve-hour flight across a continent and the Atlantic Ocean, Juliet looked...well...fabulous.

Her face lit up when she saw him waving his large bouquet of long-stem, pink roses.

Juliette est arrivée en France!

Juliet fell in love with Paris all over again as they sped into the city in a taxi full of her hefty luggage. The spring blossoms that had run riot the last time she was in France for Easter had matured into the full summer foliage of late May. The streets near the Trocadero were leafy bowers casting cool shade along the avenues. Couples strolled beside the Seine in shirtsleeves and cotton sundresses. For her part, Juliet couldn't wait to abandon her knee-high boots that she'd had to wear because she couldn't fit them in her luggage.

She and Finn weren't inside the pilothouse ten minutes before, as one, they scrambled down the wooden steps to his stateroom and fell into each other's arms.

"God, I missed you," Finn growled, pulling her tightly against him as they lay, fully clothed, on the bed.

"I was jumpy and nervous about everything the entire trip, but now that I'm here..."

Before she could finish her sentence, Finn cupped her

face in his hands and commenced to kiss her long and thoroughly. When they finally came up for air she whispered against his ear, "You need to know that this wench started taking the pill the minute we hung up the phone."

"And if you look in the top drawer of my bedside table," he murmured against the hollow of her throat, "there's probably a lifetime supply of condoms in there."

"Good man." She giggled and slowly began unbuttoning his shirt so she could scatter kisses on his chest. "We have enough complications facing us as it is."

"Good lady." He firmly pressed his arousal against her midsection to telegraph how very happy he was that she had come aboard his boat. "But you are one complication that I'd like to explore for a very long time, tonight."

"Well then, get busy, flyboy, and pull off my boots because I have a few discoveries about you that I intend to make as well…"

CHAPTER 27

In Juliet's first week of *plein air* landscape classes at *L'École*, Finn pointed out various overt examples of an increasing number of security measures that had been put in place all over Paris since her last visit. In addition to soldiers with long guns assigned to the major metro stations throughout the city, purses and bags were routinely checked where significant numbers of people gathered, including department stores, theaters, stadiums, schools, and even at the fashion houses on Avenues Montaigne and Georges V.

"I doubt the major cities in Europe, just like in the States after 9/11, will ever be the same," Finn noted one afternoon when they were held up for half an hour waiting to go through a metal detector before entering a food trade show they'd both wanted to attend.

"Still, we can't *not* go places and let the terrorists win," she insisted.

Finn bent down and kissed her on the nose. "You are a very good influence on me, you know that?"

"Really? Why do you say that?"

"Because I'm in here today."

He glanced around at the crowds surging through several doors leading into the Food Hall where rows of booths filled with all manner of fancy comestibles were on display. He had felt a tightening creep into his chest, and fought off a suffocating sense of claustrophobia as unknown bodies hemmed in the two of them. He seized Juliet's hand as they moved further into the convention space that appeared to be a couple of acres in size. He beckoned that she walk to one side with him, away from the surging hordes.

"Give me a minute, okay?" He inhaled a few deep breaths.

Juliet glanced around at the crowds flowing past them and gave a small nod of understanding. "That's fine. Take your time. You know how eager these foodies are to locate the best *fois gras*. We can wait a bit till things thin out."

Finn put one arm around Juliet's shoulder and focused his thoughts on how good it felt to have her next to him. He said, "Combat vet that I was, I would have been majorly spooked six months ago by coming into a crowded place like this. Now I'm only mildly spooked."

A smile quirked at the corner of her mouth as she surveyed the milling hordes. "I don't like big crowds much, myself," she agreed, "but these truffle-stalking folks seem pretty harmless, don't you think?"

Finn laughed and squeezed her elbow, relieved that he'd so swiftly recovered his sense of the here-and-now and felt normal again.

"Not if they want to fight me for the last pot of homemade whole grain Dijon mustard from that purveyor over there. C'mon! Tonight I'm going to make you the best *Poulet Dijonnais* that you ever ate in your life."

"That's plain old chicken thighs in a yellow sauce, right?" she teased.

"*Sacré bleu*! Not 'plain old...yellow!' There's finely chopped fresh tarragon, shallots, and garlic, and mustard, of course, and don't forget the dry white wine and—"

"Now you're making me hungry, so you have to buy me a slice of *clafouti* and a coffee over there." She replied gestured toward a pop-up café in a corner of the vast hall.

Finn smiled down at her. "First we buy the mustard. Then we go over to the *pâtisserie* section and look for that cherry dessert, deal? Only the best for us, right?"

"Deal." Juliet smiled back, and Finn could tell that the lady in his life felt happier than she had in a long, long time—and that made him feel happier than perhaps ever before.

Juliet and Finn's routine soon settled into "work weeks" and "play days," with her full schedule of classes Monday through Friday at *L'École*—along with lunches with Avery. She also spent a fair amount of time exploring Paris on her own and with Claudine Deschanel as her sometimes guide. Finn's days consisted of student assignments to fly drones in areas all over France as he drew ever closer to earning his civilian commercial drone pilot's certification.

Beginning at the food show they'd attended, Juliet snapped photos on her mobile phone nearly everywhere she went and launched her *France Unafraid* blog under the byline "Ex-Pat Painter." Often, she'd use her location photos as the basis of sketches and small watercolor renderings of the sights and scenes she was encountering all over the city as she explored her new home.

Finn's Aunt Claudine had been one of the blog's biggest boosters.

"It's a new kind of journalism!" she declared enthusiastically when Juliet sent her a link to ask her to review her work. And then Claudine invited Juliet to meet for lunch at one of her favorite eateries, Brasserie Lipp on *Boulevard Saint-Germain*. Juliet recalled that the tasty fare served there had been extolled by Ernest Hemingway in *A Moveable Feast*.

Claudine was dressed impeccably, as usual, with her "good" jewelry, including the spectacular emerald and diamond ring that never left her hand.

"I've been meaning to ask you, Claudine," Juliet said. "Is that ring a family piece or an antique you found at an estate sale? It's the most beautiful setting I've ever seen."

Claudine glanced down at her hand embracing her coffee cup. "No, it was given to me on my engagement by the man I was to marry." The sad smile on her lined face was an expression Juliet had never seen before. But before she could apologize for raising an obviously painful subject, Claudine continued, "I was a career woman in my early thirties and our parents were both in the military." She raised her hand and gazed somberly at the ring. "Jonathan was a widower and a career officer. He wanted to delay getting married because he was heading overseas for nine months on a very dangerous job. Eight months later, he died commanding a swift boat in the Mekong Delta in Vietnam. I've never taken it off."

Impulsively, Juliet took Claudine's hand and gave it a gentle squeeze.

"I wouldn't either. Forgive me for bringing up such a sad memory."

"Don't apologize," Claudine replied. "Talking about this ring keeps my love for Jonathan alive." She took a last sip of her coffee and declared, "But now, let's discuss this blog of yours."

Relieved that she hadn't spoiled their lunch, Juliet pleaded for Claudine, as a retired editor, to offer her uncensored professional opinion, along with any specific wordsmith suggestions about her blogging efforts. "After all, I'm a painter, not a writer."

"I wouldn't change a word!" Claudine beamed. "I love the way you write those introductory 'Wow...I didn't know that!' paragraphs. Then, you put those snappy captions beneath each photo incorporating your take on what you've seen and done. It's captivating, my dear!"

"Really? You think what I'm doing isn't... well... amateurish?"

"No!" Claudine replied fiercely. "Not in the slightest. It has a charming, 'Dear Diary,' quality I adore and I'm sure you'll build up your readership as you go along."

"'Paris' as an Internet keyword is the trick, I guess," she said with a rueful smile. "As of this morning, I have nearly five hundred subscribers."

"Already? That's wonderful!"

Juliet basked in praise that had been so sorely lacking within her own family circle. "So far, it's mostly Facebook and art school friends in California that I emailed as soon as Jamie launched the blog for me. And they then shared the link with their friends and it kind of took off. Some of my followers even asked if each watercolor at the end of the posts are for sale!"

"Well, me dear, why *don't* you offer little watercolors for sale? They're fairly simple ink sketches with watercolor added, right? Postcard-size, aren't they? How hard would it be to duplicate the sketch and then add the color by hand on each one? Could you do, say, twenty original copies a week? Sell them for twenty or thirty dollars each, or even more, eventually."

"What an interesting idea..." Juliet turned the possibilities over in her mind. "Subscribers could order them online, pay me with PayPal or something, and the money could drop electronically into my bank account over here." She could feel her excitement building over Claudine's suggestion. "I could ship them from the post office near school. At least it might keep us all in coffee and croissants."

"And if you made a few slightly larger sizes, you might earn a nice, supplementary income while you're here so you won't deplete all your savings."

"No wonder you were such a success in the magazine

business, Claudine." Juliet gave her a hug and got one in return. "I love it! I'll offer my next one for sale and see if I get any takers."

"*C'est ma fille!*"

Claudine's "That's my girl!" rang in Juliet's ears as she took a photograph of the small sketch she'd made of the chateau at Chantilly, located an hour outside Paris by train. She'd rendezvoused with Finn earlier that morning after he'd spent a week flying drones over a six-thousand-acre forest nearby. While he'd finished up his assignment and packed his equipment in the MG, she'd unpacked her portable paints from her tote bag and drew from real life the scene of the fairytale chateau with its turrets, balustrades, and the reflecting pools that encircled it. She'd finally begun to feel like a genuine *plein air* artist, thanks to instruction at *L'École*.

She'd just added the last touches of the color wash overlaying her ink sketch and taken its photograph with her iPhone when Finn appeared behind the spot where she'd set up her easel in the mansion's gravel courtyard. He held off interrupting her until she'd tucked her cell phone into her pocket.

"Ready for a coffee?" he asked.

She whirled in place. "Oh! Hi! Am I ever." She smiled up at him. "I had a great day. Just let me finish packing up my stuff."

By the time Finn locked the MG's doors for the second time with Juliet's art gear stowed inside, there was barely space left for the two passengers in the front. His arm around her shoulder, he led the way to the tearoom lodged in a former servants' quarters.

"Your aunt is such a total sweetheart," she told him after they'd had their afternoon pick-me-up and were strolling the manicured grounds. "I would never have thought to sell copies of what I post on the blog, but here I am...pulling in four or five hundred dollars a week! That is, if I can keep up my output and still have time to go to class—which is why I'm supposedly here in France, after all."

"You and Claudine make a pretty dynamic duo." He bent down to kiss her on the top of her head. "The next thing you know, she'll be launching another magazine and you'll be the art director."

"No," she scoffed at his teasing, "but the blog has given me hope that I may be able to make some sort of living from my art, after all, and I think Claudine gets a kick from my bouncing ideas off her."

"I know she does."

Twenty minutes later, they parked the MG in front of the charming guesthouse Finn had booked for them that night.

"How about a glass of wine to celebrate the day's labors?" he proposed.

"Heavenly, but I insist...*I'm* buying with my new winnings—including your bottle of Perrier—and while we're at it, let's toast Aunt Claudine!"

To Juliet's shock, early June brought rains to France in historic proportions. With *L'École* on a term break, she'd signed up for a week's painting workshop at an event called Art Colony Giverny, commencing June 10th. She'd spent the previous days creating scores of hand-painted copies of her popular sketch of Chateau Chantilly for the burgeoning numbers of subscribers to her *France Unafraid* blog.

"I had to pull an all-nighter to get everything finished and in the mail," she'd reported earlier on the phone to Finn, away all that week piloting his drone along several routes that the *Tour de France* cycling race would travel in a few weeks' time. "I haven't done anything like that since college—but it's all good."

Now that her painting and mailing scramble was behind her, she couldn't wait to board the train to Giverny. She was excited to meet Caroline Homes Nucholls, an American painter who had organized the workshop in France that annually offered a seven-day, action-packed session for artists specializing in landscape painting. The week's schedule was to feature art instruction, as well as after-hours entry into Monet's garden with its spectacular roses and the celebrated lily ponds.

"The price also includes accommodations at a lovely-looking Bed and Breakfast," she told Finn excitedly over dinner at *La Caléche*. "It's called *Les Moulin des Chennevieres*, which the brochure says is within easy walking distance of Monet's house. Any chance you could do something with your drone that week and end up there on the last Saturday of the class?"

Finn quickly did an online search of the Giverny region in Normandy.

"The Seine flows through the heart of Vernon, which is just a few miles away from Giverny." He shot her a grin. "There appears to be a number of bridges that might need inspection. I'll see what I can do to hustle an assignment somewhere around there."

They watched the rain pelting down outside, filling the street with more than six inches of water.

"Isn't this unusual to have this kind of downpour in *June*?" Juliet wondered aloud.

"More's predicted," Finn said, taking a sip of espresso. "I saw on my news feed that the Loire Valley is getting hammered. Many of its tributaries feed into the Seine."

"I hope Giverny will be okay next week," she said worriedly.

By June 3rd, the Eiffel Tower was all but shrouded in mist and the quay that ran beside the moorings of *L'Étoile de Paris* was beginning to fill with the overflow from the Seine. It was Friday, and Juliet and Finn planned to spend the weekend together on the barge before she left for her outdoor painting adventure.

Juliet was the first to awake and rose from their bed.

"Look outside!" she exclaimed, padding around the wooden frame of Finn's built-in queen mattress to stare out the stateroom's window at the fast-flowing river. "Quick! Come over here! There's a huge tree floating past right now. Wow! There's another one! And look at the *Ba Hakeim* Bridge! The poor tourists today. I don't think any sightseeing boats will even fit under it now."

Finn rose from the bed and stood stark naked beside her, gazing at the amazing sight of not only trees, but the side of a battered boat floating by, as well as all manner of flotsam and jetsam passing the barge at an alarmingly fast rate.

Just then, there was a loud "thwamp!" against the steel hull.

"What was that?" screeched Juliet.

"Something very big just slammed into the barge. I'd better go check on Madame Grenelle next door."

They both scrambled into their jeans just as a black blur streaked through the window that was cracked open above the radiator.

"Well, hello, Truffles!" Juliet shouted. "Smart pussycat to come in from the rain."

Up in the pilothouse, Juliet watched Finn don his heavy yellow rain slicker and brave the downpour, stomping down the deck to the entrance hatch of his landlady's side of the canal boat. When she turned her head to look at the quay, she gasped at the sight of several feet of water that now had reached midway up the concrete wall lining the river side of the spur road, *Georges Pompidou*. The barge's metal gangway at its lower level was totally submerged in water. The curve in the Seine where they were docked had turned into a catch basin for all manner of ugly river litter.

"This is getting serious," she muttered to herself, putting the water on to boil for coffee that she'd learned to make in Finn's *café presse* pot. No croissants this morning, she thought, wondering how they would get on and off the boat in the rising waters.

A few minutes later, Finn stomped back across the deck and arrived inside the pilothouse, dripping puddles on the teak floors as he removed his heavy foul weather gear. "I'm calling Pierre," he announced. "Madame has been listening to the radio all morning. The water is expected to rise some twenty feet—or more."

"On the Seine?" she said, shocked. "Here in Paris, you mean?"

"Yup." He said punched in some numbers on his mobile phone. When he ended the call he announced, "Pierre's coming over to help me rig an emergency system to get off this bucket in case the waters rise as much as predicted."

The rest of the morning, at Juliet's suggestion, she, Finn and Pierre managed to secure a small dinghy on a winch above the rushing waters off the stern of the boat, in case there was no other way of escape. The river was rising an inch an hour and the landline that connected all the barge's power systems was being strained to its full length between the shore and the boat's hull.

"If we lose electricity," Juliet fretted, "none of the bilge pumps will work, which means—"

"No toilets working. No fresh water. No nothing. It could get nasty." Finn looked at her admiringly. "How come you know so much about bilge pumps?"

Juliet shrugged. "I live on San Francisco Bay, remember. I've been on boats all my life. My brother Jamie owns a trawler that sleeps six."

"I love learning stuff about you like that." Finn kissed her on the cheek.

Juliet smiled back, but her worry for the safety of the elderly woman across the deck was increasing by the minute.

After some hastily scrambled eggs, Finn and Pierre braved the elements once more to rig a fourteen-foot ladder that had been stowed somewhere on the boat and lashed it to the river wall. Then they threaded the bottom of the land end of the gangway into the fourth rung of the ladder so "any tightrope artist could walk the plank from the edge of the barge's deck to the escape ladder," joked Finn. "Once off the boat and across the gangplank," he explained midway through their construction project, "your average daredevil can climb the tall ladder another ten feet or so, up to the top of the wall. Of course, we evacuees must then maneuver over it, try to find footing on the shorter stepladder we've set on the other side, and creep down to *Georges Pompidou*."

From the window facing the street, Juliet peered through sheets of rain at the normal morning rush of cars, slowed, this day, to a snail's pace, their windshield wipers fluttering madly. Two hours later, an exhausted Pierre and Finn shed their rain gear once more and came in for another cup of coffee. Juliet pointed to the rapidly rising level of the water that, by this time, was within two feet of topping the wall.

"The power line may very well snap," she said, "if the water rises above the predicted twenty-two-feet level. More importantly, do you think the mooring lines that hold *L'Étoile* to the riverbank are strong enough to withstand the pressure that's going to be put on them? What if they give way?"

"That would be bad," Finn deadpanned.

Pierre looked confused by their exchange in English and gave a Gallic shrug. Finn, however, followed her gaze and added quietly, "If the water doesn't stop rising before it reaches twenty-three feet, we should all definitely abandon ship. Have you heard any new rain predictions?"

Juliet looked at her cell phone and clicked the app icon for a local TV station.

"At this point they're saying it could rise very close to the twenty-three-foot level." She tilted her head in the direction of the other end of the barge. "I think we should evacuate Madame Grenelle while we still can."

Juliet kept busy making the rounds to check on the steel cables that connected the vessel to the quay. Finn said to Pierre slowly in French, "I think together... you and me...if we take your mother's arms, we can get her to the ladder leaning against the stone wall and then up and onto the street. It will be safer for her to stay with you a few days."

By this time, if anyone on the barge attempted to use the little "emergency escape boat," it would simply be swept away and crash into the nearest flooded bridge. As for exiting the barge via the submerged gangway and up the ladder lashed to the river wall, that was fast becoming less of an option.

Juliet summoned the best French she could conjure, adding to Finn's plea to take the elderly woman off the boat. "Let's get your mother to safety right now, Pierre. Finn and I will stay with the barge to keep an eye on things as long as it's safe to be here."

"No," Finn said firmly. "You go with Pierre and Madame."

"Absolutely not," she protested. "I'm the sailor around here, remember? I'm sticking with the ship!"

Juliet held her breath as Madame Grenelle was escorted by her son and Finn across the narrow gangway, its slanted foot-and-a-half-wide metal plank already underwater. The rubber-booted trio inched along until they finally reached the foot of the tall ladder. Much to Juliet's amazement and relief, the old lady gamely managed to climb the rungs until she reached the top of the river wall, mere feet above the current level of rushing water. Pierre's wife, summoned by cell phone, stood in her rain gear on the street and assisted her mother-in-law over the cement barrier and then down the shorter ladder six more feet to safety on *Georges Pompidou*. Pierre then ran the same gauntlet and waved them good luck.

That night, neither Finn nor Juliet slept much, electing to wrap themselves in blankets and stretch out, feet-to-feet, on the sofa in the pilothouse. All night, huge tree trunks and heaven knew what other debris banged into *L'Étoile's* battered hull. Every hour, the pair donned their rain gear and boots and repeated Juliet's system of checking the mooring lines along the 110-foot-barge amidst the groaning of straining cables and the clanking and thuds of anything that wasn't tied down.

By the early hours of Saturday, June 4th, the French weather service announced the waters had peaked at just under 23 feet above normal levels, and, miraculously, the rubber-encased power lines on *L'Étoile* had held.

At this news, Finn had embraced Juliet in a bear hug. "I'd have you as my tail gunner any day!"

"I think you mean First Mate, flyboy."

Both of them laughed, while Juliet stared at her cell

phone's CNN news bulletins. Along with those of the BBC, they had been their best sources of information in English. She pointed to the little screen and marveled, "In the last day and a half, the staff at the Louvre moved some one-hundred-and fifty-thousand items from the lower floors to higher ground!"

As for life onboard, Juliet was grateful they had been able to scramble eggs for their supper and breakfast, alike, and kept their mobile phones charged.

"Oh, dear!" She scrolled down a list of stories related to the historic Paris flooding. "They've announced, 'Monet Gardens will be closed June fourth through sixth, possibly opening to the public again June seventh.'"

"Just in time for your workshop the tenth," Finn reassured her, "although you'd better take your boots. I bet those famous lily ponds will be a lot bigger and deeper now."

Juliet scanned the rushing river just outside the pilothouse windows. "Look at the spaces under the bridge." She pointed to her right. "It does look as if the level's gone down a smidge." She shook her head. "What a night."

Finn strode to her side and pulled her into his arms. They clung together with shared relief that the barge had not been swept down the Seine or crashed into a bridge—and them with it.

"Let's take a nap," he whispered against her cheek. "I don't know about you, but I'm totally bushed."

"Me too," she mumbled.

"But first, let me make a call."

Juliet nodded, too exhausted to wait for Finn to tell Pierre that the boat had apparently survived the worst flooding in more than fifty years. She padded down below, stripped out of her jeans, and slipped naked under the covers.

"Great!" she heard Finn exclaim from the salon. "I'll be there June tenth."

He dropped to the stateroom in one leap. Truffles was curled up on the bottom of the bed. By this time Juliet was half asleep and simply held out her arms, inviting him to join her. Divested of his clothing, Finn crawled in and pulled her backside into the crook of his waist, chest, and thighs, spoon fashion. "Mmm...you're nice and warm," he crooned.

"Ah-huh," she mumbled, feeling herself descending into sleep despite the beguiling proximity of Finn's midsection pressing against her derriere.

"Want to hear some nice news?" he whispered into her ear.

She struggled to stay awake, sighing another, "Ah-huh."

"I'm a total genius. I just finagled a paid gig to fly my drone on an inspection tour of a bunch of bridges that were overtopped along the Seine at Vernon and—*ta-da*—nearby Giverny! We can meet up at your B and B at the end of your workshop."

"That's fabulous," she managed to mumble. "I promise to reward your brilliance another time...real soon."

And in minutes, they were both sound asleep, and so was Truffles, curled in a tight black ball on top of their duvet.

CHAPTER 28

The weather finally cleared and the trains were running again from *Gare St. Lazarre* for the hour's trip to Vernon where Rich Nucholls picked up Juliet and the other six painters who'd signed on for a week in waterlogged Giverny. Fortunately, each day, the alluvial earth dried a bit more in the quaint village where Claude Monet had lived and painted for decades.

Juliet's first stroll among the flowerbeds surrounding the painter's house bowled her over with their stunning beauty in a well-tended garden whose hardiest blossoms survived the rain. With each passing hour, the flowers seemed to revive in the warmth of the sun despite the inordinate amount of water that ran back into the river. Giverny, at least, hadn't sustained the destructive flooding that had inundated parts of Paris and much of the Loire Valley.

As for Juliet, she felt her technique in perspective and ability to mix the right colors improved by leaps and bounds under Caroline Homes Nucholls's expert instruction. She loved the camaraderie of her fellow artists slipping into the garden a few hours before hordes of tourists arrived in the morning, and then again in the soft, fragrant twilight hours when the gardens and ponds were theirs alone to command.

By the end of her week-long course, Juliet was ready to put her name down for next year's session and was flushed with excitement when she heard the sound of Finn's MG driving on the gravel approach to the stone and timbered *Les Moulin des Chennevieres*. It was an ancient Norman building, a former mill and now a first-rate bed and breakfast establishment where she and her fellow artists had lived for a solid week of painting, as if part of Monet's nineteenth-century world.

She waved and watched Finn unfold his tall frame from the pint-sized car just as Caroline Nucholls was walking in from the road that led to town. The artist was dressed in her daily uniform of an ankle-length, pale blue cotton skirt, a flowing, white poet's shirt, and straw sunhat.

"Oh, wonderful!" Caroline said with a wave to her pupil. "You're still here."

"I'm staying one more day," Juliet informed her. She pointed toward Finn as she and her Master Teacher approached his car. "I'd like you to meet a good friend of mine."

After introductions were made, Caroline said to Finn, "I'm sure it's no news to you, but Juliet has genuine talent and proved it with the stunning work she did here this week."

"Actually, she's only shown me sketches," Finn replied, "but never any of her full-fledged landscape paintings." He shot Juliet a challenging grin.

"Well, you've got lovely technique, my dear," said Caroline, "especially with your rendering of water and the land surrounding it."

Aww," Juliet joked, "I bet you say that to all your pupils."

The veteran artist narrowed her eyes and shook her head. "No, I do *not* say that to all who participate in my workshop. This is not a juried group, as I'm sure you noticed. We always have a wide variety of talent and abilities in this particular session. The first seven or eight who apply and pay are admitted, as I assume they are the most enthusiastic. That's what *I* care about!" she declared emphatically. "I want to be surrounded by people who embrace the joy of creativity." She gazed directly at Finn.

"Juliet not only showed creativity, but she actually produced some wonderful, finished paintings. Be sure she lets you see them."

Duly chastised, Juliet ducked her head and said, "Thanks, Caroline, for such kind words. It's been an incredible week and a huge learning experience. I can't thank you enough for letting me be a part of all this. I had a totally stupendous time with you and Rich. You two were just wonderful for all you did for our group."

"It was a good session," agreed Caroline. "One of the best, despite the rocky start, thanks to the weather." She offered a cheery wave. "You two enjoy Juliet's last day here, won't you?" Her long skirt swished as she walked toward the inn's entrance. Over her shoulder she called, "Hope to see you next year, my dear, so get your application in early!"

Finn enfolded Juliet in his arms by way of a proper greeting and admitted he was famished. She suggested they walk the short distance into town to avoid the parking nightmare in a village crowded with art lovers visiting Monet's garden on a sunny day.

"I want to take you to my favorite local restaurant where we all hung out when we weren't painting. You can get a full French meal or a delicious *salade composée* with salmon or chicken or ham."

As they walked hand in hand, Juliet described her amazing week of nonstop painting and classwork where she created a full canvas every single day. "Though I have no idea how in the world I'm going to get all of them back to Paris."

"We can wrap them in my car blanket and strap them to the trunk," he assured her, "but you have to promise to let me see every single one."

"And if you like any of them, you can have your pick to lean up in the pilothouse somewhere," she said, adding quickly, "and if none seem to suit, I won't get hurt feelings. Art is very personal."

"Lean against the barge's bulkhead, hell! I'm *buying* one of those babies to hang in the stateroom down below next to Avery's portrait of you. I plan to stare wistfully at both when you're not on board."

She turned and threw her arms around him. Except for her father, she'd rarely received encouragement for her dream to become a truly fine artist, and here was Caroline, full of praise, and Finn offering to buy a painting of hers, sight unseen.

When she released him, he chucked her under the chin and said, "Well, with a reaction like that, I'll buy *two* paintings."

Soon, they were walking among the bright coral-colored umbrellas of *Bistro Baudy* with its al fresco setting next to the main restaurant that was surrounded by a circle of full-leafed trees casting the outdoor tables in delicious shade. When they had both placed their orders for lunch, Juliet asked, "How did your drone survey go? Did the bridges suffer any serious damage in the floods?"

"Actually, the wooden bridges around here fared miraculously well," he reported, "although the video I took showed one or two places that will definitely need repairs."

"And was it fun, or nerve-wracking to fly that little spider in and out and under structures like that?"

"A bit of both." His expression grew serious and he looked off into the trees on his left as if he were suddenly in a world of his own. "I had to get up really early to avoid people and cars," he murmured, as if observing a scene in a movie, "…and at one point, a boat with a kid and his dad suddenly appeared floating under an arch. A dawn fishing trip, I guess, but I nearly choked when I saw them coming so close to the drone that I was planning, at that same moment, to pilot under the bridge. It sent me right back to…" Finn swallowed and grew silent.

"Hey," Juliet put a hand on his, "close calls like that are bound to happen once in a while." Finn continued to gaze off into the distance. "You didn't hurt anyone. You didn't crash the drone, did you?"

"No, but my hands shook plenty on the controls. I managed to veer away and cleared the bridge. The video is pretty dramatic, though. It probably flew within ten feet of their boat."

"Finn!" she exclaimed, alarmed by the far-away look she hadn't seen on his face since the first week they'd met. "This only proves that you automatically made the moves that only an experienced flyer knows to do…and you did it really quickly." She touched his sleeve. "Maybe this happening was a *good* thing. It proved you still have all the instincts of the great pilot you were when you flew the real deal. You took quick action and avoided a collision."

Finn pulled his gaze away from the surrounding trees and leaned back in the pale blue metal chair that didn't quite fit his large frame. Juliet could see him turning her words over in his head as he studied her. "What you just said could have come out of the mouth of the good Doctor Abel," he told her with a look of incredulity. "You're amazing, you know that?"

He leaned forward and kissed her, his lips and tenderness a reminder of how much she'd missed him this week, despite the wonderful time she had in the workshop. What a strange combination of feelings: she had longed to see him even as she had rejoiced for having an entire week to herself to pursue her art. And now that he was here, sitting beside her, it all felt so…right. So as it should be.

"Oh, Finn…"

"Ms. Thayer, you are truly… somethin' else."

She was unable to pull away from his intense scrutiny, his eyes the precise shade of cobalt she'd used to paint the sky arching above the lily ponds and green painted bridges in Monet's garden. He kissed her again just as their waiter approached and placed their food between the neat rows of cutlery spread out on the metal table.

Finn's thousand-yard stare had vanished, replaced with one signaling that they would eat their lunch rather quickly and head straight back to their room at the B and B.

Back in Paris, their routine returned to what it had been before the floods. Finn was gone from the city during the week, while Juliet resumed summer classes at *L'École* and spent time with Avery, whose shoulder and arm had nearly recovered the mobility they had before the November terrorist attacks.

"And Alain?" Juliet asked, sitting on an artist's stool in the atelier that Avery now called home.

Large and small canvases leaned, one against another, next to a wall. A chaise lounge with a single upholstered rolled arm sat in one corner, a beautiful red and gold tapestry fabric draped over it and across its seat cushion. In the loft above their heads was a thick mattress covered by a puffy, white, down-filled duvet. A blue-and-white porcelain lamp sat on an old wooden box next to a gold-framed mirror on the floor that leaned against the wall. To Juliet, it looked like a set for a movie about Degas or Renoir.

"Is everything all right with your...arrangement, here?" she pressed Avery.

"It's eighty percent all right," Avery replied with a shrug. "Alain's here most nights during the week, but goes...to...the St. Cloud house on the weekends."

"To be with his wife and family?" Juliet asked bluntly.

"His youngest will be off to college in a year or two.

After that, well...who knows? It's fine for now."

Juliet detected an edge of defensiveness in her friend's tone, but she was unsure whether Avery intended it to protect her pride or Alain's reputation as the decent sort of man Avery was convinced he was.

"I'm living the opposite schedule," Juliet said, trying to lighten the atmosphere. "Finn is flying spider drones all over France, Monday through Friday, while I'm taking classes, and then I meet him on the barge on *Le Weekend.*"

She wasn't particularly disapproving of the affair between Avery and Alain; she simply worried her closest friend would receive the short end of the arrangement, as had happened to Avery a few times in the past. Changing the subject, she said, "By the way, I've been meaning to ask you for ages...have you heard from your father, recently?"

It had been months since Juliet had forced Avery to leave word with Stephen Evans about being shot.

"I heard from him when he returned from the Far East that time. You'd gone back to San Francisco."

"And you didn't tell me he'd gotten in touch? Avery!"

"He just wanted to know if I needed money."

"That was it? Did you ask him to come over for a visit?"

"No. And he didn't offer."

"Well," Juliet said, exasperated, "maybe he thought you didn't want to see him?"

"Maybe he didn't want to bother seeing *me.*"

"Well, maybe he was waiting for an invitation?"

"Maybe *I* was waiting for his offer to come for a visit?"

"Oh, Avery," she said with a sigh. "It is so hard to get things straightened out when they've gone sideways for so long, isn't it?"

"Yeah." She flashed a sardonic look in Juliet's direction. "Case in point. Mildred Church Thayer."

"*Touché.* People in glass houses, and other poems,"

Juliet agreed, keeping to herself the small breakthrough she felt she'd had with her mother just before she'd left home. Still and all, she hadn't heard a word from her mother, despite emails and links she'd sent to friends and everyone in the family—except brother Brad—that displayed her *France Unafraid* blogging efforts. Her father and Jamie had been enthusiastic and supportive, but as for Mildred Thayer—nary a word.

It is what it is... she thought with an inward sigh. To Avery she said, "I really thought your dad would come through this time."

"Not in this life, I guess," Avery said with studied nonchalance. "Hey! I've got a good idea!" She seemed determined to change the subject. "Let's go see the newly refurbished Rodin Museum this afternoon. You can't say you've lived in Paris if you haven't touched the base of The Thinker!"

Within the hour, the two were strolling through Rodin's former home, *Hôtel Biron* on *Rue de Varenne,* amid the smaller-sized sculptures and plaster casts that populated the many rooms of the mansion. After close inspection inside, they moved out into the vast gardens featuring straight lines of trees marching across the property like soldiers on parade and providing deep shade for Rodin's monumental works cast in bronze. As they drew closer to the iconic Thinker on its pedestal, Juliet and Avery shared a laugh watching a constant stream of tourists flexing their right arms and tucking their hands under their chins while having their pictures taken on mobile phones.

Juliet had brought her sketchpad and spent more than an hour drawing the mammoth statues of lesser-known Impressionist artists Jules Bastien-LePage and Claude Lorrain. Avery eventually abandoned her in favor of the outdoor café and a *café crème,* content to rest and people-watch until Juliet finally appeared.

Sinking onto a metal chair, Juliet said excitedly, "Could you believe how Rodin captured those artists standing there in solid bronze, six feet tall, holding their full-scale palettes? Aren't they simply wonderful?"

"Yeah," Avery agreed with a grin. "That's why I pointed them out to you."

"Did you read the display cards? It said they painted near the end of the nineteenth century and called themselves 'naturalist painters.' Bastien-LePage was the *leader* of the '*plein air*' school of landscape painting! He was the one who said landscapes couldn't be true-to-life unless the painter is right there! *In* the scene! I took a zillion shots and I can't wait to post about these two guys on *France Unafraid*. I bet half the American tourists who come here never get past the museum."

Avery nodded in the direction of the counter where beverages and pastries could be ordered. "Go get your coffee, *mademoiselle*, though at the rate you're spinning, I don't think you need any more caffeine."

Early July marked the end of the classes Juliet had been taking and the commencement of the annual French summer-holiday season. She bid a reluctant farewell to Finn and boarded the TGV fast train to Lake Annecy south and east of Paris where she had enrolled in a month-long course in a lesser known art school—an institution happy to take the tuition money from visiting foreigners, including a number of Americans. The city of Annecy sat at the head of a lake of the same name in the *Haute Savoie* section of the French Alps, an hour across the border from Geneva, Switzerland.

"It's absolutely gorgeous here," she related to Finn on the phone after she'd booked into the *Hôtel du Château*, right across the street from the twelfth-century *Château d'Annecy* and at the top of a hill that featured a commanding view not only of the water, but also of the soaring Alpine mountains that surrounded the lake. She negotiated the high-season rate for her tiny room down from a hundred euros a day to eighty-five, and had purchased some flowers to cheer herself up.

"Only one star," she explained to Finn, "but it has a glimpse of the lake and I'm not here much, anyway. Tomorrow we're going to the little village of Talloires to set up our easels in the exact spot Cezanne chose when he came here to paint. It's going to be great for the blog, which, if I can brag a little, has just hit a thousand subscribers and my Facebook page, fifteen hundred!" She paused for breath. "Where are you tonight?"

"Back in Paris on the barge, missing you."

Juliet's heart skipped more than a beat. "Me, too, you," she admitted without even trying to pretend otherwise. "In fact, when I get back to this teeny cubicle, the bottom sort of drops out and I really, *really* wish you were here with me. Two is way more fun on these junkets than one."

"Well, here's some hopeful news… Our class's next assignment is going to be railroad tracks. They've got us fanning out all over the place. Maybe I can get them to send me in your direction. "

"Great idea!" The prospect of seeing Finn over the Fourteenth of July national holiday was exactly what she'd hoped. "Ask for the Lyon-to-Annecy branch. The fast train section pretty much stops in Lyon and the old track takes the train at normal speed from there to where I am. I'm sure it needs a *close inspection*," she added, her tongue planted firmly in her cheek.

"I'll do my best."

Juliet was amazed when Finn, in fact, did manage to wangle the precise assignment that would bring him to this eastern region of the country. He arrived in Annecy right before the weekend of Bastille Day celebrations that were scheduled all over the country and were similar to America's 4th of July festivities. Fortunately, as of Wednesday, July 13th, she had booked them into a charming hotel she'd spotted when she was painting *à la Cezanne* in Talloires, a village of five hundred souls where tiny, twisting roads banked along the foothills. Their room overlooked the lake and faced the ancient *Chateau de Duingt*, looming on the opposite side of the water, its high walls and turrets clad in pointed roofs made of slate.

L'Hôtel Beau-Site was exactly that: a hostelry within sight of the beautiful lake. The Alps soared above their heads—some peaks still covered with small patches of last winter's snow—and below, tall trees and sloping lawns marched down to the crystalline water. Juliet described it as being "a French-speaking Lake Tahoe with better food, better architecture, higher mountains, and minus billboards and casinos."

Finn suggested they do as *Guide Michelin* recommended: drive up a mountain road to the small, World War II French Resistance museum next to a hallowed gravesite where the lives of the grandfathers of current Talloires and Annecy residents had been extinguished in a massacre in March of 1944.

"By August that year, the Germans were in retreat after Allied landings at Normandy that June," Finn related, having read the section on the battle of the *Plateau de Glières*. "But, four months earlier, German forces had slaughtered the remnants of some four-hundred-and-fifty resistance fighters who had endured the Alpine winter up there."

Next to the museum were 105 neatly laid out graves, each one with a cross or Star of David, along with a metal placard noting each man's birth and death date. Most of the deaths occurred the same day in March, so tragically near the end of the war in Europe.

Finn pointed to the escarpment that rose hundreds of feet above their heads marking an outer rim of the plateau, the rock walls surrounding it like a curtain of gray granite. They returned their gaze to a stone slab that told the rest of the story in French. Pointing to the incised script, Finn translated slowly. "It says that the few resistant fighters who survived in towns and villages of this region liberated Annecy themselves soon after this massacre, even before the Americans came rolling through. Poor bastards," he murmured, turning away. "They were sitting ducks up there."

She could see that a mantel of melancholy had Finn in its grip. "Sweetheart, what's going through your mind right now?" she asked softly.

He faced her then returned his gaze to the graves in front of them. "Even a supposedly 'good war' has terrible aspects that can't be glossed over by clinging to the notion of duty, honor, country."

"But the resistance fighters were defending their very country...*this* soil," she countered softly, "these beautiful mountains."

"Well, at least a better case can be made for what happened here than unmanned drones shooting off Hellfire missiles from northwest of the Las Vegas Strip at people in another desert, half a world away."

Their somber mood continued even when they arrived back at their hotel for a late dinner. When they walked into the pleasantly updated lobby, they noticed immediately that everyone was glued to the television mounted in the corner above the bar. On the screen was a video showing a large, white refrigerator truck streaking down a street in the seaside resort of Nice, France. Juliet and Finn stood motionless, watching the vehicle's massive bulk mow down scores of bystanders who'd been enjoying the Bastille Day celebratory fireworks display traditionally scheduled for the night before July 14th. On the screen flashed "Terrorism?"

"Oh God, no...not again," moaned Juliet, her eyes glued to the screen, as the scene played over and over and television broadcasters related the unfolding horror story. She could only imagine the thoughts whirling in Finn's brain. No one in the room seemed able to stop watching the terrifying images that had just taken place in one of France's most beautiful seaside cities facing the Mediterranean Sea.

Finally, Juliet urged, "C'mon, Finn. Let's go upstairs. They're just running the same video, over and over again. We'll get them to bring our dinner to the room."

Finn nodded and they walked in silence toward the elevator that would take them up to the second floor. Juliet figured that the romantic interlude they had planned for their weekend getaway was now shot to hell. She was startled when Finn turned to her as soon as they'd shut the door to their small suite and pulled her fiercely into his arms. His words were harsh in her ear. "I don't want to think about what's just happened! I want to shut it all out. I just want *you*, Juliet. I just want *us* in this room. Otherwise, I think I'll go completely nuts!"

Juliet clung tightly to him and rocked back and forth as they stood next to the bed.

"Just us," she repeated, her voice hoarse with unshed tears. "Yes. It's all we can do. Love instead of hate. It's our only weapon."

Finn drew back and clasped her by her shoulders as if she were a life raft. In mere minutes they both were naked in bed, loving each other and crying for the lost and wounded—doing what little they could to blot out the nightmare unfolding on television screens throughout the world.

CHAPTER 29

An hour later, their dinner was delivered to their room. Finn had ordered them leek and potato soup and toast with the region's *Reblochon* cheese melted to creamy perfection, but neither felt much like eating.

Without preamble, Finn put down his fork and demanded, "Will you marry me?"

Juliet was completely unprepared for his question, and for a moment, her mind went blank. Then, the urgency of his request set off alarm bells instead of filling her with joy. She could see by his troubled expression that he was struggling to keep at bay the memories of other people being killed in villages and towns in the Middle East. *He will probably always face these ghosts,* she thought, searching his face and willing him to understand her next words. She rose from her chair and stood beside him.

"Ask me again," she said, leaning down to encase his face between her hands. "Ask me to marry you on an ordinary day, a day when we both don't feel like howling to the moon over what's happening to our world." She pulled him toward her, the side of his head pressed against her breast. She scattered kisses on the top of his head, wanting him to feel her love, her care for him, but knowing in her heart that he had to be sure he truly wanted *her,* not just someone to cling to when horrible things were happening.

Finn pulled away and his lips crooked upward in a half smile. "The timing of my proposal is all wrong, huh?"

"Only slightly," she said, assaulted by a gloomy sense that he might never ask again. "But there is no one on this earth I'd rather say yes to...on a different day."

Unfortunately, events on the following days of their supposed getaway only got worse. On Bastille Day itself, when all of France was in mourning for 84 dead and 202 injured as a result of the rampage in Nice, Juliet's cell phone rang in their hotel room just before eight, as they were about to go downstairs for breakfast. It was a call from Jamie.

"You heard about Nice, right?" Juliet said. "Finn and I are in a little Alpine town, nowhere near what happened. We're fine."

"I'm glad to hear that, but that's not why I called. Just as you predicted, there's another takeover bid in the works and Brad's making moves that could jeopardize Mom and Dad and the Bay View, big time."

"Oh, shit!"

Finn reared back and gazed at her with a questioning look. *Why is life repeating itself so disastrously*, she wondered? First, another horrible terrorist attack in France and now, yet another takeover war breaking out in her family's business.

"What's Brad doing now?" she demanded. "Can't he just beat them off like he did last time, whoever they are?"

"These are apparently very big boys in the video-game industry. Brad's now demanding that the parents increase the equity loan up to practically every penny the Bay View's worth, and he's seeking funds from some very sketchy sources to stock his war chest."

"And the parents say what?"

"The usual, of course. Mom says they should do what Brad demands and Dad doesn't think it's wise to mortgage the hotel any further, as they could lose everything. However, he hasn't put his foot down and Brad is bugging him every minute to sign a bunch of papers."

"So what's going to happen?"

"That's why I'm calling you. You've got to come home. Dad and I can't fight this without you."

"Why me?" she protested. "I only own the stock I could have sold starting July first, but I've been too busy even to do that. You three have all your stock, plus your stock options. That should give you some clout. And think of it this way… maybe you'd do better if the takeover *happened?*"

"Brad says all our holdings will be diluted if there's a change of control, and they could actually end up worthless if the takeover guys win."

"And you believe him? What does Adelman, the lawyer, say?"

"That's why you've got to come home!" Jamie insisted. "Adelman told me that with you here, there's a better chance we four Thayers can come out of all this with something decent, whoever ultimately controls GatherGames."

Juliet felt a rock in the pit of her stomach. Finn had turned from her during the conversation and was staring sightlessly out the window at the lake. There went their weekend. There went her session at the art school in Annecy, along with a month, prepaid, at the little hotel up the hill. *Does it also mean I'm jeopardizing something else*, she wondered, gazing at Finn's stiff, erect stance. *Am I giving in when I should stand firm? Let Dad and Mom and Jamie fend for themselves?* "Let the chips fall where they may," would Finn say? *But the Bay View Hotel is sacred ground*, she thought with an aching heart. *Can I simply stand by and allow Brad to run roughshod over our family's proudest legacy and leave our parents in a ditch?*

She heaved a resigned sigh.

"Okay. I'll get there as fast as I can. But only for a

week or so. Just to see if we can help straighten out this mess."

Downstairs in the dining room, Finn and Juliet ate their soft-boiled eggs and buttered toast in silence. The lake outside was a smooth, blue carpet this somber July morning. They both gazed without comment at several boats pulling water skiers carving curling wakes on its pellucid surface.

"So, off you go," Finn said, finally. "Juliet to the rescue."

She ignored his pointed comment, saying only, "It turns out that I can fly out of Geneva. The man at the desk, here, said there's a bus from the Annecy train station that goes right to the airport in a little more than an hour."

Finn nodded, but didn't comment.

"Would you mind driving me into town? I can just make it to a flight that goes to Heathrow, and from there, get a nonstop to San Francisco. With the time change, I'll get there at about eleven o'clock at night, California time."

"I'll drive you to Geneva."

"You don't have to do that. I-I can take the bus from Annecy."

"You want to make sure you make your flight, don't you? I'll drive you."

A wall had risen between them that Juliet ascribed to both Finn's disappointment that everything about their getaway had gone so awry, and also that Juliet was playing rescue ranger for a mother who—he'd surely surmised from everything she'd told him—was going to side with her elder son, as usual, with no real concern for the welfare of the rest of her family.

"You're wondering why I'm trying, one more time, to

help Jamie and my parents save the Bay View when I've failed so often before?"

"That and...well, a lot of other things. As you said before, maybe our timing is wrong."

"Please, Finn...hear me... I'm not abandoning ship! You must realize by now that I can't imagine my life with anyone other than you, but for both our sakes, we have to be sure that when we do get together, it's for all the right reasons...and not when your divorce papers are barely dry, or because we've both been horribly jolted by what happened in Nice." She touched his sleeve. "I'm not the bad guy in all this."

Juliet watched the shuttered expression on the face of the handsome man sitting across from her in one of the most romantic places she'd ever been.

"They're all using you, you know," he said, his voice barely audible. "Jamie's a great guy, but he's been under the influence of a weak father and a pretty abusive brother...and he may never have the guts to break away. He's wanting you to shore him up, even when there's not much in it for you. Except money, I guess."

Even though Juliet knew that Finn's brutal assessment was mostly accurate, she felt thrown totally off balance by his last remark that struck her as one below the belt.

"You may find this hard to believe," she replied, cut to the core by the implications of his last words, "but my going home is not about the money!" She'd never told him about her plans to donate a significant portion of her profits—once she got them—to nonprofit organizations she believed in, but still, Finn should know her better, by now. Her flying home was not about her portfolio. "Look," she pleaded, "you've lived all over the world, never really even having a place to call your hometown. I've lived in San Francisco in my family's hotel my entire life, and so have generations of Thayers that came before me. I can't just leave it to the fates of a bunch of Silicon Valley predators, Finn. Don't you understand at all what I'm feeling? I want to fight to hold on to the Bay View for *myself*, yes, but just as much as for my family."

"But what about your art? Your decision to become a serious painter."

"I haven't any less burning desire for all that," she protested, "but, surely, it can wait a week or two? What's going on at home can't. I'll come back to France as soon as this is settled, one way or the other."

"Maybe you won't," he challenged, with a distant, closed air. "Maybe you'll discover there's more to keep you there than bring you back."

"Finn! That's not going to happen!" she cried, unable to keep the exasperation from her voice. "I want to be here. With *you*. Believe me, I'll be on the first plane to Paris once Jamie, the lawyers, and I see if there's a way to keep my dad from losing everything he's worked his entire life for!"

"You sound very convincing, so I guess we'd better put your suitcase into the car and get the hell out of here," he said with studied politeness, as if they were mere, casual acquaintances.

"I guess we'd better," she murmured, her heart sore as she rose from her chair. She glanced out the window at the lake where she'd never even dipped a toe, and headed upstairs to their room to retrieve her luggage.

"On top of everything," Jamie complained as they headed out of San Francisco airport close to midnight and drove up Highway 101 toward the city, "Brad hired a new head attorney, even before he learned about a second takeover. The guy's as much of a self-satisfied jerk as Brad, and won't give Dad or me the time of day."

"Where'd Brad find him? Some Stanford crony, no doubt."

"A fraternity brother, of course. Gavin, somebody. I don't know the guy."

Why does that name sound vaguely familiar? She shook her head and stared through the windshield.

Jamie warned, "And I hope you've girded yourself for the big family powwow at lunchtime tomorrow."

"Oh, I'm ready, all right." She suddenly remembered where she'd heard the name 'Gavin.' "And, by the way, I smell a great, big rat in all of this!"

"Gavin Linley's m'man," Brad announced smugly when his siblings and parents were gathered around the table in their small family dining room. "He's a total ace in fighting the VCs in these predatory takeover bids. He'd won three in a row before I got him to come over to us to help beat down this thing."

"Where did you find this paragon?" Juliet asked, wanting to confirm her suspicions.

Brad shot her a glare. "Stanford buddy, what else? Only the best." He turned to his father. "Look, Dad, Gavin says you can't put it off any longer. He's going to need you to sign the paperwork to increase the equity loan. He's also lined up some other deep pockets, and we may need to let one of them take over your board seat."

Even Mildred Thayer looked surprised at this announcement. Brad senior frowned and shook his head. "You're asking us for more money *and* you want me off the board?"

"That's only a possibility," Brad hastened to assure him. "We just have to be prepared for all eventualities. It's all for a good cause, of course…holding on to what we have."

"What *you* have," their father commented with an unexpected show of displeasure.

Juliet was amazed to hear Jamie speak up before she could even open her mouth. "Don't do it, Dad! Don't sign anything!"

"Shut up!" Brad snapped. "You're small fry in all of this, as usual, and you'd better back off if you don't want to lose every nickel in time and treasure you've invested in this family enterprise of ours. Just let me take care of things."

Juliet looked over at her father, who was now staring at his untouched plate of food. She stood up and threw her napkin on the table. "I'm begging you, Dad," she pleaded, worried that his show of pique wouldn't last very long if their mother started to work on him, along with Brad. "Jamie's right. Don't sign *anything*! We four need independent legal counsel and I'm going to get it!"

"Juliet!" warned her mother. "Don't make things any worse than they already are. Let Brad handle this."

"Which Brad?" she demanded. "The one who owns this hotel, or the one who doesn't give a damn about it?" And before anyone could say anything else, she stormed out of the room, raced down the hallway, and used a master key everyone in the family possessed to let herself into Brad's hotel suite.

Once inside his rooms, Juliet remembered exactly where her brother kept his Stanford yearbooks in a prominent place in a wall of bookshelves at the far end of his small sitting room. She flipped to the index of the one for his senior year and searched.

"Linley…. Linley…Gavin Linley," she muttered. "Bingo!"

She flipped to the pages next to Gavin Linley's name, and sure enough, he had been a fraternity brother and also a member of Brad's college squash and track teams. Under

Gavin's Stanford senior picture were the words, "Life's Ambition: Killer Lawyer." He had also been the young Turk who'd looked her up and down on both her visits to Adelman and Marx, Attorneys-at-Law. Jamie had not been on the receiving end of that blatant Male Gaze and so hadn't even noticed the guy as they were leaving.

She tucked the yearbook under her arm and closed the gap among the remaining three yearbooks, praying Brad wouldn't notice the one now missing from his shelf. Thirty seconds later she was out the door and scurrying down the hallway to her own suite of rooms. As soon as she entered the sanctuary of her own bedroom, she called Finn's mobile phone and let it ring until it went to voice mail, leaving a short message that she'd made it home safely— and that she missed him terribly. A few minutes later, she also sent him a text with a similar sentiment, and then punched in the number of Edward Adelman.

That afternoon, with Brad's yearbook stowed out of sight in her tote bag, Juliet set off down the hotel's fifth floor corridor to meet Jamie in the basement garage for the appointment she'd just scheduled at Adelman and Marx. When the elevator doors opened on her floor, she found herself face to face with her older brother, who apparently was headed to his room. He stepped out, blocking her path, and let the doors close behind him.

"You really upset Mom and Dad, you know, storming out like that."

Juliet pushed the button to summon the next elevator. "So tell me," she said, ignoring his comment, "what made you think of hiring Gavin Linley away from the law firm that already represented Jamie and me."

"What makes you think that's true?"

"Because it is and you know it."

"And how was I supposed to know you'd sneak behind my back like that?"

"Even if you didn't know—and I suspect you *did* very early on—Gavin Linley now has a very big problem called 'conflict of interest'—or doesn't Stanford Business or the Law School teach that anymore?"

"What are you talking about? Gavin probably hasn't a clue who you are and I'm sure he didn't know you were a client at Adelman and Marx."

"How did you know that was the firm I went to see?" she said, her eyes narrowing.

Brad shifted his glance to the wall behind her. "I— Jamie told me, I think, when I finally pried it out of him what you were up to after I fired your ass and you lost your stock options. I figured you'd go to see if you could sue me for wrongful termination or some shit like that."

"Jamie didn't tell you a thing," she said in a low voice. "I went to see a lawyer long before you canned me. You found out from your buddy, Gavin, that I'd hired the senior partner in his old firm—and probably why I was there. The question is—how much did *he* know of my business there?"

Just then, the down elevator pinged and the solid brass doors opened revealing a well-dressed matron holding a beautifully groomed tri-color Cavalier King Charles Spaniel in her arms.

"Where are you going?" Brad demanded of Juliet.

"Down in this elevator with this adorable dog." She smiled sweetly at the guest as she entered the car. "Lovely to see you again at the Bay View, Ms. Streisand."

Without responding to her brother, she punched the elevator button for the floor below in order to make a short visit to her parents' rooms before she rendezvoused with Jamie in the garage. The elevator closed and then soon opened again and Juliet strode down the hallway.

"Oh, honey..." her father began as soon as she entered the room, but before he could say anything further,

her mother overrode his next words.

"Well, you made a fine spectacle of yourself at lunch."

"With good reason," Juliet countered. "Look at this!" She pulled out the Stanford yearbook and pointed to a guy in the line-up of the track team standing three members down from a college-aged Bradshaw Thayer.

"That's Gavin Linley. He worked at the law firm Jamie and I consulted a few months back before the first takeover threat. Linley saw me there, so he knew—or made it his business to find out—what Jamie and I were there for at his old firm. If he revealed to Brad that we'd consulted his boss, Adelman, and what we'd consulted him about, it would be a major conflict-of-interest to come work for this company."

"They're a big firm, with hundreds of clients," protested her mother. "How would Gavin Linley have any knowledge why you were seeking counsel at that firm—or even that you were? You could have been getting a Will done, or something totally unrelated. I don't see his coming to work for Brad as any big conflict."

"He saw me there," Juliet asserted. "Gave me the once over. I got the feeling he knew who I was and, by the way, he was very chummy with *my* lawyer. Asked him to play squash with him that coming weekend."

"That proves absolutely nothing. You are just stirring the pot, Juliet, because you're still resentful about Brad's firing you."

Juliet saw that the leopard's spots were right where they'd always been.

"His firing me was the best thing that happened to me all year!" she shot back. "I'm just trying to find out what is actually going on around here, Mother, and hoping you and Dad won't lose everything you own in the process!"

She saw by her mother's tightly clasped hands that, despite her automatic defense of her eldest son, Mildred

Thayer was worried. Juliet sought her father's glance. "Dad, I want you to come with me to Adelman and Marx, even if Mother won't. At least, let's find out if there's been any conflict of interest that could jeopardize all our futures—but especially yours and the hotel. Don't you get it? The guy who used to work at Adelman and Marx is the very lawyer working for Brad who is pressuring you to sign away every last bit of equity you have in this place! Gavin Linley probably now knows the strengths and weaknesses of Jamie and my wanting to get what's owed all of us if there is a change of control of GatherGames. Gavin can *use* that insider's knowledge to Brad's advantage, not ours, if—or when—the takeover happens."

Mildred addressed her husband: "Brad Junior wouldn't do anything like that! I'm telling you, Juliet, you're just stirring up more trouble when we've got plenty already."

Her father said in his usual appeasing tone, "Your mother may be right about Gavin Linley's working for Brad not being an issue of conflict-of-interest. For certain, San Francisco is a tiny town where everybody knows everybody, but Brad hiring Gavin could be perfectly innocent. And even if Linley did know who you were that time when he saw you at their office, I'm sure he didn't have access to your lawyer's files—"

"We don't know any of that!" Juliet said with frustration. "What if he found a way to see whatever he wanted to before he left that firm?"

"That's sheer speculation and slanderous to Gavin Linley," Mildred retorted.

"Well, I'm not so sure it's speculation, but I damned well am going to find out!" She turned on her heel and left her parents' suite without further argument, more certain than anything in her life that Gavin Linley had egregiously violated moral ethics by telling Brad she'd consulted one of the partners at his old law firm—and maybe why she was there.

But was it a breach of legal ethics? What if Gavin was engineering her father's removal from the Board of Directors to give her brother a stronger hand to protect his own, selfish interests in a second takeover fight?

Less than an hour later, Juliet and Jamie took seats opposite Edward Adelman at his highly polished desk. Juliet inhaled deeply and began, "As you know, your former colleague, Gavin Linley, has joined GatherGames as chief counsel, hired by my brother."

Edward Adelman's features were expressionless and he merely nodded. Her look to Jamie telegraphed, *he knew!* In some ways, San Francisco was, as her father said, a truly tiny town, and she groaned inwardly.

"Did you or anyone in this firm identify Jamie or me as siblings of Bradshaw Thayer the Fourth, or reveal that we were your clients and were here to get legal advice on how to protect our interests against our brother's greed?"

"Of course I never discussed with Gavin Linley why you and Jamie had come to see me!" he said, clearly offended by such a notion.

"Well, if you or anyone else in your firm did," Juliet replied, coolly, *"that's* what lit the match as far as my elder brother is concerned and got me fired, along with causing me to lose my valuable stock options.

By this point, Juliet didn't give a fig about her options, but she wanted to make Adelman plenty worried that Linley's actions had "grievously harmed her" financially.

"Even worse," she continued, "now that Linley is Brad's official counsel, the rest of the Thayer family stands to get screwed in this new takeover fight. I'm sure that Linley has been behind Brad's move to make everyone sign an agreement not to sell their stock unless Brad says they can." Her gaze narrowed as she looked at the man she'd originally hired to represent Jamie and her. "And now Linley is urging my father to increase his equity loan against the hotel and surrender his seat on GG's Board of Directors to someone Bard has picked!"

Juliet could tell that Adelman recognized these were serious charges of ethical violations against him and his firm.

"I repeat," he said in an even tone, "I never disclosed anything about you and your brother Jamie consulting me."

"And can you vouch that no one *else* in this firm did?"

Adelman hesitated. His next words shocked both Jamie and her. "I'm afraid I cannot. Gavin didn't tell the partners of this firm, including me, he was being hired away by GatherGames. He just said he needed a break from the grind and was quitting to think over what he wanted to do next."

Jamie jumped into the conversation. "Well, he must have taken all of five minutes to 'think it over' because he came on as our new general counsel only a week or so after Brad fired Juliet, a move that then disqualified her from exercising the options to buy more stock at a lower price somewhere down the road." He glared at Adelman. "This, of course, put even more stock options under Brad's sole control."

Adelman raised his fingers and pinched the flesh between his eyes. "I reiterate, I had no idea Gavin was such a loose cannon. He's about ten years younger than I am, and a pretty bright guy, but this…"

"*This*," Juliet filled in for him, "puts Adelman and Marx under threat of a major lawsuit from Jamie and me– or at the very least—severe disciplinary action if we file a complaint with the California Bar Association against you."

"Hold on a minute! My firm has my name on the door

and I promise you, I will get to the bottom of this. In fact, there's someone on staff I'd like to speak with. Can you wait a few moments?"

"Off the clock?" Juliet demanded.

"You won't be charged," Adelman replied, tight-lipped.

Mystified by the attorney's abrupt departure, Jamie and Juliet sat silently in their luxurious leather chairs until the man reappeared with a younger man in pale pink shirtsleeves who was introduced as Roland Miller.

"Roland is a recent hire who had the office next to Gavin Linley's until he departed the firm." He turned to the nervous young man, who had taken a seat beside his boss, and barked, "Tell them what you just told me when I asked you if you ever overheard anything unseemly from Gavin Linley when he had the office next to yours."

CHAPTER 30

Juliet judged that Roland Miller looked pale as the filet of sole served at Tadich's Grill. He shifted his gaze anxiously to the pair sitting in his boss's impressively large office. He swallowed hard before speaking. "Ah...well...the walls between some of the offices of the junior partners, here, are pretty thin, and with the divider between Gavin and mine, if either of us was speaking very loudly, the other could hear every word."

He glanced at the founding partner at his firm who gave him a sharp nod. "Go on, Roland."

"About two months ago, I overheard Gavin chuckling about the fact that his buddy, Brad Thayer, had persuaded his own father to surrender his stock options during the first takeover fight at GatherGames."

Shocked to hear this, Juliet interrupted. "The *first* takeover fight?"

Roland nodded. "From what I could gather, Gavin's college buddy wanted more options under his control so there'd be enough to offer a new board member who supposedly was bringing in a needed infusion of cash to fight the dissident VCs."

Aghast to have this fact confirmed, Juliet turned to Jamie. "Did you know Dad was pressured to give up *his* options months ago, just like I was forced to when Brad fired me?"

Jamie shook his head. "Dad never said a word."

"What else?" Adelman demanded of his underling.

Looking embarrassed, but apparently aware his own job was on the line, he said, "Not too long ago, when Gavin was on the phone again, I heard him say on his end of the conversation that he admired Brad Thayer's...ah...brass balls... threatening his father that he wouldn't hesitate to default on some equity loan if his dad wouldn't give up his board seat to a new investor. Gavin congratulated Thayer junior on following his advice."

"I knew it!" Juliet exclaimed to Jamie. To Adelman she said, "So, *your* employee, Gavin Linley, was giving advice to *my* brother before he'd even left your firm, even though *I* was a client, here, with opposing interests to my brother's—and probably as a ploy to land himself a plum position as house counsel at GG!"

"So it would seem."

To the shaken young lawyer she demanded, "Did you hear anything about the family-owned stock in this fight?"

Roland nodded. "Gavin told Brad he'd write up a document for all family members to sign stating that they wouldn't sell any family-owned stock unless Brad said it was okay, thereby keeping it in one bloc to give Brad more leverage on the board and against the continuing threats from outside."

Juliet turned to Adelman. "What are the penalties for someone acting as counsel for my brother's selfish interests—and against our father's interests and Jamie's and mine—when we were already clients at the same firm?"

"Reprimands, dismissal...disbarment," he replied.

"Gavin had to know intimate details about why Jamie and I consulted you!"

Jamie chimed in. "How the hell did he do that?"

Before Adelman could answer, Roland swallowed hard and raised a trembling hand to get their attention. "I'm guessing somehow he'd seen your client logs, Mr. Adelman, and it's even worse than that," he admitted with another glance at Adelman. "Gavin figured I'd probably heard a lot of what he'd been saying to Thayer. He even joked to me in the men's room about what he'd advised Brad's fallback position should be."

"Which was?" Juliet asked, gripping the sides of her leather chair.

"If Gavin's first plan didn't work, he told Brad that your older brother could always make a side deal to leave as CEO if he was given his full complement of stock and options, plus a big bonus as a kiss-off deal with no exit provisions for the rest of his family." He paused, inhaled, and added, "In the men's room, Gavin threatened to destroy my chances for advancement if I breathed a word of anything I'd ever overheard."

"And do you know what Mr. Linley ultimately recommended regarding the outstanding equity loan against the Bay View Hotel?" Juliet demanded.

The young lawyer visibly gulped. "Gavin said in that second scenario, to harvest enough money for Brad's golden parachute of stock and vested options, plus the bonus, he'd tell the new owners just to let the equity loan default on the Bay View Hotel."

"Oh, my God," Jamie said on a long breath.

Roland Miller nodded. "Brad's logic was that he'd never monetize his share of the hotel until his parents were dead and his siblings agreed to sell—which Brad had told Gavin he was sure they—you—never would agree to unless you had no other choice."

Jamie looked at Juliet in disbelief, and then turned to Adelman. "So, in other words, a guy still working in a firm that represents *us* advised our brother it might even be *advantageous* to his bottom line if the rest of his family were thrown under the bus."

Adelman shifted an icy gaze toward the junior member of his firm. "Please leave us, now, Roland. I thank you for being so candid in your responses. I will inform you later what I decide to do about your future in this firm, but you might let it be known among the other juniors if *ever* anyone at Adelman and Marx knows about such obvious conflicts going on in this office—and he or she doesn't say anything to a senior partner—I will personally turn these individuals over to the Bar Association with a recommendation of disbarment."

"Y-Yes sir."

"You may go back to work, and I better not learn that you've repeated anything you've heard in this room, or anywhere else… is that crystal clear?"

"Yes, sir." In the next instant, he slunk out of Adelman's office.

Juliet was the first to speak. "Thanks to Gavin's advice, Brad could appear to be fighting the takeover and then just make his own side deal with the wannabe buyers and to hell with the losses that the rest of us will suffer."

"But I don't understand," said Jamie, "how did Gavin even know who you were?"

Juliet mused aloud, "I got the eeriest feeling Gavin recognized me that first time I came to this office. Maybe Brad invited him to my thirtieth birthday bash, or something? He could have gotten in touch with Brad right after we consulted this firm and told him that he'd seen me here and saw it as an opportunity to troll for a bigger job at GG?"

"Or maybe Gavin and Brad still play squash together, or see each other at the Pacific Union Club and trade gossip," Jamie speculated. "Who knows in this town?"

"But Edward," she pressed, "wouldn't Gavin be required to reveal to his firm if he wanted to advise Brad as a client, in order to be sure there was no conflict-of-interest among all the clients you represent—even if Gavin *wasn't* angling for a bigger job?"

"Yes, of course," Adelman replied. "There are rules about this. However, it could be that he approached Brad after he figured out who you were, saying he knew something that would be of interest. Everyone in San Francisco heard about that first takeover bid."

"But how would he even know the specifics of what I was doing here if you never said a word about the substance of our meeting?" Juliet said, her skepticism returning.

Adelman pointed to a large notebook on the table with LOG printed on its cover.

"Roland had the answer. Gavin could simply look in here. It's standard practice to note in our phone-and-meeting logs the name of the person a member of the firm is seeing and jot down what issues were discussed in order to justify our billable hours."

"You mean Gavin Linley could have seen me here," Juliet protested, "put two and two together in the light of rumors of the first takeover, and then snuck in here and stolen those pages to entice Brad to hire him as Chef Counsel?"

"It's possible," Adelman agreed carefully. He opened the log on his desk to a page he had marked. "Look…the pages are here, but there is no need to steal them or even 'borrow' them for a while." He pointed to a shelf behind his desk full of identical notebooks. "Some lawyers keep notes electronically, but I like the privacy of paper." He inhaled a deep breath, continuing, "But now it's clear even *that* system depends on the trustworthiness of your fellow employees not to snoop. I could have been in a conference down the hall or at a meeting outside the building, and all Gavin would have to do is slip in here, pull out his cell phone, and photograph the pertinent pages of my notes to peruse at his leisure. He could have later downloaded the images and emailed or printed them to show Brad why you two had come to see me, in exchange for the offer of chief counsel at GatherGames."

"Holy shit!" breathed Jamie.

"Gavin's advice saved Brad's ass that first time, no doubt," Juliet said to Adelman grimly. "Well, not *this* time around! If those pages about our meetings with you exist somewhere other than in that log there," she tapped the notebook in front of the lawyer, "we're going to find the copies he made. Brad's having that information cost me my job and a lot of money! If Gavin purloined those notes from your log, they're either in Brad's possession or in a file in Gavin's new, corner office!"

"Or on his laptop—or Brad's," Jamie reminded her with a bitter laugh. "I'm head tech guy at GG, remember. If they're somewhere other than in this log, I'll find them."

With a sideways glance at Adelman, Juliet asked her brother, "Can you hack into their two computers? What about their phones?" Looking back to the discomfited lawyer, she added, "You didn't hear that, but we have to fight fire with fire, now."

"You are correct. I didn't hear that," their lawyer repeated.

Jamie said, "I have legal ways to access our office intranet system." He pulled out his key ring and grabbed a slender one made of brass. "Even better than a hack... here's a master key to the entire office. Let's do a little 'borrowing' of our own!"

"I didn't hear you say *any* of that," Adelman broke in, "but I do want you to know this...if you can find proof that Gavin Linley took client-sensitive property belonging to my law firm, I'll see to it he's disbarred."

"But what about the damage to us he's already done," demanded Juliet, "to say nothing of the havoc he could wreak on our family in the future?"

Adelman paused and Juliet could tell he was carefully considering his next words. "If you two get the proof, I will be able to persuade my partners to provide you the full firepower of this office, *pro bono*, to help you mount the best fight possible to preserve your family's stake in the coming battle over control of the company." Then he hastened to add, as any lawyer would, Juliet figured, "Of course, we can't promise a miracle, but I swear on the integrity of Adelman and Marx, we'll have your back on this until the Fat Lady sings."

Half a world away, Finn hiked his heavy backpack onto his shoulders and headed down the steep incline behind the native guide toward what he hoped was a riverbank and shelter of some kind. The sun was blistering and the air so filled with creatures flying in swarms, he hoped his spider drone would function in these extreme conditions. His mobile phone certainly didn't work, although that was most likely due to the fact that this particular Third World nation barely had running water, let alone functioning cell towers. The rest of the party trudged behind him, their boots caked with dirt and sweat seeping through their khaki shirts.

Cut off from civilization is exactly where a guy like me belongs right now. And who gives a shit if danger lurks just around the next rock?

For the briefest instant, a vision of Juliet loomed in his mind's eye.

She would give a shit…and so would Aunt Claudine…

But Juliet Thayer was caught up in a world so foreign to Finn's own, right now, he couldn't imagine the lady from California sparing him a moment's thought.

Not true, Deschanel…and you know it.

Juliet and Jamie chose the following quiet Sunday to display before their parents' photo copies they'd found in

GG's electronic files of the purloined phone logs from Adelman and Marx, along with other proof of the betrayal of their eldest son. They also related the unsavory details of Brad's sexual harassment of Avery Evans and her subsequent flight to Paris.

After silence descended in the sitting room of the family's suite, Mildred rose from her chair, walked over to the bay window with its spectacular view, and shook her head from side to side in disbelief. "I'll never forgive you if you've distorted the facts."

"Look again at the phone logs, Mother," Juliet said quietly, almost sympathetic to a woman whose own son would allow the hotel to go into default on the outstanding equity loan. "Jamie found Adelman's log notes in Brad's Inbox, courtesy of Gavin Linley. Gavin wanted a job, and Brad wanted to win this takeover fight, no matter what. It was like a video war game to him, I think."

Brad, senior, also stood up and crossed the room to stand behind his wife. He placed his hands gently on her shoulders. "This time, Millie, even you cannot condone his behavior—nor ours," her husband insisted in his quiet voice. "It's true. Brad twisted my arm to surrender our stock options in the first takeover fight. It was spineless of me not to tell you, Jamie and Juliet, I'd done that. Now Brad wants to remove me from the board and leverage the hotel to a dangerous level. He didn't even look after *your* welfare, Mildred, let alone the rest of us. Surely you see that, now?"

Juliet took a step toward her mother and took her hand. "Mother, please know that Jamie and I feel horrible to have found all this out. Brad's our *brother*! But, the evidence we've shown you means that our only chance of saving the hotel from receivership and ending up with some of the money owed us all is for the four of us to grant our proxies to the board members who are in favor of the takeover—provided they pay back the loan on the Bay View and grant us our fair share of what we founding family members invested in time and money."

Juliet's father remained standing behind his wife. "Mildred, you and I must face up to the fact that we're partly responsible for Brad's...lack of empathy, I guess we'd have to call it...toward anyone but himself."

Mildred Thayer whirled in place and glared at her husband. "Isn't what you're really saying is that *I'm* responsible for the way Brad is?" Hands on hips in her typical, combative stance, she confronted the man she'd lived with for forty years. "Well, maybe it's time, now, to tell your other children how you skipped out on me when I was pregnant with our first child and—"

Juliet interrupted her.

"Jamie and I both already know that story," she revealed as gently as she could. "We had another brother, also named Bradshaw," she recited. "He was born dead when Dad was in Vietnam and is buried in Arizona. When Dad came back, you had a second son you also named Bradshaw. Since Day One, you clung to him and used him as a weapon. Dad stood by and let you do it. End of story." She turned and gazed out the bay window at the sparkling water a mile away. "It must have been painful for you both, but that was then and this is now, and if you care about your other two children—or yourselves—you'll join us by giving your proxies to the board members who are the only ones that can dig us out of this mess."

Juliet was startled to hear a little sob, and turned to put an arm around her mother's heaving shoulders. "Mother, I know this is hard, but I have to know. Can Jamie and I count on your proxy, or do you want to be thrown under the bus with the rest of us?"

"Do you know which board members you'd trust to approach?" Mildred asked, barely above a whisper.

Jamie spoke up for the first time. "Yes, I know which ones they are, and since I still work for the company, our lawyers at Adelman and Marx advise me that I can demand a meeting with the dissident members of the board. We can then offer to strengthen their hand in the outcome of this fight by giving them our four proxies and cut a deal so that *we* can survive, too."

Mildred bowed her head in defeat, her hands no longer defiantly on her hips but trembling, now, by her sides. Tears rimmed her eyes and her voice caught.

"Where do I sign?"

"Hey, Deschanel!" somebody yelled from the foot of a rickety set of mobile stairs leading to the open door of a prop plane that looked as if it would never get off the ground. "Get a move on! We're leaving!"

Finn slowly reached for his mountainous backpack squatting in the orange-colored dirt and slowly rose to his feet, slinging it with a thud around his shoulders. Once he got to his next stop, what did he do then, he wondered? Sleep in another mosquito infested mud hole? Eat another serving of food brought back to life by water that might give him the worst case of dysentery in his life?

What the hell am I doing?

Tadich's Grill was brimming with customers and noisier than ever when four members of the Thayer family entered its hallowed interior at the height of the dinner hour. They were taken directly to one of the larger booths positioned behind the paneled walls of the restaurant's main front room.

"Will you ever forget our dinner here, the night Brad fired you?" Jamie whispered as they followed the *maître d'* toward their destination.

"Yeah...the beginning of the end of GG, as we knew it," she whispered back.

And the true beginning of her love affair with a certain former Air Force flyer she hadn't heard from in two-and-a-half weeks despite repeated attempts to contact him. The regret she felt about her last day in Talloires left her feeling hollowed out inside.

She couldn't think about that now, she warned herself. *Just focus on the crucial meeting that's about to take place.*

The restaurant's host pulled back the heavy curtain cloaking their booth and the Thayers took their seats. Edward Adelman and his partner, Martin Marx, were already present with seven of the thirteen board members around the linen-clad table where drinks and Tadich's famous French fries were already on display. Squeezed beside these attendees were two potential Silicon Valley investors whom the Thayers had never met in person but knew by their tough reputations. After introductions were made, lawyer Adelman took charge of the meeting.

"My hand-delivered memo has informed you why we requested to see you privately with my clients, Mr. and Mrs. Bradshaw Thayer, the Third, and their adult children, Juliet and James—all of whom were among the founders of GatherGames."

Adelman swiftly confirmed that the four Thayers, together, owned a significant amount of the family stock and would be willing to grant their proxies to those in favor of a change of control at the firm. "That is *if* the new owners will both retire the ten-million-dollar equity loan Bradshaw Thayer, here, granted the company in its start-up phase, and secondly, accelerate the right of these family members to exercise their remaining stock options at the time of the sale—as well as simultaneously allowing them to sell their preferred shares to the new investors—all in one, coordinated transaction."

Adelman allowed his gaze to roam from one end of the table to the other.

"In return, the Thayers will grant the members of the present board who wish to sell the company to *you* gentlemen," he said, nodding at the newcomers, "their executed proxies of agreement. In this way, the family members who worked so hard to make a success of GatherGames will be granted what is fairly due them for their five years' work—and you, gentlemen, will be able to purchase the company that's proven to be extremely profitable in the video-game industry. Everybody wins."

The silence in their private booth only emphasized the loud chatter and clank of dishes beyond the walls in the main dining room. Then, into the void, one of the team of investors asked, "And what about the CEO of GG? The younger Bradshaw Thayer. Can we have his proxy too?"

Adelman responded with a slight shrug of his pin-striped shoulders. "We do not represent Bradshaw Thayer, the Fourth," he disclosed in a neutral tone of voice, "so I expect you'll have to negotiate separately on that score." With a look in Mildred Thayer's direction he added, "However, Mrs. Thayer has made a request that her eldest son be granted the right to maintain the stock and options presently due him, plus his salary for the entire year."

He turned to the Thayers and suggested, "While these gentlemen consider our proposals, why don't you four, plus Mr. Marx and myself, move to another booth I've reserved for dinner?"

The Thayers, along with Adelman and Marx, were shown to another private booth at the other end of the restaurant. Juliet couldn't eat a bite of the dinner she ordered, and the rest of her fellow diners—with the exception of their two lawyers— pushed around their food in a similar manner. Just as dessert and coffee were being served, one of the board members poked his head into their booth, a broad smile on his face. He waved a piece of paper and then placed it in front of Edward Adelman. "Here's the term sheet," he said and laughed. "You got practically everything you asked."

"What *didn't* we get?" Juliet said, her heart speeding up.

The dissident board member glanced at Mildred Thayer and announced, "If the current CEO resigns his position, he will be granted the stock and salary due him to date, which is still quite considerable, you'll remember. However, he will be granted only half his stock options to be exercised over a five-year period. If he balks, he can always sue," he said with another swift glance at Mrs. Thayer. "The investors don't want young Brad in any position to challenge their authority in future. That's the deal. No negotiation."

All but Bradshaw Thayer IV's mother declared simultaneously, "We'll take it!"

All eyes shifted to Mildred. Juliet reached for her mother's hand and gave it a gentle, sympathetic squeeze. Mrs. Bradshaw Thayer III slowly nodded her assent. When they had all signed the Letter of Agreement and paid their restaurant bill, even the senior Thayers seemed relieved to have the drama finally over.

Juliet wondered, however, why she only felt horribly depressed?

An hour later, in the sitting room of her suite, Juliet flipped on a single lamp and sank into the silk-covered slipper chair in front of the fireplace. She was spent from the strain of the evening but was determined to make one more call before she fell into bed. Once again, she punched in Finn's cell phone number, certain that her name appeared on his phone's screen whenever she tried to contact him.

It rang...and rang. Still no human answered. When his familiar, deep voice asked callers to leave a message, she described the night's momentous events as quickly and succinctly as she could. Her heart beating at an accelerated pace, she told him once again how much she missed him.

"But I won't come back to Paris without an invitation, Finn. It's up to you. I love you. I love you so much, and I hated the way we were together the day I left. But hear me now, flyboy," she warned, her voice shaking. "I-If you've decided...*whatever* you've decided...please, at least let me know and there'll be no more calls from me."

Two days passed and—nothing.

On the third day, Juliet couldn't stand the thunderous silence any longer and decided she'd head further north up the coast to paint. This resolve was a prudent move, given that the change-of-control at GatherGames was to be publicly announced this day. She figured making herself scarce would be an excellent strategy, given also that proceedings to disbar attorney Gavin Linley had been filed with the California Bar Association—another bombshell she preferred to miss.

Juliet started to pack her small, wheeled bag, only to toss it back into her closet since its presence reminded her painfully of her collision with a tall, handsome figure in front of the American Hospital in Paris. Instead, she pulled a canvas sailing bag from under her bed, threw in two pairs of jeans, a sweatshirt and several T-shirts, along with her tights, a pair of tennis shoes, and enough underwear to last her the week. Then she headed north.

She drove across the Golden Gate Bridge on Highway

101 to the town of Petaluma and turned west to the coast road. Another 125 miles further up the coastline, the fog had burnt off and the picturesque cluster of houses known as Sea Ranch was bathed in the warm sunshine of a typical September Indian Summer. En route, she'd stopped for lunch in the town of Jenner at the River's End Restaurant, granting herself a quick look at her mobile phone before turning it off in disappointment and burying it at the bottom of her purse.

"Only one bar!" she grumbled. The entire coastal area was one of the few spots in the "wired state" of California that cell coverage was spotty, at best. *Perhaps it's just as well*, she thought, telling herself that ignoring her nonfunctioning cell phone would improve her concentration on why she'd driven north in the first place.

By late afternoon, she'd checked into the Sea Ranch Lodge and was given a lovely room with wood-paneled walls and spectacular views of the Pacific. Her king-sized bed sported a navy and taupe striped coverlet with large tailored pillows to match. Her surroundings were warm and welcoming and Juliet was determined to stop moping and start painting.

However, the first night, the distant sound of the surf pounding below the cliff kept her awake. Bitter regret, and then anger at Finn, and then remorse for her dark thoughts began to spiral in her head. How would she get back the possessions she'd left on his barge? Her winter clothes? Her art supplies? Would Avery be willing to be her go-between with Finn and send everything to her? How icky would *that* be?

"Oh, hell!" she said aloud. "Why should I care about any of that?"

And why wouldn't Finn return her calls? She turned over in bed and tried to get comfortable but hardly slept a wink.

Despite this—or perhaps because of it—she set out early the next few mornings, marching along a trail that bordered the cliff overlooking the Pacific. She had discovered a clearing that was encircled by a tall stand of majestic redwoods and set up her portable easel. Over three days, she sketched and then painted the scene that stretched before her, grateful to be thinking about something other than the former Air Force Major, Patrick Finley Deschanel.

In France, she'd taken courses in both oil and watercolor, but it was water-based paints that had become her first love. She could almost hear Caroline Nucholls' voice on color choice, along with the instructor at *L'École* advising her on perspective techniques.

This is my life's work! she thought with an unexpected and joyous rush. The rest of her life, she decided, would somehow have to take care of itself. As the hours passed with total focus on her work-in-progress, Juliet found great comfort in finally letting go of the collision of thoughts and questions about Finn's on-going silence ever since she'd returned from France.

While mixing the pigments she would use on the nearly completed piece propped up on her easel, she mulled over an idea for a new project that she'd had while driving to Sea Ranch—a series of watercolor land-and-seascapes of the Northern California coast where there wasn't a single human in sight. She figured she could display her finished work in a small room off the Bay View's main lobby, along with the paintings of other local artists she admired, and run the space as a boutique art gallery for the tourist trade.

With the sun rising higher in the east warming her back, she dabbed shaded colors on her work that represented the curving coast in front of her. Dipping her brush in the glass jar of water, she thought about the host of photos she'd taken in Europe that she had yet to use in *France Unafraid.* Should she continue her blog posts and offer the resulting watercolor "postcards" for sale, or would it merely be a painful reminder of Finn and her magical time in Paris, like picking the scab off a wound two times a week? Maybe she should simply shut down the blog as a chapter in her life that was over?

But France belonged to her just as much as to him!

And then there was Avery...and Claudine.

Suddenly, she realized with a sinking heart that her thoughts had circled back where she started. Pangs of yearning invaded every cell of her body. She savagely seized a larger paintbrush, mixing black with purple to create a threatening sky that didn't exist in the actual scenery that lay before her. She wondered, then, if she were painting a story devoid of a happy ending, now that Finn had completely disappeared from her life.

In fact, how had so many aspects of her existence gone awry? Her eldest brother had cut off communication with the entire family, made plans to move out of the Bay View Hotel to Silicon Valley, and was already involved in another video war-game start-up. And thus far, poor Jamie had no success getting an editing job at Pixar Studios.

Meanwhile, her parents were barely speaking to one another, although Jamie insisted that Mildred had finally accepted which of her children truly had her welfare at heart. Juliet tried to take solice in her younger brother's prediction that Millie and Brad, senior, would eventually return to their lifelong status quo, "Maybe acting even a bit nicer to each other in their golden years," he'd added with a droll smile.

Juliet swished more black into the small well of purple where she'd been mixing her paint, wondering if she'd ever have the courage to go back to France at some future date? Given how hard she and her younger brother had fought to retain the Bay View Hotel, there was little doubt that her roots were set deep into the bedrock of Nob Hill.

I am a San Francisco Thayer, after all, she ironically reminded herself. Her links to this part of the world were stamped into her DNA. She and Jamie had already begun to take up the reins of running the hotel, along with a professional manager her parents had finally given their blessings to hire in the wake of the recent family debacle. She'd also taken the time to write a substantial donation to a charity devoted to halting youthful cyber bullying.

Crashing into these thoughts, a vision of the Eiffel Tower glittering through Finn's window made her suck in her breath, her paintbrush poised in the air.

"We'll always have Paris," hadn't Finn joked once?

All she had was scores of iPhone pictures and a craving for croissants and *tarte tartin*. Truth was, Paris would be Paris, whether she ever returned there or not.

She dipped the tip of her brush into the angry hue she'd concocted, and then gazed again at the cloudless, azure sky meeting the green-blue water of the sea stretched out before her. Life truly imitated Art, she decided, as the day's perfect weather had demonstrated. She tossed the blue-black water she'd just mixed into the grassy bank. The sun would come up tomorrow—just as it had today. Life would go on.

Even without Finn Deschanel by her side.

CHAPTER 31

By noon on her fourth day at Sea Ranch, with the sun directly above her, Juliet was so hungry she could hear her stomach rumbling. She was also suddenly conscious of an annoying buzz and turned to look behind her. Dumbfounded, she spied a small, four-cornered object overhead, whirling its way in the direction of where she and her easel had been positioned all morning, perched on the edge of the cliff that overlooked the broad Pacific and the curving coastline.

"Be quiet! Go away!" she shouted at it, shaking her paintbrush at the heavens.

The move only showered her hair and forehead with the green paint she'd been using to create the stand of redwoods that appeared in the upper portion of the watercolor she'd been slaving over for hours.

The whirring machine flew ever closer—and lower—regardless of her stream of protests at having such a bucolic scene disturbed by the whooshing, insistent sounds of what could only be a pesky drone.

A drone? It can't be...

The mechanical spider landed not ten feet from where she sat. Heart pounding, she stood up from her painter's stool and peered more closely at a net pouch attached to the drone's frame—now soundless—as if obeying her command. She glanced around the broad meadow behind her and squinted at the enormous stand of trees that ringed it. Disappointment flooded her chest. There was nothing unusual in view.

Probably some kid staying at the lodge...trying out his Christmas present...

Then something turquoise caught her eye. She took a few tentative steps toward the drone and saw that within the confines of the net was a small, highly recognizable Tiffany box with hand-printed letters on the outside that said, "Open Me."

"What the—?" she murmured, advancing a few more steps. Her heart felt as if it had done a backflip above her ribs. With a trembling hand, she leaned down and liberated the box from its carry pouch. Her fingers shook even more when she opened the lid and saw that a tiny note had been squeezed inside.

> *I just got back from a month in the jungles of*
> *Africa on a drone job with no Wi-Fi for miles.*
> *P.S. You asked me to propose to you*
> *"on another day," so I am:*
> *Will you marry me?*

Again she scanned the meadow, a quizzical smile beginning to pull at her lips. With a whoop, she tossed aside the skinny watercolor brush in her right hand and then freed a small velvet box from inside the turquoise one made of glossy cardboard. She pried open the second box to find a vintage emerald and diamond ring that she instantly recognized—and gasped. It was the very engagement ring that Claudine Deschanel had worn all these years after the love of her life had been killed on a swift boat in Vietnam four decades ago.

"Where *are* you, Major Deschanel?" she shrieked to the clear skies above.

The open velvet box clutched in her hand, Juliet looked up to see a tall, familiar figure in a leather flight jacket emerge from the woods. Even at a distance of a hundred yards, she could see he was holding a black plastic rectangle with a joystick. As she had with her paintbrush, he tossed the controls aside and came galloping toward her.

"Did you see the message?" he shouted.

"Yes!" she shouted back, running toward him.

"And what's your answer?" he demanded, heading right for her.

"*Yes*! Of course I'll marry you!" she yelled across the tall grass, "but how did you find me and why did it take you so long?"

And then he was a foot away. He caught her in his arms, crushing her entire length against his body.

"I was stuck in Kenya—with no Wi-Fi—in the rainforest. And your brother Jamie told me how to find you."

"Oh, God, Finn, no Wi-Fi? I just want you to know I am *never* traveling to Africa!"

Between kisses he glanced around. "Man, you live in one, beautiful part of the country, and let me tell you, it's *great* for flying drones! The civilian kind, I mean." He leaned back and asked, "Where's the ring? Did you put it on? Claudine guessed you were a size five and had it sized." His eyes scanning her paint-spattered face and hair, he asked, "Do you always splatter paint all over yourself?"

"At least it's green and matches the ring," Juliet said, giddy with amazement. "I was shaking my brush at that annoying sound buzzing above my head and paint went everywhere!" She brought her right hand between them, the opened velvet box still clutched between her fingers. "Now, let's see this ring in all its glory." She pulled it from its nest and handed it to him.

"It was Claudine's engagement ring."

"I know," whispered Juliet with a catch in her throat. "I can't believe she took it off her finger."

"She and I hope it fits."

Juliet looked up at him. "How about you do the honors? Then I'll know this isn't a dream."

"I'm a little creaky with my left leg, you understand, but here goes..."

Finn slowly sank onto his right knee with a barely audible groan. "*Mademoiselle Juliette*," he said in an excellent French accent, "*Allez-tous tous marier de moi et mon épouse bien-aimée?*"

He slipped the emerald and diamond ring in its eighteen carat gold setting onto the second finger of her left hand and smiled up at her. It fit perfectly and the jewel sparkled in the noonday sun.

"I understood the first part of what you just said...'will you marry me,'" she said gazing down at him, one knee still on the grass, "but then—?"

"I said, 'Will you marry me and be my beloved wife?'"

"Oh, Finn," she said, tears filling her eyes, "*oui, mon amour*...absolutely *oui!*"

Finn grinned up at her. "We've got to work on that accent."

She offered him a hand as he struggled to his feet. Once upright, he pulled her into his arms again.

"Where, *exactly*, have you been, again?" she demanded, her question muffled by his chest. "And why didn't you find a way to contact me?"

Leaning back, he replied, "Like I said, in Africa. The same day you flew home, a rich client of the guy who runs the drone school in Rennes got a big assignment in Kenya. Feeling as rotten as I did after you left, I talked him into taking me with him."

"I'm glad you felt rotten," Juliet declared. "You went totally cold on me in Talloires."

Finn cast her a guilty look. "I know. It took me a full week piloting these gizmos over jungles, along rivers with flying snakes, and above preserves of endangered animals before I finally realized what had happened to me in Talloires."

"You thought I was just giving in to what other people wanted of me."

"No. I thought you were dumping me, just like Kim had."

"*What?* That's crazy!"

"Kinda," he agreed. "But you'd just turned me down when I asked you to marry me, and then you left. I *felt* left—and I didn't like it. It brought back a lot of unhappy memories. Now I know that I went directly into zombie mode that lasted ten days."

"But Talloires wasn't at all like what happened with you and Kim," she protested.

"Of course it wasn't. It just *felt* like it was. My bad."

"When I didn't hear from you, I thought…"

"I know, sweetheart. You thought I was dumping *you*. Once I got it through my dumb skull that my own personal baggage had hijacked me when you flew back to San Francisco—and that your having to fly home for a perfectly valid reason wasn't what I thought it was—I had no way of getting in touch until I got back to Paris. Then I heard all your messages as soon as my plane landed and…here I am."

"I'm not *ever* dumping you—as you so elegantly put it—so don't you dare do that to me again!"

"I promise, never again. I took the Africa job right after you left because I was a pretty sad dude and going to the back-of-the-beyond seemed like a good solution."

"The old bear-in-his-cave defense?" she shot back. "That's never a good solution!" She stared at him a moment and added, "But I suppose it's better than jumping off the Eiffel Tower or the Golden Gate Bridge—which is what I felt like doing."

"Or into a river with flying snakes."

"Listen to me, flyboy, it was absolutely horrible on my end when you went into that radio silence." She realized she had started to cry.

"Oh, sweetheart…never, ever again" he repeated,

kissing both her eyelids. "You and I were meant to be together the second we crashed into each other that day."

"You think so?" she sniffed, wondering at how disgusting she must look on her engagement day with tears streaming down her cheeks and paint on her forehead and in her hair. She clasped him even tighter, reveling in how blessed it felt to feel safe and loved.

A sudden thought made her frown and she gazed up at her newly intended.

"What?" demanded Finn, as always, attuned to her every mood.

"Where on God's earth are we going to *live*? You've developed clients in Europe and I have committed to my parents that I'll help with the management of the hotel. And then there's my art, which hasn't started to make money and—"

"Not a problem," he insisted, seizing her left hand and admiring his aunt's ring winking on her engagement finger. "I'm a military brat! I'll live anywhere you want —except in Colorado or Nevada. And there's a great VA hospital around here, I'm told."

"I've never been to Colorado," Juliet said, the rush of happiness and relief making her slightly dizzy. "I'm sure it's a nice place, but we never have to set foot in that state, if you don't want to. And as a girl who loves fog and cool weather, I'm fine about giving a pass to Nevada, too! But what about *your* work? Did you get your final certificate? And what about France?"

Finn raised his gaze from the sparkler on her hand to cast her a mischievous look.

"Yup, I passed everything in France and possess a good-as-gold commercial drone pilot's license." He shot her a grin. "And today, I applied for one here."

"You did? In California?"

"It shouldn't take long to get it, given my resume. I

also had a meeting at the San Francisco Airport yesterday with a high-level security company that's forming here with a plan for expansion as grandiose as the company in Rennes. Just like in France, they'll be independent contractors using small drones to inspect railway lines, power plants, stadiums before big events…basically infrastructure assignments all over the country, plus Canada and Mexico. The guys I met with are also former U.S. Air Force pilots and drone operators. We signed an agreement late yesterday guaranteeing me a place as one of the partners as soon as all the paperwork is filed here in the great state of California."

"No! You did all that since you landed here?"

Finn flashed her a grin and put his arm around her shoulders, guiding her back to her easel that still sat near the cliff's edge.

"I started putting the pieces in place as soon as I heard and read all your sweet messages that you left everywhere for me."

"Well, why didn't you put me out of my misery and call me when you got back from Africa?"

"I did, but nothing went through on your phone."

Chastened, she nodded. "Not quite as bad as Africa, but there's spotty cell service up here." She cast him a sheepish look, adding, "Plus I just realized…I turned off my phone in disgust four days ago and threw it in my purse."

"Your bad," Finn said, deadpan.

"But I hadn't heard from you once since I'd flown home!"

Finn squeezed her hand. "I know. My bad—*again.* When I couldn't get hold of you, I called Jamie and he gave me more gory details on the family fireworks finale regarding the takeover ruckus. He then told me you'd headed north to 'lick your wounds,' as he put it. I caught him up about what I'd been doing in Africa and that I needed time to get my ducks in a row before... well... before I showed up here on barely bended knee."

*And all that time, I'd been filled with doubt and misery. Oh, ye of little faith...*she silently scolded herself.

Finn leaned down and brushed his lips against hers, murmuring, "I figured I'd better have a profession lined up before I asked Bradshaw Thayer the Third for his daughter's hand in marriage."

Juliet could only shake her head and say, "Finn...you are so amazing."

"It feels pretty great to have as a goal keeping civilians safer in this New Normal we've created for ourselves."

"Amen to that, but let's just hope one day soon somebody designs one of these critters to fly a lot more quietly."

"Compared to a jet helicopter, they're whispering— but I hear ya!" He grinned. "And, believe it or not, the guys I'm partnering with are working on it."

Juliet shook her head in wonder as she began packing up her easel and paint supplies. Finn took a few minutes to gather up his own equipment and then the two of them trudged along a well-worn path to the lodge.

"The new company has leased offices in downtown San Francisco," he disclosed, "in one of those rehabbed piers near the Ferry Building."

Juliet halted, mid-path, to offer him a rueful smile. "I used to stare down at the Ferry Building from my old office at GatherGames. The clock tower was practically the only thing left standing after the quake of 1906. Who'd ever dream my future husband would one day be working on the Embarcadero?"

Back at the lodge, Juliet opened the door to her room and they walked inside where Finn leaned the easel he'd carried for her against one wall next to her paint box that she'd placed on the floor. Then he deposited the small drone and the control box beside her art equipment.

"Um...and by the way," Juliet said cautiously, "I have to ask you something."

Ever attuned to the slightest nuances of her tone, Finn's own countenance grew wary. "What?"

"In these months of flying civilian drones, did it ever trigger any more bad memories of your time in those unmarked trailers at Creech?"

Finn turned his back to stare out the window at the spectacular ocean view fanning out beyond the cliff. "Aren't you really asking if it's ever going to be safe to be with a guy like me?"

"No! I'm asking about how it's *been* for you, working in the same arena that caused you so much pain before! You've just told me you've committed to a profession that deals with these machines so you could stay in California, and—"

Finn turned, his apology evident in his eyes as well as his words. "I'm sorry. It's just that...well...the truth is, my worry that I'll suddenly flip out is always in the back of my mind, which is why your question just got the reaction it did. But all I can say is that, so far, flying civilian drones in France and on that project in Africa became part and parcel of the therapy I did to try to rewire those memoires."

"Rewire? How does that work?"

She sat on the edge of her bed and patted the space beside her. Finn joined her and seized one of her hands, his thumb drawing small circles in her palm. "Well, as Doctor A says, laying down good experiences can sometimes override the bad. If I start to get wiggy, I just keep telling myself that I'm flying these machines for the good of people...and that I'm using the skills Uncle Sam's taxpayers paid to teach me for things that will help, not hurt our country."

"You know something?" she said without fanfare, cupping her other hand on top of his. "You are the dearest and most amazing man I've ever known."

"What do you mean?" he asked, his doubt evident.

"Because you are one of the few males of the species I have ever met who was willing to admit he needed help—and then you went out and got it."

"It was that or...well...you know what I thought my only other choice was back then. Thank God I figured out that wasn't the answer."

"And you never gave up. That's what I so admire about you."

Finn wrapped his arms around Juliet's shoulders while she melted against his chest, tucking her head under his chin.

"Meeting you," he murmured against her ear, "made me see that life could be good again. You were something ...someone...to try to get well for."

"Oh, Finn," she whispered. "You had to get well for yourself."

He held her at arm's length. "Of course, but bumping into you in front of the American Hospital made my recovery much more interesting," he replied, joking now. "I'll probably never be perfectly okay, you know?" he warned, serious again. "There will be the nightmares. The thousand-yard stare. And I'm sure you'll see me diving for cover from time to time. You need to know that...and you need to be willing to accept it and live with it. So do I."

"I *do* accept. And you need to accept that I often jump to conclusions and have to remind myself to get the facts, first—and be willing to act in my own, selfish interest some of the time. If it wasn't for meeting you, I doubt I would ever have had the moxie to leave the stupid life I had at my old job and go to Paris to study art."

Finn wrapped his arms around her again.

"By the way," Juliet asked, looking into the dark pools of his blue eyes, "how do you feel about...living in a hotel atop Nob Hill?"

"The Bay View? The hotel your great, great granny designed and built? I'd be honored."

"You haven't even seen it!"

"Yes I have. I sneaked in to meet Jamie there briefly for coffee before the rental car was delivered. But I do have one question."

"Uh oh...what?"

"Do we have to use room service all the time with this deal?"

"Sometimes we'll want to," Juliet answered, relieved at his amused tone, "but I'll also wrangle kitchen privileges for you, if you want, so you can cook for us whenever you feel like it. And maybe the chef will even let you *sous* chef for him once in a while."

"That seals it. You're on!"

"Oh, and I can offer Aunt Claudine her own suite whenever she comes for a visit *if*," she added with a smile spreading across her face, "you and I can spend part of each year in France, right? I still want to take more classes at *L'École*."

"*Boot oov course*," Finn teased in a phony French accent. "Once I help get the new company up and running, let's plan to spend holidays, birthdays, and anytime we can afford it over there."

"On the barge?"

Finn's grin practically spread ear to ear. "Of course on a barge!"

Juliet threw her arms around her soon-to-be husband, kissing him soundly.

"*Vive La France!*" she whispered.

"I solemnly promise that we Deschanels will, upon occasion, return to our floating home in the Motherland..."

He gently pushed her down on the hotel bed, its plush coverlet a smooth landing place for them both. Juliet held her arms open and Finn soon lay beside her.

"Home?" she murmured. "It's *us*, Major Deschanel. Wherever we happen to be."

EPILOGUE

By late August, Finn had completed his commercial drone courses and certifications in France, the U.S., and California, settled into his new job, and plans for a spring wedding were well underway.

"It certainly is handy to already have a hotel venue for the reception," joked Juliet.

As their chosen best man, Jamie was the first to be informed of their engagement, followed by excited calls to Claudine Deschanel and Avery Evans in Paris.

Finn had been introduced to his prospective in-laws at a small dinner in the family's private dining room with everyone in attendance except Brad IV. Afterward, Finn and Juliet's father disappeared down the service elevator to his basement office. The two men emerged, an hour later, wreathed in smiles, with the joyous news that Juliet and her mother had a wedding to plan for in early spring.

"I don't even get to be Bridezilla," Juliet was soon complaining good-naturedly to Finn. "Mother has taken complete control, planning the wedding *she* never had."

"Let her," Finn counseled, nuzzling his bride-to-be as they lay on the bed she'd slept in since childhood. "I already feel married."

For appearances sake, however, Mildred had given Finn her eldest son's old suite, down the hall from his prospective bride. Even so, each night, he slipped into Juliet's room with no one fooled in the slightest. Juliet had, after several heated discussions, succumbed to her mother's pleas to include brother Brad in the wedding.

"It's traditional for the eldest male sibling to be Head

Usher!" Mildred insisted. "I doubt he'll accept, however," she added sadly.

Juliet, her jaw dropping, could only stare at her mother. Finally, she demanded, "And what about the way he treated *you*?"

For the merest second, a stricken look invaded her mother's eyes—a moment that soon was replaced by a frown. "He was under tremendous pressure at that time."

Once Finn had talked Juliet down from the trees after that particular exchange, he gently reminded her, "Let's just be grateful the equity loan against the Bay View has been repaid, and your parents can retire this year."

He kissed her soundly and urged her to swallow hard and write the invitation to Brad to serve as head usher, which she did on crisp stationary from Gumps.

"I mailed it to his business address in Palo Alto where his latest venture is incubating," she reported to her fiancé, grumbling, "let's hope he throws it in the trash!"

Much to everyone's surprise, Brad accepted the honor, although Juliet told Finn she was under no illusions that he "had changed his spots."

In the end, her mother's planning came off brilliantly the day in early May when Finn and Juliet's nuptials were held before a gathering of sixty friends and family in a chapel at Grace Cathedral, three blocks from the Bay View Hotel.

The organ was echoing a thunderous rendition of Marc-Antoine Charpentier's *Prelude on the Te Deum* at the moment the entire Thayer family assembled in the vestibule. Juliet had just entered the back of the church, awash in her elaborate gown, chosen by her mother, of course. She took her father's arm, relieved to see that Jamie was already a few feet down the aisle, escorting Aunt Claudine to her seat. In front of the bride and Brad senior, Mildred had just slipped her arm through the crook of the younger Brad's elbow in preparation for her own grand entrance as Mother-of-the-Bride as the glorious music resounded off the soaring walls of the massive cathedral. The *Te Deum* was a favorite of both Juliet and Finn and played often at weddings held in Paris' Notre Dame.

"Oh, Mother," exclaimed Juliet with genuine pleasure, "you were finally able to persuade the organist to play the *French* processional. Thank you so much!"

Mildred turned around and met her daughter's smiling gaze. Then she pulled her arm from her eldest son's and embraced Juliet, clinging to her for a long moment. A faint, "I hoped you'd be pleased," was whispered against her daughter's ear.

"I am...very much," she replied, a catch in her throat. "It's going to be a beautiful wedding, thanks to you."

Mildred's smile contained a strange mixture of gratitude and triumph. She turned, resumed her place next to her son, and the pair took their first, measured steps toward the front of the chapel, where Finn was standing at the altar.

Sitting on the groom's side, Aunt Claudine had taken her honored position in the front pew, joining Avery Evans and Alain Devereux, over from Paris, along with "The General" as Mildred reveled in describing Finn's father. Resplendent in his uniform with a chest full of ribbons and medals, along with three stars gleaming on his shoulders, Andrew Deschanel was accompanied by Finn's sister, Maureen, and her husband, also in formal attire as an Army Lieutenant Colonel.

After the ceremony concluded, the General stayed only for the champagne toast at the reception held in a walled-off half of the Bay View's grand ballroom. He was due the next day, he apologized, for a conference in Washington, D.C. with the Joint Chiefs and had an aide whisk him to the airport for his flight to the East Coast.

At about the time that the last bottle of champagne was poured, the newlyweds were driven by their best man to San Francisco International themselves to catch their night flight to France. Both were exhausted from the excitement of the festivities and once on board the plane, they sank into their Business Class flat bunks and slept all the way to Paris.

When the taxi at De Gaulle had been loaded with their luggage, Finn gave instructions to the driver before he entered the cab. Juliet leaned back in her seat and closed her eyes, still fatigued from the trip and all that had gone before. She was half asleep when they drew up to the embankment on the opposite side of the Seine from where the *L'Étoile de Paris* was moored. She had gathered her tote bag and other possessions inside the cab before she noticed they were parked across the water from Finn's barge.

"Wait a minute! What are we doing here?" she asked.

"I have a little surprise for you." Finn announced, paying the driver who swiftly sped off to catch his next fare.

"What surprise? Aren't we spending our honeymoon on the boat?"

"Follow me and I'll show you. Look down there." He pointed in the direction of the quay below.

Just like the Right Bank where the Grenelle's barge was moored, this side of the river was also paved in cobblestones. Here on the Left Bank, too, a series of gaily-painted vessels dotted the water's edge. The base of the Eiffel Tower was only a few hundred yards from where they stood next to their suitcases. Finn led the way down the ramp past two other barges and halted at a black-hulled boat with the name *Adriana* incised on its prow in large, gold letters. In contrast to the weathered barge where Finn lived across the water, the craft on this side of the Seine sported teak trim both around the windows up top as well as encircling a series of portholes embedded in the hull. Pots of flowers—mostly red, yellow, and purple—dotted the decks. Forward, near the prow, handsome teak chairs and a matching table with a jaunty red umbrella invited the boat's passengers to while away the days on deck sipping cocktails and eating *hors d'oeuvres* before descending into the grand salon.

"C'mon," Finn said, gesturing toward the open hatch. "Let's go below."

Juliet obediently followed her husband up the gangway. "What in the world…?"

A few more steps led them along the deck and then down five wooden stairs into the barge's beautifully appointed main cabin—featuring even more teak accents. It was luxuriously furnished with an elegant, built-in sofa and a sea-going, antique Louis Vuitton trunk topped with a thick sheet of glass doubling as a coffee table.

"You like?" Finn asked.

Juliet could see he was anxiously awaiting her response as she turned in a circle to take in every detail of the decor.

"Like? I *love* it! Whose is it? And what are we doing here?"

"It's a wedding present…to both of us."

"For our honeymoon?" She clapped her hands, mentally comparing it with the comparatively bare-bones furnishings on board *L'Étoile*. "She's stunning! And, oh my! Will you look at the gas stove!" she exclaimed, peering over the teak bar into the galley, an onboard kitchen at least three times bigger than the area where Finn had previously produced some amazing meals on only two burners.

"Come see the staterooms," he urged, leading the way past a tapestry curtain and down a highly-varnished passageway that led to two cabins, both featuring built-in double beds and high-gloss, wood-paneled wainscoting below white bulkheads where the portholes offered views of the Seine.

"Oh, Finn," she said, turning to throw her arms around him. "How did you arrange this for us?"

"Aunt Claudine, of course," he said, nose to nose. "She saw the ad and—"

"One of those short-term rental websites?"

"No." Finn was grinning now. "The advertisement said 'For Sale.' Congratulations, Juliet! You and I now *own* this bucket."

"What? Oh, my God...we *do*? It's gorgeous!" she squealed. Then, a worried frown creased her brow. "But how can we afford it?"

"Aunt Claudine bought half of it for us as a wedding present and I bought the other half with my savings and the hefty hardship pay I got from working those weeks in a pretty dangerous part of Africa. Claudine insisted she be part of the deal as soon as I said I was flying to San Francisco to ask you to marry me."

"She did?" Juliet could only shake her head in amazement.

"When Claudine and I came to see it the first time, she told me I was already in her will and so why not have some of my inheritance *now*? It's an eighty-five-foot former lumber craft that some hotshot American ex-pat bought and refitted to a fare-thee-well, as you can see. Recently, he was unexpectedly transferred back to New York and put it on the market." Finn cast her a worried glance. "I want you to know that I will never buy anything major like this without your input, but I had no idea if you'd say yes to me, and I didn't want to have missed out if you *did* agree to be my wife. People were swarming all over her the first day she went on sale."

Juliet gave an embarrassed laugh. "Well, after you'd heard my anguished voice messages saying how much I loved and missed you, I guess you thought it was a pretty good bet I'd say yes, right?"

Finn leaned forward and gave her a kiss. "I sure hoped so."

Juliet sank down on the corner of the double bunk in the second stateroom, suddenly completely speechless. She could only stare in wonder at the soft-as-snow cashmere throw she recognized from Claudine's apartment that was now folded across the arm of a small chair in the corner. Then, she was filled with confusion. "But, if we now own this in Paris, what about living in—"

Before she could finish her question, Finn assured her they would still be based in San Francisco, as they'd agreed. "But since we don't own or rent in California, thanks to living in the Bay View, I figured this can be our condo-on-the-water whenever we're in Paris. And when we're not, we can loan it to friends. Avery has already said she wants first dibs."

"Oh, Finn," Juliet said, still staggered by the notion they were the boat's proud owners. "She's so beautiful! Our perfect Paris *pied-à-terre* when we come here."

Finn sat down beside her and gathered her in his arms. "So what do you say, sailor? Shall we launch this honeymoon?" Finn gently pushed her down onto the stateroom's built-in bed. Sunlight poured through the half-opened porthole and they could hear the rhythmic slap of the Seine's ever-flowing current against the hull. "I vote that the honeymoon officially begins...right now."

For the next ten days, Juliet and Finn left the barge only to secure supplies and take long walks along the embankment that led to the base of the Eiffel Tower. Seeing the mammoth structure from a different angle among the spring foliage had taken some getting used to, now that they were moored on the Left Bank side of *Bir Hakeim* bridge.

On a Wednesday around noon, they heard someone trilling outside the grand salon, "Yoo-hoo! Permission to come aboard!"

"Aunt Claudine!" they said in unison.

Fortunately, they were both dressed and so the couple scrambled on deck to greet their visitors, who were standing below them on the quay. Behind the slender, erect figure of Finn's aunt, clad in chic, camel-colored gabardine slacks and a matching sweater set, stood Avery and Alain. Their arms laden with flowers and champagne, Finn motioned for the trio to mount the gangway while he and Juliet hastened to relieve them of their burdens.

"So how was your time in San Francisco after we left?" asked Juliet as the party descended below deck. "I hope the flight home wasn't too awful, Aunt Claudine."

"First of all, hello, my darlings!" she exclaimed, kissing them both effusively. "I told Avery that I had to give myself two days to recover from jet lag before we came over. We had a glorious time in your hometown, Juliet, so to celebrate, I've brought *Veuve Clicquot* for us all—except Finn, of course!" She held up a bottle of Perrier that she presented to him in a grand gesture.

Finn began to open the champagne as Juliet threw her arms around his aunt a second time to thank her for the role she'd played in purchasing the barge and offered quick hugs to Avery and Alain as well.

Avery announced, "We also came to help you christen the boat. What shall we name her?"

"Her name is the 'Adriana,'" Finn declared, warning, "...and they say it can be very bad luck to change it. So how about you all just drink the champagne and we'll sprinkle a little of it and some of my Perrier water onto the bow as her new owners—and leave it at that?"

"And anyway," Juliet chimed in, "Finn and I *love* the name!"

Her groom began to pour the bubbling wine into tall flutes that had apparently come with the furnishings. Taking her proffered glass, Juliet thought dreamily to herself that the broad deck on the stern was going to make a perfect place to paint.

Paris would always be Paris. True, they would never forget the suffering of the Grenelle family, nor Avery's struggle to recover from her wounds. The city would mourn its losses and its valiant citizens would carry on as America had after 9/11 and a host of terrorist events that followed. There were sure to be more attacks and tragedies, she thought, and for a moment she felt the familiar clutch of fear for the future hovering over their happy group. She inhaled deeply and then made a deliberate and conscious choice not to think about that now. She would be happy in the moment. She and Finn would face whatever was to come...together.

"To the *Adriana*," Avery murmured, holding up her glass in a toast with the arm now healed, despite the scars. Juliet's best friend glanced around at the *Adriana's* interior. "Yep!" she declared in vigorous agreement. "The name's perfect!"

Juliet turned to her right to absorb the sight of the husband she adored raising his glass of sparkling water, a man who had fought his demons and remained steadfast in all he believed. Her mind flew to the memory of them clinging to each other in their room in Talloires beside beautiful Lake Annecy in the wake of the Bastille Day terrorist attack.

Love instead of hate or despair, she reminded herself fiercely. It was their best weapon in any battles that lay ahead in this unpredictable world they were part of...

And then another thought washed over her.

Adriana is a lovely name for a little girl...after we have one named Julia Morgan Thayer Deschanel, of course...

AUTHOR'S NOTE AND ACKNOWLEDGMENTS

"Ripped from the headlines" was never my original intent for this novel. As a former medical and health reporter for a number of years for the American Broadcasting System in Los Angeles, I was one of the first in the media to begin doing stories on the men and women returning from Viet Nam with what previously was referred to (usually in whispers) as "shellshock." I chronicled the years of struggle it took for service men and women to have the condition formally recognized by America's medical and military communities. And then, after nearly two decades of America's involvement in foreign wars in the Middle East and the horrifying statistics of returning veterans committing suicide, a story began to form in the far reaches of this writer's brain where these things can percolate virtually for years.

Another impetus for this novel is my love of France, and the fact that my husband of forty years and I have reason to travel there nearly every June, and have encountered many ex-pat Americans who have found life there to have that *Je ne sais pas quoi* element that they can't find anywhere else. Paris, despite the tumult of recent years, is—like my own San Francisco—one of those cities where the beauty and culture of the place can soothe the soul.

Central to the setting of *That Spring in Paris* was the sheer luck of finding the *Orion* on an AirBnB listing for stationary barges to rent on the Seine. Of course, the fact that we came aboard on the very week when a "Fifty Years; Flood" occurred, with the river's waters rising some twenty-three feet above flood stage, merely added to the drama. In the novel, recounting that experience in fiction provided an exciting sequence for the main characters to learn what good partners they made under extreme duress, and despite the hero's battles with PTSD. My deepest thanks go Brigitte and Eric Sautot for their incredible hospitality—and for finding us a swell hotel—Hôtel Eiffel Trocadero on *Rue Benjamin Franklin*—when it was finally decided it was no longer safe for even former boat owners like my husband and me to remain on board!

Other Parisians that provided guidance include Philippe Pellerin, owner of *La Caléche*, the restaurant across the street from #7 *Rue de Lille*, where Juliet and Finn enjoy several lovely meals and find themselves under an outdoor table when a car backfires soon after the terrorist attacks of November 13th. As for the other restaurants and bistros mentioned in the novel, I can highly recommend them all and thank their proprietors for their culinary skills and warm welcome.

And speaking of delicious meals, we had occasion to meet up with another barge owner, American Charlie Downer at a wonderful restaurant in the Passy, along with my high school pal, Lacy Williams Buck. When we couldn't board the *Orion* due to the extreme flooding that week in Paris, Charlie later sent me gorgeous pictures of her interior that are lovingly described in the last chapter. Leslie de Galbert, an American originally from New Orleans, and now long-time resident of France, treated us to superb dinner in their apartment with a head-on view of the Eiffel Tower and was a great source of help along the way.

And if you love feasting your eyes on images of delicious food, *Paris Breakfast* blogger, Carol Gillott, who takes incredible pictures of Paris and environs and offers her delightful watercolors for sale online, was the inspiration for the way in which the heroine initially could support her "artist habit" when she first moved to Paris. The minute I spied Carol's photo of the wisteria-draped café, I knew I had to have it for the book's cover. (Just Google "Paris Breakfast," sign up for free, and enjoy weekly doses of the City of Light—and color!).

Huge thanks are also due Rich and Caroline Nuckolls who operate the wonderful Art Colony Giverny where both experienced and fledgling artists can live near and paint *in* Monet's Gardens each summer. What an experience it was to be admitted with Caroline's gaggle of painters "after hours" into the Impressionist's magnificent garden and trod across the green bridge spanning the lily pads beside weeping willows in the soft, golden light of oncoming dusk. Anyone interested in her classes can contact her at info@artcolony-giverny.com .

With regard to the military aspects of the story, I am great indebted to a number of U.S. Air Force members—some retired and others still on active duty—who set me straight on everything from the age at which a pilot who attended the U.S. Air Force Academy and had served in Iraq and Afghanistan would reach the rank of Major, to the responses that drone pilots experienced in those unmarked white trailers in the desert of Nevada. Gentlemen, you know who you are, and you have my undying gratitude. Any mistakes or misstatements, however, are my own.

And then there are the "Ciji's Betas." These are friends and colleagues willing (and brave enough) to read my early drafts of some 400 pages of manuscript that often reach eight or nine versions before I'm through. Liz Trupin-Pulli—pal, editor, and an ace of an agent—helped me immeasurably on this one, as did the critique of bookstore partner, dog-walking pal, and writer herself, Cheryl Popp. Additional writer-betas include Kim Cates, Janet Chapman, Diana Dempsey, Kate Moore and Cynthia Wright. The other sets of sharp eyes belonged to Diane Barr, Linda Hammond, Dean Stolber.

Like most writers who have once been working

reporters, I often seek out "sources" to interview in the course of writing fiction that can show me the intricacies of their unique worlds. I am grateful to my childhood friend and distinguished graphics designer and artist, Marcia McGinnis Shortt, who helped me to sketch in the background for the heroine, Juliet Thayer—a woman that transitions from a designer of video war games packaging to a fully-fledged landscape painter.

As usual, my thanks to formatter Pam Headrick and of A Thirsty Mind Book Design for the mechanics of getting the book ready for publication.

In the dedication, I mentioned the members of my own family that have served in the nation's military during times of war—and peace. I could not have written this novel without the encouragement and support of former naval Lt. Anthony Cook, who floated around Viet Nam as "officer of the deck" in his youth, and has been a steady hand on my shoulder during the wild ride that became the publishing business. After four decades of marriage, we've figured out a way to have *fun* researching my projects and bringing them to the page with an "out-fox-'em" attitude that has served us well. Thank you, darling, for everything you are—and do.

I hope my beloved son, Jamie Ware Billett, his amazing, lovely, and talented brain scientist wife, Dr. Teal Eich, and their precious boys will inherit a world far more peaceful than the one described in this novel. Our family association with beautiful Talloires in the Alps all these years has been one of life's great blessings. *Vive La France!*

Meanwhile, may we all hold on to each other tightly—with abiding love.

Ciji Ware
San Francisco, California

The Four Seasons series – Book 1
That Summer in Cornwall

Meredith Champlin, the newly appointed guardian of an unruly "Beverly Hills brat," decamps from her settled existence in Wyoming with her charge and her Welsh Corgi to spend the summer with her English relatives at Barton Hall, a shabby-chic castle perched on the remote cliffs of UK's West Country.

Meredith's summer escape gets even more complicated when former British Army Lieutenant Sebastian Pryce, veteran of a bomb- sniffing K9 squad in Afghanistan, proposes they join forces to found the Barton Hall Canine Obedience Academy, along with signing her up for his volunteer rough-and-ready Cornwall Search and Rescue Team.

Even with an assist from a novice search dog named T-Rex, the odds seem long that a mere three months in the land of Meredith's Cornish ancestors can transform her troubled ward into a happier child, heal the wounds suffered by her soldier-turned-significant-other, and save the Barton-Teague estate from pending disaster.

"Ware again proves she can intertwine fact and fiction to create an entertaining and harmonious whole." – *Publishers weekly*

"Ciji Ware's award-winning storytelling should come with a warning—Do not start unless you want to be up all night!" – *Romantic Times*

Available at all online retailers or cijiware.com.

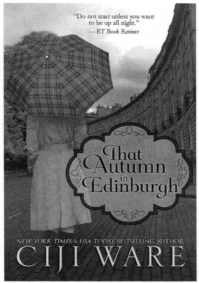

"Do not start unless you want to be up all night."
—*RT Book Reviews*

NEW YORK TIMES & USA TODAY BESTSELLING AUTHOR
CIJI WARE

The Four Seasons – Book 2:
That Autumn in Edinburgh

Can memories of a tragic, eighteenth century love triangle be passed down through a descendant's DNA?

When Fiona Fraser's mercurial boss dispatches the American designer to Edinburgh to create a Scottish Home Furnishings Collection, the chemistry deepens instantly when she and tartan manufacturer Alex Maxwell discover their ancestral bonds to the star- crossed lovers Thomas Fraser—the "Lost Lieutenant"—and Jane Maxwell, the flamboyant 4th Duchess of Gordon who died in 1812.

From the cobbled streets of Edinburgh's Royal Mile to the tartan and cashmere mills of the Scottish border country, the modern lovers grapple with the imminent threat of financial ruin to their respective firms, along with ancient wounds echoing down through time...and a heartbreaking mystery, hidden for more than two centuries, that will dictate Alex and Fiona's own destinies...

"A deep, complex novel exploring love, betrayal, healing, and renewal in the human heart." – *Affaire de Coeur*

"Vibrant and exciting…" – *Literary Times*

Available at all online retailers or cijiware.com.

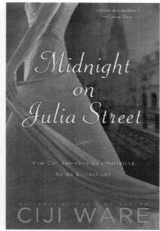

The Four Seasons Quartet Book 3
That Winter in Venice is a sequel to
Midnight on Julia Street

If you enjoyed meeting Kingsbury Duvallon and Corlis McCullough in *That Winter in Venice*, you will love reading their own story in *Midnight on Julia Street*, a novel of scandal that transcends time in the Big Easy.

The sultry streets of pre-Katrina New Orleans, the glamorous Garden District, derelict riverfront cotton warehouses, and gritty back alleys come alive in this time-slip novel of a feisty reporter who inexplicably glides between the nineteenth century and the modern world. A long-forgotten drama of blackmail, swindles, and a love affair that is still changing lives leaves Corlis and King wondering if their burgeoning, unholy attraction will render them pawns in a matrix of mystery and deceit.

"Vibrant and exciting...an intriguing plot full of rich characters that I couldn't wait to see what happened." – *Literary Times*

"Wonderful storyteller, Ciji Ware is in rare form with this intriguing and terrific novel." – *RT Book Reviews*

Available at all online retailers or cijiware.com.

ABOUT THE AUTHOR

Ciji Ware is the *New York Times* and *USAToday* bestselling author of ten novels, a novella, and two nonfiction works. She is the daughter, niece, and descendant of writers, so writing fiction is just part of the "family business." She has been honored with the Dorothy Parker Award of Excellence and a *Romantic Times* Award for Best Fictionalized Biography for *Island of the Swans*, and in 2012, was shortlisted in the prestigious WILLA (Cather) Literary Award for *A Race to Splendor*.

An Emmy-award winning television producer, former radio and TV on-air broadcaster for ABC in Los Angeles, as well as print and online journalist, Ware received a BA in History from Harvard University and has the distinction of being the first woman graduate of Harvard College to serve as the President of the Harvard Alumni Association, Worldwide. As a result of Ware's first novel, *Island of the Swans*, she was made a Fellow of the Society of Antiquaries of Scotland (FSA Scot), and in 2015 was named to the "Martha's Vineyard Writers-in-Residence" program—both honors she treasures.

The author lives in the San Francisco Bay Area and can be contacted through her agents, Celeste Fine at Sterling-Lord Literistic (nonfiction), and Elizabeth Trupin-Pulli at Jet Literary.com, (fiction), or at http://www.cijiware.com.

Research photographs of Ciji's travels relating to her novels can be seen on www.pinterest.com/cijiware or follow her on www.facebook.com/cijiwarenovelist and join *Ciji Ware's Readers Roundtable*, a Facebook group.

Made in the USA
Middletown, DE
10 December 2021